Praise

Last Call is a wonderful heartwarming story that is a perfect way to spend a relaxing day. *Last Call* will pull you in with the first chapter and will hold your interest all the way through the last page.

The heroine in this novel is a young woman that has faced the many challenges in her life with determination and an amazing sense of strength. Novalee decides to treat herself to a fun trip to Vegas. She awakes on the last morning of her vacation to find that she had had too much to drink the night before and had gotten married. She sneaks away and hurries home in the hopes that she can go on with her life and pretend that it never happened.

The groom, Dean, is handsome and wealthy and is embroiled in a battle with his drunken father over his Grandfather's estate. The conditions of the will state that Dean has to be married in order to inherit the estate.

Enter the problem - Two years has passed and now Dean needs Novalee to testify that they are married and that it is a real marriage. How does he approach her and persuade her to testify for him and not hate him for tricking her? How can he keep her from taking him to the cleaners in anger?

Can these two come to an agreement? Can they be honest with each other or will they be too busy protecting their hearts and their assets? Can they find a way to forgive after the deceptions and lies finally come to light?

Ms. Schmidt has a real talent for telling a story. I enjoyed every minute that I spent curled up with her story. If you are looking for a fun, light and beautifully written story - I urge you to lose yourself in this touching story.

Kat Terrell – *The Review Lounge*

Jennifer Schmidt

Last Call

First published by The Writer's Coffee Shop, 2011

The Writer's Coffee Shop
(Australia) PO Box 2013 Hornsby Westfield NSW 1635
(USA) PO Box 2116 Waxahachie TX 75168

Paperback ISBN- 978-1-61213-064-4
E-book ISBN- 978-1-61213-065-1

A CIP catalogue record for this book is available from the US Congress Library.

Cover image by: Claudio Monni
Cover design by: Jennifer McGuire

www.thewriterscoffeeshop.com/jschmidt

About the Author

Growing up in a small town in the Interlake region of Manitoba, there wasn't always a lot to do. Having to entertain one's self, Jennifer soon discovered a love for reading, and later, one of writing.

She wrote her first novel at the age of 15. Six hundred hand written pages later, it was put away and forgotten about. It wasn't until she found an online writing community that she took the first step and, hiding behind a pen name, posted her work. After some persuasion from family and friends, Jennifer shed the pen name and entered the 2010 TWCS Original Fiction Contest and won for best romance.

After moving and living in a couple of different cities around the country, Jennifer came back home to Ashern where she lives with her two young sons, Hayden and Nicholas.

Dedication

To my boys, Hayden and Nicholas, who not only find new ways every day to drive me crazy, but who have taught me that a little bit of craziness is a whole lot of love.

My parents, family, and friends who encouraged me and believed I could accomplish this goal when I had no belief in myself.

And Nick for lending Dean his ink, threatening to kick my ass when writer's block became so bad I wanted to quit and give up, and helping to inspire the naughtiness that fills these pages.

xoxo

Prologue

Even without meeting his gaze, she could feel his eyes on her. She kept her gaze locked on her cocktail glass, her hair around her face to hide her smile. He had been sitting there for a good ten minutes now, watching her. Normally it would creep her out, make her stomach flip to the point of being nauseous, to have someone stare at her like he was doing. But oddly she liked it.

Flirtatiously, she twisted her shoulder while still keeping her eyes on her glass. She turned her body, slowly twirling on the stool so her bottom half faced him. She began to swing her leg back in forth slowly, lazily. She didn't have to look to know his eyes were now on her legs, probably drifting up to where her skirt ended just above her knee.

She softly giggled at her actions, knowing what it was doing to him. She felt sexy sitting four barstools down from a total stranger, knowing she was turning him on. Or at the very least that he was captivated by her for the moment.

The bartender must have been making her drinks with a little splash of something extra tonight. She'd never behaved like this in all of her twenty-six years.

But she was in Las Vegas, and everyone knew what happened in Vegas stayed in Vegas.

Not that there was anyone she knew to witness her actions anyway. She had come alone, her first real vacation, and knew no one in the city. It was a time to be by herself, to celebrate how far she had come in the past few years, and to welcome the different woman she was becoming with open arms.

And apparently that new woman liked to tease strangers in Las Vegas casinos.

She giggled again at the thought.

"Excuse me?"

She looked up, meeting the eyes of Mr. Four Barstools Down. She opened and closed her mouth, the innocent game suddenly at a whole new level now that he had approached her.

This is where she would normally smile nervously, maybe let him engage in chitchat for a few minutes and then excuse herself so she could hurry away.

But for reasons she would never be able to explain to anyone, including herself, no part of her wanted to flee. She stared into the blue eyes of the man before her and wanted nothing more than to stay. She felt a surreal pull towards this man, making it impossible for her to want to run away.

"I couldn't help but notice you were alone," he said. His voice was deep, yet soft. "Could I buy you a drink?"

She looked down at her glass as if realizing she had one in front of her and then back up at the man.

"Okay."

Immediately she wanted to smack herself for such silly response. *Okay?* The man asked to buy her a drink and all she said was okay?

He smiled and took the seat next to her, signaling the bartender for another round.

She smiled shyly at him when the drink was set in front of her, even though she felt anything but shy in that moment. His leg bumped hers as he made himself more comfortable on the barstool and she had to bite back the grin that wanted to spread across her face at the contact.

He apologized and then introduced himself; she told him not to worry about it and did the same.

"What brings you to Vegas?" he asked.

"Vacation," she answered. "I needed a little bright lights and big city."

"You don't seem like the bright lights and big city type," he said. She raised her eyebrows at the assumption. "I don't mean that in a bad way," he assured her quickly. "There's just something about you that doesn't fit in here."

"Fit in how?" she asked, genuinely curious about his answer.

"I don't know. Maybe it's the innocence." He grinned.

She laughed.

"I am far from innocent," she said, and then frowned.

No, that wasn't exactly true. In some ways she was innocent, even to the point of being naïve. But in other ways, she had experienced more than most young women of her age.

She glanced back up at the man beside her, puzzled by why she was sitting there talking to him. He smiled kindly at her, his eyes vibrant as he watched her, and yet, not once did she feel like he was checking her out in a sleazy way.

His eyes didn't stray to her breasts, they didn't travel up and down her body—although she would bet dollars to donuts he *had* been eyeing her legs earlier. But even that didn't make her skin crawl.

There was something oddly comforting about this man. She couldn't say what it was, but for the first time in years she didn't feel like she had to be on guard.

"Have you enjoyed your visit with us so far?" he asked, taking a sip of his drink.

She nodded.

"I have, but honestly, you were right, I'm not much of a city girl. At least not a city this size." She smiled. "I'll be glad to be home tomorrow."

"Well, if it's your last night I insist on making it a memorable one." He turned around in his seat and glanced towards the casino. "How are you at blackjack?"

She chuckled, "Horrible. I'm more of a slots girl."

"In that case," he stood and held out his arm to her, "care to accompany me to the slots, ma'am?"

She looked from his arm up to his face and bit her lip, slowly nodding her head.

"Sure. Why not?"

"Now, there's a trick to this," he told her once they were standing in front of a machine.

"Is that so?"

"Yes. Let me show you."

Gently, he put his hands on her hips. The touch was so light she had to look down to make sure she hadn't imagined him doing it.

He must have caught her look because he pulled his hands away slightly and asked, "Is this okay?"

She nodded, swallowing over the lump that had suddenly formed in her throat at his touch.

He put his hands back on her hips and moved her to stand directly in front of the slot machine.

"Now," he said, sliding his right hand down her arm and gently grasping her hand, lifting it to the lever, "the key is to pull down really slow," he murmured.

"Why slow?" she asked, thickly.

"Everything's better when it's slow the first time," he answered just as huskily.

Her heart beat faster at the words and she let him help her pull the handle, her head feeling as if it were spinning right along with the images in the tiny display windows.

"Are you okay?" he asked when her breath hitched.

"Fine," she all but croaked. "I think I need a drink."

He smiled.

"Let me get it for you."

He ended up getting them both a few drinks, and what could have been hours later, they were laughing at every attempt they made to play the games around them. He excused himself to take a call during the middle of their fun and she watched him out of the corner of her eye. His demeanor seemed to change while on the phone and she couldn't help but notice he seemed a lot tenser than he was before the call.

"Everything okay?" she asked, even though it was none of her business.

"Fine," he replied, but his smile was tight and forced.

"I've had a great time. Definitely a few too many of these," she added with a laugh, holding up her glass, "but a great time."

This time the smile he gave her was genuine.

"I'm glad."

"I've never done anything like that before!" she suddenly exclaimed. "At least not for a long time. It feels so good to let loose. It kind of makes me want to do something crazy," she added with a laugh.

He watched her, shook his head and she swore she heard him curse under his breath, before he looked back up and asked with a charming smile, "Just how crazy do you want to get?"

"As crazy as you want to be," she answered in almost a whisper.

She couldn't help it. It was that damn smile. Those dimples that carved his cheeks made her feel all weak in the knees. And he made her feel whole again. It was messed up and made no sense but he made her feel like a real woman again.

Something no one had been able to do for a long time.

He leaned forward and also whispering said, "You know, there's a chapel just a few blocks down that does mock marriages. Feel like getting hitched?" he asked, wiggling his eyebrows.

She laughed, but shook her head.

"I couldn't do that!"

"Why not?" He shrugged. "It's all phony. No harm done. We say some sappy vows, take a few pictures for a laugh and you go home having done something wild and crazy."

She bit her lip as she thought of what he said.

"And what do you get out of the deal?" she asked.

"Me? I get the memory of once having a very beautiful bride," he teased. "Something that will make all my friends jealous."

Finding his charm irresistible, she set down her glass with a little too much enthusiasm and cried, "What the hell! Let's get married."

"Seriously?"

"Seriously." She laughed again, a definite sign she'd had too much to drink. She was never this giddy. "What harm could it do?"

Her head throbbed, making it almost impossible to open her eyes. When she finally did manage to crack them open, fractions at a time, the lights were so blinding she had to slam her lids closed again. The small action caused a rush of pain to surge through her forehead.

She moaned and covered her face with her hands and slowly turned onto her side to bury her head under the pillow. Under the protection of the thick material, she attempted to open her eyes again, groaning from the effort.

What the hell had she done last night?

She shifted her body, trying to stretch out, when her foot brushed against a very hairy leg.

Gasping, she jerked her foot away and held her breath, afraid any noise or movement might wake the stranger.

Oh my God!

Who had she done last night?

She heard him mumble something in his sleep and the bed shifted as he moved.

Please don't wake up, please don't wake up, please don't wake up.

She stayed as still as possible until his soft snore filled the room. Breathing a quiet sigh of relief, she slowly inched her way to the side of the bed. The mattress squeaked from her slight weight and she froze, squeezing her eyes shut and biting her lip so hard she tasted blood.

To her relief her companion continued to snore beside her despite the noise. Hoping he was truly a heavy sleeper, she said a silent prayer and slid the rest of the way to the edge of the mattress. However, she misjudged the amount of room she had and rolled right off the bed, landing on the floor with a loud thud.

She instantly curled up into a ball, covering her nakedness as best she could from prying eyes. Her cheeks burned as she thought of being caught bare-assed in that position, but the room remained silent except for the cover hog's snoring.

Inhaling a shaky breath, she sat up, darting her eyes over the room in search of her clothes. Her jeans lay on the floor at the foot of the bed bunched up as if she'd taken them off in a hurry. Not bothering to look for her underwear first, she reached for her pants and squirmed into the heavy material while still lying on the floor.

After successfully wiggling into her jeans, she spied her purse on the seat of the armchair and quickly snatched it up, then crawled to the other side of the bed—*his* side—and saw her blouse peeking out from under the bed. She stretched out as far as she could to reach it, not wanting to get any closer to him than necessary. Finally, her fingers brushed the soft fabric and she pulled it to her, yanking it on as fast as she could while still being quiet. Then she grabbed her shoes and held them to her chest as she slowly got to her feet and backed away from the bed, her eyes never leaving the sleeping form.

If the circumstances had been different, she'd definitely think he was a good-looking guy. His brown hair was spiked in the front—although it had flattened from sleeping—and his nose had a slight bend to it as if it had been broken at one time. His chest was bare, and she was pretty sure the rest of him was as well, revealing a very nice set of biceps. His face suddenly flashed in her mind and she knew he had brown eyes and dimples when he smiled.

She forced her mind to focus back on quietly escaping, when her bare foot landed on a piece of paper. The crinkle echoed through the room, making her cringe. She bent down and ripped the paper off her foot, quickly glancing at it to make sure it wasn't something of hers.

Her eyes widened when she saw the words that were staring back at her, making her stomach roll and vomit rise in her throat.

No fucking way.

She tore her eyes away from the paper and looked at the man sleeping in the king-size bed. His soft breathing felt all wrong compared to how her heart was hammering in her chest. This man, this stranger, was—

He rolled over, grumbling again in his sleep, causing her to jump. She had to get out of there before he woke up.

Frantic now, she turned and bolted from the room, not caring if her hasty exit woke him, just as long as she got away. As she ran down the hall she could only hope he would wake up as confused as she had been and unable to remember anything.

Especially her.

Chapter 1

"When was the last time you got laid?"

Novalee Jensen almost dropped the glass she was drying.

"Whoa, someone's jumpy," Cali Donavon commented to her jittery friend.

"You just startled me," Novalee disagreed, placing the glass on the tray.

"Nov, I've been standing here drying glasses with you for the past half-hour."

Novalee frowned. She hated that irritating nickname, and if it had been anyone but Cali, she would have corrected them. "I know, I . . . I guess I'm just in my own world," she muttered, picking up another shooter glass.

"Well, now that you've rejoined this world, answer the question."

Novalee looked at the woman next to her and saw she was frowning. "Why do you want to know?"

"Because I haven't gotten any in almost two months. Two months!" she cried, looking totally disgusted. "I thought breaking up with Adam meant I'd get more tail."

Novalee chuckled. "Why would you think that?"

"Uh, because I'm single and smoking hot and work in a bar," she answered stating the obvious. "Plus I'm fun, smart, and fucking fantastic in bed."

"Not to mention totally modest," Novalee teased.

Cali laughed and lifted one shoulder, shrugging coyly.

And it was true; men should be hitting on Cali left and right. With her honey-colored hair that hung halfway down her back, piercing hazel eyes, small waist, mile-long legs and a great rack to boot, she looked more like a Playboy centerfold than a bartender in a small city.

"Maybe they think you're still with, Adam," Novalee said. "The guys that come in here are regulars and know you fall into the 'look but don't touch' category."

"*Fell* into that category," Cali corrected. "But I flirt with them all the time."

"You always flirted with them," Novalee reminded her with a snort.

"Well, how long has it been since you got some?" she questioned again.

"I don't know," Novalee muttered. "A few months, I guess."

If there was an award for understatement of the year, she'd definitely win. A few months were more like twenty-four months. Two long years.

Not that she hadn't had the opportunity. Men flirted and asked her out, blatantly told her they'd like to take her home for a night she'd never forget, but she just couldn't do it. Ever since waking up in Vegas two years ago with *him* and realizing what they'd done—what she still hadn't dealt with—being with other men felt wrong.

As soon as the plane landed and she was back in Missoula, Montana she should have taken the necessary steps to have the issue resolved, but she hadn't.

Honestly, it was too embarrassing. She didn't want to admit to herself, let alone anyone else, about her intoxicated mistake back in Nevada. She hadn't even told Cali, her best friend since daycare days, what she had done. If she couldn't tell the one person who would never judge her no matter how fucked-up she made things, how could she tell anyone else?

"A few months?" Cali's voice broke into her thoughts, and she heard the frown in her voice. "I don't remember seeing you with anyone for . . . Hell, I don't even remember how long!"

Novalee stashed the full tray under the bar, ignoring the comment.

"Who was the last guy you were with?" Cali pressed.

"I don't know . . . Maybe it has been longer than a few months," she snapped.

"Damn." Cali shook her head, pity coloring her tone. "That Rabbit must be getting a good workout." Novalee scowled at her. "Hey, it's nothing to be ashamed of. Mine and I are like this," she said, crossing her fingers.

"I'm surprised you need one," Novalee retorted. "Your little black book is like a huge black binder."

"Dry spell, remember?"

"Still, you weren't with Adam that long," Novalee mused. "All your men couldn't have disappeared."

"You wouldn't think so." Cali slid closer to her and whispered, "Seriously, I'm so horny Tony is starting to look good." She cast a glance at the cook who'd just come out of the kitchen.

"Oh my God!" Novalee gasped in horror. "I'd disown you, Cali!"

"I know!" she moaned, covering her face. "I feel so dirty just thinking about it."

Tony was a nice enough guy and a decent cook, but he was a total douche when it came to women. What could you expect when your nickname was "Tony the Pony?"

"Call Adam," Novalee demanded.

"No." Cali removed her hands and shook her head. "I refuse to crawl back. My BOB will do just fine, thank you."

Novalee rolled her eyes, although she wished she could say the same about her battery-operated boyfriend. She may have survived the past two years, but sadly her Rabbit hadn't. She still remembered the sad little groan it made as it shuddered one last time and died for good. She'd actually managed to kill her vibrator. Who did that?

Women who do stupid things in Vegas and go without sex for two years because they have a twisted conscience.

Oh, right.

"Hey, Tony," Cali called, "what size are your shoes?"

"Huh?" Tony looked at her with a goofy expression on his face.

"What. Size. Are. Your. Shoes?" she repeated slowly.

"Uh, sixteen."

"Really?" Cali's voiced pitched in surprise.

Oh Christ, she wouldn't.

"Is it true what they say?" she asked. "You know, about men's shoe sizes?"

Novalee cast a glance at Tony and saw him shifting from foot to foot looking uncomfortable. Tony was uncomfortable? That was a first.

"Uh . . . I haven't been with any men to know that, Cali."

Novalee held back the laugh that wanted to burst forth. Okay, he may be a good guy, a decent cook, and not bad looking, but no one said he was bright. She looked at Cali, who rolled her eyes. "I mean, is it true in your case?"

He suddenly grinned and lost all the self-consciousness he'd shown seconds before. He was nothing short of cocky now.

"Why don't you come back to my place and find out, honey?"

Novalee clamped a hand over her mouth to keep from vomiting on the floor, but still tasted some of the acidy substance on her tongue. Her stomach rolled again when it looked like Cali was actually considering it!

"I'm not sure," her friend finally replied.

He shrugged. "Your loss."

"That's the thing." Cali leaned against the bar, placing her elbows behind her on the smooth surface, thrusting out her breasts in the process. Tony's eyes traveled up her legs and stopped at her chest. "Would your cock be satisfying enough to make my loss of friendship worth it?"

And she did.

This is where she and Cali differed. It was amazing they were best friends, considering how opposite they were. Cali was an extrovert—an overly friendly, loud, opinionated extrovert. She said whatever was on her mind regardless of how inappropriate it was. Women tended to see her as a pushy, obnoxious skank and because of that she had very few women friends. In fact, Novalee was sure she was Cali's only female friend. Men flocked to her like bees to flowers however, and she wasn't one to turn down their . . . pollination attempts.

Novalee was more of an introvert, although she hadn't always been so reserved. Life and its unpredictable curve balls had made her that way. She used to be as social and outgoing as Cali, and there was a time when she was the life of the party. Granted, she didn't collect men like her friend and could count on one hand the number of men she'd slept with in her twenty-eight years—the number was incredibly depressing—but at one time she was just as spontaneous and fun as any other female her age.

Over the years she'd disappeared into a shell of the person she once was. She didn't party anymore, didn't socialize with other people other than Cali and the patrons that came into the bar, and she didn't date. She really didn't live.

And the last time she had taken a spur-of-the-moment trip and was spontaneous, look what happened.

"Uh, yeah, sure," Tony answered, looking at Cali as if she was crazy. He tore off the apron and said, "You know where to find me," before leaving.

Cali giggled and looked at Novalee, who was still fighting nausea.

"You look green," Cali commented.

"Uh, yeah! I just pictured Tony the Pony naked and sweaty!"

Cali rolled her eyes. "Don't worry, I won't go there."

"The problem is *I* just went there." Novalee shuddered.

They finished cleaning up and exited the bar through the back employee entrance.

"Going home to Ben and Jerry?" Cali asked as Novalee locked up.

"Who else would I go home to?"

They walked to their cars together, always sure to park next to one another since they didn't leave until after closing. Safety was in numbers after all. Novalee's headlights flashed as she hit the button to unlock her door.

"You'd better go home to your BOB," she warned Cali as she opened her door.

"Like I said, I won't go there, Nov," Cali promised.

Novalee waved and got into her car, locking the doors. The soft melody of a country song came out of the speakers as she started her car. She followed Cali out of the parking lot and to the first light, but that's where they parted. Cali turned left, giving a quick honk as she did, and Novalee continued straight ahead. They lived at opposite ends of the city, but since Missoula wasn't that large, they weren't too far from one another.

Novalee lived closer to the bar—her bar. She'd purchased the rundown building seven years ago on her twenty-first birthday. The previous owner had been pretty desperate to get rid of it and her real estate agent told her it was a steal even with the amount of work she'd have to put into it.

Cali told her she was crazy opening a business she knew nothing about, but like the awesome friend she was, she was by Novalee's side from closing bid to opening day. It had taken them a year of hard work to get the old place ready. Novalee had decided to gut the building, removing all the old booths and tables and even the bar itself. They ripped up the stained floor and put something new and shiny in its place. The shelving and counter space behind the bar was removed and redone, and a deep mahogany wood took the place of the old chipped counter that had been there. The floor looked like hardwood but was actually something much cheaper, and the booths and tables were a dark color to match the bar. Cali had suggested adding a new jukebox and a pool table for the younger crowd as well.

She also replaced all the old appliances in the kitchen with newer ones, but that had been the extent of the makeover in that area. Novalee didn't want to run a restaurant, so she saw no need to spend a butt-load of money in the kitchen when the majority of the food served would be hamburgers, fries, and sandwiches.

At first people only came in out of curiosity, but after a while she got some regulars, and within eighteen months the business really took off. What seemed like a foolish idea was now her meal ticket.

Novalee turned into her driveway and slid her shiny red sports car into the garage. She nervously glanced into the review mirror as she pressed the button to close the garage door behind her and shut off the engine. Even after all this time she was still anxious that someone might be hiding in a dark corner waiting for her to park and slip into the garage after her. Out of habit, she still packed the pepper spray in her purse and it somewhat comforted her that if she needed it at any time, it was there.

She exited the car, making sure to lock it behind her even though it was in the safety of her garage, and hurried around the vehicle to the door that led straight into her house. That was a must for her when she'd been house hunting. There had to be a door in the garage that led straight into the house.

As always, she was greeted by Ben and Jerry as soon as she opened the door. Ben, a white Persian, jumped up on the entryway table demanding attention, while Jerry, a chocolate Lab, panted at her feet. She scratched behind Ben's ear before bending down to give some love to his companion.

"Mama's good boys," she said in a soothing tone. "Are you guys hungry?"

She patted Jerry's head one more time and went to her bedroom to change into the sweats and tank she slept in before going into the kitchen to fill their water and food dishes. She let Jerry out into the backyard through the sliding glass doors in her kitchen so he could do his business for the night. He was back within seconds, and she grabbed the fruit bowl she'd prepared that morning out of the fridge and shuffled to the living room, curling up on the couch with the remote. She clicked through her DVR list until she found her favorite sitcom from earlier that evening and settled in to watch.

She popped a grape into her mouth as Ben poked his head under her arm to snoop inside the bowl.

"I'm not sharing this time, buddy," she said. "My food." She selected a piece of melon this time and looked back at the T.V., ignoring the cat's pestering. Jerry flopped down beside the couch, resting his head on his paws, waiting for any food she might drop.

She must have dozed off sometime during the show, because suddenly a loud crash startled her awake. She jumped up, spilling the contents of her bowl and Jerry was beside her in seconds in full protective mode. Before she could panic, she saw what had caused the noise: Ben had climbed up onto the bookshelf and knocked over a picture, which in turn had knocked down the other objects next to it in a domino effect.

"Damn it, Ben," Novalee grumbled as she saw the cat perched next to the mess. "You scared the shit out of me."

She bent down to scoop up the spilled fruit and carried it back to the kitchen to dispose of it. After washing her hands and rinsing out the bowl, she went back to the living room and shooed the mischievous cat off the shelf to clean up the mess.

Picking up the picture, she immediately felt the familiar pang of loss as she looked at the image. Her parents, Joseph and Amelia Jensen, stood arm-in-arm in front of their first home. Amelia was several months pregnant with their first, and only, child. Their smiles lit up the old photograph; the love between them so strong it would be evident even to a stranger.

Tears stung her eyes as she traced the faces of her parents with her fingertip. Her mother stared back at her, identical to her daughter in every way. Both had eyes the color of the ocean, thick, curly blonde hair, heart-shaped faces and full pouty lips. Their figures were similar also: both slender yet curvy in all the right places, although Amelia's hips were a little fuller after having a child. And they stood the exact same height at five feet six inches tall.

Novalee had grown up in the small town of Superior, Montana where her parents owned and managed a local hardware store. It wasn't much, but in a town with less than a thousand people it was a small success. Joseph had had dreams of retiring on a ranch one day, a place he and his wife could sit on the front porch and relax after years of hard work, perhaps watching grandchildren play in the yard.

Novalee had dreamed of escaping the town and moving east. She'd wanted to live amongst the bright lights of the big city. She'd wanted to go to Broadway shows and spend hours window-shopping or wandering around the large parks, people watching. She'd wanted the chance to live and experience the things her parents never got to.

The day her life had changed forever started out as any normal day. She was sixteen and a sophomore in high school. She and Cali skipped the entire afternoon and hung out at her place instead. Her parents had gone to Missoula, an hour from Superior, for some shopping and wouldn't be home until later that night. At five, Cali left to go home and Novalee had expected her folks to be home any minute. By six they still hadn't shown up, but she'd figured they had just stayed later than planned. By seven she'd started to worry, and at eight she was panicking. Her parents never went this long without checking in on her and never got home any later than seven when they went out.

Finally at nine, lights had shone through the living room window, but instead of her father's car, a police cruiser sat in the driveway. To this day, Novalee couldn't remember the officer coming to the front door, nor Patrick and Ann, Cali's parents, arriving, and she couldn't remember the blood-curdling scream she'd apparently let out.

All she'd remembered was feeling empty and dead inside as the officer informed her that her parents were dead. Joseph and Amelia had been driving home when a tractor-trailer lost control in front of them. Despite any effort Joseph may have made to avoid the collision it had been inescapable and neither the truck driver nor her parents had walked away from the accident.

Being the planners her parents were, they'd made arrangements in case such a thing ever happened. Patrick and Ann, who'd had always been like a second set of parents to her, became her guardians. Novalee hadn't had to worry about finalizing arrangements when it came to their personal or business lives either; they'd made it all quite clear in their will what they wanted. That had come as a relief to a sixteen-year-old girl who had just lost her entire world. Who wanted to make decisions about how that world would be put to rest?

She'd been surprised after the funeral to learn that her father had managed to put away a fairly large amount of savings over the years. That was on top of the two-million dollar life insurance he'd had. Novalee remembered feeling sick when the lawyer had smiled at her and told her she was indeed a very wealthy young lady. Everyone around her had seen endless possibilities for her future with that kind of money. She'd only seen it as blood money. Her parents had to die in order for her to have that money. She would have traded it all and lived in a box for the rest of her life if it meant she could have them back.

At eighteen, she had gained control over her father's savings and the hardware store. The life insurance money had stayed in a trust fund. She'd received half on her twenty-first birthday and would get the rest on her thirtieth. Patrick and Ann had managed the store until her eighteenth birthday and then handed it over to her. She'd had no idea what to do with it. She hadn't felt like she couldn't sell it because it was all she'd had left of her parents, but at eighteen she had no idea how to run a business. All her friends had left and gone off to college, including Cali, and even though she'd been only a few hours away, it had felt like she was across the country. At times it seemed to Novalee that she'd been left behind.

All those dreams she'd had of leaving the small town she grew up in didn't seem as important. Superior had been the last place she'd been happy with her parents and she'd been unable to turn her back on that.

So she'd decided to stay and keep the store open. With Patrick's help she'd slowly begun to catch on and found it wasn't as hard as she'd feared. Then, just when it had seemed like she was putting her life back together, Dalton entered the picture . . .

Novalee shuddered, snapping herself out of the past. That was a memory lane she didn't want to go down. She sighed, thinking instead of when she'd sold the store three years later just before her twenty-first birthday and moved to Missoula. That's when her life had really begun, and she hadn't looked back since.

She carefully put the picture back on the shelf and wiped her tears. A glance at the clock told her it was almost four in the morning, and she groaned. She had to stop coming home and watching T.V. instead of going straight to bed. She should have been ready to pass out from exhaustion when she walked through her front door at three thirty every morning, but she never was. She always needed to unwind after being at the bar all day and as much as she hated it five a.m. was usually her bedtime.

Checking once more to make sure she'd locked the doors, she shut off the lights and made her way to her bedroom. Yawning, she pulled back the covers on the queen bed and crawled in. She wasn't alone long before her boys made themselves comfortable on the bed. She smiled as Ben's purring filled the room and let it lull her off to sleep.

She was in her office by two that afternoon. Okay, maybe "office" was a loose description of the space. There was a small apartment over the bar that she'd turned into her office space when she'd bought the place. It was equipped with a small kitchenette and bathroom and enough room for her desk, filing cabinets, and a couch Cali had insisted she have. Novalee had to admit the couch had come in handy on nights she'd been too tired to drive home.

She was going over the books when Cooper, her deliveryman, poked his head in.

"Hey, Miss. J!"

She looked up and smiled. "Hey, Coop. How many times do I have to ask you to call me Novalee?"

He smiled sheepishly. "Sorry. I have the order downstairs if you want to come take a look."

"Great." She stood and grabbed her keys off the desk and followed Cooper downstairs.

He'd just handed her the clipboard to look over and sign when Cali walked in. Her huge sunglasses hid her eyes, but Novalee could smell the guilt dripping off of her without having to see it in her eyes. Plus, she was carrying two cups of very expensive coffee, something she only did as a peace offering when she'd done something she knew Novalee would disapprove of.

Novalee quickly signed the receiving order and handed it back to Cooper. "Thanks for unloading it," she said, giving him a smile.

"No problem." He grinned and nodded good-bye to Cali before leaving.

Novalee turned and crossed her arms, eyeing her friend. "Do I even have to ask?" she questioned.

"I know. I know. I'm a horrible person!" Cali whined, putting the coffee on the bar.

"You screwed Tony," Novalee stated, not even needing her to admit it.

Cali sighed. "If it makes you feel any better, Karma really is a bitch." She pushed her glasses on top of her head and squinted against the light.

"Was the shoe theory wrong?"

"Oh, no, the shoe theory was not wrong at all. That guy is hung like a horse." She grimaced. "But he doesn't know how to use it. At all."

Novalee laughed. "That does make it a little better, but you still chose dick over friendship. You're disowned."

"But I didn't get dick!" Cali cried. "I thought that's what I was choosing, but instead I got horrible jackrabbit sex. Remember Carrie Bradshaw's awful jackrabbit sex in that wedding episode?" Novalee nodded. "Times that by a hundred and you have Tony the Pony."

"Oh my God!" Novalee giggled, covering her mouth with her hand.

"Oh my God is right. And not in a good way. He hurt me, Nov!" she exclaimed. "Something that big should not be attached to a man who doesn't know how to properly fuck a woman." Cali shook her head. "Mother Nature is a bitch for unleashing him on us unexacting horny women."

Novalee couldn't help it and burst into giggles again.

"You have to forgive me!" Cali begged. "Believe me when I tell you my poor vag is paying for all the damage caused to our friendship by this mistake."

"Well, don't expect me to kiss it better for you," Novalee warned. "Although, I'm sure Tony would be happy to oblige."

Cali scowled. "He and his ten-foot-pole are never getting near me again. You know how he's never with the same woman twice? I don't think that's by choice. They run away and go into witness protection."

Novalee laughed. "Don't you mean pussy protection?"

"Good one." Cali grinned. "Yes, pussy protection. I wish there was such a thing."

"I'm sure he'll be crushed to hear it."

"Not as crushed as I am," Cali moaned. "That's a penis I could have married."

"Ew." Novalee wrinkled her nose. "No more sharing."

"Here." Cali thrust a cup at her. "Will you accept my peace offering?"

Novalee glanced at the cup and then back at her friend, pretending to ponder the question. "Fine. But remember, if you ever betray me again I'm sending Pony Boy over for round two."

Cali cringed. "Scout's honor."

Novalee rolled her eye. "That's not very assuring. You were kicked out of Girl Scouts."

Cali smirked. "Trust me. I want to keep Little Miss Muffit in one piece."

Novalee took her coffee and grinned. "There's some ice in the kitchen if you need to stuff your panties."

"If I thought ice would help I'd be sitting on a pile right now. The poor girl is never going to be the same again."

Novalee took that as her cue to leave. "I need to check the kitchen stock," she said, escaping before Cali could go into detail.

Tony arrived for his shift a few minutes later, strutting around the kitchen with a big-ass grin on his face. Cali hid out front making sure to busy herself with the customers once they opened. A couple of times Tony tried to make conversation with her, but she'd quickly scurry off, finding some task that needed her attention. By the time happy hour hit there was enough tension between the two of them to suffocate everyone in the building.

Novalee was in the storage room getting another case of beer when Cali came in grinning from ear-to-ear.

"What?" Novalee asked when she stood there without saying anything.

"Someone's at the bar asking for you."

"Is there a problem?" Because if there was and Cali was standing there with that goofy look on her face, she was going to smack her.

"I don't think so. He just asked where he could find Novalee Jensen."

She frowned. "He's not a regular?"

"Never seen him before in my life." Cali wiggled her eyebrows. "Spending time with someone other than Ben and Jerry, are we?"

"Don't be ridiculous," Novalee scoffed. "As if I could keep something like that from you."

"He's hot, Nov. Like, make-my-broken-Muffit-feel-better hot."

Novalee rolled her eyes. "So much for never being the same again." She picked up the case of beer and handed it to Cali. "Let me go see what he wants."

Cali was right on her heels as she left the storage room and crossed the kitchen to enter the bar. She pushed open the swinging door and stopped dead in her tracks. Cali, obviously caught off guard, ran into her and almost dropped the beer.

"What the hell, Novalee?"

Novalee continued to stare at the man who was sitting at the far end of the bar. His short brown hair faced her as he played with his Blackberry, but she didn't need to see his face to know whom he was and that this was the man looking for her.

Cali nudged her with the box, pushing her out the door a little more. Panic filled her chest and she spun around and pushed past her friend, pressing her back against the kitchen wall out of sight.

"What the fuck is wrong with you?" Cali said as her eyes widened.

"The guy at the far end with short brown hair, brown eyes and a nose that's kinda crooked as if it has been broken once . . . is that the guy?"

"Yeah. Hey, how can you see his eyes and nose from here?" Cali poked her head out of the door before Novalee could stop her.

She pulled her back into the kitchen. "Don't," she hissed. "He might see you."

"Hell, I wouldn't complain if he did." This comment earned a death glare from Tony. "But the question is why don't you want him to see you?"

"Please, get rid of him," Novalee begged. "Tell him I left."

"Why?" Cali looked worried now.

"Please, just do it for me, Cali." She sounded almost hysterical now.

"Nov, what's going on? Are you in trouble?"

"Yes. No. I don't know! Just get him to leave!"

"Not until you tell me why!" Cali gripped her upper arms and forced her to calm down. "Who is that guy?"

She looked into her best friend's eyes and shook her head. Fear made her heart pound in her chest as a night from two years ago came flooding back to her.

"Novalee, answer me, dammit!" Cali said, gripping her arms harder and giving her a little shake.

She let out a sob as humiliation filled her.

"He's my husband."

Chapter 2

Two months earlier . . .

He knew she was coming before the clicking of her heels on the tiled floor announced her approach; the expensive perfume she wore assaulted him the minute she entered the hotel bar. The fragrance was alluring to most men; it had been to him the first time he'd met her, too. Now, it just reminded him of money and cheap sex. Or maybe it wasn't cheap considering the amount he paid her to be his lawyer.

He didn't bother looking up when she slapped a bill on the cool surface and informed the bartender, in a voice that told him not to mess with her, that he'd had enough.

"Are you trying to ruin my buzz, Abigail?" he mumbled into his glass.

"I'm here to make sure you get to your meeting on time," she snapped.

"So that would be a yes."

"Dean, it's ten in the morning and you're sitting in a bar when you should be in the conference room." Her tone became softer. "I need you sober."

"I'm not drunk, I'm relaxing."

"You sure do a lot of relaxing lately"

"I wonder why," he said under his breath.

Abigail snatched the drink out of his hand and placed it out of his reach.

"How do you think this is going to look, Dean?" she hissed.

He finally looked at her and gave her a half-assed smirk. "You look good enough for the both of us, Abby."

She glared at him. "Will you be serious?"

"Oh, I'm serious," he said in a smarmy tone, reaching to swat her ass.

She smacked his hand away and threatened to cut his balls off and serve them with his liquor if he touched her again.

He sighed. "You used to be more fun, Abby."

In truth, Abigail had been a lot of fun to a lot of guys. They had met when she was working as an exotic dancer in a Las Vegas club to earn enough money to put herself through law school. Her witty banter and smart-ass attitude had made Dean like her instantly. The fact that she was smoking hot didn't hurt either.

She kept her raven black hair long, but always wore it pulled back when working. Dean remembered the days when her hair was a wild mess around her face, being tossed this way and that from her dancing. The days when she hadn't been so put together and prissy.

Her eyes were so dark they were almost black and somehow they managed to turn even darker when she was pissed. Truthfully, it used to turn him on knowing that beneath her conservative exterior lay a vixen. Plump C-cup breasts, a tiny waist with a navel that sported a diamond piercing, and hips that begged to be touched. And when you touched them, *she* begged.

"Well, I hope those thoughts of how much more fun I used to be keep you warm at night when you're living on the street," she quipped. "Because that's where you're going to end up if you don't get your fucking act together."

Dean snorted. "I'm not going to be homeless, Abby. I own this fucking hotel and ten others like it."

"At the moment. But maybe not for much longer."

"You worry too much," he said, brushing off her concern. "Besides, I can always live with you."

"This isn't funny, Dean! Your entire life, your entire financial well-being, rests in the hands of those men that are waiting for you today."

He stared at the spot where his drink had been, his hands clenching into fists on their own.

"Do you really think they can go against my grandfather's will?" he asked.

"Richard is pissed and out for blood. He thinks he should have been the rightful heir to your grandfather's estate."

"He does have a point," Dean agreed, even if he hated to admit it.

His father, Richard Philips, should have been the one to inherit his grandfather's real estate. Instead, the old man had left every single hotel across the country to his only grandson. Richard still got an enormous chunk of change, but it wasn't enough for the greedy bastard. He wanted to control it all and he wouldn't be happy until he did.

His grandfather, William Philips, had owned a chain of luxurious hotels across the country. Years of blood, sweat, and tears had gone into making his dreams come true and in the end he'd created WIP Hotels, an empire that astonished even him at times. At a young age, William had seen something in Dean that he hadn't in his own son. He'd taken the boy under his wing, showed him the ins and outs of the business, and groomed him for the day he would take over. Hoping to expand his chains outside of the country, William had sent Dean on scouting missions to Canada, Europe, and Australia, giving him more responsibility than he'd ever entrusted to Richard.

With great effort on his part, Richard tried endlessly to get his father to see Dean as only a child, too young to understand what really went into running the hotel empire, but William would hear none of it.

Richard knew of his father's decision well before it was written on paper, and they had fought about it constantly. William told his son outright that it would be a cold day in Hell before he handed his hotels over to him. Richard was irresponsible and a gambler, and William knew if he left his livelihood to Richard it would be sold and lost to the family the second the deeds landed in his hands.

However, William did agree to put in one stipulation: Dean had to be married before he came into full control; a stipulation presented by Richard, of course.

Dean hadn't understood it and the only reason that made a little bit of sense for his father to want *that* was because he knew William's health was failing and Dean had no prospects of marrying any time soon. Richard knew his son was a playboy, the non-commitment type, and marriage was the only way he would gain control himself. Dean was sure his grandfather only agreed to shut Richard up.

It was two years ago when Dean was in a Las Vegas casino that he'd gotten the call from Abigail that his grandfather had suffered a heart attack and was in rough shape.

"He told me he needs you to do something for him, Dean." Abigail's voice sounded nervous, almost upset.

"Anything."

And when she told him what William needed, Dean had suddenly understood why he hadn't cared about putting in Richard's stupid stipulation.

There didn't need to be a real wife, only a marriage.

Dean had been talking with a pretty little blonde at the time of the call and as soon as Abigail had hung up on him, promptly denying his proposal in a huff, he knew what he had to do.

So he did it.

And he felt like the shit he was every single day since.

His grandfather had recovered, but was never the same. Dean had gained control of power of attorney above his father because of that simple piece of paper he had presented.

His father had flown into a rage when he'd found out. "This is bullshit!" he screamed, throwing the papers across the table. "It's a conspiracy between the two of you to keep me from what is rightfully mine!"

"What you think is of no concern to me, or anyone else, Richard," William replied calmly. "The boy is married. Control lies with him."

Richard pushed back from the table so hard he knocked his chair over. He rounded the table and pointed his finger at his son. "You'll pay for this," he threatened. "He won't live forever and when he dies, we'll see just how real your marriage is. Be prepared to lose everything."

"You already made me lose everything, Richard," Dean answered coldly. "Remember?"

Little did his father know he had lost the last remaining thing that was important to him when his grandfather had passed away. It had been six months and the pain was still as fresh as ever. His father had wasted no time in trying to contest William's will and prove Dean's marriage was nothing more than a fake.

"It doesn't matter if he has a point or not," Abigail said. "This is your grandfather's dying wish, and he wouldn't want you sitting here drinking yourself stupid when you should be up there fighting for what's yours."

Dean glared at her and leaned over the bar, grabbing his drink from behind her.

"Don't tell me what William would have wanted, Abigail," he snarled before downing the rest of his drink, and then looked up to meet her eyes. "No one knows better than I do what he wanted. Look what I did to make sure of it."

"Then stop beating yourself up and act like it matters," she snapped.

"I am!"

"No, you're not."

Dean groaned and shook his head, frustration, and anger tensing his shoulders.

"Dean." He rolled his eyes towards her. "You have to do this for him. You have to finish this and then you can go and make everything right."

Dean looked away and stared off into space. He knew she was right. There was no other way but to go up and face the waiting army of men his father had hired to take him down. And then he could right the wrongs he'd made two years ago.

"Did you find the information I asked you for?"

She smirked. "I found everything you'll need." She patted her black leather briefcase. "It's all in here."

"Is there anything I should know before going up there?" he asked, keeping his eyes on the briefcase. His fingers itched to grab it and devour everything in there.

"Like?"

"Like anything they may ask me," he barked.

"You mean, like where she lives? What she does? Who her family is? And why no one has ever seen you with this woman in the past two years?" Abigail matched his glare with one of her own. "Don't play stupid with me,

Dean. You know everything about this woman. You've been obsessed since you met her." She brushed her hand through her hair and rolled her eyes.

"She's my wife," he said.

"On paper. Don't fool yourself into thinking it's more."

"Will there be any surprises? Anything they know that we don't?" He wasn't in the mood for her games, either.

"I guess we'll find out when we get up there," she answered coolly.

"Did you take care of the other matter?" he asked, staring at the bar's smooth surface.

She hesitated before answering. "All the paperwork is in order and just needs your signatures." She paused. "It's been too long to ask for an annulment. You have to file for divorce."

"Fucking perfect," Dean muttered, suddenly craving another drink.

"I'm sorry, Dean. There's nothing I can do."

"It's not your fault."

"Oh, I know." She smiled. "You made this mess all on your own."

"I know."

Abigail clicked her tongue and tapped her sliver watch. Taking the not so subtle hint, Dean pushed to his feet and stood to his full six-feet-three-inch height. He looked down at Abigail and jerked his head, indicating he was ready to face his father and the waiting firing squad.

"I asked Andrew to be there," Abigail informed him once they were in the elevator. Andrew Percy had been his grandfather's attorney. Now he was one of Dean's. "I told him to bring his partners if he thought it would help."

"Sure." Dean didn't care who was there as long as one of them made his father back the fuck off once and for all.

"Don't get emotional in there, Dean," Abigail advised.

"I'm not going to fall to my knees, crying and begging for Richard to drop all of this if that's what you're worried about," he replied dryly.

"What I'm worried about is you losing your temper. You can't take this personally."

They reached the top floor which housed an office and a medium-sized conference room on one side and a personal penthouse—his personal penthouse whenever he needed it—on the other. All of his grandfather's hotels were built the same. The main floor had the bar and restaurant, three ballrooms, four small conference rooms, and an indoor swimming pool and spa. Each area had its own private terrace and access to the outdoor pool and patio. The twenty other floors were luxurious suites, each designed by William Philips himself, guaranteed to make any guest feel like royalty. The top floor was always private with the same style office and conference room and the penthouse.

All business was usually conducted in his grandfather's office downtown. Dean still had a hard time thinking of the offices as his. Richard had insisted they meet at the hotel today, though. Dean figured he didn't want to waste a minute throwing Dean and his belongings out on the sidewalk if everything went his way.

"This is personal, Abigail." He stopped walking and waited for her to turn around and acknowledge him.

She did, but she looked annoyed more than anything. "No. This is business." He ground his teeth together to keep from snapping at her. "Keep your personal shit out of this meeting. I'm warning you."

"Or what?" He didn't like being threatened.

"Or your father will win," she answered simply, turning to enter the meeting room.

Dean's hands fisted and he had to press his lips together to keep from snarling at the saucy minx in front of him.

Richard couldn't win. He'd already taken too much from Dean as it was, and he'd be damned if he would let his father stomp on his grandfather's last wishes. The only thing Richard Philips deserved was to rot in Hell where he should have already been fifteen years ago.

How could he keep things from getting personal when he wanted to rip the man apart piece by piece and make him feel the kind of pain Dean had felt every day for the past fifteen years? How could he go in there and look at the bastard who had shattered his life? How could he keep from killing the son-of-a-bitch who had killed *them*?

The faces of the two most beautiful people a person could have ever known flashed in his mind. Their blue eyes shone with an excitement for life and their smiles lit up any room they were in. One had a voice so soft and soothing it could calm you down and take away your fears in seconds. The other was still almost childlike, eager to explore the world and find her place in it. Both were filled with so much love and compassion for every living thing, human or otherwise, that they could only be described as angelic.

His mother and sister had been his whole world; the only two people, other than his grandfather, who he had loved unconditionally and who had loved him the same way. Until he'd come home one evening and found his world shattered and smeared all over the living room—

"Dean?" Abigail said gently, breaking the images up before they could get any worse. He looked up at her, recognizing the sympathetic look on her face. She knew where he'd just gone. She always knew. But what could she say?

"I won't let him win," she promised. "Listen to me, trust me, and I won't let him win."

And that was enough for Dean.

Inhaling deeply, he forced a tight smile and nodded. "I trust you, Abby. You're the only one I have left to trust."

Affection flashed in her eyes, but it was gone as fast as it had appeared and she was back to her aggressive, cold self.

"We'll do this together."

She nodded and jerked open the door, leaving Dean to follow behind her. He entered the room seconds later, noticing Andrew Percy and his two law partners already seated at the table. On the other side sat his father's lawyer, the seat next to him empty. Dean was more than a little surprised the man sat alone. Where was the army Dean was expecting?

"Good morning, gentlemen," Abigail greeted briskly.

"Ms. Knight." Andrew nodded at her and stood to shake Dean's hand. "Mr. Philips."

"Andrew." He nodded his greetings to the other attorneys and took a seat between Andrew and Abigail, his eyes narrowed.

"Where's your client?" Abigail asked before Dean had the chance.

The man lazily lifted his gaze to her and smirked. "Why are you here, Abigail? This is a business matter pertaining to the late Mr. Philips."

"She's my attorney," Dean answered. "Just as much as the men are."

Charles Tanner snickered. "Need all of the team to take me down, Mr. Philips? Are you that afraid you'll lose?"

"The only person that should be afraid, Tanner, is your client. Of me," he said. Abigail laid a restraining hand on his arm and glared at him, warning him to shut up.

"Now, that sounds like a threat."

Dean shrugged. "Take it how you will."

"I think," Andrew said, "what my client is trying to say is that your client has no case."

Charles smiled slyly. "We shall see."

Just then the door opened and Richard Philips sauntered in, a smug smile on his face when he saw everyone waiting on him.

"Dean." He sat across from him. "You still have one last chance to negotiate."

"By 'negotiate,' you mean 'hand everything over to you?' " Dean asked.

Richard's lips twitched. "That's how it should have been."

Dean stared at his father as he leaned across the table. "You'll never get your fucking *bloody* hands on any of this."

Richard stiffened, taking the threat exactly how Dean had intended.

"Let's get this bullshit over with," Richard huffed, looking at Charles.

Charles cleared his throat. "We all know why we're here. Two years ago, Mr. Dean Philips willingly entered a fraudulent marriage to obtain control over the late Mr. William Philips's estate."

"There's no proof that my client's marriage is a fraud," Abigail interjected. "Mr. Philips assumes my client's marriage is a fake simply because he has never met Mrs. Dean Philips."

"Yes, where is Mrs. Philips?" Charles asked with that sly grin again. "*Who* is Mrs. Philips? The only proof we have she exists is a marriage certificate from some sleazy twenty-four hour chapel."

"If you mean 'sleazy' as in it was officiated by an Elvis impersonator, then you couldn't be more wrong." Dean grinned. "Elvis was never in the building."

"Of course he wasn't in the building!" Richard said. "There was no fucking wedding."

"We have documents that say otherwise." Andrew spoke slowly.

"So, I'll ask the question again: where is Mrs. Philips?" Charles inquired.

Dean looked from Abigail to Andrew, waiting for one of them to answer like they were supposed to.

"She's away at the moment," Abigail replied.

Dean fought the urge to roll his eyes. *Yeah, that answer was going to satisfy Richard and the shark.*

"At the moment?" Richard snorted. "This woman hasn't been present since this farce began."

"In all fairness, how often has Dean been in your presence these past two years?" Abigail asked.

"Often enough to steal what is mine!" Richard bellowed.

"That's enough." Charles gave him a stern look before shifting his eyes to Abigail again. "We figured that would be your response, Ms. Knight, so we did some digging of our own."

Dean stilled, his heart rate steadily increasing.

"What do you mean *digging*?" he asked.

With the smug smile in place, Charles flipped open the folder in front of him and withdrew a sheet of paper. "Information on your wife, Mr. Philips."

Dean watched as Abigail snapped the paper from his hands, her eyes roaming over the sheet in front of her before passing it to Andrew.

"Good. Then that proves that Mr. Philips is indeed married and this meeting and attempt at stealing what is legally his is over," she said confidently.

"Not so fast, Abigail," Charles replied calmly. "If they are indeed married, then why does Mrs. Philips reside in Montana?"

"Maybe you need to reread your own information, *Charles*." Abigail smirked. "Mrs. Philips has a permanent residence and business in Montana. My client does not have a permanent residence in Las Vegas, or anywhere else for that matter, so he resides with Mrs. Philips in her home when he's not travelling." She paused and Dean watched as Charles Tanner lost a bit of his smugness. "You can check my client's credit card records and see for yourself. You'll find there have been many trips to Montana in the past two years."

Of course there would be. His grandfather had wisely insisted he cover his tracks and make it look as real as possible in case this moment did happen.

"Charles, this is absolute bullshit!" Richard exclaimed. "It's obviously all fake; a very devious plan set up by the old fool to keep me out!"

"If I do recall, Richard," Andrew said, "it was you who insisted Dean get married, and William agreed."

"Well, yes, but—"

"You just didn't think it would be a problem."

Anger flashed in Richard's eyes. "Very convenient, wasn't it? The old man gets sick and suddenly wonder boy shows up fucking married!"

"What's wrong, *Dad*? Have you already gambled and drunk away the money he left you?" Dean snarled. "Need something to pay your debts with? Maybe this time they'll get the right person and not take out innocent victims!"

Richard was on his feet in an instant, Dean following suit. They glared at each other while their lawyers told them to sit down and shut up.

"Clearly, this is going nowhere," Abigail said once everyone had calmed down.

"Clearly," Charles agreed dryly.

"Obviously we're not going to resolve anything amongst ourselves," Andrew added, his partners nodding in agreement. "That only leaves one option."

Dean knew it would come down to this, but his stomach still knotted. "I'll get a court date."

Charles and Richard stood. "We'll be in touch."

They left the room and Dean immediately jumped from his chair, anger rolling through his body.

"Dean—"

"What do you think our chances are?" he demanded.

Abigail exchanged looks with the men.

"Depending on the judge, I think we'll do okay," Andrew said carefully. "You have the evidence regarding your visits to Montana."

"Worst case scenario—"

"He wins," Dean said. "That's the worst case scenario."

"The worst-case scenario," Abigail repeated through clenched teeth, not liking to be interrupted, "is the judge will want physical proof."

Dean stopped pacing and stared at Abby. "Physical proof? You mean . . ."

"I mean, he'll want to meet your wife and have her confirm your story."

As he locked eyes with his lawyer only one thought crossed his mind.

He was definitely fucked.

Four weeks later they had sat in front of a judge, repeating everything they'd said to each other a few short weeks ago.

"Mr. Philips," Judge Benning said, directing himself at Dean, "you acknowledge your trips to Montana were to visit your wife, is that correct?"

"Visit his wife: was a stretch. The truth was that he'd been to Montana trying to find out as much about her as possible. That was almost the same thing, right?

"Yes, I do, Your Honor" he answered.

"And if I were to ask her she'd tell me the same thing?" he questioned, narrowing his eyes.

Dean swallowed. "Yes, Your Honor, she would."

Judge Benning watched him for a few seconds more before nodding. "Mr. Philips, how you and your wife live and what you do is your business, but this marriage is in question because of a legal matter. You've been accused of fraud, and that's very serious. Do you understand that?"

"Yes, Your Honor," Dean answered thickly.

"Then I have no choice but to demand you produce your wife in this court within thirty days."

Dean felt Abigail tense up next to him.

"If she confirms what you've told the court, the will stands. However," he continued, "if she, for whatever reason, does not show, I will grant Mr. Philips's request to contest the will." Dean nodded, not trusting his voice to answer. "Until then Mr. Dean Philips remains in control of the late William Philips's estate."

Dean glanced at his father and saw the arrogant bastard smirk in satisfaction. Abigail waited for the judge to dismiss court and leave before turning to him.

"Well, I told you this could happen."

"Yes, you did."

"So, what now?"

"I guess I have no choice, do I?"

Her mouth dropped open. "You're not seriously going to just hand him control, are you?"

"Fuck no!" Dean said. "I have to go to Montana and bring her back."

Abigail pursed her lips. "And how are you're going to do that?"

"I don't know." He glared at his father as he cockily walked out of the court room. "But I have thirty days to figure it out."

"Are you going to tell her the truth?"

Dean frowned. "Who knows what she knows? She never made any attempt to contact me or annul the marriage."

"You think she really doesn't know she's married?" Abigail asked, sounding amused.

"I don't know."

"Okay," Abigail said finally. "You go work your magic in Montana and I'll do what I can here. What about the divorce papers?"

"Hang onto them. We'll need them after all this mess is over with."

"Dean." Abigail bit her lip and suddenly looked concerned in more than just a lawyerly way. "You do realize if you divorce her she's entitled to her share."

"Maybe she won't want anything."

"Maybe she'll be in the mood for revenge after the truth comes out."

"So, what do you expect me to do?" Dean asked, frustrated. "Stay married to her?"

"No." Abigail shook her head and sighed. "Just be careful."

Two weeks later he was on a plane to Montana, and now here he sat in what he'd learned was his wife's bar.

He took a seat on one of the bar stools and looked around. The place was busy and he assumed business must be good if it was like this every night. A group of young men played pool while a table of business men and women sat around winding down from a long day. He saw a couple in a corner booth looking a little awkward, but interested in each other. He guessed it must be first date jitters.

He peered behind the bar and saw a honey blonde pouring a drink.

"Hey, miss," he called, signaling her over.

She held up her finger, indicating he needed to give her a minute. She finished pouring the drink and slid it to the guy with a wink.

"What can I get you, honey?" she asked, placing her hands on the bar and leaning closer.

"Scotch."

"Straight up?"

He nodded and watched her get the drink. "Do you know where I can find Novalee Jensen?" he asked after she placed his drink in front of him.

She raised an eyebrow and looked at him more closely. "What do you want with Novalee?"

He smiled his charming smile. The one that showed off his dimples. "It's personal."

The blonde laughed. "That bitch lied to me! Going home to Ben and Jerry my ass."

Dean choked on his drink. "Excuse me?"

"Forget it. What's your name, honey?" she asked, grinning.

"She'll know my name." *Hopefully.* "Do you know where she is?" he asked again.

"Yeah. I'll get her for you." She giggled again and hurried into the back.

He shook his head and took out his Blackberry and sent a quick text to Abigail.

Found her and will talk soon. Wish me luck.

His phone chimed a minute later.

You need more than luck. You need a fucking miracle.

He smiled and looked up from the phone just in time to see a flash of blonde disappear behind the door again. After a good ten minutes of waiting, his patience got the best of him and he wandered behind the bar and pushed open the door that led to the kitchen.

An annoyed-looking cook glanced up at him and frowned.

"Customers aren't allowed back here."

"I'm looking for Novalee Jensen," he said to the young guy, stepping farther into the kitchen.

The cook shrugged and pointed to a door marked Employees Only. "She's up in her office."

"Can I go up there?" Dean asked, already walking toward the door.

"Dude, I don't care. If she's up there it's fine."

Dean nodded his thanks and opened the door that would lead him to his wife.

Chapter 3

"Do you want to explain to me how the hell you have a husband?" Cali exclaimed, shutting Novalee's office door behind them. Cali had dragged her up to the office after Novalee had made her confession and started to hyperventilate.

Novalee dropped to the couch, her head swarming with too many questions of her own to pay attention to Cali.

Why was he here now? After all this time, why had he decided to show up? Did he just find out about their marriage? Did he come to demand answers? An annulment? Was it too late for an annulment? If it was they'd have to get a divorce.

Novalee's blood ran cold. Was that it? Did he find out what she was worth and came to demand his share in a divorce?

"Novalee?" Cali sat beside her and grabbed her chilled hand. "Talk to me, Nov."

"I don't know . . . I . . . Why is he . . . ," she babbled to herself.

"Breathe, babe," Cali instructed, rubbing her back. "Calm down and tell me how that guy is your husband. Who is he?"

"His name is Dean Philips," Novalee said, making sense for the first time.

"Okay. How did you become Mrs. Philips? *When* did you become Mrs. Philips?"

Mrs. Philips?

"I . . . Oh God," Novalee moaned, dropping her head to her hands as shame filled her.

Everyone was going to know now. The secret she had kept hidden for the past two years had just walked into her bar. Two years ago she'd been prepared for this. Two years ago she'd expected to see the handsome stranger from her wild and reckless Vegas weekend. Who wouldn't come looking for the mystery woman that they'd married? Every time the door opened she'd held her breath, fear tightening her chest that it might be him.

But he'd never showed. Days turned into weeks, weeks into months and months into years and still he never came. She'd finally begun to breathe easier after the first year and stopped looking for him in the crowed.

And now he was here. She'd stopped expecting him and now he showed up. What the hell did he want after all this time?

"Novalee, talk to me," Cali pled.

"I'm so ashamed, Cali. I don't know how I let this happen."

"Let what happen?" Cali asked again, starting to sound impatient.

Novalee let her hands fall away from her face and looked at her friend as tears filled her eyes. "Remember my trip to Vegas two years ago?" she asked slowly. Cali nodded. "On my last night there I was at a casino and I started talking to a guy. Some idle chitchat and a few drinks later . . . I wake up in bed with the guy the next morning." Cali's eyes widened and she opened her mouth to speak, but Novalee shook her head. "I snuck out of the room before he woke up," she continued, "but not before I found a copy of a marriage license on the floor."

"Holy shit!"

"And a week later I received the marriage certificate in the mail," she concluded.

"You married that hot piece of ass in Vegas after a night of drinking?" Cali asked, just to rub it in.

"Yes."

"Was the sex good?"

"Cali!"

"What?"

"How can that be the first thing you want to know after everything I just told you?" Cali raised her eyebrows and Novalee rolled her eyes. "Forget it. I almost forgot who I was talking to."

"Was it?"

"I have no idea," Novalee confessed. "I don't remember anything from that night. I don't even remember the wedding."

"Now that's the kind of wedding I want," Cali teased. "If you can't remember marrying the guy, how can you expect to remain faithful?"

"Cali, please try and be serious right now."

"Trust me, I'm serious." Novalee glared at her and she sighed. "I don't understand how you could have been that drunk. That's not you."

"I know!"

"Why didn't you tell me? Why didn't you have it annulled right away?"

"I was embarrassed," she admitted, shifting her eyes away. "I got drunk in Vegas and married a stranger. I was ashamed."

"In your defense, he's a smoking-hot stranger."

"Sure, that makes this all better," Novalee snapped.

"Okay, fine I get that you were embarrassed." Cali turned to face her, tucking her leg underneath her. "But you didn't have to tell anyone. You could have filed for an annulment and not made a peep about it. But you stayed married to the guy."

Novalee bit her lip and nodded.

"Have you talked to him since? Has this been an ongoing relationship?"

"No! I haven't seen nor heard from him since that night."

Cali frowned. "Well, that doesn't make much sense either. Why wouldn't *he* file to dissolve the marriage? Why stay married to someone you don't know, or have no intention of knowing?" Cali cast a thoughtful look at her. "Do you think he just found out?"

"I was notified. I mean, I got the marriage certificate. Why wouldn't he?"

"Then why show up after all this time?"

"I don't know, Cali." Novalee shook her head. "I never thought I'd see him again. At first, yeah, but not now." She looked down at her hands.

"Do you think . . .?" Cali let her sentence trail off.

Novalee looked up. "What?"

Cali shifted her weight, suddenly looking uncomfortable. This wasn't good. Cali never looked uncomfortable.

"What?" Novalee asked again.

"Maybe he did some digging and found out about the money your dad left you, and this bar, and he's sniffing around for his share," she said, voicing Novalee's earlier thoughts.

"But how would he find out about the life insurance?"

"It's pretty common knowledge to anyone who knows you, sweetie." Cali's eyes suddenly widened as she thought of something else.

"What?" Novalee's heart dropped to her stomach.

"You don't think he could know Dalton, do you?"

"Dalton?" Novalee jumped off the couch, her heart thumping loudly in her chest.

Cali reached for her. "Nov, it was just a thou—"

"Do you think it's possible?" she asked, panic setting in. "Do you think Dalton would actually set someone up on me like this?" Her stomach rolled.

"Nov, calm down," Cali soothed.

"I mean, yeah, he was pissed at me. And yeah, he's dangerous and crazy and . . . totally capable of doing anything to get his hands on what he wants." Novalee kept thinking about it, panicking more and more. "He *could* be behind all this!"

Cali grabbed her hand and yanked her back down on the couch. "Novalee, look at me," she demanded, holding her shoulders now. "I'm sorry I mentioned it. I just want you to be safe and to be sure you can trust what this guy tells you."

"What if you're right?" Novalee whispered fearfully. "What if Dalton is back?"

Cali pulled her in and wrapped her arms around her quivering body. "Then we go to the police," she answered.

"But what if—"

A knock at the door cut off Novalee's next frantic concern. She pulled out of Cali's embrace and nervously glanced from the door to her friend.

"It's probably just Pam," Cali said. "No doubt she has more orders than she can handle and needs a hand. She's as useless as tits on a boar."

"We could always send Tony after her." Novalee tried joking. "Didn't he give you a helping hand?"

Cali shuddered. "I don't think even Pam deserves that."

Another knock, this time a little louder than the first.

"I'll deal with it," Cali said, standing. "You stay here until you feel like coming down."

"He's down there," Novalee reminded her.

Cali shrugged. "He'll either wait around or get bored and go away."

Novalee doubted it, but nodded anyway, leaning her head back on the couch and closing her eyes. She heard Cali open the office door and then her sharp gasp.

"Hello again," said the deep voice.

Novalee froze.

"Uh . . . um . . . hi," Cali stammered.

"I was told I could find my . . . Miss Jensen up here."

Miss Jensen?

"Well," Cali hesitated, "she's not—"

"It's fine, Cali." Novalee sighed, opening her eyes. The last thing she wanted to do was talk to him, but how long could she possibly hold him off? It might be best to get it out of the way now so they could both move forward.

Cali looked over her shoulder at her and Novalee nodded, indicating she was sure.

"Okay." Cali stepped back and gestured for him to enter.

Novalee felt as if the air had been knocked out of her as he walked into the room. He was taller than she remembered, with broader shoulders. A lot broader. Her mouth went dry as she looked over his body. His hair was shorter than it had been two years ago, and his eyes no longer had the spark they'd had the first night they met. His brown eyes had been full of life then, bright with excitement.

Her gaze drifted down to his chest, and then to his stomach, where she was positive rock-hard abs must be hidden by his shirt. The sudden urge to reach out and lift the shirt to reveal such treasures rocked her to the core. She felt a sudden spasm shoot between her legs as her imagination went wild with what lay beneath the material.

Whoa, down, girl. If that's the kind of reaction she had to just his stomach, she sure as hell had better not let her eyes roam lower.

And as if magnetized, her eyes indeed dropped lower, below his waist. Jeans that fit him in a way that would make any female pant stared back at her. She couldn't remember exactly what lay waiting behind that zipper, but she'd bet it was just as impressive as the rest of him. And she wasn't a betting kind of woman. She bit her lip to keep from blurting out for him to turn around so she could check out the rest of his goods.

Lazily, she dragged her eyes back to his face. He was giving her a half-assed smile, and the dimples she remembered that carved his cheeks didn't show.

Of course, he was probably nervous about this awkward reunion. To Novalee, he looked like he was carrying the weight of the world on his shoulders.

And yet, even though he appeared to only be a shadow of the man she'd had met in a casino all those nights ago, her stomach suddenly filled with butterflies and her heart rate increased.

This man was her husband.

"I'm sorry for barging in like this," he said. "I don't know if you know who I am, or if you remember—"

"I know," Novalee whispered thickly as the sound of his voice made her heart grow wings and flutter in her chest. "I remember." Awkward silence fell between them as they stared at each other.

Cali cleared her throat and said, "I'm going to leave you two alone." She looked at Novalee. "Unless you want me to stay, Nov."

Novalee bit her lip again and looked from the man in front of her, to her best friend. Cali raised her eyebrows questionably.

"No, it's okay, Cali. Thanks."

"I'll be downstairs if you need me," she said, giving Novalee's visitor a once over before leaving.

Novalee shifted her eyes back to him and just as quickly looked away again. What the hell was she supposed to say now?

She peeked at him from the corner of her eye and saw he was checking out her office.

"So, you own this place."

It didn't sound like a question, so obviously he knew the answer without her telling him. However, she did answer with a clipped, "Yes."

He nodded. "Is it always this steady? Good business?"

Novalee stiffened. What was it to him? Unless her instincts had been right and he was sniffing out what he would get from a divorce.

"I do okay," she answered coolly.

He looked at her, surprised by her tone, and then smiled sheepishly. "I'm sorry. I'm a businessman, so my first impulse is to ask about business. I'm not here to take anything from you," he assured her.

Novalee felt relieved but didn't fully believe him yet.

"Why are you here, Mr.—"

"Dean."

"Okay. Then enough with the Miss Jensen stuff." She forced a smile. "It's Novalee."

She stood from the couch and relocated herself to the chair behind her desk, motioning for him to take the seat opposite her.

"Why are you here, Dean?" she asked once he sat down.

He raised his eyebrows, obviously surprised by the question. "Isn't it obvious? You are aware that we're married, right?"

"Trust me, I'm aware," she said. "But why now?"

He hesitated before answering, shifting his gaze from the only window in the office to her.

"I only found out," he finally answered.

Now it was her turn to be surprised.

"Just recently?" He nodded slowly. "But that makes no sense. Weren't you mailed the marriage certificate?"

"No. Perhaps your address was the only one we wrote down," he replied quickly.

"But . . ." Novalee licked her lips and swallowed over the lump in her throat. "How did you find out?"

"Ah." He cleared his throat and squirmed in his chair. "Well, see, my fiancée and I went to get our marriage license and lo and behold, I'm already married to someone else."

Novalee sat there, stunned.

"You . . . you're engaged?" she forced herself to ask.

"Not anymore." He grinned. "Truth be told, our marriage probably saved me from a big mistake."

He was going to get married? Something that felt an awful lot like jealousy rose in her. She had felt guilty even looking at other men, and here he'd been about to get married! What a lying, cheating bastard!

Not that he'd had any idea that he already had a wife staying faithful to him just a hop, skip, and jump away, but still.

"If you've known all this time, why didn't you take care of it?" Dean asked, breaking into her thoughts.

"I . . ." Novalee felt heat rise in her face. "I was embarrassed."

"Embarrassed?" His narrowed eyes quickly, then changed to amusement.

She glared at him, not finding it amusing at all. "Yes, embarrassed. I don't normally wed strangers in Vegas," she snapped. "I didn't want anyone to know."

"But didn't it occur to you that someone else's life was being affected by this?" he accused.

Novalee flushed again. "Yes." She looked down at her hands. "It's been two years and you never once tried to contact me to straighten it out."

"I didn't know," he reminded her. "This could have all been handled quickly and easily if you had just dealt with it."

Even though he never once raised his voice, she couldn't help but feel as if she'd been reprimanded. Novalee was not the kind of woman to let any man reprimand her. Her spine stiffened and she glared at him.

"So you're saying this is my fault?" she snapped. "Did I force you to walk down the aisle?"

"I never said it was your fault," Dean argued. "I just said you were the one who knew and I wasn't. How could I take care of something if I have no idea it has happened?"

"I understand that, but it wasn't easy for me either. I had no idea what the hell I had done. I have no idea how I came to be your wife. The last thing I remember is having a few drinks with you and then I wake up next to you in bed." She dropped her gaze again. "Naked."

"That's all you remember? Nothing else?" he inquired.

"That's all, Dean," she said in almost a whisper, trying to ignore the way her body responded to his name coming from her mouth. "All I know is I woke up next to some stranger who, apparently, was also my husband. I didn't even think you could get married if you were that intoxicated."

"Why didn't you wake me up?"

"Oh, yeah, I'm sure that would have been a pleasant conversation. 'Hey, wake up, good-looking. Do you remember me? I'm your wife.' " She rolled her eyes.

A grin spread across his face, flashing those damn dimples that she was sure had been her downfall that night. "You think I'm good-looking?"

Novalee fought to keep from smiling and shook her head. "You're missing the point."

"You're right, it would have been awkward. But it also would have been better to know than having to deal with it all now."

She nodded. "I know."

"Do you want a divorce?" he asked, raising his eyebrows.

"Why wouldn't I?"

"You tell me." Brown eyes locked with blue, both refusing to break contact.

"Why would I want to stay married to you?" she asked, bewildered. "I don't even know you!"

He pressed his lips together as if to keep his comment to himself. Wait. Did he want to stay married? Novalee felt her heart begin to pound and she fought the urge to wipe her brow to see if she had indeed broken out in a cold sweat.

That was ridiculous. Why on earth would Dean Philips want to stay married to her? Who committed themselves to a one-night-stand?

If that's all she had been.

What if there was some other motive for him wanting to keep their marriage intact? Did she really believe he just found out? Or was it more convenient for her to swallow his lies to hide her embarrassment?

Was Dean playing her?

Before she could open her mouth to express her concerns, he stood.

"All right. I'll call my lawyer and have her draw up the paperwork for a divorce," he declared.

"Divorce?" She swallowed hard, seeing him at his full height again.

"Yes. That is what we both want, right?" he asked, narrowing his eyes again.

"A divorce will take longer. Can't we just get an annulment?"

"I'm afraid we've waited too long for that, Novalee."

She shivered, liking the way he said her name.

Oh, this wasn't good.

"Right," she said. "And I guess we already . . . consummated the marriage."

Something in his eyes darkened, causing her to smother a gasp. He was looking at her with more smoldering desire than she could remember anyone ever looking at her before.

Was he remembering their night together? Was it good? Great? Had *she* been great? Had he? Did he think about it as often as she had the past two years? Replaying that night over and over in her mind, wishing she could remember what had possessed her to jump not only into bed with this man, but marrying him as well.

As far as husbands go she could have done a lot worse. As she looked over his body again she actually didn't think she could do much better than Dean Philips. Did they even make them better? If they did, she sure as hell hadn't seen it.

She didn't have to remember their night to know he would be a fantastic lover. She could read it all in his confidence, in the way he spoke, the way his eyes bore into hers making her stomach flutter and her girly parts perk up in interest, something that hadn't happened in a very long time.

This man, her husband, was sex on a stick. She had never understood that saying until now. Dean Philips was like a popsicle. A huge, yummy, mouth-watering popsicle that she wanted to lick all over.

Jesus Christ.

And yet, she knew she'd never get the pleasure of finding out just how amazing he was between the sheets again. Too bad she couldn't remember the first time.

"Novalee?" he said.

"Hmm?" She blinked at him, seeing his amused smile and eyes that sparked with mischief.

She blushed, realizing she had probably been staring at him for God knew how long now.

Hey, there was no law forbidding you to ogle your own husband.

Unless that husband happened to be a stranger, and then even if there was no law forbidding it, it no doubt came across as rather creepy.

"Sorry. What?" she asked, tearing her eyes away from him.

"This is where I'm staying," he said, putting a hotel business card in front of her. "I've also written my cell number on the back for you."

"Oh. Um . . ." She looked down at the card so she wouldn't have to look at him. It was close to the bar. "Thanks."

"Would you prefer I call here for you if I need to get in touch?" he asked.

"How long are you planning to be in town for?"

"Until we get this sorted out and have the divorce papers drawn up, I suppose."

He was staring at the floor.

She pulled one of her own business cards out of her desk drawer and jotted her cell number on the back.

"I'm here most evenings," she explained as she slid the card to him, "but it would probably be easier to reach me on my cell also."

Dean took the card, his fingers brushing hers in the process. A shiver ran from her fingertips, up her arm, and down her spine. She quickly pulled her hand back and shoved both of them between her knees before she was tempted to do something stupid. Like grabbing him by the collar and kissing him while dry humping his leg.

Novalee shook her head as heat filled her body.

Where the hell was this coming from? Her libido had been quite happy tucked away and forgotten about all this time. Now, suddenly in the presence of her husband, it decided to make its comeback with a vengeance.

Damn hormones.

She watched as he took the card and slipped it into his pocket.

"I'll be in touch then."

Oh, yes, please touch.

Novalee bit her lip and nodded, avoiding his eyes.

He walked to the door, paused, and turned back to her.

"Novalee?" Hesitantly, she looked at him and met his eyes, which suddenly looked sad and full of regret. "I'm sorry."

She furrowed her brow and asked, "For what?"

"For doing this to you. I know that doesn't make up for all that happened, or what will happen, but I am sorry." He tried to give her one last smile, but failed, and instead shut the door and walked away.

Novalee sat there staring at the closed door for several minutes before finally getting up and leaving, locking the door behind her.

She caught Cali just before she took a tray of drinks out.

"Can you lock up for me tonight?" she asked.

"Sure, hun." Cali looked her over. "You okay?"

Novalee shrugged. "Yeah, I'm good. I just need to go home tonight."

"What's going on with tall, dark, and handsome?"

"A divorce."

Cali cocked an eyebrow. "Why don't you sound happy about that?"

"I'm just confused about all of this."

"I don't blame you there."

"Thanks for closing up." Novalee forced a smile and fled to the kitchen, mumbling a good-bye to Tony before rushing out the back door and to her car.

Ben and Jerry were waiting for her as always when she got home, and she stopped to show them some love before changing into her shorts and tank.

Deciding it was still early enough, she clipped Jerry's leash to his collar and took him for a walk rather than letting him out in the backyard.

She still couldn't wrap her head around the fact that Dean had actually shown up after all this time. The thing that she had feared the most had finally happened and yet it hadn't been nearly as bad as she had anticipated. If anything, it had been pleasant.

Very pleasant, if her tingling body meant anything.

Novalee had expected Dean to be pissed-off and resentful towards her over all this, even if it hadn't been entirely her fault. After all, there had been two of them to blame. She hadn't gotten intoxicated alone and married herself.

But he'd actually been reasonable and pretty understanding about it all. Even somewhat sympathetic for her if his parting words meant anything and he had been the one to lose a fiancée over it all.

And what did he mean by that anyway?

He sounded as if he blamed himself as if this entire mess was his fault. But that was ridiculous, right? He wasn't solely to blame, just as she wasn't. In fact, if anything, she was more to blame than he was. She had known about it this entire time and hadn't done a thing about it. He was the one that had been in the dark until recently.

At least, that's what he claims.

Novalee frowned, the little voice annoying her as she watched Jerry mark his territory against a tree.

Why would he lie to her about just finding out? What purpose could he possibly have to stay in a marriage with her? If he didn't want anything from her as he claimed, why wait years to come forward and lie about knowing?

Unless there was something else.

Maybe he didn't *want* anything from her, but *needed* something.

Novalee's stomach twisted.

What could he possibly need, though? What did she have to give him?

Jerry's bark interrupted her thoughts, indicating he was finished. She let the Lab lead her home as thoughts and concerns over the situation swirled in her head.

Her first instincts had told her to be wary of Dean Philips. No matter that he was technically her husband and had apparently revived her dead libido within minutes of seeing him again. She didn't know this man from Adam. How could she be positive that Dean wasn't working her?

Simply put, she couldn't.

Her mother had always told her to trust her gut and listen to her woman's intuition, and that it would always steer her in the right direction.

Right now her intuition was telling her to ignore those tingles he gave her and be very cautious of her husband's sudden arrival.

Chapter 4

Dean slammed the door a little harder than necessary as he entered his hotel suite, dropped his large duffel bag, and headed straight for the mini bar.

He grabbed the bourbon, filled a glass half-full, and drained the contents in one gulp. The slight burn he felt was almost comforting and he refilled the glass, this time taking one sip at a time to enjoy the taste. It warmed his belly and strangely started to lift the fog that had formed around his brain the second his eyes had landed on Novalee Jensen again.

She looked exactly as he'd remembered her. From the top of her beautiful blonde head to the toes on her small delicate feet and everything in between—and he did mean *everything*—Novalee was still how he pictured her after all this time.

Her blue eyes pierced him the same way they had the first night he'd met her. Vibrant and captivating when she smiled, yet behind that glow was a haunted look that tugged on his heart. Her eyes told him a story that her lips might never tell. This woman, his wife, had lived through her own personal hell.

It was her eyes that made him feel like the complete shit he was for lying to her two years ago, not to mention fifteen minutes ago. She already had so much pain and heartache buried inside her and he was an asshole for purposely putting more there to help himself.

He'd taken advantage of the situation and put her in turmoil. He'd seen it on her face when she'd looked at him, heard it in her voice when she'd spoken to him. Novalee blamed herself for the mess they were in. And what did he do? Like the true fucking tool he was, he let her. He sat there and spewed lie after lie about not knowing about their marriage. Without so many words, he blamed her for not coming forward and ending the charade.

He hadn't intended to go in there and make her feel like shit, but that's exactly what he'd done.

Dean slammed the empty glass on the smooth countertop, surprised when it didn't shatter from the force, and muttered a string of curse words.

He knew he couldn't go in there and confess the truth to her if he wanted to get on her good side. He needed her in his corner when this all fell apart. He needed her to save his grandfather's last wishes, to save his inheritance from his greedy bastard of a father, and to keep things right.

Simply, Dean needed his wife to save his life.

And he had no fucking idea how he was going to pull that off.

His cell vibrated in his pocket and for one split second he thought of Novalee. Why would she be calling him so soon, though? He dug the phone out of his pocket and wasn't surprised to see it wasn't her. The feeling of disappointment was unnerving, however.

"Hello, Abby," he greeted, dropping onto the bed.

"Do you still have both your balls?" she asked, sounding half-amused, half-serious.

"Yes." He almost smiled.

"Hmm. What lies did you spin in order to keep them?"

With a heavy sigh, Dean told his lawyer/best friend the conversation between him and Novalee earlier that evening. Abigail listened quietly, not even interrupting him to add her own comment, which wasn't like the outspoken Abby he knew.

"If you ask me to play the part of your ex-fiancée, I may cut your jewels off myself," she responded after he was finished.

"No," he chuckled. "But if you have to, please play along with the story."

There was a long pause on her end that made Dean shift uncomfortably. Abigail was rarely ever silent about anything. Whatever she was thinking wasn't good.

"Spit it out, Abby," he said, his stomach tightening anxiously.

"I don't like what you're doing, Dean," she finally said.

"You think I do?" he snapped. "You think I enjoy lying to this woman? Do you think I want to hurt my wife, Abigail?"

"No, I don't think you want to hurt *your wife*," she answered sharply. "But that's exactly what's going to happen."

"I can't tell her the truth. Not yet. You know that."

"Have you thought of another way? Instead of spinning more lies, have you thought of maybe giving her a little incentive to want to help you?"

Dean frowned.

"What do you mean?"

"Do I have to spell everything out for you, Dean?" Abby snapped. "Money."

"What?"

"Tell her the truth about everything, tell her why you really married her, and throw a dollar amount her way."

"You want me to bribe her?" Dean asked, half amused, half pissed-off at her for even suggesting it. "You want me to buy a court appearance from her?"

"Yes. The right amount of money can make anything go away, Dean. You just have to name her price," Abby said simply.

"No fucking way," he spat.

"Why the hell not?"

"Because, for one, she doesn't need money—"

"I highly doubt that," Abby muttered.

"And two," Dean continued, ignoring her interruption, "what if she said no? What if she laughed in my face and threw me out, Abby? Where the hell would I be then?"

The other end of the phone stayed silent.

"You know that's a risk we can't take. We need her on our side. We need her to appear in court. Throwing money at her and hoping she takes the bait is too big a gamble."

"I know," she said softly, the sharp tone gone from her voice.

"I need her to trust me, and right now, this is the only way I can think of. She wouldn't take money, Abby. I can tell she's not that kind of person."

"I just have this sick feeling this is all going to backfire."

"Just let me worry about that," Dean said, rubbing his temples.

She snorted. "I know how you deal with stress, Dean. How many empty bottles has housekeeping already cleaned up?"

"Are you implying I have a drinking problem?" He wasn't surprised if she was, but still kind of annoyed with her for thinking it.

"Two years ago I would have said no. Now, you're walking a very fine line," she replied, almost sounding sad.

Sure, he drank more now than he had before. The bottles seemed to empty faster and he re-stocked quicker than even he liked at times. But he wasn't a fucking alcoholic. He didn't *need* a drink to get through the day, but at the end of the day it sure was great to have one. Or two. But that didn't mean he had a damn problem. It was the same to him as chocolate or shoes were to women.

No, on second thought, he wasn't *that* bad. Someone could take his drink and still walk away with all their hair and both eyes. He sure as hell wouldn't want to be the one to tell a woman like Abby she couldn't have her rich treat or stylish pumps.

"What's the old bastard up to?" Dean asked, changing the subject.

"He's fairly confident you're going to show up empty-handed in court."

"He's always underestimated me," Dean said as he closed his eyes against the rage inside him.

"I never have, and yet, I'm worried he may be right," Abby confessed.

She paused and then her breath hitched, cluing Dean in that whatever she was about to say next he probably wouldn't like. "Dean, there are rumors."

His body stiffened. "What kind of rumors?"

"That your father owes big money to some big people."

It was Dean's turn to snort. "What's new?"

"No, this is different. It's so much money there's talk if he wins against you, he could still end up losing."

"Are you telling me that son of a bitch has gambled away my grandfather's worth?" he screamed, clenching his fists and seeing red.

"That's exactly what I'm telling you," she replied calmly. "If she doesn't come through for you, it's all gone. Maybe not right away, but how long do you think it will take for Richard to destroy everything William made for himself?"

"I'll get her there, Abigail. There's no fucking way he'll win," he seethed.

"Even if it means telling her the truth?"

"I'll do whatever I have to do to keep him from winning," he declared through clenched teeth.

"As your lawyer I hope it doesn't come down to that, but as your friend, I hope you do tell her. This guilt you've been carrying around has gone on long enough."

Dean closed his eyes and bit back the words he wanted to throw at her. He'd already decided he was going to tell Novalee everything after all this was over. He owed her the truth.

"Just be careful, Dean," she advised.

"Is that my lawyer or my friend talking?"

"Both."

"Keep me updated on what he's doing, will you?" he asked, knowing he didn't have to explain who 'he' was.

"Of course." Abby sighed. "Keep me posted on how you're doing."

He smiled against the phone. "You just want billable hours."

Abby laughed, a sound Dean wasn't used to hearing too often from her. "Sweetie, after all this is over, I think I'll take a nice long vacation with the check you'll be writing me," she teased.

"You deserve one."

"I know. So hurry your ass up and get this over with because the beach is calling my name."

He chuckled. "I wouldn't want to keep you and your little bikini away from the sand."

"Who said anything about a bikini?" she taunted.

Despite the stress and frustration he was filled with, his groin tightened when he thought of a bikini-less Abigail, a sight he'd seen many times in the beginning of their friendship. A sight he wouldn't mind seeing again if his head wasn't so messed up by Novalee.

His relationship with Abby had been strictly platonic since she'd become his lawyer three years ago. She'd said she didn't want to mix business with pleasure, but Dean couldn't help but feel it was more than that. They'd become each other's best friends while sharing each other's beds when they'd met ten years ago. As they'd slowly begun to learn about one another and started to care, they stopped turning to each other for mindless sex. Sure, it had still happened on occasion until Abby accepted his offer to be his personal lawyer. He'd understood why their sexual relationship had to end. His life was already conflicted enough without adding banging his new lawyer to the list. But that didn't mean he didn't miss their carefree romps.

Hell, he missed *all* carefree romps. He hadn't seen any action in far too long. The night his wife had passed out in their bed was the last time he'd seen a woman naked.

Novalee's blissfully naked sleeping form flashed in his head, replacing the one of Abigail in an instant. His cock now strained against the close confinement of his jeans as he thought about touching *her* soft skin.

He groaned silently as his neglected body part twitched inside his pants, practically begging for attention from the sweet little bar owner.

Fuck it all to hell. This wasn't good.

"Dean?"

He pushed aside his naughty thoughts to concentrate on Abby.

Good fucking luck with that.

"Huh?"

"Mention bikinis and beaches and you disappear," she remarked. "Going through a dry spell?"

"I'm in the desert, dearest Abby. In the fucking desert," he muttered.

"Don't do it, Dean," she warned, catching on to where his thoughts had just been. "Do not fuck all this up and complicate it further by screwing this woman."

He grinned. "She's my wife. It's my sworn promise to take care of her every need."

"Think with the head on your shoulders, Playboy, not the little one in your pants."

"Little?" He acted wounded. "Honey, we both know 'little' is not the proper description of what's in my pants."

Abby groaned. "Please."

"See? You do remember," he teased. "You're moaning the same things to me now."

Abby snorted. "Don't flatter yourself, Philips. If I ever begged you, it was only for you to hurry up so I could get on with more entertaining things."

"Ouch!"

"I mean it," she warned again, losing all the playfulness in her voice. "Don't fuck her."

Can she fuck me?

The question was almost out of his mouth before he could stop himself. He was sure that would just lead to an angry lecture. One he wasn't in the mood for.

"Okay, Abby," he agreed feebly.

"I mean it."

"I know you do."

She sighed. "But you don't."

"I promise I won't screw this up," he said seriously. "It means too much to me."

"The case or the girl?" she asked just as serious.

Dean hesitated long enough for Abby to click her tongue.

"Ab—"

"No, Dean, I get it," she snipped. "It doesn't matter how you look at it; someone's going to get hurt, and you have a lot more to lose than she does."

Truer words had never been spoken.

After a hasty goodbye to Abigail, Dean took his time refilling his bourbon glass once more before pulling the file from his briefcase. A feeling of guilt suddenly washed over him as he brushed his fingers along the top of the folder.

Wasn't this wrong? It was like an invasion of her privacy. He shouldn't be learning about her from a stack of papers. Of course there were things he already knew. He hadn't been obsessed as Abigail had accused him of being a few weeks ago, but he had done the basic research on his wife after their night in Vegas.

Thanks to a basic Internet search he knew she had been orphaned and left to be taken care of by family friends. The accident had happened almost twelve years ago when she was just sixteen.

It didn't escape his notice they had been around the same age when they'd both lost their loved ones, even around the same time of year. The night she'd been mourning the loss of her parents, he'd probably been in the strip club pawing Abby and trying to forget his own loss.

Talk about ironic.

She was twenty-eight, just four years his junior, had grown up in a middle-class family unlike his own. She was an only child, like himself, and had moved to the average-sized city she now resided in a few years after her parents' death. Before then she had been managing her father's hardware store, and now she owned the bar he'd been in that night. He figured she must have inherited some money from her parents to be able to live as she did, although the simple search hadn't told him how much.

Was he more than a little curious to know? Definitely. He'd be fool if he didn't want to know how much Novalee had to her name, especially considering how much *he* had to his. Had she sunk all her money into her business and now lived off the patrons that she served every night, or did she have savings to fall back on? Did she think of her future and the consequences of her actions, or did she live day-to-day, enjoying life's unexpected twists?

Dean stroked the cover of the file again as his brain overloaded with questions faster than he could keep up with them. All he had to do was flip open the folder and find out all the answers to his questions. At least most of them.

A month after his grandfather had passed away, Abigail had forcefully suggested he hire a private investigator to get the dirty details on Novalee. He'd bristled at the idea and shrugged off the suggestion until Andrew told him the same thing. They needed to know all they could about his absent wife to ensure the façade looked real. Dean had finally relented and let his lawyers handle it.

Two months ago the detective had handed over the information he'd gathered, collected his check, and walked out. Dean had never spoken to him, instead letting Andrew and Abigail continue to handle the matter. They'd reviewed the contents of the folder and offered it to Dean, but he hadn't bothered to take it. Not until the morning after their court appearance. The file had burned a hole in his briefcase these past two weeks, but hadn't given into the urge to peek.

Until now.

He swallowed the last of his liquid courage and cast a glance at the object in front of him.

If he wanted her to be on his team then he should know something about her, right? He needed common ground to stand on to be able to handle this properly. Right?

Right.

Stop being a fucking pussy and read the damn papers, Philips.

Dean flipped open the cover and his eyes greedily took in everything.

Novalee Taylor Jensen was born June 5th to Joseph and Amelia (nee Taylor) Jensen. The report confirmed what he already knew about her upbringing, her parents' accident, and living with Patrick and Anne Donavon.

He skipped through all that, pausing at a large sum that jumped out at him. She had inherited two million from her father's life insurance, half of which she'd already received and the rest would be handed out to her in four years. Two million. Now it made sense to him how she could afford to open the bar.

Of course two million wasn't close to his net worth, but it made Dean breathe a little easier to know she had her own financial means.

He skimmed over the everyday things, searching for something, anything really, that would tell him the personal side to his wife.

And there, a few pages in, he found it. Although it wasn't what he'd been expecting at all.

Eight years ago she'd had a lengthy hospital stay. Dean's blood boiled as he read the report. Words like "broken bones," "intensive care," "physical therapy," and "restraining order" jumped out at him, blurring everything else until only one thing was clear: someone had hurt Novalee. Badly. Someone had physically put their hands on her and broken her.

Badly.

He shook his head trying to clear it as he scanned the pages looking for a name, but there wasn't one.

He slammed the file closed, muttering curse after curse to himself. It was more than he'd expected to find. It was more than he wanted to deal with. It hit too close to home for Dean. They sure had common ground, but it wasn't what he wanted at all.

He pushed away from the desk and stomped into the bathroom, tore off his clothes, and jumped into the shower, hoping the hot water would ease the tension in his body that the alcohol had failed to do.

Why had he read the damn file? Now he knew something that he should have only known if she'd wanted to share it with him. Any man who put his hands on a woman and beat her to within an inch of her life, which is damn well what it sounded like that asshole had done, deserved a taste of his own medicine.

Dean shuddered with rage as he imagined Novalee's sweet body almost lifeless lying in ICU. The bastard had better be behind fucking bars for his own sake if Novalee ever opened up and told him about the incident.

Shame filled him in that second. What right did he have to get protective of a woman who he'd tricked and lied to and would inevitably hurt also? He may not use his fists to scar Novalee, but he was no better than the scumbag who had beaten her.

And yet, not moments ago he'd been thinking of her bare and sleeping in their bed. He knew he was bad for her, that his actions were going to cause more damage than he could fix, but he still wanted her.

He closed his eyes and titled his head up, letting the water flow over his face and down his body. The droplets touched him in ways that he wished were someone's hands. Or mouth.

His dick jerked in response again, and he groaned. He wiped the water from his face and grabbed the bar of soap, coating his body in the thick offensive film. He had forgotten his own brand of body wash in his bag, so the over-fragrant hotel soap would have to do.

As he washed, his hand brushed his jutting erection and he was helpless to stop himself from wrapping his hand around himself. Lubricated by the soap, he thought of *her* hot, wet mouth and jerked his hips into his hand as he moaned. He stroked faster and shuddered a few minutes later as he shot onto the stall's floor as the evidence of his lonesome tryst was rinsed down the drain.

Dean shut off the shower and got out feeling disgusted by his actions. What kind of sick fuck was he to jack off while thinking of her after what he'd just learned?

He quickly dried off, dropped his towel on the bathroom floor, and yanked on his boxers. Not bothering to clean up, he headed to bed and wished for sleep to come.

Tomorrow was Sunday. He doubted Novalee would be at the bar and maybe they could get together and talk.

The dirty part of his brain couldn't help but think if she was willing to do more than just talk that would suit him fine as well.

Asshole.

After tossing and turning most of the night, sleep had finally found him. He hadn't gotten up and relied on the whisky to use as a sleep aid, and the last time his eyes had landed on the clock it had read three a.m. He figured he couldn't have been awake much longer after that.

It was now just after seven a.m., and despite only having four hours of sleep, Dean was wide-awake and ready to face the day. Better yet, he was ready to face Novalee.

If she was ready to face him.

Her business card laid beside him on the nightstand, the number of her cell facing up so he could stare at it. He longed to reach for his phone and dial her this second, but not knowing her usual routine on a weekend and not wanting to wake her up, he restrained himself. Barely.

To distract himself, he changed into a pair of blue shorts and a matching muscle shirt, grabbed his key card from the desk, and went downstairs to the gym, pushing thoughts of Novalee out of his mind by over-working his body with cardio. It seemed to work, too, and then he suddenly wondered if she worked out and pictured her in little bicycle shorts.

Damn it!

What the hell was wrong with him? Since when did he only think of this woman he barely knew? His mind had been full of her since last night and he couldn't shake the images and thoughts that roamed his brain. He wasn't acting like Dean Philips. Dean Philips did not obsess over women. Dean Philips had more women than he knew what to do with.

Correction. He used to have more women than he knew what to do with.

That's what this all came down to: the fact that his dick hadn't seen any action in two goddamn years. That's *all* this fascination was. Well, that and the fact that she was pretty important to his future.

Instead of thinking of her legs in short shorts, or nothing at all for that matter, he should be more worried about getting her on his side and seeing him as a friend and not the enemy. Which, let's face it, he was. He needed her to believe him when he told her he had no idea of their marriage and not to question his motives for suddenly showing up in her life. He needed to concentrate on how he was going to pull this whole thing off, while keeping the damage on her end as low as possible. He didn't want to hurt her any more than he already had.

Right now was the time he needed to focus on getting her back to Las Vegas with him and somehow persuading her to tell the Judge what he needed to hear to keep his grandfather's empire in his hands.

He had no idea how the hell he was going to pull that miracle off, and he wouldn't figure it out if he didn't keep his mind on business instead of the pleasure they could have together.

Since cardio was no longer working in his favor, he skipped the rest of his workout and went back upstairs to his room to shower, placing an order for room service before sliding under the warm spray, careful to avoid Mr. Happy this time as he lathered himself up with his own soap. His dick seemed even more alert this morning since there was a chance of seeing the blonde beauty today.

His head may have plans to play this safe, but obviously his cock had his own plans in mind. Horny little fucker.

He rinsed off and wrapped a towel around his waist just as room service knocked on his door. Not bothering to dress, he grabbed a few bills out of his wallet for a tip and opened the door.

Room service was not on the other side, however. There, staring at him as if she had just seen a ghost, was his wife. Her mouth was open, just enough for him to see her tongue, her eyes were wide and her hand hung in the air as if she was about to knock again just as he'd opened the door.

What the hell was she doing here? Didn't she know it was dangerous to knock on the door of a man who had been thinking of all the naughty things he wanted to do to her since the night before unless she wanted to be taken against the wall fast and hard?

She licked her lips and her eyes traveled over his body, pausing at where the towel wrapped around his waist. A blush crept into her cheeks and he couldn't stop the smile that spread across his face due to her innocent reaction.

Oh yeah, she definitely wanted him just as much as he wanted her. Of that Dean was sure.

Chapter 5

Novalee slid out of bed, finally giving up on sleep at seven thirty the next morning. Her encounter with Dean the night before had left her feeling anxious, excited, and frustrated as hell all night. Every time she closed her eyes she saw him swagger into her office with those big, bad, broad shoulders.

The more she thought of his shoulders, the more she started to think about other parts of him, like his chest and stomach that begged to be scratched by her nails. And if she was scratching his stomach she might as well do his back too; his back led to his butt, which she got a very nice peek at as he'd walked out the door yesterday. It was nicely hugged by his designer jeans, just waiting to be squeezed.

So much for ignoring the tingles.

She puttered around the kitchen making coffee as she cursed herself for feeling this way. The last thing she needed to muddle her already muddled brain was sexual urges to jump her husband. Her libido couldn't have perked her horny little head up at a more inconvenient time.

Novalee stood at the counter, her hip cocked against it, drumming her fingers on the surface as she waited impatiently for her coffee to brew. The rich aroma filled the air, making her stomach growl.

She needed to sort out how she felt about Dean other than the way he made a party come alive in her panties. As sincere as he'd seemed to be about not knowing about their marriage, she didn't know if she should believe him. Her gut told her he was hiding something.

She poured her coffee into a mug that read, 'Life is better when he's bigger,' a gift from Cali, as she pondered what his sudden arrival in Missoula could mean. The problem with that was she didn't know anything about Dean, so how could she even attempt to figure him out? Her husband was a total stranger, one that could be around to cause a lot of trouble for her.

Glancing at the clock, she smiled when she saw the early hour and reached for her phone. Cali wouldn't be awake yet, but Novalee figured if she could betray her by bedding Tony than she could call her this early without getting her head ripped off. She wandered into the living room and sat down just as Cali answered.

"The sun is barely out. What the fuck do you want?" groaned a raspy voice on the other end.

"I need to talk to you." Novalee smiled.

"Call back later."

"But I need my best friend. You know, my bestie who said she'd never sleep with our cook and betray our friendship?"

Cali groaned and Novalee heard the rustle of bed sheets. "Payback is a bitch and her name is Novalee Jensen." She yawned and mumbled, "Talk."

"I need to get to know Dean so I can figure out what he's up to."

"I thought he just wanted a divorce," Cali muttered sleepily.

"That's what he says. How do I know it's true?"

"You think way too much for this early in the morning, hun." Then she sighed and asked, "What do you know about him?"

"Nothing. Not a damn thing," Novalee answered, annoyed.

"Google him."

"Excuse me?"

"Google him," Cali repeated through another yawn.

Novalee frowned. "That's kind of creepy."

"Whatever. Everyone Googles everyone. It's how you get all the nitty-gritty."

Novalee bit her lip as she thought about it.

"What if I find something I don't want to know?" she wondered out loud.

"Well, at least you'll know now instead of later. Isn't that better?"

"Maybe I should invite him to dinner," she mused.

"Why?"

"To get to know him in a way that doesn't scream stalker," Novalee replied, rolling her eyes.

"Fine. Invite him to dinner and feel him up."

She snorted. "I think you mean 'feel him out.' "

"Oh, no, I definitely mean 'up.' All that rock hard muscle has got to lead to a nice piece of me—"

"I think you should go back to bed, Cali."

Cali giggled. "An excellent suggestion. Call me after you Google."

"I'm not going to Google."

"You will Google. And, babe?"

"Yes?" Novalee sighed.

"This phone call at this ungodly hour makes us even."

She smiled. "Of course."

Novalee's eyes immediately landed on her laptop as she ended the call. A simple search couldn't hurt, right? If he had nothing to hide then nothing would show up. It wasn't as if she was digging through his private papers; whatever she found on the web was public knowledge.

She gnawed on her lip.

To Google or not to Google?

If she wanted to get a step ahead of him and figure out what he wanted, she needed help. She needed information. She needed public knowledge.

To Google.

She reached for her computer and flipped open the screen. With shaky fingers she clicked on the website and type in two simple words: Dean Philips. Closing her eyes, she took a deep breath and hit enter. A few seconds later she peeked.

Whoa.

Who knew so much would show up? How did she know which was *her* Dean?

Her Dean?

Focus, Novalee.

She pushed the possessive thought out of her mind and turned her attention back to the search results, landing on what appeared to be a newspaper article with the headline, *A Fight for Fortune.* She read the little blurb, catching Dean Philips amongst the names, and clicked on the link to read the article. She chewed her thumbnail as she read the news piece, eyes widening with each paragraph.

No, this couldn't be her Dean. Could it? This Dean had inherited WIP Hotels, a chain of luxury hotels everyone was familiar with. This Dean Philips was now in a court battle to keep his newfound wealth from his father.

Novalee continued to read, unable to close the article and move onto something else, growing more and more appalled with each word. She didn't know this Richard Philips from Adam, but from the comments he made, he sounded like a pompous ass.

She reached the end of the page and clicked on the image link. The photo that loaded made her gasp.

The scowling man staring back at her was her Dean.

Holy shit!

She was married to a multimillionaire. Novalee stared at the picture as her heart pounded and her palms grew sweaty. She licked her lips, tasting the dry skin. Is this why he had come? She thought *he* was after *her* small wealth, but what if *he* thought *she* was after his? Did he come, not to snoop out what he could get from a divorce, but to see what she could possibly want from one?

Her mind filled with questions. Did he plan to tell her who he was? Or was he going to hide it from her to protect himself? Did he think she knew who he was when she'd married him?

Oh no!

The blood drained from her face and her stomach rolled. Did he think she married him for his money? That she planned to run into him that night and seduce him?

No, that was ridiculous.

Wasn't it?

Novalee closed her eyes and tried to think back to that night. Who'd approached whom? She remembered sitting at the bar, nursing a frilly drink with an umbrella. He had suddenly appeared beside her, flashing that dimpled smile at her. He'd definitely initiated the conversation, but who had made the first move? Whose idea was it to get married for Christ's sake?

Novalee shook her head, wishing she didn't have these black pockets regarding that night. She had never drunk so much that she didn't remember the night before or recall her actions. That wasn't her. So what had come over her that night?

Frustrated, she slammed the laptop closed and pushed it away. If Dean did think she was after his money, she needed to squash the idea, pronto. She couldn't go up to him and tell him she had been snooping and now knew who he was. But if she tried to be nice to him and smooth things over, would that confirm her motives to him?

She laughed at the small humor in the situation. Some one-night-stands had awkward morning-afters. Her one and only one-night-stand had led to an awkward marriage and possibly a messy divorce if things got out of hand.

She sighed and leaned her head back against the couch. She had to get Dean to see she wasn't a gold-digging whore. If he indeed thought she was, well, things could get ugly.

So how could she do that?

Dinner? She'd mentioned to Cali that she was thinking of having him over for a meal, but that was before she'd known who he was. Was dinner still a good idea?

God, she was being utterly stupid. It was just food. What could go wrong?

Still, the thought of him being in her house, of them being alone, sent a round of butterflies off in her stomach.

Oh, grow up, Novalee. You're not twelve and he's not your first crush.

She snatched her coffee cup off the table and went into the kitchen. She had just set it in the sink and was rinsing it out when her foot landed in a small puddle of water. Or at least she hoped it was water and Ben wasn't boycotting his kitty litter box.

Squatting down, Novalee opened the cupboard below the sink to investigate. She groaned when she saw the leak from the sink's drainpipe.

She knew from working in the hardware store that the flexible drainpipe that was installed didn't work very well; she'd had countless customers come in and complain about them. She, however, hadn't had a problem until now. She may know the parts she needed, but when it came to actually fixing the damn thing, Novalee was clueless. She wasn't a plumber, after all.

And it was Sunday, which meant an actual plumper probably wasn't available.

Dammit!

She huffed and glared at her sink. Really, how hard could it be? She knew what she needed and it couldn't be that difficult to put it back together.

Deciding on her plan of action, she stood and went to her bedroom to get dressed, yanking on a pair of jeans and a white blouse, and stopping long enough to apply a little makeup. She grabbed her keys and was poking around in her purse before heading out the door when she found the business card Dean had given her. She knew she would be driving almost right by it on her way to get the pipe; maybe she should stop in and invite him to dinner.

It occurred to her, of course, that a simple phone call would also get the job done, but calling wasn't nearly as personal as asking him face-to-face.

Oh, yeah, right.

A little grin spread across her face as she locked up the house and skipped to her car.

Skipped?

She was definitely too giddy over the thought of seeing "her husband."

Her nerves started to get the best of her the closer she got to his hotel. Her stomach flipped so much she thought she might actually throw up, and she almost changed her mind a half a dozen times in fifteen minutes.

She was still battling with herself when she pulled into the parking lot, the knot in her stomach tightening as she glanced at the building.

Maybe she should have just called. Leave a message and ask him to get back to her. Who knew if he was even awake yet? Maybe he slept in on Sundays. Maybe he went to church. Then she wrinkled her nose. Dean really didn't seem like the religious type. But what did she know? She was only married to the man.

Still, calling would probably be more appropriate.

She was reaching for her cell when her backbone suddenly spoke up telling her she was ridiculous. Hiding in the parking lot while calling him was not Novalee Jensen. She didn't survive all the shit in her life to suddenly become a shy little girl in the company of Dean Philips. He was just a man after all.

A sexy man. A man that made her want to drop her panties and spread her legs and beg him to take her. *Nothing shy about that, was there?* asked

Libido.

Confidence, supplied by Backbone, was overcome by lust, supplied by Libido. A warm rush heated Novalee's skin as she thought of Dean slowly dragging his hands up her legs as he licked her earlobe. His teeth biting into her flesh and his tongue flicking it as his hot breath tickled her, dragging a moan out of her. He would reach her most sensitive area just as his tongue would slide into her mouth, both entering at the same ti—

Oh, she was definitely going up to his room.

As quickly as her shaky legs would carry her, she entered the building and crossed to the front desk. The attendant looked at her with bored eyes and a smirk.

"Checking in?"

"No. I'm looking for Dean Philips." She smiled at the young man. "He checked in yesterday and gave me his card, but forgot to tell me his room number."

Bored and Brooding tapped on the keys a few times and glanced at the computer screen.

"Three oh two," he said.

She was sure it was against hotel policy to give out guest information, but if he didn't have a problem with it, she sure as hell wasn't going to complain.

"Thanks!" She grinned at him again and turned to the elevators.

The doors seemed to close extra slow, the numbers lighting up at a snail's pace as she tapped her foot impatiently. And then suddenly she was in front of his door, inhaling deeply so she wouldn't pass out. Her heart pounded in her chest, her stomach pleasantly flipped and, thanks to Libido, her lady bits were going crazy.

Sweet baby Jesus, if he could do this to her without even being in the room, what would it be like if he actually touched her?

She made a mental note to update her will just in case she didn't survive. Ben and Jerry would have a good home with Aunty Cali. The obituary Cali would write after she died of having amazing sex made Novalee giggle and she had to wait a few seconds to calm herself before knocking. Deciding it was now or never, she softly rapped on the door and stood waiting, holding her breath.

He didn't answer.

Disappointment filled her. Maybe he wasn't in. Or maybe he was still sleeping and didn't hear her knock. She raised her hand to do it again, but stopped. What if he was sleeping? She didn't want to wake him up just to invite him to dinner when she could have called in the first place.

She suddenly felt foolish for showing up unannounced at a stranger's hotel room. But before she could make a quick getaway, the door opened and he was in front of her.

Wet.

Wearing only a towel.

Wet.

She opened her mouth to speak but couldn't. Instead, she stood there gawking at him like some creepy stalker with her mouth hanging open and her eyes bulging out of her sockets.

Real sexy.

Novalee snapped her mouth shut and licked her lips. It was nerves that made her do it, she told herself. It wasn't to make sure drool hadn't pooled in the corners of her mouth and was now dripping off her chin.

Do not check him out. Do not check him out.

However, her traitorous eyes didn't get the message her brain was sending out and on their own her gaze lowered down his body. She swallowed, coating her dry mouth due to the sight of his abs and then she looked lower and her crotch sang "Hallelujah."

It took all her willpower to keep from reaching out and tugging the towel from his waist. Heat filled her cheeks and she knew she was blushing like a prude on a nude beach, but she still couldn't look away.

Vaguely, she heard him clear his throat and she forced her eyes up to his face. He was smiling and she knew she was busted checking out his goods.

"Novalee, I'm surprised to see you here."

"I'm sorry," she apologized quickly. This was a bad idea. She needed to go. Now. She took a step back and said, "I should have called, but I was in the area getting some pipe and I thought I'd drop by and see—"

"Getting some pipe?" He smiled.

Oh, God!

"I—" *Getting some pipe?* She tried to keep from smiling. Of course he would take that the wrong way. She rolled her eyes instead of grinning like a fool that his thoughts had gone that way. "My kitchen sink decided to be a bitch this morning and is now in need of some fixing."

Surprise filled his face. "You're going to do it?"

Was he implying she couldn't? Yes, she technically didn't know how, but he didn't know that. Just because she had boobs that meant she couldn't give her sink the TLC it needed?

"What? Because I'm a woman I can't fix things around my house?"

"Of course that's not what I meant," he said.

Liar.

"Look, I'm sorry for stopping by. I can see you're . . . busy." Against her will, her eyes traveled over his body again. Damn, the towel was still there. "I'll call later."

She turned to leave just as he said, "No," and grasped her hand. His touch was warm and hard and the sexual jolt she felt from the gentle brush of his hand made her gasp and pull away. She froze as her body came alive, crying out for more of his touch in other places. Her nipples hardened and she stared at him, praying he didn't notice her reaction.

He watched her carefully, as if he was afraid she was going to take off running at any second.

"Please, don't go," he said. "You're already here you might as well come in." He stepped back into the room, opening the door as an invitation. "I'll even put some clothes on if it will make you more comfortable," he teased, grinning at her.

She smiled, grateful for his attempt at humor to put her at ease. Almost shyly, she entered his room. The soft click of the door closing behind her made her heart leap in her chest.

What the hell was wrong with her?

She nodded when Dean told her he'd be right back as he grabbed his clothes and locked himself in the bathroom. She wondered how flimsy that lock was and if it was strong enough to keep a horny, single woman out if she decided to barge in.

She had to sit down before she fell down.

She dropped to the bed, which she knew instantly was a bad idea. She was on a bed and he was only feet away. He could open the door and be next to her in seconds, pushing her back onto the bed and crawling on top of her body.

Goddamnit!

She scooted as close to the edge as possible without landing on her ass. This is what not having sex for years did to a person. She was going to scare the next man who took her to bed with all her built up sexual aggression. Maybe *he* wouldn't survive.

The bathroom door opened and Dean stepped out, eyeing her quickly before looking away.

"I have breakfast coming up, complete with coffee if you would like some," he offered.

Do I get to drink it off your body?

"No, thanks. I can't eat you." *Oh. My. God.* She did not just say that! Damn dirty thoughts muddling her brain. "I mean, I can't eat *with* you. I'm not hungry. I ate. Earlier. Before I came." Not true. Wait. *Before I came?* "Here!" she added. *Oh, dear God.* "I ate before I came here," she mumbled, wanting the floor to open up and swallow her.

Dean laughed, which only added further embarrassment on her part to her word vomit.

"Stupid sexually frustrated woman," she whispered under her breath. She peeked at him and saw he was still chuckling while watching her.

She held her lips together to keep from grinning. Damn, he was fine when he laughed. Even his chuckle sent chills down her spine.

"What can I do for you, Novalee?" he finally asked.

Oh, the possibilities in answer to that question were endless.

"I just wanted to . . ." Suddenly, she felt nervous again. She played with her hair while looking around the room, avoiding looking at him. "Since it's my entire fault that you had to come all this way here to fix this —"

"Novalee, it's not your fault," he protested.

She held up her hand.

"Please. We both know it is." She smiled. "Anyway, I just wanted to stop by and invite you to dinner tonight. We can talk about all this mess and it will be the start of my way to make it up to you."

He grimaced. "Novalee, you don't have anything to make up to me," he almost whispered.

Oh, my. If it was possible he sounded even better in hushed tones. *Must. Get. Control.*

"Does that mean you don't want to come to dinner?" she asked sadly.

So much for extending an olive branch.

"Oh, I'll definitely come to dinner." He smiled and her stomach did crazy things. "How crazy would I be to turn down a home-cooked meal?"

She watched him as his acceptance slowly sunk in and panic spread in her chest. She'd never invited anyone to her house. Only Cali came to see her; no one else even knew where she lived. And here she had just invited her husband/stranger/sexual fantasy to her home.

Why did she feel she could trust this man without even knowing him?

She bit her lip, a nervous habit that she had tried to break, and opened her purse to find something to write her address on. Then she stood and looked at the scrap of paper for a second before handing it over.

"Is five o'clock okay?" she asked, still not believing what she'd done.

"Perfect."

She continued to chew on her lip knowing she should be leaving, but unable to move. She saw his eyes lower to her mouth, watching her.

He took a step closer and her legs grew weak. He was going to kiss her. The way he stared at her, his nostrils flared and his eyes on fire, made her weak in the knees. She longed to kiss him. To snake her fingers through his hair and inhale his clean scent. Her body screamed for her to press herself against him and feel the hardness of the man in front of her.

And yet, he continued to stare at her mouth, not making another move.

"Dean," she whispered, inviting him to do as he pleased. Telling him it was okay to claim her.

But a knock at the door interrupted them before they could start. Dean closed his eyes and Novalee shook herself out of her sexual daze and made herself back away. His eyes still burned when he opened them was. Her entire body screamed in protest, but she ignored it, grateful when the person knocked again.

Dean opened the door gruffly, startling the guy on the other side.

"R-room service," she heard him stutter.

Taking that as her cue to leave, she walked to the door once the waiter had come in.

"You don't have to go."

"Yes, I do. I have errands to run." *Like buying a new Rabbit, maybe a bullet, a variety of dildos, and any other toys that can take care of my needs the way I want you to.*

The soft touch of his hand on her arm made her look up at him.

"Five o'clock still?" he asked.

"Yes. You can come earlier if you like."

She looked at his hand on her skin, smiled at him once more, and then hurried away before her hormones got the best of her. Once inside her car she groaned and banged her head against the steering wheel.

Could she have been any more of a moron? The comment about breakfast . . . she cringed. It couldn't have been any more obvious what she was thinking if she had worn a huge "Do Me" sign. And now she had to face him at dinner tonight.

" 'You can come earlier if you want'," she mocked herself. "You might as well have just thrown your panties at him."

She started the car, still grumbling to herself. She made a quick stop at the hardware store, finding the parts she thought she would need before heading over to the supermarket. As she pushed her cart, she wondered what to make tonight. Should she impress him with her culinary skills and go for something difficult and fancy, or something simple like steak? Every man liked meat, right?

Novalee stood in front of the noodle section contemplating her choices. How much of an effort did she want to make for this man? This wasn't a date after all. He was coming over to talk about their divorce.

The idea that she was thinking of impressing him while he was only there to end their marriage made her laugh, earning her a curious look from her fellow shoppers. Yes, people, pasta really was that stimulating.

Steak it was. It would give her a chance to use her grill, which usually sat in her backyard lonely and neglected.

She grabbed a couple of baking potatoes along with the steaks and a few veggies for a simple salad. She was heading for the cashier when she detoured, deciding if she was going to make it through tonight without jumping him, she would need something after dinner to satisfy her. Chocolate Pistachio Cream Pie sounded just about right.

She paid for her purchases, smiling at the cashier a little too brightly for a Sunday morning if her dull stare was any indication, and hurried home to play with her pipe.

Okay, maybe that sounded wrong.

She laughed out loud as she loaded her car, suddenly eager for the night ahead.

Once she got home, she put both dog and cat outside so they wouldn't be in her way as she worked. Ben, always annoyed to be put outside and away from his scratching post and catnip, tried to scurry back in between her feet. She closed the screen door on him and received an appalled meow in return.

Ignoring the cat, Novalee hunkered down to her leaky problem. All confidence she'd thought she had was quickly lost as she started to examine the sink's piping more closely. Performance anxiety set in and she doubted herself. She wasn't a damn plumber. What if she screwed it up even more and had to pay double to have a professional fix her mistake?

She frowned, looking from the dripping pipe to the new one she had purchased. It wasn't leaking *that* bad. She could probably put a small plastic container underneath and catch all the water until she got it fixed. Properly. By someone who knew what they were doing.

Besides, she had a mile-long "to-do" list if Dean was coming to dinner. She had a house to clean, or at least straighten up, a meal to prepare, and dessert to make. She didn't have time to play with the pipe now. Not today. Right?

Right.

Satisfied with her reasoning, she nodded and stood back up, letting her boys in from the backyard much to Ben's delight, who went straight for his catnip. She made a marinade for the steaks and put them in the fridge to do their thing.

Next, she tackled the dessert, sampling the pistachio pudding after she made it. As she licked the green pudding from her finger, an image of Dean doing the same thing to her invaded her mind, his lips wrapped around her finger, his tongue swirling around the tip as he held her wrist securing her finger in his mouth. That led her to thinking about his mouth in other places.

She shivered, the image popping like a soap bubble from her mind as she forced herself to focus on the task at hand.

Down, girl, or else he won't only be filing for divorce but a restraining order as well.

She spent the rest of the afternoon tidying up the house, doing a load of laundry, and trying to ignore the ticking of the clock and her hammering heart. She filled the sink with water and did the dishes, letting her mind wander again as her hands worked in the soapy warm water. After she finished washing the last dish, she mindlessly pulled the plug to drain the sink when it gurgled back at her.

Oh, that couldn't be good.

She hesitantly bent down to check under the sink at the same time the pipe burst and water gushed everywhere.

"Oh, no! Oh, shit! Oh, crap!" Novalee chanted, standing quickly in search of towels only to slip and land on her butt, eye level with the gushing water.

She sputtered, coughing as water hit her in the face, soaking her. She screamed, making Jerry run into the kitchen to investigate. He ran right into her, knocking her over in the process.

"Jerry! Down! Sit!" she screamed as he licked her face.

The water finally stopped attacking her and was again a slow drip. Jerry stuck his head under the sink, sniffed, and gave a small whine before trotting out of the kitchen, leaving wet paw prints in his wake.

Just then the doorbell rang.

"That's just fucking perfect!" She glanced at the digital clock on her stove. Too early for Dean.

Carefully getting to her feet, she grabbed a clean dishtowel as she tried to dry off as best as she could. Maybe the visitor would take pity on her looking like a drowned rat and kindly fix her sink.

She snorted as she opened the door . . . and froze.

Oh sweet Jesus.

Of course it had to be *him*. She hadn't embarrassed herself enough today in front of him and, apparently, God needed another laugh today as well.

His eyes roamed over her body, pausing on her chest, which she realized was so exposed she might as well be standing there topless. His mouth opened and closed, but no sound came out. He just stood there staring at her in bewilderment.

Say something, dammit!

"My pipe burst and got me wet when I wasn't expecting it!" she blurted.

Anything but that!

His shoulders started to shake and he pushed his lips together, but it was no good. Laughter spilled out of him, doubling him over as he wrapped an arm around his middle.

Novalee stood there drenched, cold, embarrassed, and flashing half her neighborhood, but she couldn't help but smile at the man practically rolling over with laughter.

This was the man she was planning to divorce, and that realization gave her heart an unfamiliar tug.

Chapter 6

"Novalee, you sure do know how to break the ice," Dean teased through his laughter.

"I'm glad I amuse you," she muttered, frowning.

He grinned at her. "Sorry. I wasn't laughing at you, I was . . ." *Thinking of all the ways I could get you wet.* Novalee crossed her arms and arched a brow, waiting for him to finish. "Okay, I was laughing at you."

The corners of her mouth perked as she tried hard to resist smiling. Dean wrestled with the impulse to lean over and kiss the frown from her face. He'd never wanted to taste and explore someone as badly as he did this woman. Finally she caved and the smile appeared as she awkwardly laughed and ran her hands through her hair.

"I must look like a mess."

When she moved her arms she revealed that lacy pink bra again. Dean's dick hardened, delighted by the sight of this personal wet T-shirt contest. He was sure if he looked closely enough he'd see her nipples beneath the thin material. He was also positive if he tried to look closer it would earn him a slap in the face and signed divorce papers before he could blink.

He shifted his eyes away from her chest and cleared his throat, hoping his voice didn't come out sounding hoarse.

"You look a little wet is all," he mumbled. "Not a mess at all."

She blushed and looked down at herself, crossing her arms again to hide her breasts that were playing peek-a-boo with him. She opened her mouth to say something when an elderly woman appeared at the end of her driveway, calling to her.

"Novalee? Is everything all right, dear?" She cast a suspicious glance at Dean. "You look like someone tried to drown you."

"I'm fine, Mrs. Bailey." Novalee smiled at the woman Dean could only assume was her neighbor. "My kitchen pipe sprung a leak."

The old woman's eyes lit up and she shuffled her way closer to them.

"You know, Grayson is visiting me today, and he's great with things like that. I'm sure he wouldn't mind popping over and giving you a hand."

Dean raised an eyebrow, amused by the woman's obvious matchmaking ploy. For all she knew he and Novalee were an item and yet here she was trying to set his woman up with this Grayson character right in front of him.

He looked at Novalee, curious as to what her reaction would be. For all *he* knew, Grayson and she had been together before he reappeared in her life. Maybe he was an ex that she had recently broken up with who she still had feelings for. Maybe the old woman wasn't trying to match make at all, but ignite an old flame.

Fortunately, Novalee's eyes didn't light up. If anything, she looked uncomfortable. She smiled, but he could tell it was forced from the tension around her lips.

"That's sweet of you to offer, but I think we can handle it."

"Oh." Mrs. Bailey's face fell and she narrowed her eyes at Dean. "I don't think I've ever seen you around here before."

"I'm—"

"This is Dean Phillips," Novalee quickly introduced. "Dean, this is my neighbor Mrs. Bailey."

He smiled at the woman and extended his hand. "Pleased to meet you, ma'am."

She stared at his hand for a moment before limply placing hers within it, and then snatching it away just as quickly.

"How do you know Novalee?" she inquired.

"We're—"

"Old friends," Novalee interrupted again.

Damn. Was the woman ever going to let him speak?

He looked at her questionably and saw panic widen her eyes. Was she afraid he was going to blurt out they were married? From his experience, women tended to gossip and he'd bet old Mrs. Bailey would be on the phone within seconds of entering her house, spreading the word of Novalee Jensen's well-kept secret. The last thing he wanted was to do anything, or say anything, that would embarrass her. Didn't she know that?

Of course not. How could she know she could trust him when she didn't know him? And really, could she trust him? Look what he'd already done to her life.

"Old friends," he mimicked, turning his attention back to Mrs. Bailey, smiling.

She grunted and said to Novalee, "Friends shouldn't walk around half-exposed in front of each other," before turning to leave.

Novalee blushed and crossed her arms tighter over herself.

Dean watched the woman depart as quickly as she could and chuckled. "She's got spunk."

"She meddles but means no harm."

Dean looked at her and nodded. "She is right, though. You should put some dry clothes on. Not that I'm complaining about the view." He winked at her and she smirked as she took a step back.

"Come in."

Dean stepped into the house, looking over what could be seen of her home slowly. A person's home was their sanctuary, a place they could truly be themselves. Anything he needed to know about his wife would be found here.

Before he could comment on his surroundings, a low growl snapped his attention to his right where a large chocolate Lab stood baring his teeth. He swallowed, afraid to move in case it set the animal off. It moved closer just as Novalee calmly said, "That's enough, Jerry."

And just like that, the dog's teeth disappeared and his tail wagged as he sat at Dean's feet looking up at him for attention.

"He won't hurt you," Novalee assured him. "Unless I tell him to," she added wickedly.

He glanced at her grinning face and breathed a little easier. Turning his attention back to the dog, he slowly offered his palm for the Lab to sniff, which he did eagerly.

"You're just a big softy, huh," he said to Jerry, squatting down to scratch him.

"Um . . . I'm just going to change," Novalee said from behind him. "Make yourself comfortable in the living room. You'll obviously want to avoid the kitchen until I clean up."

Dean patted the dog's head one last time and stood.

"I've got a better idea. Why don't you show me where you hide your mop and I'll start the cleanup while you change?" he offered, smiling.

Her eyes widened and she shook her head.

"No. I couldn't let you do that. You're here as my guest."

"I'm also here as your husband." He shrugged. "That's what husbands do, right?"

She bit her lip and stared at him.

Shit. Maybe he'd gone too far.

"C'mon. You can't expect me to sit around and watch as you clean up a mess and do nothing, can you?" He grinned, flashing the dimples he knew drove most women wild.

"It's okay. I can do it," she insisted.

He sighed. "Novalee, it's not a big deal. Let me help."

He watched her, deciding if she refused his offer again he'd drop it and go search for the damned mop himself. But he realized he wanted her to let him do this. It was a simple gesture, not a big thing at all really, but he had the feeling Novalee Jensen wasn't the type of woman to let anyone do anything for her, despite how little the offer was.

She licked her lips and finally nodded. "Okay. I'll get the mop for you."

She hurried toward the back of the house, waiting until she disappeared to let his curiosity overtake him. He wandered into the living room, stopping at a bookshelf that held an old photo of a smiling couple. The resemblance between the woman and Novalee was so strong he knew that he was looking at her parents.

On the shelf below were two more pictures: one of two little girls and beside it two young women in graduation gowns and caps. He looked closer at both photos, assuming the little blonde was Novalee with her arms wrapped around the other child.

He picked up the graduation picture and glanced at the younger version again, noticing the same girl was with Novalee in both pictures, arms still wrapped around each other the same way, only ten years older. He squinted at the brunette as a nagging feeling of recognition filled his gut.

"That's Cali and me," Novalee said. He turned to face her, looking up from the picture. "You met her at the bar," she added.

Right. Of course. He nodded and put the picture down, pointing at its mate.

"You and her as well?"

She smiled. "We've been friends since diaper days."

His gaze drifted back up to the picture of her parents and he heard her sigh as she came to stand beside him.

"Cali's parents took me in when my parents were killed in a car accident," she explained. "We're more like sisters than just friends."

Of course he knew that, he knew more about her than she could ever guess.

"I'm sorry," he said. "How old were you when it happened?" he asked, knowing it was something someone would inquire about if they didn't already know the answer.

"Sixteen." She shrugged and he could tell it was her way of dropping the subject. "It was a long time ago." She turned and went back towards the kitchen, carrying the mop. "You really don't have to clean up my mess."

He took the object from her hands and shook his head. "You really have difficulty accepting the smallest amount of help, don't you?" She looked like she was about to say something else, but he waved off her silent words. "Go change," he said, turning his back on her to start his task.

As he mopped he could feel her eyes on him for what felt like hours until he finally heard her turn and walk away. He smiled, liking that he could fluster her so easily. The way she stared and stammered at the front door, blurting out words that made her turn red, told him just how much he affected her.

And then there was the way her body reacted to him earlier at the hotel when he was seconds away from kissing her. She wanted him just as much as he wanted her. If that damn kid hadn't shown up with room service at that exact moment, he would know what Novalee's lips felt like instead of wondering.

He knew he should back off. As much as he didn't want to admit it, Abby was right. The last thing he should do was mix pleasure with business. He shouldn't be thinking of ways he could seduce this woman into bed. The situation he'd created was already so fucking complicated and wrong without adding sex into the mix.

She was going to hate him at the end of all this. How could she not? And if they slept together . . . How would that make her feel after the truth came out? Cheap? Used? Degraded? Would she think he was no better than the asshole that beat her?

His grip tightened on the mop. He'd never raise a hand to a woman, but what he'd done to Novalee by tricking her into a marriage, was he any better than the anonymous prick? His actions wouldn't leave physical scars, but there'd be scars nonetheless.

"I said you didn't have to clean up, you don't have to break the handle to get out of the job."

He looked at her, confused. She raised an eyebrow and nodded at his hands and he saw his knuckles were white from the grip he had on the mop. He loosened his hold, his hands slowly going back to their normal color.

Gently she took it from him, glancing at him with a worried expression on her face. He took a step back, running his hands through his hair as she finished cleaning up the mess.

"I'm sorry. I just . . . I don't know—" She looked at him and he closed his mouth to keep from rambling some more nonsense.

"Are you okay?"

He nodded. They stared at each other for a few moments before she broke eye contact, grabbed the mop and bucket, and left the kitchen.

"Fuck!" he swore under his breath, his hands clenched into fists. He needed to fucking relax. He'd almost snapped her stupid mop in half as she'd watched him freak out over nothing. He didn't need to scare her away before he even had a chance to win her over.

She came back into the kitchen then, watching him cautiously from the entryway.

"Uh, do you want me to call a plumber or something?" he asked, sheepishly meeting her gaze.

She shook her head. "It's Sunday and will cost an arm and a leg to get one out here. As long as I don't use the sink it should be okay until tomorrow."

"Are you sure? I can handle the cost if—"

"No!" she said firmly, suddenly looking angry. "I can afford it; I just want to wait until tomorrow."

"I'm sorry. I didn't mean to imply that you couldn't pay for it. I just wanted to help."

"If you want to help you can grill the steaks instead of flashing your money around," she said, opening the fridge and pulling out a dish.

Flashing his money around? As in all the money she knew he had? Did that mean she knew *who* he was?

He narrowed his eyes at her as she got the get ingredients together. Should he ask her? If she did know, how long ago did she find out? *How* did she find out?

She turned around to pass him the dish with the steaks, but stopped when she caught him staring at her.

She swallowed, clearly nervous by his intense stare. "What?"

He waited a moment before reaching for the steaks and shook his head. "Nothing."

"Dean—"

"I assume the grill is out back," he said, not waiting for her reply as he walked toward the patio doors.

He quickly fired it up and threw the meat on, closing the lid as he got lost in his thoughts. So what if she did know? It was a bit hypocritical of him to be pissed at her for finding out, considering what he knew about her. She was bound to find out sooner or later anyway. She *had* to know sooner or later because of the circumstances and what he needed from her.

Or maybe she didn't know anything at all. Maybe it was just an offhanded comment because he offered to cover the plumping expenses. But if she did know who he was, did that mean she also knew about—

"Do you want a beer?" she called from inside the house. "Or I have soda or water."

"I'll take a beer."

She appeared with the cold refreshment, handing it to him carefully so their fingers didn't touch. He brought the bottle to his mouth and took a long pull, keeping his eyes on her.

She sat down in one of the patio chairs, pulling at the beer label as she avoided looking at him.

He turned his attention back to the steaks when he heard her whisper, "I Googled you."

He froze, the metal barbeque spatula paused mid-steak-flip.

"I . . . wanted to know about the man I'd married," she continued. "I wanted to try and understand why I would do such a thing with someone I didn't even know."

He clamped his teeth together, forcing himself to listen and not just react.

"I didn't find out much. I just typed in your name and clicked the first article I saw." He heard her shift in her chair and the bottle being set down on the glass tabletop. "The only thing I know is that you're an heir to your grandfather's hotels." His heart rate slowed down a little and he relaxed his jaw. "And that you're fighting your father for it," she added. "I'm sorry about your grandfather."

He nodded, not trusting himself to speak.

"Dean, I swear that's all I know." The pleading in her voice for him to believe her was hard to miss. "I read the little blurb about you and your father and that's it. It's not as if I did a background check on you. Of course there are things I want to know, but I don't want to find them out from some computer. It felt like an invasion of privacy. I want the answers from you when, and if, you're willing to give them."

Guilt washed over him, making any anger he felt disappear. She wanted answers but wasn't willing to go behind his back to find them as he had with her. She really was better than the shit he'd put her through.

"Dean, I understand if you're angry—"

"I was just surprised," he said, sounding gruffer than he'd intended. He inhaled deeply and tried to focus on grilling again. Anything to not have to face her right now. "I understand wanting to know more about the person you're married to. I don't fault you for that."

"But you weren't honest about who you are because you have a fortune to protect," she concluded. "You're afraid I'll go after whatever I can get from a divorce."

He remained silent. Of course she was right . . . to a point. However, he was more afraid of what she'd find out if she dug into his past.

"I don't want anything from you, Dean" she assured him, sounding insulted that he might even think that. "I don't need anything and I'm not looking to take what's yours."

"Awesome. Now that we've established you don't need me, can you please get me a clean platter for these steaks?" he snapped.

Her sharp intake of breath told him his tone surprised her. In all honesty, it had surprised him, too. But hearing her say she didn't need him stung in ways he couldn't explain. It may not be a real marriage, but he was her husband. She should need him. She should want him. And it made no fucking sense that he felt that way since they were only married on paper. All he knew was that it hurt to be so easily discarded, even though she was telling him exactly what he should want to hear.

"Here." She thrust the clean plate at him, snatching up the dirty one and going back inside.

Dean took his time moving the steaks off the grill and turning it off. Inside a confused, and possibly hurt, woman awaited him. He didn't want this evening to turn awkward, where they ate in silence, the only sounds coming from the clanking of the silverware as it scraped against the plates, and ending with a clipped goodbye at the front door. This was like a first date. If he wanted to get another invite, it all had to go smoothly.

He found her in the little dining room area just off the living room. The table was set, complete with a large bowl of salad in the middle and a baked potato still wrapped in foil on each of their plates. He took her cue and placed a steak on each plate, returning the empty dish to the kitchen before sitting down to join her at the table.

As she passed him the salad bowl the awkward silence he'd feared fell around them. He glanced at her out of the corner of his eye and suddenly found the humor in the situation. His chuckle earned him a raised eyebrow from his dinner companion.

"What's so funny?"

"This. Us." He gestured between the two of them with his fork, grinning. "You're upset about something I said; I have no idea what to say to make it right. So now here we sit in silence."

"And this amuses you?"

"It's just such a married thing to do."

She looked at him. He winked, and despite the attempts she made to keep from smiling, she failed.

"It's our first married misunderstanding," he declared and she laughed.

"Wow. That didn't take long. It hasn't even been twenty-four hours yet," she joked.

"Technically it's been two years," he corrected with a smirk. "I think we've done damn well."

"Sure, until we're in each other's company. I guess that's a sign we work better apart than together," she said, taking a sip of water.

He thought about that and then shook his head. "Apart there's no making up."

"Just because we're together doesn't mean that will happen either," she countered.

He laughed. "You're quite stubborn, aren't you?" She shrugged, smiling coyly. "I get the feeling being married to you will be an adventure."

"Being married? You mean for the few days until the divorce papers arrive?" She rolled her eyes. "I think this hardly counts as a marriage, Dean. We don't even know each other."

And there it was again. That goddamned tightening in his chest when she dismissed their union as nothing. For Christ's sake it *was* nothing like a normal marriage, he reminded himself. Why the hell couldn't he remember that?

"Well, let's fix that," he heard himself say.

She tilted her head to the side. "How?"

"Usually we ask questions about one another. Isn't that how you get to know someone on a first date?"

"Is this a date?"

"You tell me. You're the one that asked me here tonight."

She fiddled with her napkin. "What do you want to know?"

Score!

"What were your parents like?" It was a risky question. She could either shut him down or open up about the people she lost too young. Thankfully, she smiled.

"They were amazing, self-employed, hard-working kind of people. We weren't rich," she smirked at him, "but I never went without anything. They were both laid-back and 'take things as they come,' but also very structured. They made sure everything was planned, but didn't worry themselves sick over detail, you know?"

"No brothers or sisters?"

She shook her head. "Just me."

"So, you were alone after they died," he said, knowing all too well what that felt like.

"No. I was never alone. I had Cali and her parents; they're family. I felt a lot of things, but never alone." She smiled. "What about you?"

He stiffened. "What about me?"

"What was your grandfather like?"

Instantly, he relaxed and returned the smile. "Strong-willed, intelligent, powerful. He looked hard on the outside, but had a heart of gold for those he loved. He was my best friend," he added.

She reached for his hand and gave it a light squeeze.

"I'm sorry," she said again. "I know how hard it is to lose people you love."

He nodded, mindlessly linking their fingers together. He didn't miss the way her breathing increased, and he'd be lying if he said it didn't affect him too. His pulse increased and the head in his pants came alive as he wondered if her skin was this soft everywhere.

Fuck. He was getting hard over a little handholding. He couldn't remember that ever happening. Was it even normal?

"He was more of a role model than my own father," Dean confessed, scowling. "My father has no right being anyone's role model."

"He sounds like an ass," Novalee blurted, turning red as soon as the words left her mouth. "I mean, from what I read, the comments he made; he doesn't sound like a nice man."

"You have no idea." He continued to stroke her with his thumb. " 'Ass' is a pretty mild description."

"What about your mom?" she asked.

His thumb stopped. "Dead."

"Oh. Siblings?"

"A sister." He pulled his hand away completely. "She's gone, too."

"Dean." He glanced at her, quickly shifting his eyes away again. "I'm sorry. I didn't mean to upset you." She pulled her hand off the table and shoved them both between her knees.

"It's fine. I just don't talk about them."

She nodded. "I get that. I don't talk about my folks either."

She picked up their dishes and took them into the kitchen. Grabbing what was left on the table, he followed her and set them down on the counter for her.

"Thanks." She held a cup up to him. He nodded, understanding she was offering him coffee, and she poured some in her cup.

"Dessert?"

"Maybe later. I'm stuffed." He smiled and patted his stomach. "Thanks for dinner."

"It wasn't anything fancy."

"Doesn't have to be fancy to be good."

She shrugged and wandered back out to the living room, leaving him no choice but to trail after her. They settled on the couch and it was then he noticed the ball of fur in the corner.

"You have a cat, too?"

She grinned. "That's Ben."

"Ben and Jerry?" he chuckled.

"Named after the two greatest men in my life."

He eyed the feline. He was definitely more of a dog person.

"You don't like cats." She guessed.

"Not as much as dogs, no."

"I had always thought I was more of a cat person, until I needed something bigger."

He cocked an eyebrow. "Needed something bigger?"

Her eyes widened as she realized what she'd said, the color almost draining from her face.

"I, uh, wanted to feel safe when I moved into my own place." She sipped her coffee, avoiding his eyes.

"Was there any reason you shouldn't feel safe?" He pressed her, wondering if she'd tell him about what happened.

She shrugged. "Just a precaution. You know, single woman living alone, coming home late at night. Gotta be careful, right?"

"Of course," he agreed, noticing how tight her body had become. "So, why did you open a bar?"

She relaxed again and finally looked up at him. "I wanted something of my own. I had just moved here and was living with Cali for a while. I had inherited some money from my parents and one day Cali and I were walking downtown and saw the 'for sale' sign. The rest is history."

"But why a bar?"

"Why not a bar?" she questioned back.

"There wasn't anything else you wanted to do?"

"The place was already set up as one. It just needed a little TLC." She grinned. "Okay, maybe a lot. But it had potential and was in a good location for business. I'd had experience running a business before, so I figured 'why not?' Took a lot of work, and a lot of time and effort, but it was worth it."

"If last night was any indication, it seems you do very well."

She nodded. "We do okay."

"We?"

"Cali and me. She may not own it, but I couldn't have done it without her." She looked down at her coffee cup. "I couldn't have done a lot of things without her."

"I'm sure it helped to have her when you lost your parents."

"It did, but she's done more than just hold my hand through their loss."

"That's what best friends do." He was able to read between the lines, but he wanted her to say what she was hinting at.

"I owe my best friend my life," she said.

His heart stopped as he asked the next question, "What did she save you from?"

Novalee's head snapped up, suddenly looking panicked. She bit her lip so hard he feared he'd see blood. Setting his cup on the coffee table, he scooted a little closer to her. Slowly, he reached out and traced his thumb over her bitten lip, and smiled.

Their eyes locked as he cupped her face and she released her lip, and she gently rubbed the bitten flesh, pretending not to notice when her breathing hitched. He'd scared her by asking the question. Obviously it had something to do with the douche who'd hurt her, and he understood if she didn't want to confide in him yet. But he also didn't want to freak her out and demand that he leave. He had to calm her down, to take her mind off what she had just revealed to him.

"You're going to hurt yourself if you keep doing that," he said.

"Would you kiss it and make it better if I did?"

Chapter 7

He stopped caressing her lip and they both sat motionless.

What the hell had she just done?

Her heart raced as what she'd said sank in. She'd just asked him to kiss her!

What. The. Hell?

She'd spoken before she could think; going on impulse by what she was feeling. What he made her feel. Things didn't need to become physical between them. She knew that would only lead to trouble, but that didn't stop her from opening her mouth and inviting him to explore it.

For the third time that night she had said what shouldn't be said. First in the damn kitchen when she practically told him she knew about his multimillion-dollar empire. How could she not explain the random comment about not flashing his money after that?

And then just moments ago when she'd told him about needing to feel safe and how Cali had saved her. But there was no way she was going to explain that to him. She didn't even like thinking about that time in her life, let alone sharing it with anyone else.

And now here she sat, staring at the man who was her husband on paper if nothing more, after just asking him to kiss her. Really, what the hell had she been thinking? Worse yet, what was he now thinking?

Their eyes were still locked on each other, their breathing almost matching, but he made no attempt to take her up on her offer. Talk about feeling like a total fool.

She licked her lip and his eyes dropped to her mouth. He still cupped her face, which she normally would have pulled away from, but it felt . . . nice. Comfortable. Safe.

Safe?

She swallowed, trying to coat her sudden dry mouth. Safe wasn't something she felt with men anymore. Not completely, anyway. There had been men she had casually dated after Dalton that she was comfortable with and was fairly certain wouldn't hurt her, but she never felt entirely safe with any of them. So, what made Dean the exception?

She closed her eyes, knowing she had to say something to break the silence, but she didn't want to look at him when she did. She was already embarrassed enough by his rejection; she didn't need to see his relief when she pulled away.

She opened her mouth to speak, but before she could utter a sound she felt warm breath on her face just as his lips pressed against hers. Her eyes snapped open in shock as he drew away. Dean's face was so close, his brown eyes burning into her as he watched her, waiting for her reaction to the peck he'd placed on her lips. But she sat there too stunned to react.

She wanted to say something. She wanted to *do* anything that told him it was okay and to please continue. Her hands ached to reach run her fingers through his hair as she pulled him back to kiss her. But she hadn't expected him to actually act on her impulsive invitation, and she had no idea what to do now that he had.

Suddenly, she felt very self-conscious. It had been so long since she'd had any physical contact with a man that she doubted her ability to be with one again. What if he thought she was a lame kisser? What if her lack of response made him think she was frigid? Could a person become frigid and boring from lack of sex?

Oh God! What if she couldn't remember how to do it?

Was it possible to forget? Would every move she made feel awkward not only to herself, but to him as well? Would he feel like he was with an inexperienced virgin?

Jesus. She felt like a virgin again. She may have lost her innocence almost ten years ago, but she couldn't remember feeling as nervous as she did right now with Dean. She wanted to please him, but how could she when she doubted her sexual ability?

However, the response she lacked on the outside was more than made up for on the inside, which told her she had no reason to fear becoming frigid. Her heart was hammering so hard in her chest she was afraid it might stop any second from overexertion. Her stomach was one twisted ball of excitement, and she was certain if she stood her legs would collapse.

And that was all just from a goddamn little peck!

His lips were parted as if he was about to say something. Panic suddenly rose in her chest that she would hear, "I'm sorry."

She didn't want him to be sorry! She'd basically asked him to kiss her and when he did as she'd requested, she'd turned to stone. She didn't want him to think that was his fault, or that she hadn't wanted the kiss. She sure as hell didn't want him to think she didn't want him. And if he uttered those two words it would mean all of that.

"Novalee . . ."

She looked at him, knowing the words she didn't want to hear were about to be said if she didn't do something.

"Novalee, I'm—"

She leaned in and silenced him the only way she wanted to. He only took seconds to respond to her actions. The kiss was soft, slowly allowing her to grow used to the intimate touch. Gradually, Dean's lips became firmer, pressing harder as he cupped the back of her neck.

Novalee ran her hands up his arms, feeling the hard muscle beneath her palms. A thrill shot through her from the touch, giving her the boost of confidence she desperately needed. His mouth parted and his tongue swept along her bottom lip, tasting her for the first time just as she snaked her fingers through his hair.

She moaned and needed no further encouragement to open her mouth to him, and a shiver ran down her spine, causing her nipples to harden and scrape against the lace of her bra in an almost painful, yet pleasurable, way. If his mouth wasn't already occupied, she would have begged him to give them some attention

And for that reason alone it was probably a good thing. She had already thrown herself at him, and although he didn't seem to have any complaints, she didn't need to embarrass herself further by begging for sex. Which was exactly what some very neglected, very horny parts of her were telling her to do, sending a painful reminder that she hadn't felt pleasure that didn't come from her own fingers or silicone in two long years.

She was sure if her nether regions had a voice they would be screaming for attention. Demanding that Dean work his hand lower and explore other areas than just the side of her face. Those parts longed to be filled by real flesh, not some fake stand-in. It had been far too long and a toy just wasn't going to cut it anymore.

Maybe if she just . . .

Novalee shifted, hoping he'd take the hint if she moved closer and move his hands lower. But the movement caused the seam of her jeans to rub against her, sending a jolt of sexual desire all the way to the very tips of her nipples. She arched her back to better grind him, thus thrusting her chest to his.

The sudden change of posture caused Dean to pull away and Novalee was positive she heard her lady bits weep with frustration.

He still cupped her face as he stared into her eyes. Novalee was afraid to blink, worried that he may pull away altogether if she did. Her tongue felt thick in her mouth, which might have been a blessing in disguise since she was sure she wouldn't be able to form words that weren't *please, don't stop*, and *fuck me*. She bit her lip to stop herself.

She realized her fingers were still tangled in his hair and she slowly lowered her hands until they rested on his chest. Then she grasped his shirt, afraid that if she let go he would get up.

So holding him against his will is a better idea?

Novalee sighed and loosened her hold, flattening her palms against his chest instead. He felt hard, muscle built up from years at the gym perhaps. The heat from his body radiated through her fingers even through the fabric of his shirt and warmed her skin. Her eyes roamed over his upper body as she tried to remember what he felt like bare and pressed up against her.

Shouldn't she feel . . . something? Some sense of *déjà vu*? Shouldn't images be flashing in her mind right now from their night together, reminding her of what they'd shared? His touch, his kiss, should feel familiar, but it all felt . . . new.

There wasn't anything vaguely recognizable about him. Oh, sure, she knew she knew him. She could remember meeting him that night, but his body wasn't familiar to her, his touch was alien. She would just like something, *anything*, to help her remember what had made her decide to marry a man she didn't know.

"What was the point of kissing it better if you're just going to continue to chew it off?" he teased. Novalee snapped her eyes back up to his and he grinned. "I kind of like how both your lips feel. It would be a shame to lose one," he said.

She blushed and ducked her head, causing his hands to fall away.

"It's an old habit."

"Old habits are hard to break."

"Some are," she agreed. "I guess it depends if you think breaking them will benefit you." She shrugged. "Biting my lip is better than reaching for a cigarette or drink every time I'm anxious. I'd be drunk all the time if I did that."

Dean laughed and Novalee smiled, loving the sound.

"I see your point." He watched her for a minute before asking, "Why are you anxious now?"

"I guess I was waiting for the "ah-ha" moment."

He furrowed his brow. "The what?"

"The moment when everything clicks and falls into place and I suddenly remember everything from that night."

He narrowed his eyes, looking at her even more closely now. "Why did you think that would happen?"

"The kiss." She glanced at him quickly before looking down at her hands as she played with the hem of her shirt. "I thought something about it might feel familiar and bring back some memories."

"And did it?" he asked, sounding tense.

Novalee shook her head. "Nothing."

"Is there anything you do remember?"

She hesitated, throwing it back and asking him a question instead. "Do *you* remember anything?"

He sighed heavily and ran his hand through his hair.

"I remember talking with you and . . . taking a phone call." He glanced at her, looking very much on edge. "Playing a few slots . . ."

"How is it possible neither one of us can remember?" She was frustrated. "It doesn't make any sense! One of us had to have the bright idea to . . ."—she waved her hand back—"you know."

He smirked. "Hook up?"

"Sex is one thing, marriage is another. I could understand if it was just sex, but I can't understand this." She shook her head and crossed her arms, a defensive move she always made when feeling conflicted. "It's almost as if we were roofied."

Dean's eyes widened. "Jesus, Novalee, you don't think I'd do something like that to you, do you?"

"I said 'we,' as in both of us," she reminded him. "I never pointed the finger at you."

"You didn't answer the question," he said, so low she barely heard him.

Novalee looked at him and saw the hurt clearly written across his face. Did she know this man, like really know him? No. Did she think there were things he wasn't telling her? Definitely. But she couldn't fault him for that since there were things she wasn't willing to share with him either; However, she couldn't help but think he knew more about their night together than he was letting on.

Did that mean she thought he was capable of drugging her?

Novalee learned a long time ago that the person you thought least likely ever capable of hurting you had the power to do it in a blink of an eye. She had put her trust and faith in a man who'd showered her with affection and gifts one minute, only to turn around and slap her across the face in the next.

Dalton had been charming and had the ability to make her believe he meant it when he said he was sorry and that it would never happen again. He really had sounded sincere in his apologies, always making sure he brought some small token of his love to give to her after one of their fights.

"I'm just so crazy about you, Nova. My passion for you is so strong that sometimes it feels like it's all too much and I can't think straight! My body reacts before my mind can comprehend what it's doing, baby. I would never purposely hurt you."

He brushed the hair off her swollen eye, grazing it gently with his fingertips as he made a show of cringing.

"This is how strong my love is for you," he whispered. "I love you so much you make me lose my mind. You understand, don't you, baby?"

She nodded, not understanding at all, but not wanting to question him and risk him losing his temper again. And really, was it such a bad thing when someone loved you so much they felt crazy from it at times? At least she had someone who loved her.

"Tell me you forgive me, baby," he begged. "I swear it will never happen again. I promise, Nova. I can't stand to see you hurt." Her smile

was shaky, but she nodded. "Tell me. I need to hear the words," he demanded.

"I forgive you, Dalton," she rasped, her throat still sore from all the screaming and crying she had done.

He wrapped his arms around her and kissed the top of her head.

"It's always going to be like this, baby. You and me. No one can, or will, love you like I do."

His embrace suddenly became a little too tight . . . His words suddenly sounded a little too threatening . . .

"Novalee?"

A hand touched her arm and she flinched. She looked down and saw Dean quickly remove his hand, then looked up at his concerned expression and immediately felt guilty for making him think she doubted him.

"I'm sorry, I don't know . . . ," Novalee started to explain, but he cut her off.

"No, don't apologize. It's clear I've made you uncomfortable." He looked around the room and nodded. "I should go."

When he stood to leave Novalee grabbed his hand, forcing him to stop and look at her.

"You don't make me uncomfortable, Dean. And I don't think you'd do anything to hurt me, including drugging me. That's not what I meant when I said that."

"But just now—"

"Just now I went on a trip and didn't leave the room." She grinned at her lame attempt at a joke. "I just remembered something that took me back to a time in my life that wasn't so great. It had nothing to do with you."

"But I brought it on. I made you remember," he said with sadness in his tone.

"No." She shrugged, trying to play it off as nothing. "Sometimes it just happens. Certain words, sounds, places . . . It just happens," she repeated.

He sighed and his shoulders relaxed as he smiled down at her.

"Well, that's a relief. I mean, that it wasn't me, not that you remember shitty past experiences," he explained quickly.

She chuckled and gently pulled on his hand. "I wouldn't be alone with you if I thought you had done something like that," she added.

"Do you trust me, Novalee?" he asked seriously, staring at her intensely so she was unable to look away. She swallowed and nodded. "Why?"

"I don't know," she admitted. "Maybe I shouldn't. There are obviously things you're hiding, and I'm not judging you," she assured him. "There are things about me you don't know that I won't tell you either."

"Ever?"

"I don't think we'll know each other long enough for me to really feel I can," she stated.

"I wish that wasn't true."

She blinked, surprised by what he'd said. Did that mean he wished she would tell him, or that he wished they'd be together longer?

"I do, too," she replied, knowing her answer was the same for both.

They stood and sat in silence, staring at one another, each lost in their own thoughts until Dean gently squeezed her hand and said, "I really should be going. It's late."

Novalee glanced at the clock hanging above the fireplace and was amazed to see it was after nine. Not late by any means, but she didn't think they had been hanging out so long.

"You don't have to." She blushed at his grin. "I mean, obviously you have to eventually, but it's still fairly early and there's still dessert if you're interested."

"Oh, I'm definitely interested." He wiggled his eyebrows suggestively and she giggled. She actually fucking giggled like a schoolgirl. "But I've already been tempted once tonight."

Her heart fluttered as the butterflies in her stomach took flight. She tried to keep what she feared would be the biggest, silliest grin from spreading across her face. She shifted her eyes from his face and coyly asked, "You find me tempting?"

"More than you know," he answered hoarsely. He dropped her hand and headed for the door, leaving her on the couch, grinning like the fool she feared she looked like. She scrambled up and followed him.

"I'm glad you came, Dean," she said.

Even if it wasn't in the way that I really want.

Whoa. Down, girl.

"Thank you for inviting me."

She folded her arms across her stomach, grasping the sides of her shirt, suddenly feeling awkward saying goodnight after sharing a kiss with him. She hadn't intended for the night to go this way, but now that it had, now that they had crossed that line, did that mean it would happen again? Was it something she wanted to do again, even? She sized him up once his back was facing her, her eyes landing on his fine ass and her breath hitched.

Oh, yeah. She definitely wanted to do it again. "It" being so much more than just kissing.

Dean turned and Novalee quickly averted her eyes before he could catch her staring. She could only hope her expression didn't give her away.

"So, can I call you tomorrow?" he asked, shoving his hands in his pockets.

As the schoolgirl inside happy-danced in a shamefully embarrassing way, the grown-up calmly nodded, acting like it wasn't a big deal. "Sure. I'll be busy at the bar in the afternoon until closing, though, just in case you call and don't get me." She shrugged. "Or you could come in."

"Not much else to do, huh?"

She winked. "You'd be surprised."

He raised his eyebrows and grinned. "Maybe you'll have to show me sometime."

"You make it sound like you'll be sticking around for a while."

"Would that be a bad thing?"

"Not bad. Surprising, though. Don't you have . . . affairs to get back to?" she asked, trying to be as delicate as possible where his business was concerned. "I thought you were only waiting around for the divorce papers to be drawn up and sent out."

His jaw tensed and his eyes lost the flirty tease that had lit them up seconds ago. His body suddenly stiffened and any sign of ease he had displayed all evening vanished.

Novalee wanted to kick herself for bringing up his business back home. She should have known better than to mention anything considering how he'd reacted earlier. But she didn't actually ask about it, she'd only presumed he had to get back to attend to whatever was going on. So why did he just go from hot to cold in two point five seconds?

"As soon as my lawyer sends them, I'll give you a copy for your lawyer to review and I'll be out of your hair," he said, almost gruffly.

Ah, crap. Maybe that was why.

"Dean, that's not what I meant." She frowned. "I just assumed you had dealings back home to get back to, not that I wanted you to blow town as soon as our . . . business ended."

"Business?" He smirked. "Our marriage is a business deal to you?"

"Well, it's not exactly a marriage," she said carefully, sensing she was offending him.

"No. It's just ironic *you* would think of it as a business deal," he said.

"What do you mean *ironic*?"

"Nothing." He dismissed the comment with a shake of his head and forced a smile. "So, tomorrow? I'll call you."

She hesitated a moment, debating if she wanted to press him further on the subject, but finally nodded, letting it go. "Okay."

He took a small step forward, watching her face as he did and slowly leaned toward her until he brushed his lips against her cheek, right near the corner of her mouth.

"Good night, Novalee," he said.

The sound of him whispering her name had a strange effect on her body.

He brushed his hand against hers as he pulled away, and she shivered.

"Night," she croaked, blushing from the hoarseness of her voice.

He flashed her one last smile before leaving. The click of the door closing behind him snapped Novalee out of her sexually frustrated haze long enough to lock up. After checking to make sure everything was secure, and letting Jerry out for his nightly sniff, she changed into the boxers and tank she used as jammies and crawled into bed. Unfortunately, Ben's purr wouldn't help her mind to shut off as easily as it usually did with.

When she closed her eyes she saw Dean's face. She felt his lips and the soft touch of his hands on her cheek. The butterflies came alive in her stomach again for the umpteenth time that night, and she groaned, frustrated by her body's reaction to him.

Goddamn, she was going to spontaneously combust soon if he didn't put his hands on her. If she thought investing in another Rabbit would help she would run out first thing in the morning to get one. Sadly, the BOB would probably die from over-usage again. Especially if she spent too much time in the company of Dean Philips.

No man should be allowed to smell so fucking amazing and sound so fucking sexy and look so fucking . . . fuckable when he was supposed to be hands-off. Wasn't screwing your husband one of the perks to marriage? And yet, here she was trying *not* to screw him. Married life was not what it was cracked up to be.

It was crazy to feel this way. No good would come of her crushing on her soon to be ex-husband. The divorce papers would arrive, they'd sign, he'd leave, and that would be that. End of marriage number one. And possibly the only marriage she would have.

Novalee frowned. She wasn't the type to get swept up in the idea of matrimony, but the thought this might be her only chance was downright depressing. Who wanted their only experience with wedded bliss to be a drunken night in Vegas with a man who didn't remember her until he went to marry someone else?

Oh, yeah, definitely shrink-worthy depressing.

Her phone buzzed from the nightstand, indicating a new text message. She reached for it telling herself she would feel this exited to get a text from anyone. It wasn't because she hoped it might be *him*.

The disappointment she felt when she saw the familiar name told her otherwise.

You'd better be having hot sweaty NON-jackrabbit sex since you're ignoring my calls.

Novalee smiled, shaking her head over her perverted best friend.

No sex of any kind going on here. At least none that involves another person.

She could be pervy too.

Why the hell are you going solo when you have a man there? Man left?

She grinned as she sent off another message.

But he did kiss my booboo better.

Novalee snorted when her cell rang five seconds later.

"You'd better not be talking about that Yogi Bear stuffed animal collection you have," Cali threatened. "And by 'booboo' you had better mean 'hoo-hah.'"

Novalee laughed. "No hoo-hah."

"Explain."

"My lip-biting habit may have helped me out a little tonight," she teased, being vague.

"Need more info."

"He said I was going to hurt myself if I kept biting it and I asked . . ." Novalee grinned, remembering the moment.

"Hello? And you asked what?" Cali screeched.

"If he'd kiss it and make it better if I did."

"Oh my god! Nov, that is so corny!"

"Hey!" Her *former* best friend giggled in her ear.

"I'm sorry, babe, but that's a pretty corny line."

"Corny or not, I was getting some hot tongue action. What were you getting tonight?" Novalee fired at her.

"Okay, shut up," Cali grumbled back. "Hot tongue action, huh? Guess that answers my question if he's a good kisser or not."

"If what he can do with his mouth is any indication of what else he can do . . ." She let the sentence trail off and sighed. "Too bad I can't remember."

"Just stay sober this time and you will."

"This time?"

"Oh, puh-lease. You so know you're going to bone him. Don't act all innocent with me, Miss Thing."

"There will be no boning," Novalee disagreed much to her hoo-hah's disappointment.

"You don't want to?"

"I never said that. Trust me; I want to. It took every ounce of willpower I had tonight to not spread my legs and beg him to take me."

"Fuck willpower!"

"Cali, do you know how complicated that would make things?"

"I see nothing complicated about it," Cali stated.

Novalee rolled her eyes. Of course she didn't. This was Cali after all.

"Really, Nov, it's not. So you're hitched on paper. Big deal. It's just paper; it means nothing in this situation. Treat it like what it really is: a guy you met, who you have fun with and who you could have even more fun with. Hook up and move on as you would normally. Just with a few dotted lines to sign in between romping."

"Wow. You're totally right. I feel so much better now," Novalee replied dryly. "You really have no boundaries, do you?"

"I draw the line if it involves fur, but other than that anything goes."

"You're unbelievable," Novalee said, rolling her eyes again.

"That's what she said."

Novalee snorted in an unladylike way and shook her head. "I'm screwed."

"No you're not. That's the problem," Cali teased.

"You know not everything is fixed by being laid, right?" Novalee said, punching her pillow in frustration.

"Said by the woman who hasn't gotten any in . . . how long?"

"None of your damn business!"

"Touchy." Cali paused. "Dinner went well, then?" she asked, wisely changing the subject.

Novalee sighed. "Yes. No. Good." The urge to slap her forehead was overwhelming. "It was fine."

Cali chuckled. "Wow. I hope you were more articulate than that with him."

"I told him I Googled him," Novalee admitted.

Cali groaned. "Dude, you never confess to the Google. Nothing says creepy stalker more than a woman who has fingers itching to search the web."

"You told me everyone did it!"

"They do! They just don't fess up to it. How did he take it?"

She grimaced. "He wasn't happy I don't think. But then I told him I didn't read any more than one article about him and stopped because I wanted to find out who he was from him, not the computer."

"Nice save. What did you find out?" Nosiness asked.

"Are you familiar with WIP Hotels?"

"Who isn't?"

"Guess who *is* WIP Hotels."

A small gasp was followed by, "No fucking way!"

"Yes fucking way. Now do you understand why I told him? I didn't need him thinking I was after his money."

"Man, Nov, you sure do know how to marry 'em." Cali whistled.

"And divorce them," she pointed out. "Without taking a cent."

"Oh, I'm sure his lawyers will be all over that."

"I have no doubt."

They ended the conversation a few minutes later, Cali making her swear she would fill her in on any dirty things that happened.

Novalee had just snuggled into the warmth of her bed when her cell buzzed again. Cursing Cali for the being the irritating twit she sometimes was, she grabbed the phone prepared to read some unfiltered sex remark.

I can't stop thinking about our kiss

Libido kicked up lust upon seeing those seven words, while her heart did funny things in her chest. He was thinking about her! Yes, the schoolgirl came out with an unusually high squeal that sent Ben scurrying off the bed.

Taking a deep breath to calm herself, she pondered if she should reply with something witty. Sexy? Something that made it sound like she really didn't care?

Thoughts like that will only lead to trouble . . .

It was pretty hot, wasn't it? My lips are dying for a repeat performance . . .

What kiss? Oh, right . . .

Novalee stared at the little screen, reading the words over and over again. Playing coy games didn't feel right, especially when he'd taken a chance and sent a text he didn't have to.

She inhaled deeply and sent the only message that felt right to send.

Neither can I.
Is it too high school of me to say I can't wait to see you tomorrow?

She grinned. Considering she had just squealed like a twelve-year-old, she didn't see the problem. Not that he would ever know that.

Yes, but I'll overlook it since I am too.

Her phone remained silent for a good three minutes, and she was beginning to think he wasn't going to respond again, but just as she was about to snuggle back into bed another text buzzed giving her goose bumps.

Good night, wife

Mrs. Dean Philips.
Dammit!

Chapter 8

Dean impatiently waited for his phone to chirp again.

Nothing.

Maybe he'd pushed it too far by calling her "wife." He didn't even know why he had. The words were written and sent before he could have second thoughts, but now he was second-guessing himself.

Why the hell had he texted her in the first place?

Sure the kiss was on his mind, but Christ, he'd actually *told* her it was.

Fucking pussy.

And it wasn't to get in her good graces by sucking up and telling her what he knew women loved to hear. He told her because he wanted her to know he was thinking of her.

That kiss had been fucking torture just as much as it was pure pleasure. He'd quickly been reminded of how soft her lips were. She may not have been able to remember their night together, but it was one he would remember until his dying day. Every single detail from that night was forever branded in his brain. Everything they did was always right there at the forefront of his mind.

Along with everything they *didn't* do.

He roughly dragged his palm down the side of his face, feeling the roughness of his five o'clock shadow scrape against it.

If he wasn't such a douche he would tell her the truth about that night. But how could he? If he acknowledged what he knew, his cover story was blown and any chance of her helping him was shot.

He could only hope when this all came to light that she would forgive him and wouldn't always see him as the asshole who tricked her into marriage, but as the guy who didn't take advantage of her drunken state.

Didn't take advantage? You're fucking crazy, Philips.

Okay, he took advantage. But not physically. Not in the way she'd been trying so hard to remember. His conscience may be warped to have married her, and he was positive there was a special place in hell just for him, but there was no way he would have taken her to bed in that state.

Damn, she had been eager though.

He chuckled at the memory of Novalee practically ripping off her clothes as soon as the hotel room door closed, leaving him staring wide-eyed at the beauty in front of him. Wide-eyed and totally fucked. How did a guy tell his new bride he couldn't have sex with her? Luckily, she'd passed out and it hadn't come down to him crushing her confidence and her crushing his nuts.

Although he was sure his nuts were still in jeopardy when she found out the truth.

He still had no idea how he was going to tell her. First, he needed to get her to Vegas. Or maybe first he had to tell her so she'd come to Vegas.

No, if he confessed first, she would flip out before he could explain shit, and then he'd have no chance in hell of getting her to cooperate and appear in court on his side. She had to be on his home ground so she couldn't run. He needed the advantage to make her listen; to try and explain and get her to understand why he'd done it. She had to know it wasn't his intention to hurt her. He did it all for his grandfather, to protect everything from his bastard father. He hadn't purposely picked her out; she had just been in the wrong place at the wrong time. It could have been anyone he married.

Oh, yeah, that's exactly what every woman wanted to hear.

"Honey, you were a means to an end. Anybody with tits could have filled your place."

Charming. That would score him big points.

He groaned and dropped to the bed, lying back as he covered his eyes with his forearm to block out the light.

He didn't need the twisted ball in his gut to tell him what he already knew: Novalee was going to hate him. She would see him as just another man she couldn't trust. Another man who made her feel as if she wasn't safe.

He could clearly see she still lived in fear of the bastard who'd hurt her. The way she spoke of needing her dog spoke volumes of how her past still affected her. It killed him to think that there were still times in her life that the dark probably scared her, or that she felt as if someone was watching her, waiting for the moment she was alone to make his move.

It killed him to think that she may feel like his mother had. That she lived through the same hell Lilly Philips had. His hands balled into fists. He'd witnessed his mother's life; too many bruises, too many flimsy excuses.

Novalee may have gotten out broken, but at least she had gotten out alive.

And how did Cali play into all of it? It was obvious they were close, and only natural that she would have been there to help Novalee through that time in her life, but Novalee had said she owed Cali her life. That sounded like a lot more than a little handholding through the experience.

It was so fucking frustrating not to be able to ask questions. All these lies had piled up around him and he was starting to feel suffocated by it all. The only person Dean could talk to about everything was Abby. She'd listen, not spare him the bullshit sympathy, and help him figure out the solution if there was a problem.

Abby was great. She was the best person to have on his side, both personally and professionally. If not for her, Dean would have been alone after his grandfather's death. If it hadn't been for Abby checking up on him, dragging his ass out of bed and pouring the booze down the sink when all he wanted to do was drown in it, who knows where he would have ended up.

In a way, he owed Abby his life. She had kept him afloat when all he'd wanted to do was give up and sink.

But it wasn't his best friend he wanted to talk to right now. He wanted to open up to Novalee and have her open up to him. He wanted to know about the dark secrets that still frightened her. He wanted her to share the trauma she had lived through, to know that she trusted him and could count on him to be there for her. It startled Dean to realize just how badly he wanted to protect this woman, to chase away her demons and keep her safe.

Aside from his mother and sister he had never felt the need to protect anyone. And he'd done a piss-poor job of that hadn't he?

The anger and pain filled him instantly. He couldn't protect his own family, the people he loved and cared for, the people he knew. What right did he have to want to be Novalee's knight in shining armor? If she was smart she would run as far and as fast as possible away from him when this was all over. It would be better that way for both of them. He was too damaged to give her what she deserved, and she was too decent for him to deserve her.

But knowing all that didn't stop him from wanting it.

Their kiss tonight just proved how bad he wanted it. He thought he had died and bypassed that reserved spot waiting for him in the pits of hell and gone straight to heaven's gate when she'd asked him to kiss her. She had looked so lost, so vulnerable as she whispered the words, and he hadn't known if he should comply with her request. He'd sat there, stunned by what she was asking, wondering if she was even aware of how powerful her words were. Dean couldn't help but feel as if she'd been asking him to heal much more than a bitten lip, and he wasn't sure if he was up for the challenge. There was so much of himself he couldn't fix, how could he heal someone else? Especially someone he would have a hand in hurting.

Then she'd closed her eyes, but not before he'd seen rejection in them. He made her feel like shit as if she wasn't worth healing. And Dean was damned if he was going to make her think of herself that way. So he'd kissed her, but her response wasn't what he'd thought it would be.

Fear replaced rejection, uncertainty making her body rigid. The last thing he'd wanted was to scare her and he'd been about to apologize when she'd turned the tables and kissed him.

Dean was the one that was lost then. Lost in the feel of her lips, the touch of her hands and her soft moans, and all he'd wanted to do was push her back and sink into her.

Every part of his body had ached to explore the rest of her. His cock had gotten so hard so fast he was surprised he hadn't passed out from the blood loss from his head to, well, his other head.

But Dean had been content just holding her face. As badly as the rest of him wanted to release the sexual beast within that hadn't been satisfied in far too fucking long, he'd just wanted to hold her.

Until she'd gone and pressed against his chest and he'd felt her hardened nipples. At that point he'd known if he didn't stop he would have taken it too far. It didn't help knowing she'd obviously wanted it as much as he did.

His dick came to life as he thought about all the ways he wanted to explore Novalee's body. He wanted to know what the swell of her breasts felt like, how she would sound when he traced his fingers over her flesh. To see her body's reaction to him, watch as her nipples hardened and goose bumps broke over her skin. He wanted to hear her moans, to know she wanted only him as she sighed his name.

He was now painfully pressed against the fly of his jeans, begging Dean to make his fantasies reality, and he was just about to reach down and give himself a little self-love when his phone finally chirped, making his heart jump into his throat.

It fucking jumped into his throat.

He eagerly reached for the device and the three little words he read was all the encouragement he needed.

Good night, husband

Dean had tossed the ball into her court and she had tossed it back. Unintentionally he had started a game he knew no one would win, but he sure as hell was going to try.

The shrill ring of his cell woke him the next morning. He groaned and pried his eyes open, hating the caller instantly for disturbing him from the best sleep he'd had in months.

Groggily he glanced at the nightstand clock and knew from the time glaring back at him who it was without even having to check the I.D. Only one person could get away with calling him so damn early.

"Whataya want, Abby?" he grumbled, closing his eyes again.

"That sounds like the voice of a man who's hung over," she greeted him, sounding way too chipper for five thirty in the morning.

"No. It's the voice of a man who was sleeping."

She paused. "Sleeping? Like honest-to-god sleeping?"

He chuckled deeply, knowing she was shocked he hadn't needed alcoholic aid.

"Honest-to-god sleeping, Abigail. Just me, my pillow, and blanket. Best threesome I've had in a while."

"Shit." She sighed. "I thought you would be awake. I'm sorry."

"Don't worry about it." He yawned, tasting the staleness of morning breath. "What's up?"

"Honestly, nothing that couldn't have waited, but I'm in court all day and have plans tonight, so I thought I'd call now and check in."

"Plans?" His voice pitched in surprise. "What kind of plans?"

"I'm calling as your lawyer this morning, Dean," she replied.

"So?" And then it clicked in his exhausted brain. "Do you have a date?"

"As your lawyer, my personal affairs are none of your business," she snapped, sounding defensive.

"No, but as your best friend they are. Do I know the guy?"

She laughed. "Jealous?"

His lips curved against the phone. "Just looking out for you, babe."

"I can look out for myself."

"Doesn't hurt when someone else has your back, too," he said gently.

She sighed. "How are things on your end?"

"As my lawyer my personal affairs are none of your business," he teased.

"There had better not be any personal affairs; it all comes down to business."

He ignored the comment and stayed silent.

"Dean?" she pressed.

"Abigail?"

"Christ," she swore, anger clear in her tone. "Do I have to supervise you twenty-four-seven with this woman? Do not toy with her."

"I'm not toying—"

"I'm serious. Did you forget she has the power to fuck you over faster than you can blink?"

"She wouldn't do that," he said, rolling over onto his back and looking up at the ceiling.

"You don't know that! Jesus, Dean, you've fed her all this bullshit and you don't think she'll be angry when she—"

"I know she'll be angry," he said. "But she wouldn't want revenge."

Abby's silence said more than her words ever could, but she didn't have to say anything for him to know what she was thinking. She feared he'd put too much faith in a woman he didn't know. She was wrong, though. Dean may not know all the things that made Novalee who she was, but he could tell what kind of heart she had.

"I'm worried." Abby admitted.

"There's nothing to worry about. Richard won't win."

"I wasn't talking about the battle with your father. I'm worried about what will happen to you if you fall for her."

"That . . ." He swallowed, coating his dry throat. "That's not going to happen." The words sounded weak even to his ears.

"I think it's already started," Abby said, voicing what they both knew was the truth. "I think it started that first night. She's haunted you, and now you've found your ghost very much alive. No good will come of this."

"How do you know that?"

"How do you think it can?" she asked. "You can't build on something based on deception. That's what your entire relationship is right now."

"It won't be for long."

"You're serious?" Disbelief raised her voice. "You think you can work this out? Make it real?"

"I don't know." He ground his molars together, tired of being interrogated about his feelings for Novalee.

"Do you want to?" Abby asked quietly.

"I don't know," he answered. "Maybe."

"Why?"

He blinked, surprised by the question. He hadn't really thought *why* he wanted to be with Novalee, only that he did.

"Our upbringings couldn't have been more different." Dean thought out loud. "Yet our experiences in life and losing people we love are so similar it's . . ." He let the sentence trail off. "There's something there, Abby. I feel it, and I know she does, too. I thrust us into this whole mess and I know it has no chance of working. But . . . I can't help but think that if it was given a real shot, a do-over with just her and me and no lies, it could work."

"Dean . . ."

"My grandfather used to say, 'nothing happens by chance; it's not always your choice, but everything happens for a reason.' "

"I remember him saying that," she recalled fondly. "But what does that have to do with this?"

"There's a reason I met her that night."

After what seemed like hours, leaving Dean time to wonder where his balls had suddenly gone to make him think like such a pansy, Abby asked, "Are you sure you haven't been drinking?"

Dean laughed. "Yeah, I get it. I sound like an idiot."

"Maybe a little," she agreed, teasingly. "But then who am I to talk?

Apparently some women like that sweet romantic shit. As long as it gets you what you need, tell her the cheesiest pickup lines for all I care."

He rolled his eyes, deciding to drop it before he made a bigger ass out of himself.

"Andrew and I are working on everything we'll need to prep her with. Questions about you she should know. It's your job to handle the personal stuff."

"What do you mean?"

"C'mon, Dean, now is not the time to play dumb. Every couple, especially one that's married, knows the personal side to each other. They'll want to know what she likes for breakfast, favorite color, tattoos, if she has a patch of freckles on her inner thigh, childhood sicknesses. Whatever."

"They'll ask all that?" he asked, already wondering if Novalee had freckles on her inner thigh.

"Better to be prepared than to look like we're making this up as we go along," she stated.

"Okay."

"You should check in with Andrew," she instructed. "I gotta run."

"Have fun with your plans tonight." He grinned, knowing he had just received an eye roll.

"Be careful, Dean," she advised one last time before hanging up.

Be careful, indeed. *Be careful not to answer the phone so early unless you want a lecture.*

Dean tossed the cell back onto the nightstand and covered his head with the blanket, blocking out the light that would soon threaten his sleep. With thoughts of Novalee's possible patch of freckles dancing in his head, he drifted off to sleep.

A few hours later he woke feeling more rested than he had in a long time. He showered and ordered room service after making a quick call to Andrew while he waited for a lecture from him as well. Dean found Abby hadn't wasted any time filling in his other lawyer on his extra-curricular activities.

"I don't think it would be a bad thing to get close to Miss Jensen," Andrew said thoughtfully.

Dean snorted. "You and Abigail differ in your opinions."

Andrew chuckled. "I have very high regard for Ms. Knight's professional opinions; however, in this case, I believe they are clouded by personal involvement." He paused, giving Dean time to disagree. When Dean made no attempt at a challenge he continued. "It's very clear you and Abigail are close."

"We were friends long before she was my attorney," Dean confirmed.

"Yes. So, it's only natural she would be concerned for your well-being outside of the courtroom."

"What are you getting at, Andrew?" Dean asked, not in the mood for another lecture.

"As much as I care about you, Dean, I care about keeping your grandfather's will intact more," he said bluntly.

"As you should."

"So, you could understand why I think it wouldn't be a bad thing, given that you can handle the emotional fallout, to have Miss Jensen become fond of you. It would be more convincing in court if you appear to have a bond," he added.

"Andrew, I think I've done enough to Novalee. I won't add sleeping with her to the list just so we look more like a couple in court," he said firmly, offended the man would even suggest it.

"I didn't say you had to have a physical relationship, only that you are . . . friendly," he suggested.

"Friendly?" Dean smirked. "Look. I like this woman. If I become *friendly* with her it's because I want to, not because it'll look good to a judge."

"Fair enough."

"Have you heard from Tanner lately?" Dean asked, needing to take the heat off him and Novalee.

"Of course I've heard from Charles. He's trying to keep as close tabs on your progress as possible."

Dean hesitated before asking, "Abby mentioned Richard's debt." He hated to ask but he had to know.

"His debt?"

"I'm sure you've heard, Andrew. Don't treat me like a child and pretend otherwise," Dean snapped more harshly than he intended.

The man on the other end sighed heavily. "Yes, I've heard the rumors, Dean, and it wouldn't surprise me one bit if they're true."

Dean clenched his jaw to keep the anger at bay. If he lost to his father for whatever reason and the bastard went and handed everything over to a bunch of no-good goons, he would kill the SOB himself.

"Try not to think about that, Dean," Andrew advised. "It's out of your control anyway. Focus on your task at hand."

Dean ended the call shortly after, the good mood he had half an hour ago fading quickly.

Damn his useless fucking father and his gambling addictions. He couldn't remember a time his father hadn't gambled and it just got worse over the years.

Richard Philips had been the prince to WIP Hotels back when Dean was a boy. His family wanted for nothing, there was always an endless flow of whatever money could buy. Entertainment, parties, vacations, private schools; everything Dean and his sister Brynlee could dream of became a reality.

His parents had even been happy back then. He could remember the looks of affection that passed between them when they thought they weren't being watched. How his father always seemed to be touching his mother, how his mother was always smiling and laughing in his presence.

Dean wasn't sure when his father's weekly poker nights suddenly weren't enough and turned into a need for something more. It couldn't have happened overnight, but it felt like one night he and Brynlee went to bed to the sounds of their parents laughing and then woke to find Lilly with a split lip and bruised eye.

Dean was only ten at the time but could remember every detail as if it happened yesterday.

"Mommy's crying," Brynlee whispered, pulling on his arm to wake him. "Dean, Mommy's making breakfast and crying."

He rubbed the sleep out of his eyes and blinked at his sister. "Why?"

"Dunno." She shrugged her skinny five-year-old shoulders. "She hurt her face, like you did to your knee. Remember? When you fell off your bike?"

Dean jumped out of bed and raced downstairs, leaving his sister yelling after him to wait up. He burst into the kitchen just in time to see his mom wipe the tears from her face.

"Mama?" He took a small step closer to her. "Mama, what's wrong?"

"Nothing, sweetheart." She sniffed, keeping her back to him.

"Why are you crying?"

"I was cutting onions. They make me cry," she said.

Dean moved closer to his mother and took her hand, pulling at her until she looked at him. What he saw shattered his ten-year-old heart. He didn't know what happened, he didn't know who or what had hurt his mother or why, but he was in pain because she was. He wrapped his tiny arms around her waist and buried his face in her stomach.

"It's okay, Mama. Dad will make it better when he gets home."

The innocent boy didn't understand why his words of comfort made his mother wrap her arms around him tighter than ever before as fresh tears rolled down her bruised cheeks.

It was after that day Dean had started noticing changes. His father no longer looked or touched his mother affectionately. His mother no longer laughed or smiled when his father was around. She avoided looking at him as much as possible, keeping her eyes down to try and hide from her children the fear she felt.

Other changes had started taking place shortly after that as well. Material possessions disappeared and family vacations were things of the past. Dean discovered, years later, that his grandfather had put his father on an allowance so he wouldn't gamble away everything he had. Richard turned to loan sharks and later got tangled up with the mob. As his gambling debts got worse so did things at home.

After Dean found his mother crying in the kitchen there wasn't a day that he didn't wake to find Lilly with a new bruise or broken bone. The lullaby that had been her laugh to put them to sleep was replaced by screams of anger and pain, followed by her crying for hours after Richard stormed out, fleeing the destruction he'd caused. The times Dean had tried to intervene and save his mother from the beatings she received had enraged Richard all the more, and it never ended well for him or Lilly.

Why no one ever questioned the countless visits to the ER was beyond Dean. Someone should have said something; someone should have stepped in and stopped it. But no one did. William must have been aware of what was going on, but if he offered help, Lilly never took it. The only one that was spared Richard's abusive hand was Brynlee. For whatever reason Richard had never raised a hand to his daughter, the only thing Dean was thankful for when it came to the asshole.

If Lilly had just left, if she had taken Brynlee and run, maybe their lives would have been spared. Dean would never understand why she hadn't. By staying, Lilly had sentenced to death not only herself but her child as well.

Dean shook his head his head, snapping himself out of the past before visions of blood-splattered walls could come rushing back.

He poked at his breakfast, any appetite he'd had before the call to Andrew all but gone. Finally giving up on food, he cleared away the dishes and pulled his laptop out. A quick check told him he was behind on more e-mails than he cared to deal with. The same could be said for all the voice mails that had built up. But deal with them he must. Despite how the court may decide, right now Dean was CEO of WIP Hotels and that meant taking the time to sit down and return them all.

For the next four hours Dean responded to mail, called mangers back at six of the eleven hotels, checked-in with the others, and even called a few disgruntled guests to try and apologize for this reason or that. Normally he would set up dates with each hotel to fly out in person and see how everything was, but that would have to wait.

There was also a bid on a new site in Canada he had to pull out of because of all the bullshit with court dates. He wouldn't be surprised if William was rolling over in his grave at the loss of revenue that build would have earned.

Finally at two thirty, Dean shoved everything away and stretched as his stomach grumbled, reminding him he had barely eaten anything all day. Ignoring his complaining gut, he reached for his cell and scrolled through his contacts until he found the name that put a smile on his face for the first time since that morning. He hit send, figuring it was a good time to call since it was still early.

But her frazzled tone when she answered told him otherwise.

"Bad time?" he asked.

"Yes," she groaned. "I'm sorry. It's just been that kind of day already."

"Anything I can do to help?"

She laughed dryly. "I don't think there's anything even *I* can do right now." She sighed. "One of my girls left because of morning sickness and I can't find a fill-in for her today because my other two guys aren't available.

I can work the floor with Cali and Pam so that wouldn't be problem *if* my cook hadn't walked out and quit this afternoon. There's no way I can go through my applicants and find a replacement for him on such short notice. And," she added, sounding exhausted, "the only time a damn plumber can fix my sink is later today and I can't be at home and here at the same time."

"I'll be there in ten minutes," he declared, grabbing his keys to the rental and walking out the door.

"What?" She sounded distracted and he could picture her sitting behind her desk in her office, rubbing her forehead in frustration.

"I'll be there in ten minutes," he repeated.

"Why?"

"Because you need help," he said as he got into the elevator.

"Dean . . . you don't have to. What can you possibly do anyway?"

"Ouch. I think I should be insulted," he teased, stepping out of the elevator and hurrying across the lobby.

She laughed. "I didn't mean it like that."

He yanked open the door to his truck and climbed in.

"Ten minutes," he said again.

"By now it should be only eight," she kidded.

"Hush, woman, and let me get off the phone so I can drive." She laughed again and they said their goodbyes as he was pulling out of the hotel parking lot.

A few minutes later he arrived at the still-quiet establishment. He parked at the back and yanked on the handle to the side door, but it wouldn't budge. As grateful as he was Novalee was cautious enough to have proper security, it was a pain in the ass to walk all the way around to the front.

Cali looked up from behind the counter as he entered, cocking an eyebrow at him as he sauntered toward her.

"Becoming a regular?" she asked, screwing a cap on a salt shaker.

"Thinking of becoming an employee for the night." He grinned at her, but she didn't look as impressed with his dimples as most women.

Well, damn. He knew women trusted their best friends' instincts when it came to men. If he couldn't win over Cali, all hope may be lost.

She set the shaker down and narrowed her eyes. "I don't know what game you're playing with my girl, but she's been through enough shit. More than anyone deserves."

He nodded. "I get that."

"Good. So you understand that if you break her heart I'll not only break your arms and legs, but also whatever you're working with down there," she promised, lowering her eyes below his waist.

The member in question and his boys shriveled up upon hearing the threat.

"Got it."

She finally smiled a real smile and extended her hand. "Cali

Donavon," she said formally introducing herself.

He took her hand. "Dean Philips."

She rolled her eyes. "I know. The estranged husband."

"That would be me."

"Cali, if you're putting your nose in places it doesn't belong you're going to be the next to go," Novalee threatened, coming up behind her. "It's your fault Tony stormed out."

The blonde rolled her eyes again. "It's not my fault Pony Boy couldn't handle rejection."

"Maybe if you had kept your pants zipped in the work place none of this would have happened."

"Oh sure blame me," Cali huffed, picking up the tray of salt and pepper shakers and turning to Novalee. "And if I recall I was wearing a skirt that night." She winked and stalked off.

Novalee shook her head, laid tired eyes on Dean, and smiled. "Hey."

"Hey." He smiled back and barely stopped himself from reaching out and pulling her into his arms. Even dressed in an oversized sweatshirt and old jeans with her hair pulled back in a ponytail and no makeup, she was beautiful.

She saw him looking her over and blushed, running her hand over the top of her head self-consciously.

"Why is it every time you come see me I'm a mess?" she asked.

"I think you're stunning," he said. Her blush deepened and she looked away. Dean cleared his throat and glanced around the place. "So, what can I do to help?"

She sighed heavily and looked at him again. "You don't have to do anything."

"Novalee, please." He locked eyes with her until she finally nodded. "It's still fairly quiet in here. What time do you get busy?"

"Around four it picks up, but our busiest is five."

"Okay. I'll let you know up front I'm not good on that side of the bar." He pointed to where she stood behind the counter. "But you need a cook, right?"

Her eyebrows rose. "Do you know your way around this kind of kitchen?"

No fucking clue.

"How hard can it be? Fries and burgers? I think I can manage." He grinned, knowing he was giving himself way too much credit. But she needed the help and he'd be damned if he just stood back and did nothing.

She held back a smile and crooked her finger at him. "Come with me."

He couldn't stop the image of her naked and beneath him, clinging to his body and telling him those exact words in a totally different way. He followed her, shoving his hands in his pockets in an attempt to hide his overly eager dick that sprang to life at the tiniest thought lately. However, if the snicker from Cali was any indication, he wasn't fooling anyone.

Novalee led him into the kitchen and he instantly knew how much trouble he was in. Even though she tried to assure him he wouldn't have to make anything fancy, he was in way over his head.

After a quick run-down of where he could find everything, and a demonstration on how to turn on the grill and fryer—which she couldn't help but giggle at him for not knowing—she turned to him with doubt in her eyes.

"You don't have to do this," she said for the hundredth time.

He took a step toward her and she took a small step back, bumping into the island behind her.

"Are you more concerned that I'm doing something I don't really want to do, or that I'm going to burn the place down?" he asking teasingly, grasping her fingers. He didn't miss her sharp intake of breath.

"Um . . ." She looked down at their joined fingers and swallowed. "I'd really hate for the burning the place down thing to happen. I don't think I could handle another disaster today."

He chuckled and slid his hands up her covered arms until they rested on her shoulders.

"If that happens I'll build you a new one for my stupidity."

She snorted and rolled her eyes. "Does that line work on all the ladies?"

He grinned. "I don't know. I've never used it before." He moved his hands down her sides and rested them on her hips.

"Well," she said thickly, then cleared her throat and tried again. "I think it's pretty corny."

He nodded, agreeing wordlessly as he tugged her hips so she had to move closer to him and she placed her hands on his chest to steady herself. Her blue eyes bore into his and she bit her lip as she snaked her arms around his neck and pressed her body against him.

Dean lost what little control he had as he dropped his hands to her ass at the same time he kissed her.

His grip on her bottom tightened and she wiggled against him, rubbing her front *right there*, where his cock pulsed thick and hard for her.

Novalee took his bottom lip between her teeth and gently pulled it away. The noise that rose up from his chest was indefinable, and he cupped her ass and hoisted her up onto the island's countertop, pressing his arousal into her.

Her gasp went straight to his dick. He forgot they were in the middle of the kitchen in a very public place, forgot that anyone could walk in at any second, or even see them through the open partition that looked out on the lounge. All he knew was he needed this woman right here, right now, more than he needed his next breath.

She grasped his hair as he moved his mouth from her mouth to her ear, arching her neck. He licked at her lobe and she hissed, but when he sucked it into his mouth her body jerked, the grip she had on his hair tightening.

The sharp sting he felt from her tugging on his hair sent his blood boiling. He pulled her closer to him, grinding himself into her harder as he dipped the tip of his tongue into her ear.

The sounds she made filled the room, and Dean was sure it was both the sweetest and sexiest sound he had ever heard. He was just about to slip his hands under her sweatshirt when the kitchen door swung open.

"Oh my god! Shit. I'm sorry! I didn't know—"

Dean tore his mouth away from her and looked up at the stammering woman.

"Hey, you're not supposed to be back here," she said, finally finding her voice.

Novalee buried her face in his neck and her body shook with laughter. He couldn't help but laugh as well.

"I don't think the boss will have a problem with it," he answered.

The woman's eyes widened and she finally recognized the back of Novalee's head.

"Oh. Wow."

He said, "This is where you leave . . ."

"Pam," Novalee whispered against his skin, almost sending his body into convulsions.

"Pam," he managed to say.

She nodded and backed out of the kitchen without further comment.

Novalee sighed and pulled away from him once they were alone again. She kept her gaze down, avoiding his eyes.

"I, um, have to go meet the plumber," she mumbled, yet made no attempt to leave as she played with the hem of his shirt.

Dean knew he had to keep the mood light if he didn't want her to over think what just happened and get freaked out by it. It was clear she wanted him just as much as he did her, but their situation was a tricky one. Just because her body wanted him didn't mean her head was totally in the game.

"Yeah. Get out of my kitchen and let me work, woman," he instructed, brushing the loose strands of hair off her face.

She smiled and finally looked up at him. "Try not to burn the place down."

"I'll do my best."

She hopped off the island and was about to leave when she turned back to him. Then she stood on her toes and softly kissed him

"Thank you," she whispered before fleeing the kitchen out the back door.

Dean stood staring well after she was gone until someone coughed, bringing him back to the present. He turned to see Cali with her arms folded.

"Why do I have a feeling that's the only thing you know how to do back here, Casanova?" she asked with a wink. "Better pull it together, buddy. You've got orders coming."

As Dean struggled to remember everything Novalee had told him, one thing was definitely clear: Abby was right.

When it came to Novalee Jensen he was in over his head and falling hard. So fucking hard he wasn't sure he'd be able to recover when she walked away with pieces of his tortured soul.

Chapter 9

Novalee impatiently drummed her fingers on the countertop as she waited.

The plumber had promised it wouldn't take long, and yet, forty-five minutes later, she was still staring at his ass crack.

Was it so difficult for some men to wear a belt, or buy pants that actually freakin' fit?

Novalee scowled and averted her eyes from the offensive sight. She wanted him to hurry up and finish so she could get back to work. It wasn't that she didn't trust her employees, or Dean for that matter, but she worried he had overestimated himself when it came to his culinary skills.

What did a CEO of a multi-million dollar franchise know about slumming it in a bar's kitchen? He'd probably never had to work a day in his life at a minimum wage job. She could tell from the second he'd walked into the kitchen he was out of his comfort zone, but he had stepped up and offered his help anyway.

Her heart felt all kinds of mushy things. Novalee hadn't expected him to come rushing down, but when he did and offered his help any way she needed it, she had suddenly felt taken care of. Like there was someone other than Cali who wanted to make sure she was okay. Novalee hadn't had someone take care of her since her parents had died.

Cali's folks had taken her in and she knew they loved her, but Novalee sometimes felt like it was out of obligation because they were practically family.

Dean had nothing to gain by being there for her, but he hadn't hesitated to do it.

Novalee felt a pull in her chest thinking about what that might mean. Why did he want to help her? Why did he care enough to get her out of a tight spot? Did he feel like he had no other choice when she complained to him on the phone about her crappy day? Did he worry if he didn't at least offer she would think he was an ass?

Speaking of ass . . .

Peeking over, she saw the one in question still puttering around her sink.

She sighed and looked away again. She didn't like to think that Dean was helping her because he felt like it was just the thing to do and was grateful to him, but she wanted his help because he *wanted* to do it, not out of pity or obligation.

"If that happens I'll build you a new one for my stupidity."

A silly grin spread across her face. Corny as hell yes, but also kind of cute.

A shiver ran down her spine as she thought about their island countertop escapade. Practically dry humping a man in the middle of her business wasn't in Novalee's character. She didn't do PDA, or in this case PDSA—Public Displays of Sexual Aggression. Going this long without any sex apparently changed a person's character. She would have let him strip her down and have his wicked way with her right there if Pam hadn't interrupted them.

Could a person be fired for cock blocking?

Pam should consider herself lucky Novalee needed all the help she could get right now.

"Okay, that should do it," Ass Crack declared, standing and finally adjusting his pants.

Novalee smiled politely. "Great!"

He took his time putting away his tools, ignoring Novalee's hints at hurrying him along by checking her watch. She wondered if he would be offended if she finished packing for him.

Finally, he wrote out the bill and she all but snatched it from his hand.

"If you have any problems don't hesitate to call me," he said when he got to the door, handing her a business card.

"Will do." If packing his tools for him was offensive, what was pushing him out the door?

"You don't need the excuse of a leaky sink if you just want to call either." He grinned at her, showing off some questionable dental hygiene.

Novalee's stomach rolled and she was thankful she hadn't eaten much all day.

"I don't think my husband would appreciate that," she said without thinking.

She wanted to slap herself as soon as the words were out of her mouth. It was the first time she had ever acknowledged her marriage and the only reason she did was to discourage unwanted attention from Ass Crack. She had no idea if he was even a customer or how fast her well-kept secret would get around now.

Fucking idiot.

His grin turned into a smirk. "What he doesn't know can't hurt him."

Novalee glared at the sleazy douche bag and opened the door. Suddenly, she didn't care if she offended him or not.

"What he does know could hurt *you*, though," she answered coolly.

He lost some of his cockiness as he glanced down at the business card he'd just given her, uncertainty in his eyes.

"Thanks for your help, but I don't think I'll need your services again." She held out the card to him, which he grabbed and then stomped out the door.

Novalee slammed it closed after him and turned to face Jerry who had wandered in from her bedroom.

"I think you and Ben are the only decent males around," she said.

Jerry looked over to where Ben was perched on the couch cushion licking himself and then back at her, his head tilted to the side as he gave a soft whine.

Novalee laughed. "Don't judge. You do the same thing," she reminded him, grabbing her purse from the entry table. She patted his head once before hurrying out the door and to her car.

Visions of the disaster she might find in her usually well-organized bar flashed in her mind. A glance at the dashboard clock told her they were into happy hour. She just hoped Dean could keep up.

She sang along to the radio, pausing occasionally to mutter the odd curse word under her breath as traffic crept along. Just her luck she was stuck behind an elderly woman who could barely see over the steering wheel. Novalee giggled, suddenly remembering an episode of an old comedy where the old woman had to use a phonebook to drive. The show had been her mother's favorite and she recalled sick days curled up on the couch watching old reruns with her, sipping tea and nibbling toast or crackers to settle her upset stomach.

She sighed wistfully, missing her mother's contagious laugh. The twelve years they had been gone hadn't done a thing to heal the hole Novalee feared would always be in her heart.

She wondered if Dean still felt the same way about his mother and sister. Granted, she didn't know how long ago he had lost them, but did a pain caused by the death of a loved one ever really pass? She had wanted to ask about them last night, her curiosity more than piqued when it came to his life, but his demeanor when he had told her not to push the subject.

Whatever happened to his mother and sister obviously still haunted him. The anger and pain that had flashed across his face in the few seconds he'd let his guard down made Novalee think the story behind their deaths was a tragic one.

And why did he hate his father so much? Sure the guy sounded like a first-class ass on paper, but what had led to the animosity Dean felt for him? Had it always been like that between them? Had his father abandoned him and his family and Dean couldn't forgive and forget? Had he cheated on his wife? Not shown up at Dean's Little League games because he was too busy with work and Dean still resented it?

And why had Dean gained control of his grandfather's estate instead of his father? Why were they fighting for control now?

Novalee had had to bite her tongue to keep the questions from bursting out last night. She had no clue if she even had the right to ask. If he'd been a real husband, she would already know, but their marriage wasn't normal.

They weren't going to be husband and wife for much longer: soon he would be gone from her life.

Was there a point in getting to know someone who possibly wouldn't be around next week? Novalee's stomach twisted and she tightened her grip on the steering wheel.

It was stupid to get emotional over him leaving. Hell, she didn't even know the guy! But nonetheless the unexpected pang of sadness she felt when she thought of him leaving hit her like a ton of bricks.

What the hell did she expect? That he would suddenly want to stay married to her and work on their relationship? She snorted and shook her head at how stupid it made her sound.

A better question was why would she even entertain such an idea herself?

It had to be because of this afternoon. Suddenly Dean had been there playing her savior and it made her all soft and mushy and think ridiculous things.

Yes, that had to be it.

There was no way she could actually want him, other than in a purely animalistic sexual way of course, after only just meeting him

Cali was right: she needed to get laid. She needed to see this for what it really was: nothing more than lust so she could get her head back on straight, fix their mistake, and move on.

"Novalee Jensen is not the type of woman to get emotionally attached to a man she doesn't know," she reminded herself. "Novalee Jensen is realistic, and smart, and above all is not into that love-at-first-sight-fairy-tale crap. She knows the difference between lust and love and knows all this is just sexual attraction."

Good Lord, now she was talking about herself in the third person.

She finally made it to work thirty minutes later, still grumbling to herself about what an idiot she was being.

Breathing a sigh of relief that the building was still in one piece, she hurried across the parking lot and unlocked the back door, saying a quick prayer that she wouldn't find too much chaos.

"There's supposed to be a TGIF with these fries," she heard Cali whine when she walked in.

Novalee stopped in her tracks, her eyes widening at the sight in front of her.

To say the kitchen—the always clean, organized kitchen—was a mess would be an understatement. Bags of fries and onion rings laid ripped open on the counter, bits of lettuce and onions were scattered all over the floor, condiments cluttered the island, some knocked over with their contents spilled. The smell of burnt toast filled the air and Novalee spied two of the blackest pieces of bread she had ever seen peeking out from the toaster.

"Then tell him to have a good Friday even though it's Monday!" Dean hollered back.

"It's a burger, Philips." Cali laughed. "Check the menu and make it right."

"Speaking of burgers," Pam piped up, "booth five complained theirs was undercooked."

"The order said medium rare," Dean grumbled.

"Yes, but I think you forgot the medium part."

Novalee had to stifle a laugh as Dean slapped the knife down harder than necessary to chop onions. The white apron he wore was covered in grease splatter, mustard, and what she hoped was ketchup. His face was almost red and she was positive there was piece of green pepper stuck in his hair.

"Can't you see I'm busy back here?" Dean said. "Stop nagging."

"Better not distract him, Pam. He has a knife and is trying to cut vegetables. We don't need to add finger sandwiches to the special tonight," Cali teased.

"I'm beginning to understand why the other cook walked out if he had to put up with this harassment," Dean replied with a grin.

"Honey, we didn't have to ride Tony's ass. His jackrabbit speed came in handy keeping up with orders."

Novalee failed to contain her laughter this time. Dean looked up from his destructive chopping and his grin widened.

"Hello there, boss," he greeted. "How did it go at the house?"

She walked farther into the kitchen until she was standing in front of him and glanced around the room again.

"Better than it looks like it went in here." She reached up and plucked what was indeed a pepper out of his hair, held it up, and chuckled. "Did I miss a food fight?"

His smile turned sheepish. "Guess it's obvious who won, huh?"

She laughed and tossed the pepper in the trash.

"Doesn't look like you went down easy, though," she joked.

"Oh, you'd be surprised how easy I can go down," he said under his breath, leaning toward her.

The whispered words made Novalee shiver, and she unconsciously moved closer to him until their bodies almost touched.

"I don't think I would be," she whispered back, lifting her chin so her lips were an easy target. "You seem like the type of man who enjoys being thorough in whatever he does."

Dean dipped his head, and her body tingled with anticipation for the kiss she was sure was about to happen.

But he merely brushed his lips against hers and said, "I promise I won't be the only one enjoying how thorough I'll be."

Heat shot between Novalee's thighs and her legs felt like they were going to collapse from under her. She gripped the countertop to stop the wobbly feeling. Her face felt flushed and her heart was pounding so hard it would be a miracle if Dean didn't hear it.

If Novalee didn't know any better she'd swear she just came from his words alone. But that wasn't possible . . . was it? No. A woman knew when she had an orgasm, so if she had to question it than it obviously wasn't the real thing.

But it was damn close. He had her so fucking near to the edge and he hadn't even laid a finger on her. All it took was his voice in those incredibly sexy hushed tones breathing against her skin and she was almost ready to start screaming his name.

Her body wanted him in every way imaginable. Her breasts felt heavy and full, her nipples straining against the confinement of her bra cups, undoubtedly flashing Dean her excitement.

Her stomach flipped with both anxiety and delight. She was nervous about the reaction he caused her to feel toward him, and worried her lack of sexual experiences in the past few years would make her awkward. But at the same time she couldn't ignore how her body came alive around him. She wanted Dean to take her to the edge again and again, only to let her crash down when she couldn't possibly take any more.

It was unbelievable the heat generated from being this close to him. If Dean were to slip his hand between her legs he would find out how much she needed him. If he dipped just the tip of his finger inside her, she was certain her body would convulse and grip his digit as she came.

Sexual frustration didn't even begin to describe what she felt right now. No man had ever had this kind of effect on her.

Cali burst into the kitchen at that moment, pausing on her way to the storage room and rolled her eyes.

"Cut it out, you two. That's not going to get customers fed or pay bills." She grinned wickedly. "Okay, it might pay the bills, but you'd have to switch professions, Novalee."

Novalee glared at her friend who winked and continued on her merry way. Dean chuckled beside her.

"I like her," he declared.

"She's a brat," Novalee grumbled. Taking a deep breath, she looked up at Dean and smiled. "But, as much as I hate to admit it, she's right."

"About switching careers?" He wiggled his eyebrows mischievously. "It's legal in Nevada, you know. You just need to open a brothel."

Novalee rolled her eyes.

"Is that why you enjoy living there?"

He laughed. "Nah. The idea of sticking my dick where hundreds of others have been before doesn't quite do it for me."

"Hmm. So what does do it for you?" she couldn't help but ask.

He grinned. "Hot little blondes who get me drunk and marry me in Vegas."

Novalee laughed and shook her head. "Get *you* drunk, huh? You poor victim."

Dean's smile faltered, the spark that had been in his eyes just seconds before completely diminished. But before Novalee could question it, he blinked and it was gone.

"I think I'm too willing to be a victim," he said, turning back to the forgotten onion.

"Dean—"

"Hey, Nov, are you planning on helping tonight, or staying in here to ogle your hot piece-of-ass husband all night?"

Novalee ground her molars together and turned to face Cali. The woman had the worst timing ever for her meaningless interruptions.

"Do you need help?" she asked, instead of snapping at her like she wanted.

Cali snorted. "What do you think? It's just the two of us and we can't split the sections and handle the bar. Even I'm not that good."

Damn it. She had forgotten they were also shorthanded out front.

"I'll take over your section, you tend bar."

Cali nodded and Novalee waited for her to leave before turning back to Dean who wore a shit-eating grin.

"Hot piece-of-ass husband?" He nodded. "I really like her."

Novalee rolled her eyes again. "Are you okay back here?"

"C'mon, doesn't it look like I'm getting the hang of this? Don't answer that," he said when she opened her mouth. "I'm fine."

She bit her lip and nodded hesitantly. "Okay. I'll be right out front in case you need anything."

"I could really be insulted by your lack of confidence in me, you know. If I end up with a complex it's your entire fault."

"I didn't mean it like that," she insisted, feeling like an ass.

He smiled. "I'm kidding. I've lasted this long, I'll be fine."

At the door she turned and called to him, "Hey, Mr. Big Shot CEO." He looked up at her curiously. "You might want to flip that burger so it can be just as burned on the other side." She laughed and ducked out the door just escaping the handful of onions he threw at her.

"All in all it wasn't a bad night," Cali declared, wiping down the bar.

Novalee heard a snort from the kitchen where Dean was cleaning up his disaster and smiled.

She, Cali, and Pam had managed the front easily enough, and had even managed to smooth over customers' complaints about the food with a promise of a free round for their table.

Dean had failed miserably. The only thing Novalee would have felt safe eating were the fries he made. But he stuck it out without so much as a complaint, and to her that was worth every single dry or uncooked burger they had to send back or refund.

Her pocket hadn't taken such a hit since the early days, but she was still smiling. She would accept the less-than-average earnings for that night with genuine happiness because Dean had done this for her.

And that meant much more than what her bank receipt would read in the morning.

"Yeah, it wasn't bad," Pam agreed, wringing out the mop. "But that's enough experimenting with spoiled trust fund babies. We need Tony back."

"Excuse me?" Dean poked his head out of the open partition. "I'm not a *spoiled* trust fund baby." He looked at Novalee. "But you really do need a real cook if you don't want to scare away all your patrons."

"You mean the ones that survive the food poisoning?" Cali asked, flipping Dean off in return for his rude gesture.

If it wasn't for the smiles both wore, Novalee would have feared bloodshed in her newly cleaned kitchen.

"I'll start the search for a replacement tomorrow." Novalee sighed.

"By tomorrow I hope you mean today." Cali pointed at the clock that reminded her of the early morning hour.

Novalee scowled. "It's not tomorrow until I sleep."

"And on that note I'm clocking out." Pam yawned. "Night all! Nice to meet you, Dean."

"Oh, I'm sure you'll be seeing a lot more of him around," Cali sang.

Pam giggled and turned around to face them once she was at the door. "As long as he's not cooking. Good night, Mr. and Mrs. Philips."

Novalee rolled her eyes, but Dean laughed and raised his hand in acknowledgement.

Now Pam was in on it. Novalee trusted her not to say anything, but if Dean kept hanging around, people were going to start to question who he was. She wasn't ashamed of him, but she also didn't want to air her dirty laundry out for everyone. If she chose to tell people exactly who he was, she wanted it to be on her own terms, not just because people were nosey and wanted to gossip.

Speaking of people who would want an explanation . . .

"Cali?"

"Hmm?"

"Did you say anything to your parents about this?"

"About our rather interesting night?" She tilted her head to the side and looked at Novalee.

"No, thick head. About *this*." Novalee pointed to the kitchen.

"Oh! About you getting hitched!" Cali laughed. "Should I tell them they have a new son-in-law?"

"No!"

"Okay." She shrugged. "You can tell them."

"No one is telling them."

Cali pressed her lips together, a sign she wanted to say something but was trying to hold her tongue for the greater good, and threw the towel she had been using under the counter in the small laundry tub that was kept there.

"I'm going home," she announced.

"Cali—"

"You do what you want, Novalee." She cast a glace towards the back to see where Dean was and took a step closer to her boss, lowering her voice. "But maybe if you acknowledged what this is, and got out of your own way, you might find yourself being happy."

"Cali—"

"He's a good guy, Nov, and sure there's shit you don't know, but it works both ways."

Novalee sighed. "It's not real."

Cali shook her head. "And it never will be unless *you* get real."

Novalee watched her leave, the click of the back door locking back in place echoing through the silent building. She and Dean were totally alone.

Suddenly nervous, she busied herself with dumping the soiled towels into a plastic bag to take home and wash, double-checked the front cooler and liquor shelves to make sure they were full, and then hid out in the stockroom for a good ten minutes pretending to go over inventory.

She was definitely being a coward. What Cali had said spooked her. What if she did get real and opened up to Dean and he gave her nothing in return? What if she laid her horrible past out on the table and he pushed it aside and played it off because he didn't know how to relate or deal with the baggage she came with?

Or what if the opposite happened? What if she did all that and he poured his life story out to her as well and they bonded? What if she fell more than she feared she already had and he walked away in the end anyway?

Emotional rejection stung less than a broken heart in her opinion.

But Novalee knew herself too well. If she didn't do anything, if she hid out like a coward, she would always wonder what might have happened if she'd had the guts to take what she wanted.

But was the cost of knowing the answer worth the pain that would surely follow?

Novalee frowned, annoyed by the little voice.

Maybe she was getting ahead of herself. Sure, by opening up to him there was a chance she could end up hurt, but there was also a chance she could find out they made better friends than lovers. That was a possibility, right? Just because things might be hot between the sheets didn't mean everything else would magically fall into place. Great sex did not have to mean emotional attachment.

No, if she was entertaining the idea of sharing something as personal as her past than it was obvious she had developed more than just casual feelings for this man. She didn't trust anyone with the truth about Dalton. No one besides Cali and her parents knew what had happened to her. If she told Dean, that meant something to her. It wasn't just idle chitchat.

"I had a boyfriend who liked to use his fists to show his love. In fact, he almost killed me. What about you?"

Novalee groaned and exited the stockroom. Maybe it was best to keep both her mind and her body out of it.

But when she entered the lounge she knew she was totally screwed.

Dean was hunched over the jukebox, his hands pressed against the glass as he read the selections. Novalee raked her eyes over his body, perhaps staring at his ass longer than necessary. She licked her lips as her imagination went into overdrive and started undressing him. If his ass was even half as delicious as it was in her mind, she'd be one very happy little barmaid.

So much for keeping her body out of it. Hell, even her mind was involved with X-rated thoughts.

He turned around just as the jukebox came to life, filling the room with one of Novalee's favorite songs. The melody was soft and slow, with lyrics that spoke of adoration and promises to always be there for one another. Words that made you want to take things slow and explore each other in more than just a sexual way for as long as possible.

It was a song meant for lovers.

"Will you dance with me, Novalee?" Dean asked, holding out his hand to her.

She bit her lip, looking at his outstretched hand and up to his face. He looked so uncertain, like he was afraid she would reject him. Or maybe like a man who was fighting with inner turmoil, as if he wasn't sure he should be asking his simple question.

Novalee hesitated for her own reasons. Dancing used to be fun for her. At one time it had been one of her favorite pastimes. She and Cali used to have a blast taking classes and then sneaking into clubs to try out their new moves.

She had even persuaded Dalton to join them one night, thinking it would be something fun they could do together. Instead, that night brought the monster out she never would have guessed lived within him.

She never danced again after that night; the price just wasn't worth it. And even now, years later, she still hadn't been able to bring herself to pick it up again. The enjoyment of it had been beaten out of her and the act held no appeal.

Until now.

Until Dean Philips held out his hand to her, looking all shy and insecure, and she wanted nothing more than to take it and let him lead her around the room.

So she did.

Swallowing her fears of the past, she placed her palm on top of his and gently grasped his hand.

Dean smiled down at her, but neither said a word as he pulled her closer and wrapped her in his embrace. His large hand rested on the small of her back, as he keeping her close to him as he danced them around in slow circles.

Unexpected tears stung Novalee's eyes as she lost herself in the feeling of his arms and let the music wash over her. She ducked her head, laying it against his chest so he wouldn't see her sudden emotional meltdown.

She tried to focus on the beating of his heart and the spicy smell of him rather than how good it felt to be doing something as simple as dancing. But her emotions betrayed her and she sniffled, drawing his attention to her.

"Hey." He took a small step back and lifted her chin. Worry clouded his eyes. "Are you okay? Did I do something?"

"No." She shook her head and tried to tighten her hold on his waist so he wouldn't pull away. "You didn't do anything wrong."

"Well, it has to be something if you're crying," he said gently.

"It's nothing. Really, it's just silly." He stared at her, waiting for a real answer and she sighed. "I haven't danced in a very long time and it feels . . . nice. More than nice."

"Oh." He frowned. "Why haven't you?"

Novalee looked down. "I . . . had a bad experience a few years ago."

"A bad experience?"

She nodded, not wanting to explain further and hoping he wouldn't ask.

"Novalee?"

She bit her lip, trying to keep the tears away, but the way he said her name made her want to curl up and cry.

"Novalee?" Dean brushed the stray hair off her face and titled her head up again. Hesitantly she met his eyes. "I wish I could take every bad experience you've had and replace them with moments like this."

Any chance she might have had to keep her heart out of their budding friendship vanished with those words.

"I wish you could too," she whispered. "I wish it were that simple to erase everything and make me forget." She paused. "But even though you can't, maybe you can help me make new ones."

That same look of uncertainty appeared on his face again, and she worried her boldness might have been too much.

She played the words over in her head and frowned. Maybe he took it to mean she thought he was going to be sticking around for a while. She didn't mean it like that, and hated that it made her sound needy and presumptuous.

The song ended and the room was eerily quiet. Dean didn't make any attempt to comment further, and Novalee suddenly felt very foolish. She pulled out of his arms and brushed her hair behind her ear, darting her eyes around.

"I should get home," she said.

She hurried to the bar and grabbed the plastic bag full of towels and her purse. She heard Dean behind her and fiddled with the contents inside so she wouldn't have to face him.

"I'm sorry," he said, standing in front of her now.

Novalee shook her head, not really caring if he meant he was sorry about the late hour, or leaving her choking on her own words. All she wanted was to take her bruised ego home.

"Thank you for helping me tonight," she said, still not meeting his eyes. "I really do appreciate it, and I'm more than willing to pay you for your time."

"Don't insult me, please," he answered gruffly. "I did it because I wanted to, not because I expect payment."

Well, hell, she just kept making a mess of this.

"I didn't mean to offend you," she said. "I'm sorry."

How had this night gone so wrong so fast?

"If anything I should be the one offering you payment," he suddenly said.

Novalee finally snapped her head up to look at him.

"Why do you say that?"

"I figure I cost you more than I would have made." He smiled and Novalee was grateful for his attempt at lightening the mood.

"Nonetheless, I still appreciate it." She gave him a tight smile and tried to sneak passed him to the door, but he grabbed her wrist and stopped her in her tracks.

"What just happened?" he asked. "One minute we're dancing, and I know you feel whatever the hell it is going on between us, and now you can't get away from me fast enough."

She tugged her wrist free of his grasp.

"You tell me. You threw that line at me about replacing all my bad memories and then froze up."

"I meant that! It wasn't just some line."

"Then why did you hesitate when I practically threw myself at you?"

He sighed in frustration and shook his head, glancing away for a split second before looking at her again.

"Everything is so complicated, Novalee. You have no idea how badly I want you, but I feel like acting on it would be taking advantage of you."

Novalee laughed bitterly. "That didn't seem to stop you this afternoon.

Or is being with me only a turn-on when there's a chance we'll get caught?"

"What?" He looked like he was about to laugh, but her glare stopped him. "Don't be ridiculous."

She stared at him for a moment and then turned and hurried out of the building to the parking lot. She hit the automatic locks and her beams flashed as the doors clicked open.

"Novalee!" Dean called behind her.

She opened the car door and turned to face him just as he caught up to her.

"You're right, Dean. I do feel whatever the hell it is that's going on between us. Maybe it's just sexual attraction and once the itch has been scratched we'll both be left satisfied and able to move on with our lives with our marriage a distant memory.

"I'm not asking you to fulfill your end of the to-death-do-us-part deal. I'm perfectly clear on what this is. You don't have to treat me like some naïve schoolgirl you promised the world to in order to get into her pants; I'm not that easy to take advantage of. Not anymore."

Not waiting for his reply, Novalee got into her car and slammed the door on his stunned face. She sped out of the parking lot and took off down the street as she blinked away angry tears.

Who the hell did he think he was, thinking he knew what was best for her?

She screeched to a stop in her driveway, glaring at the garage door as it slowly opened. She parked inside the closure and got out, slamming the door harder than necessary.

Inside she tripped over Ben, who screamed his little cat cry and fled under the couch, causing Jerry to bark and run amok, almost tripping her again on her way to the bedroom.

"Goddamn males!" she screamed at them and slammed the bedroom door. Two seconds later she poked her head back out and muttered an apology to her boys.

She changed into her usual shorts and a tank, let Jerry out to do his business, crouched down to make sure Ben was okay, let Jerry back in, and then crawled into her big lonely bed.

Cautiously, the animals entered the room and only jumped up on the bed when she patted the mattress, granting them permission to join her.

She ran her fingers through Ben's fur, finding it almost therapeutic, and listened to his content purring to calm down. She was just starting to feel better when her doorbell rang.

Jerry growled, not use to hearing the sound at such a late hour, and jumped from the bed.

Novalee slowly slid out of bed and crept out to the living room, pausing a few feet away from the door to listen. The bell rang again and she heard her name being called on the other side.

Puzzled by what he could possibly want, she went to the door, checking her peephole just in case, and cracked it open.

Dean stood there looking almost as perturbed as she felt and she almost felt sorry for him. Almost. It was his fault after all.

"Can I help you?" she asked, feeling snarky.

"Can I come in?" he asked, instead of answering.

"Why?"

"Because I don't think you want me to make a scene out here for your neighbors. Mrs. Bailey really would have something to gossip about then." He winked and her stomach flipped.

Damn traitorous body.

She rolled her eyes but stepped back and opened the door for him to enter.

"You have two minutes," she warned him.

"What I have in mind might take longer than two minutes."

She closed the door, snapping the lock back in place, and turned around. "What's that?"

"This." Dean had her in his arms and locked in the hottest kiss of her life before she could blink.

Novalee gave as good as she got, biting down on his bottom lip just hard enough to draw a groan from Dean. He thrust his body into hers, pushing her against the front door in the process.

Novalee gasped, and dropped her head back so his mouth could better explore her neck. She wrapped her arms around his neck and closed her eyes just as Dean's tongue snaked into her ear, and she bucked her hips against him, feeling the hard outline of him pressing into her through the thin cotton barrier of her shorts.

"Dammit, woman," he said. "Do that again and this will be over in two minutes."

"What? This?" She rubbed against him again.

"Yes, that!"

Dean dropped his hands to her ass and lifted, encouraging her to wrap her legs around his waist. The move put his cock right where she needed him and she was helpless to stop herself from grinding on him.

"Fuck! Novalee—"

"Either take me to the bedroom, or take me right here, Dean," she begged. "Just don't make me wait any longer."

He tightened his arms around her as he moved her away from the door and carried her to the bedroom.

Novalee nuzzled his neck, placing soft kisses along his jaw until their lips were pressed together and he squeezed her bottom, causing her to moan into his mouth.

She refused to break the kiss even when he lowered her to the bed. She needed to feel him on top of her, to feel every inch him pressed against her. She spread her legs, and Dean fit himself between them, pressing his hardness along her heated flesh as he did.

Novalee hissed and arched into his touch. Her entire body was on fire and he hadn't gotten her out of her clothes yet.

Dean pulled his mouth away and stared down at her.

"Are you sure about this, Novalee?" he asked, tracing the side of her face with his finger.

"Am I not making myself clear enough?" She laughed.

He smiled. "Oh, you're making yourself very clear. I just want you to be sure. This will change everything, and I don't want you to regret it. Ever."

She sunk her teeth into her bottom lip as her nerves started to creep up on her. She knew this would change everything; she just wasn't sure *how* everything would change. Would it bring them closer together? Make one or both of them feel awkward and distant? She wasn't sure she was ready to deal with the feelings that might arise from being intimate with him, but she knew she wanted this, wanted him. Nothing else mattered in that moment, and if she started to think about what they were about to do she knew her insecurities would take over and she would screw it all up.

She sighed and ran her hands down Dean's back until she reached the hem of his shirt.

"I'm sure, Dean," she whispered, looking down at his chest and back up to his face. She slowly started to raise the shirt, exposing his warm skin. "Can we . . . I mean, it's been a while . . ." She felt her cheeks grow warm and she silently cursed, hating that she could be so easily embarrassed.

"Slow," Dean said, not needing her to explain. "We'll go slowly until you're comfortable."

Novalee inhaled deeply and nodded, then slid her hands under his shirt, finally feeling his skin when a thought occurred to her.

"Are *you* sure?" she asked.

He blinked, as if he didn't understand the question. "I'm the one that came to you, no?"

"But you didn't come here out of guilt or . . . sympathy, right?" His brow furrowed, and she tried to explain herself. "I don't want you to be here because of what I said in the parking lot made you feel guilty."

"You think this is a pity fuck?" His eyebrows raised in disbelief.

"Is it?"

"No." He shook his head and sighed. "Truthfully, what you said is part of the reason why I'm here. I don't think of you as a naïve schoolgirl, and I realize it wasn't fair of me to lead you on and then give you nothing back."

"So, you're here because you feel bad about turning me on and leaving me hanging?" she asked, feeling confused and more than a little annoyed and angry if that was his reason.

"No! Well, I do feel bad about that, but I'm not about to take you to bed out of guilt."

"I don't understand, Dean."

"I'm here because I want to be. I'm here because ever since I walked into your office three days ago, I can't stop thinking about you. I don't want to take advantage of you, but honestly I'm tired of thinking about it and worrying over what will happen. I just want to stop and enjoy this, enjoy you, while it lasts."

"Oh." The response was weak, but she was caught off guard by his answer and not sure what to say.

"I just don't want you to regret being with me later on," he added.

"The only thing I regret is that you still have your clothes on." She grinned and gave his shirt a little tug.

He laughed. "Whose fault is that? You keep asking questions."

"You're right. Less talk, more action."

Novalee wasted no time pulling his shirt the rest of the way off of him, dropping it to the floor as Dean kissed her again. She explored his bare back, dragging her hands from his wide shoulders, down to his waist, and slowly back up again. When her nails gently scraped his skin, Dean made a noise into her mouth. She did it again and smiled when she was rewarded with the sexy sound.

Dean nibbled the sensitive skin on her neck, kissing his way down to her collarbone. Novalee nervously bit her lip as he slipped his right hand under her tank and rested it on her stomach. The slight touch sent shivers through her body and her breathing hitched.

The anxiety she felt over her ability to please him was still there, bubbling beneath the surface, but her arousal and the way she wanted him was overpowering her self-doubt. Novalee wanted to tell him to screw taking it slow, grab his hand, and show him exactly what she wanted. She felt so tightly wound that she feared at any moment she would snap if he didn't hurry up and touch her.

"You're practically shaking." Dean observed. "Do you want to stop?"

"God, no!" she exclaimed, and then laughed at how she must sound. "That's the last thing I want."

Dean moved his hand a little higher and asked, "What do you want?"

"Exactly what you're doing right now." His fingertip brushed her breast and she gasped. "Only more." Goosebumps rose on her flesh as he slowly traced a finger around her hardened nipple. "Please," she whimpered, closing her eyes and arching into his touch.

Dean cupped her breast and rolled her nipple between his fingers, but before Novalee could scream her joy his hand was gone again. She opened her eyes and frowned.

"What—"

Dean silenced her with another kiss as he slowly raised her tank higher, only breaking away from her mouth to lift it over her head. The cool air hit Novalee's skin. Dean's eyes roamed over her naked upper body, and she fought the impulse to wrap her arms around herself. She felt as if more than just her body was being exposed under his scrutinizing gaze, and the urge to hide was strong.

Novalee licked her lips and swallowed as she watched him watching her. She wanted to ask him what he was thinking, but even if she could manage to find her voice, she dreaded it would be no more than a squeak.

She ran her hands down his arms, feeling the hard muscles beneath her palms, loving how thick and strong they felt. The hair on his forearms gently prickled her skin as she stroked him.

"You're so beautiful," Dean croaked, startling her after being silent for so long.

Novalee looked at him, suddenly feeling uncomfortable. She opened her mouth to speak, but he gently pressed his finger to her lips. "Don't even think about denying it."

He smiled down at her and pecked her lips softly before kissing his way back down her neck to the top of her left breast, licking her nipple, and she moaned.

"So beautiful," he murmured again, grazing his teeth against her as he sucked her nipple into his mouth.

"Dean!" Her grip on his arms tightened as he nipped and sucked. Then he moved his mouth to her other breast, making sure to give it the same attention.

As his mouth was busy, Novalee slid her hands down his chest and over his stomach until she reached the button on his jeans. She snapped it open and carefully tugged the zipper down, the metal teeth sounding a thousand times louder to her than it actually was. She brushed her hand against his arousal and his hips jerked.

"You're playing with fire," he groaned.

"Isn't that the point?" She grinned wickedly as she slipped her hand inside his jeans and cupped him through his boxers.

The breath hissed out of him and he thrust into her hand.

"I thought the point was to go slow," he gritted.

"Slow, yes. Not snail's pace," she teased.

His deep chuckle vibrated against her skin, causing those damn tingles to appear.

Gently, Dean wrapped his hand around her wrist and extracted her hand from his pants. He grabbed her other wrist and brought them above her head, holding her captive.

Novalee stared up at him, her heart pounding with excitement. Normally she would have freaked about being held down. It was such an aggressive move and everything inside her would scream to fight him off.

But she was not only oddly comfortable but aroused as well. Dean didn't hold her wrists tightly. If she wanted to she could easily slip her hands free, and he wasn't holding her down with his weight. He kept his upper body propped away from her so she had breathing room, but maintained intimate contact by pressing his pelvis into her.

His careful actions didn't make her feel as if she was being overpowered. It was almost as if he knew and understood her need to keep some control over the situation.

"Are you saying I'm going *too* slowly for you, Novalee?"

"No. But if you get to touch, so do I."

"Mm," he said. "I haven't even begun to touch yet."

If she hadn't already been wet for him, that would have instantly done it.

He released one of her wrists and teasingly dragged his finger down her arm. She trembled beneath him as he continued down her shoulder, over the swell of her breast and stomach, pausing at the waistband of her shorts.

"There is so much more of you that I want to touch . . . to taste," he whispered.

Novalee held her breath, sure he was going to dip his hand inside and finally relieve the ache that had been building up for days. Instead, Dean rested his hand on her hip and stopped there.

Novalee groaned in frustration and rolled her head to the side, glaring at him.

"Then stop stalling and do it!" she demanded.

He smirked. "Slow, remember?"

He skimmed his hand over her ass and squeezed her cheek, earning a yelp from her.

"Forget I said anything about going slow," she panted.

Finally, she felt his fingers back on her skin as he slid his hand into the leg of her shorts. It was his turn to groan when he discovered she wore no panties and bare, wet flesh waited for him.

"Novalee."

She saw the desire burning in his eyes when she looked up at him, and despite his attitude about taking things slow, he was just as on edge as she was.

"If I don't go slowly it will be over before I can do everything I want with you," he confessed, his voice low.

"Who said you only have tonight?" she asked.

The last of his restraint snapped and he hungrily attacked her mouth. Novalee responded just as eagerly, pulling her hands free of his grasp and cupping his face. Dean traced her with his finger.

"Please, Dean," she said, already so close to coming undone. "Don't make me wait."

"You're so fucking wet," he grunted.

He swirled his finger around her entrance. Novalee wiggled her hips, causing just the tip to slide inside her.

"More, Dean. Please."

He groaned as he plunged first one finger and then two into her depth. Novalee cried out, bucking against his hand. Dean moved his fingers in and out of her at a gentle, steady pace, but as great as it felt, it wasn't enough.

She needed more. She needed to be stretched and filled and fucked by more than what he was giving her.

"Take off your pants, Dean," she demanded, breathless. "Take them off. I need you. Now."

Slowly, he pulled his hand away from her and sat up, kneeling between her spread legs. The tattoo on his chest, just above his heart, caught her eye. Her fingers itched to reach out and trace the inked skin, but he grabbed her shorts and tugged before she had a chance to move.

"I want these off first."

Novalee lifted her hips and he pulled the flimsy material down her legs and away from her body. She was laid out before him, naked and vulnerable. Dean looked over every inch of her and she felt a blush creep into her cheeks. He licked his lips when he paused at the juncture of her thighs, and leaned forward to trail his lips above her.

He held her hips and he only stopped stroking her skin when he brushed the puckered skin of the scar on her left side.

Novalee stiffened as he traced it with his finger, slamming her lids shut as the memory flashed in her mind. It was only Dean's soft touch that kept her from going back to that night. He placed a tender kiss on the scar and a pang of *something* hit her from the intimate gesture.

Before she could speak, he was back to kissing her thighs. He inhaled her deeply, and she shuddered as he exhaled and his breath hit her private parts.

"Dean . . .

"I want to taste you, Novalee." His voice was husky. "But I'm selfish and the first time you come I want it to be around my cock."

Oh, praise the dirty-talking gods!

Novalee nearly cried in response as Dean sat up and removed his jeans and boxers. Her eyes immediately fell to his waist and she nearly died.

Oh, my.

She wasn't one to compare notes and pass judgment, but if she was, Dean definitely wouldn't have anything to worry about.

In fact, *she* was starting to feel a little nervous. It wasn't as if he was freakishly huge, but she doubted her hand would be able to wrap all the way around him and he wasn't skimping in the length department either. Nerves made the wings in her stomach flutter as the bed dipped and creaked as Dean crawled next to her again.

"Are you okay?"

"Mm-hmm."

"It's okay if you've changed your mind," he assured her.

"No." She shook her head. "And if I had I would say something. I want this. I want you."

She wrapped her arms around his neck as he lowered his head and sucked on her earlobe.

"I want you, too," he whispered into her ear.

Novalee felt his erection against her hip and she reached between them and wrapped her hand around him. Her eyes were drawn down to where she grasped him, her hand sliding up and down, unable to look away.

Dean groaned as she stroked him, thrusting his hips in rhythm with her movement. Novalee spread the drop of moisture around the head of his shaft with her thumb and he grunted, pulling away from her.

"I can't wait."

She heard the crinkle of the foil packet he grabbed off the nightstand and smirked. She could only assume he had grabbed it out of his pocket at some point because *she* sure as hell didn't have any condoms lying around.

"Do you always carry condoms around with you in hopes of getting lucky during a late night visit to your wife?" she asked, the question out of her mouth before she could stop it.

He paused in his movements and she swore a faint blush crept into his cheeks.

"Uh . . . if I tell you I made a quick stop before coming here will you think I'm a presumptuous ass?"

"Does that mean your sole purpose for coming here was for this to happen?" she teased.

He frowned as he leaned above her on his elbows.

"Okay, that makes me sound like a royal fucking jerk."

"I didn't mean it like that," she whispered, brushing her fingers through his short hair, needing to touch him in some way. "I just find it a little amusing."

His eyes darkened in a very sexy way and he grinned.

"Novalee, those are too words I will make sure you never say again while in bed with me."

She giggled and coyly dropped her eyes to his chest, asking, "What words might those be?"

"Little and amusing."

Novalee bit her lip as he brushed against her center to prove his point.

Slowly, inch by glorious inch, Dean filled her. She dug her nails into his shoulders as her body stretched around him.

"Christ," he groaned, "you feel so good, Novalee."

He pulled almost all the way out and then thrust back into her.

"Oh, god!" Novalee gasped, lifting her hips off the bed. "More, Dean!"

In one smooth thrust he was buried deep inside her, making them both moan. The muscles in his back rippled beneath her hands as she clung to him.

"Wrap your legs around me, baby," he coaxed.

She did and cried out as he sank deeper. Dean slowly pulled out until just the head of his cock touched her, and then just as slowly pushed back in all the way to the hilt.

"Dean, I can't . . . I don't . . . ," she babbled.

"Tell me what you want." He panted. "Tell me what will get you there."

"I don't know . . . It . . . feels like too much." Dean started to pull back and Novalee shook her head. "Not too much in a bad way."

He grabbed her hands and brought them over her head again. The position raised her breasts and he watched as they shook with every thrust of his hips. She closed her eyes and she licked her bottom lip, drawing Dean's attention back there.

He braced himself on his hands above her shoulders and gradually increased his speed. Novalee opened her eyes, watching his face and finding the slight sheen of sweat that glistened on his brow somewhat erotic.

She moved her hands to his shoulders and down his back, scraping his skin as his hips slammed into hers, filling the room with the sound of skin slapping skin.

The sight of his body straining above hers, the sound of their joint union, and the smell of their sweet sweat was too much for her and she began to tremble as she felt herself tightening. She dug her nails dug into his back as she climaxed, crying out his name as she came.

"Fuck." He buried his face in her neck as her walls milked him, bringing him his own sweet release.

He lay like that for a minute, close to her until his breathing slowed, and then rolled off of her. Novalee thought he was about to make a quick dash to the bathroom and an even quicker exit, but after disposing of the condom he wrapped his arms around her and pulled her back against his chest.

Without a word, he tugged the blankets over them and spooned into her heated body. Soon his breathing evened out and Novalee didn't have to look to know he had fallen asleep.

She should be just as exhausted as he was, but her mind wouldn't shut off and she reveled in how it felt being wrapped in his arms. Nothing had ever felt quite as natural as it did being with Dean.

She smiled, even as a single tear rolled down her cheek and dripped off her chin. As much as she wanted this, and as much as she knew she would never regret it, she now understood how everything had changed.

It's true that we don't know what we've got until we lose it, but it's also true that we don't know what we've been missing until it arrives.

Whoever said that couldn't have been more right.

How ironic was it that she had found what she was missing just as she was about to lose it?

Chapter 10

Dean woke hours later to a soft brushing along his abdomen. He smiled lazily, enjoying the caress, and opened his eyes to see what was responsible for waking him.

The two green eyes that stared back at him were not what he was expecting.

The white feline was perched on his chest glaring down at him as it switched its tail back and forth.

Dean stared at the cat, worried one wrong move would either anger or startle it, and he'd be left wounded and bleeding. He was never more thankful for the blankets that safely hid his dick from sharp claws.

"Shoo," he hissed. The animal cocked its head and stopped moving its tail.

Oh, that couldn't be good. Happy animals wagged their tails, right? Dean feared he had just pissed off this pussy.

"Scat!" He tried to shift to the side, hoping the cat would take the hint and jump off, but the sting of a claw digging into his chest changed his mind.

"Okay, Ben," he said, remembering the animal's name. "I take it I'm in your spot. If you move, I can get up and you can have it back."

Ben yawned, clearly not impressed with his negotiating skills.

"Fine. I'm just going to move you then," he warned, which earned him a try-if-you-dare look.

Never one to back down from a challenge, even one presented by a ball of fur, Dean slowly lifted his hands to remove the cat from his chest, and had almost succeeded in grabbing it, when Ben hissed sharply at him.

Dean held his hands up in surrender mode.

"You win. Stay where you are." He glared at the animal. "But just so you know, your attitude will not be earning you any smuggled catnip." Ben licked his lips. "Oh, yes, I have connections. You could have been living the good life. I scratch your back; you don't scratch mine. It could have been a sweet deal for you."

Dean felt the bed shake next to him and looked over to see Novalee laughing hysterically.

Busted.

"Uh, morning."

Novalee shook her head, still vibrating with laughter.

Dean sighed and glanced back at Ben.

"I hope you're happy," he said, which sent Novalee into another round of giggles. "When you finish laughing at me, can you tell me how to get him off?"

Novalee took a deep breath trying to calm herself and made a soft clicking sound with her tongue. Ben happily sprung from Dean's chest and curled up at the end of the bed.

That was it? That's all it took to get rid of the ornery little fucker? Dean shook his head in disbelief and sat up. "I'll have to remember that one." He looked down at Novalee and smiled. "Don't go anywhere."

" 'Kay," she said, wrapping her arm around her pillow and pulling it against her body.

He yanked on his boxers and disappeared into the master bathroom to take the much-needed piss that had almost been scared out of him by that damn cat.

That's not how he would have started the morning if it had been up to him. But then he hadn't planned to be standing half-naked in Novalee's bathroom either.

Showing up on her doorstep last night had been an impulse. When she'd left him standing alone in the parking lot he had every intention of doing the right thing and driving back to his hotel. The night had left him a little unnerved and he'd wanted to put a little distance between the two of them, not only so she didn't do something she might regret but so he wouldn't either.

He fucking danced with her. That shit was straight out of the kind of sappy chick flick he would normally roll his eyes at. And the thing that made him wonder if his nuts were still attached was he actually *got* why men, real men not paid actors in those horrible movies, did it.

Having Novalee in his arms was worth every second of torture his eardrums endured listening to that damn song. Unless it involved a skimpily dressed woman, Dean wasn't into dancing. The whole act was too intimate to him, and he was known to stay clear of anything involving real intimacy.

What Dean hadn't counted on was her reaction.

He didn't need to be a mind reader to know her "bad experience" had something to do with the bastard who abused her.

The pain in her eyes, and the pain that had crept into her voice tore at his gut and he'd wanted to do anything he could to take it away. But when it came down to it, he froze.

All the reasons why he shouldn't be holding her so damn close, or telling her he wanted to give her memories that would make her smile, slapped him back to reality.

He was giving her false hope, leading her to believe that he would be there for her whenever she needed him. The thing that scared the shit out of him the most was that he *wanted* to be there for her as long as she wanted him. He *wanted* to chase away her nightmares by bringing her pleasure at night. He *wanted* to be the one she turned to when she had a shitty day. But how could he do all that when she would want him as far away as possible from her when the truth came out?

Dean wanted everything Novalee was willing to give him, but how fair was it of him to ask that of her when he had nothing to give in return?

He had made up his mind to let her go home alone, pissed at him if that would make it easier for her. But her little rant had gotten him thinking, and the thinking got him driving around the city, and the driving landed him on Novalee's doorstep.

He'd sat outside her house for a good ten minutes, arguing with himself about doing the right thing and doing what he really wanted to do.

What he told Novalee about being there was true.

He was tired of thinking about what his actions had done. He was fucking sick of worrying over how this would play out. He couldn't change the past and truthfully, even if he could, he wouldn't. His decisions weren't only about saving his grandfather's legacy, but no matter what happened after all this was over, it had all brought her to Dean.

The couple of days he had been in her company were the best days he'd had in years, possibly ever. And he needed more of that. He needed her in a way that both alarmed and excited him. It was a feeling he'd never felt before, and that frightened him even more than the thought of Ben mistaking his balls for toys he could bat around.

Dean splashed water on his face, and a pang of guilt swept over him as he stared at his reflection as he dried off. He gargled some mouthwash he found, trying to ignore the knot in his stomach.

He might be tired of worrying about the fallout, but that didn't mean he still didn't feel like he was taking advantage of her. His only hope now was that she would believe him when he told her taking her to bed had nothing to do with needing her help.

Upon opening the door, he half-expected to see the bed empty. Novalee lay on her side, head propped up on her hand as she petted Ben. She was dressed in her top from last night again, and if she hadn't been lying in bed, Dean would have thought she was giving him the hint he should leave.

She looked up at him when he stepped out of the bathroom and timidly smiled at him.

"Hey."

"Hey." He returned the smile and approached the bed, wondering if the proper thing for him to do would be to dress as well.

"Ben promises to behave if you decide to join us," she teased, grinning up at him.

Fuck getting dressed if she was inviting him back to bed.

Dean eyed the cat before slipping back under the covers, mimicking her position. He glanced at the digital clock behind her head and saw it was just after ten. He watched her stroke Ben's fur.

"What time do you have to be at the bar?" he asked to break the silence.

Novalee shrugged, still petting Ben.

"Later," she replied.

He tried to interpret her body language to know if something was wrong.

"Are you okay? Did I do something?" he asked, hating that he even had to fucking ask and sound like a whiny little bitch in need of reassurance.

She sighed and looked up at him. "Sorry. Just thinking."

"About?"

She flushed and looked away. "I don't really want to talk about it."

Well, hell.

Obviously it was something, and his gut told him it had something to do with him. But he couldn't make her talk if she didn't want to. She did ask him back into her bed, so she didn't want him to leave. If she wasn't willing to talk . . .

"Come here," he said.

Novalee raised an eyebrow.

"And disturb Ben?"

"I'd do it, but he made it pretty clear he's not a fan of mine."

Novalee laughed. "You know you're out of luck when even bribery with catnip won't help."

Dean smiled and patted the space next to him.

Novalee relocated Ben back to the end of the bed and scooted next to Dean. As soon as she was pressed against him he dipped his head and kissed her, cupping the back of her neck, rubbing his thumb in circles as he explored her mouth.

She tasted like peppermint and Dean guessed she had snuck out to use the guest bathroom. Her lips were still a little swollen from last night.

Novalee's moan went straight to his dick and he knew by the way she wiggled against him that his reaction to her didn't go unnoticed.

Wrapping his arm around her, he rolled onto his back, bringing her with him so she lay across his chest.

There was nothing more that he wanted than to spread her legs and bury himself deep inside her again until she screamed his name. But he needed this time to be on her terms. If she wanted to go for round two he was more than willing, but if she just wanted to lie around in bed until she had to leave for work he was okay with that, too.

Shit. When had he turned into such a pansy?

Dean Philips was okay with *cuddling*? What the hell had this woman done to him?

Novalee pulled away and stared down at him. He caressed her back, remaining as silent as she. Her facial expression was a mix of confusion, arousal, and something else Dean couldn't quite put his finger on.

"Why were you so concerned about me regretting last night?" she asked.

He kept looking at her mouth as she spoke, and his mind clouded with all kinds of dirty thoughts when she wet her lips. Thoughts of her tongue sliding across his head rolled through his mind.

"Uh . . ." He cleared his throat and looked back into her eyes. He needed a second to clear those images.

"Is it because of our . . . predicament?"

He silently scoffed. Theirs was a little more than just a difficult situation.

"I didn't want you rushing into this." He frowned, curling a strand of her hair around his finger. "This happened fairly fast, and you don't seem like the type to jump into bed with random guys. Unless, of course, Vegas and large amounts of alcohol are involved," he teased with a grin.

Novalee stiffened in his arms and narrowed her eyes.

"How do you know what 'type' I am?"

"That's my point; we don't know each other all that well so I just didn't want last night to be a morning-after regret. Am I wrong?"

She relaxed in his arms again and shook her head.

"I didn't think so. Plus, you were the one that said it had been a while since you were with a guy."

Dean found the blush that filled her cheeks to be oddly erotic.

"I couldn't . . . I mean, even though we weren't together . . . it felt like cheating," she mumbled, dropping her eyes to his chest.

He gaped at her, shocked by her confession. She remained faithful in a marriage to a man she didn't know?

He wasn't sure why it surprised him; after all hadn't he done the same thing? He wasn't able to be with other women not only because it felt wrong, but because other women had no appeal to him.

Maybe that's why it did shock him. Their thoughts and actions were so similar it was just one more thing that made him feel connected to her.

"I guess it's hard for you to understand," she said. "You were engaged to someone else, after all."

If he didn't feel like such a shit in that moment for making her believe there had been someone else, he would have been amused by the hint of jealousy in her tone.

"Not as hard as you think," he said quietly.

Novalee raised her eyes to meet his.

"Why do you say that? Weren't you happy with her?"

Fuck. Why didn't he just keep his mouth shut? Why had he told her he was engaged in the first place? He didn't want to add to the list of lies he had already told her by fabricating an imaginary woman.

She looked at him, waiting for a reply, and the only thing he wanted to tell her was the truth.

"I've never felt as close to anyone else as I do being here with you right now."

Novalee bit her lip, staring at him and then her eyes dropped to his mouth as he had done earlier, only she leaned in and took what she wanted.

Dean let her take control as she sat up and straddled his waist. He groaned as she ground herself into him, cursing his fucking boxers and her tiny pair of shorts for being in the way. He could be sliding through her right now if it weren't for them. He dropped his hands to her ass and squeezed as he thrust against her.

Novalee ground harder on him as she moved her hips in small circles.

"Fuck." Dean closed his eyes, fighting for control over his body. If she did that again there was a chance the only thing that would be seeing any action was his boxers.

He felt her grin against his neck and say, "If you like that you're going to love what I do next."

Before he could question her, Novalee was moving down his body, pausing to place soft kisses on the foreign words tattooed on his chest. Dean watched as she kissed and licked farther down his torso until she was kneeling between his legs. She tucked her fingers into the waistband of his boxers and looked up at him.

Fucking hell that was hot!

She looked shy when she did that, almost innocent. But Dean only needed the tug she gave on his underwear to know she was thinking anything but innocent thoughts.

"Lift up," she demanded.

What kind of idiot would he be not to do as she asked?

He raised his hips, looking at her cleavage as she stripped him naked. His cock sprang free, harder than he could ever remember it being. The breath hissed out of him as she wrapped her hand around him. Her grip felt cool around his heated skin and the sensation of hot and cold nearly made him break out into a sweat.

"Novalee," he croaked, "you don't have to—"

What the fuck was he saying? There was a woman kneeling between his legs ready to blow him and he was telling her no?

"I don't recall you asking," she said. "Which means I want to."

Novalee lowered her mouth, her hot breath hitting him, and he had to fight from thrusting. Slowly, she wrapped her mouth around the head of his dick. Dean dropped his head back and moaned.

Christ. Her mouth was so damn warm, so fucking wet. Her tongue swirled around the tip and she slowly sucked more of him in.

Dean pried his eyes open to watch as he disappeared into her hot little mouth. Her head bobbed up and down, her hair falling around her face like a curtain, a private show just for him.

Novalee stroked the part of his shaft she couldn't fit in her mouth, and the feeling was almost enough to cause him to shoot his load down her throat. Then she glanced up at him, locking eyes as she sucked even harder.

"Jesus Christ!" he groaned, fighting for the last bit of control. "Novalee, stop!"

Lazily, she snaked her tongue around the underside of his length as she pulled her head up and released him.

"Why?" she asked as she continued to stroke him, smiling.

He sat up and grabbed her, hauling her to his chest. A startled look flashed in her eyes for an instant, and Dean cursed himself for being so stupid and manhandling her like that, but the look was gone as fast as it had appeared.

"I think you know why."

"I think you should tell me."

He grinned. Novalee liked the dirty talk. That was his kind of woman.

"Because your mouth feels too fucking good," he said, "and I was two seconds away from filling it with my come."

He didn't miss the way her breathing increased, or the excitement that shone in her eyes.

He trailed his hand down her shoulder to her cleavage, palming one breast over the thin material of her tank. Novalee bit her lip and drew in a deep breath.

"And when I come," he continued, playfully pinching her nipple, and then sliding his hand lower until he cupped her sex through her shorts, "it's going to be deep inside you."

"Oh, my . . ." She wiggled her hips on his hand and he found her clit through the thin cotton and flicked it.

"Do you like that?"

"Yes!" she gasped, trying to ride his hand.

He rubbed harder, watching her face show the pleasure she felt. Her shorts were damp. He slipped his hand inside, rubbing with the rough pad of his thumb as he plunged two fingers into her.

Her cry filled the room as Dean fucked her with his hand. She was so tight just around two fingers that if he hadn't already been inside her, he would worry about hurting her.

"I need you to take these off," he said gruffly, removing his hand.

She looked down at him mischievously as she grabbed his wrist and brought his fingers to her mouth.

"Take them off yourself," she challenged, sucking on his fingers.

Dean sat there a little surprised by her actions, watching as she slowly snaked her tongue around his finger just as she had before on another part of his body. If watching her licking his finger wasn't enough she closed her eyes and moaned, like she actually fucking enjoyed the taste of herself, and he snapped.

He ripped off her shorts in such a rush they got tangled around her feet. Novalee held onto his shoulders and laughed as he desperately tried to free her. He probably would have found the situation humorous, too, if he wasn't out of his damn mind with want.

Finally the blasted shorts came free and he grabbed her hips, positioning her over him.

"Ride me, Novalee," he urged.

The wicked glint was back in her eyes as she reached between them.

"How bad do you want it?" she teased, sliding him inside her.

He wasn't sure where this sexually confident woman came from, but he liked it. A lot.

He thrust his hips and said, "As badly as you do."

Novalee lowered her hips until just the tip was inside her. With agonizingly slow movements she rode him, never letting him sink into her further.

He groaned, tightening his grip on her hips a little more to convey how much of a tease she was being.

"Novalee . . ."

Dean didn't want to get rough with her—unless of course she asked for it—but he was two seconds away from pulling her hips down and ramming his dick as deep as it would go into her.

"Novalee, please," he said, almost outside of himself.

Please? Please!

There was no way he could have just said the word "please." He couldn't remember ever begging a woman to give him what he wanted.

But then there was no woman who could drive him to the edge like the one teasing him right now.

She squeezed him over and over again.

This woman was going to kill him.

Just when he thought he couldn't take any more, she dropped her hips and took all of him in one thrust.

"Fuck!"

And just as quickly she was gone again.

"Jesus, Novalee—"

"Condom."

Shit. How could he forget the fucking condom?

"Pants pocket."

Novalee left him only long enough to grab the little square packet, rip it open, and roll it onto him. She rocked her hips as he dragged his hands up her body, lifting her shirt over her head. He cupped her breasts, her nipples poking his palms as he squeezed them.

Dean looked up from Novalee's chest to her face as she threw back her head, biting her lip.

Dean dropped his hands, freeing her breasts to sway with each thrust of her hips. He covered her with his hand and moved his thumb to rub her clit. Her hips bucked and she groaned.

"More," she panted.

Dean sat up and she wrapped her arms around his neck as he crushed his lips to hers, grabbing her ass and then pulling his mouth away to nip at her ear.

"More?" He lifted her so just his head was surrounded, and then slammed her hips back down. "Like that?"

"Yes, like that!"

She gripped him, squeezing with every thrust. She snaked her hands through his hair, pulling the short strands as she rode him.

She felt so good. So fucking wet and warm and so damn tight that Dean soon felt the pressure build in his balls and knew he wouldn't last much longer.

"Dean." She gasped, digging her nails into his shoulders.

His hold on her ass tightened as she tensed in his arms and rocked her hips one last time before crying out her release.

"Dean!" She cried out again, withering against him as her orgasm took over her body.

He swiftly rolled them over so she was lying beneath him and he muffled her sounds of pleasure with his mouth as he thrust harder. Deeper. Faster.

Novalee raked her nails down his back until they landed on his ass and she dug them into his flesh as she tried to pull him deeper inside of her.

Dean groaned from the mild sting of her actions, thrusting as deep as he could go as he gritted his teeth and stiffened with release.

Novalee's grip on his ass relaxed and she ran her hands up his back and down his arms. Dean pecked her lips, mumbled he'd be right back, and disappeared into the bathroom to rid himself of the offensive latex. He quickly cleaned up and then crawled back into bed, pulling Novalee to his side.

"Good morning," he said, making her laugh.

She draped her arm over his chest and laid her head on her bicep, smiling at him.

"What?" he asked as he lazily trailed his fingers from her shoulder down to her hip and back up again.

"Can I ask you something?"

He stopped stroking her skin, caught off guard by the request. All the questions she could possibly want to ask ran through his head, and more than half of them he didn't want to answer. Not because he didn't want to give her the answers, but because in doing so it would no doubt mean telling her more lies. And he was sick to death of lying to this woman. She deserved so much better than that, especially now after giving her body to him.

But what the fuck was he supposed to do now? Confess his sins to her and hope she didn't kick him out and slam the door in his face when he needed her the most?

Fuck it all to hell!

Dean inhaled deeply and started mapping her skin again.

"Sure."

"Did you even crack open the menu last night to see how each burger was made?"

Dean stared blankly at her, unsure if he heard her right.

"Because I don't think one burger looked how it was supposed to." She paused and frowned. "Of course, it was hard to tell under all the blackness."

He continued to stare at her, mouth open, as she grinned and finally burst into giggles.

That was what she wanted to know? Whether he had followed the menu?

"I think you need to take some of those big bucks you have and invest in some cooking classes," she said.

He cocked an eyebrow.

"Cooking classes, huh?" he mocked, finally finding his voice.

"Well," she said thoughtfully, "if you can find a class that wouldn't mind possible fires."

"Hey, woman, there were no fires!"

She laughed again and smiled at him. That smile . . . it felt like his lungs were constricted and he'd never get enough air again.

What the hell was that about?

"Another question?"

"I don't know." He mulled in mock consideration. "Will my ego be further bruised?"

"I can't promise anything."

"Mm-hmm."

"Favorite ice cream?"

Dean guessed a game of twenty questions was about to begin.

"Rocky Road," he answered.

"Sports?"

"I used to play football in high school and I'm still a fan of the game."

"How many hotels do you own?"

"Eleven."

"Which one is your favorite?" she asked.

His brow furrowed. "They're all the same."

"No, I mean which location?"

"Oh." *Dumbass.* "I don't really have one. I spend most of my time in Vegas, but after a while all cities pretty much became the same."

"Have you always lived in Vegas?"

"No. I grew up in New York and moved to Nevada after . . . the funerals."

"Oh."

He glanced down at her and saw she was biting her lip again. He might not have known her very long, but it didn't take him long to figure out that was her nervous habit. Whatever she was thinking she was struggling with the decision whether to ask or not.

Finally, she said, "Did your father come with you?"

Dean exhaled noisily. He figured it had something to do with *him*, and he hated that he had to bring the SOB into their conversation, but the more she knew the better it was in the end, right?

"No. My grandfather was living out there and I moved in with him."

"Your father just let you leave?" she asked, sounding surprised.

He snorted. "Believe me; he was glad to get rid of me."

"Why? Have you two never gotten along?"

He clenched his jaw shut and remained silent. He really didn't want to get into that.

She traced her finger over his tattoo and asked instead, "What does this mean?"

He swallowed over the lump that had suddenly appeared.

"It's Greek," he replied.

"You speak it?"

"No." She looked up at him curiously and he sighed. "My mom's favorite place in the world was Greece. She loved the language, the culture, the history. Everything about it drew her in. She used to tell my sister her beauty reminded her of one of those Greek goddesses." He smiled at the memory.

"So . . ." Novalee nipped at her lip again and glanced back at the ink. "It's meant for your mom?"

"No." He closed his eyes and rubbed his hand across his forehead. Tension filled his body knowing he'd have to explain. "The language it's in represents my mother and sister, but the words define me."

"What does it mean?" she asked again.

Dean wanted to tell her. He wanted to expose all the pain he'd kept hidden inside for so long and he only wanted to do it with her. But it was easier said than done. Even though he wanted to, he felt himself shutting down. He was seconds away from jumping out of her bed and leaving.

He stilled his hand on her hip and he felt the scar under his fingertips. He wanted to ask her what had happened, but the first time he'd touched it last night she froze. There was a story behind it that he wanted to know, but how could he ask? How could he expect her to open up when he wouldn't?

Why the fuck was this so hard? The words were there, right *there*, and he felt like he was choking on them. Dean wanted to speak, he wanted the words to come out so damn bad, but they wouldn't.

He just couldn't.

So she did.

"The scar on my hip," she began in no more than a whisper, "is a reminder of the abuse I put up with for far too long."

Every muscle in Dean's body tightened. He held his breath, both willing and apprehensive to hear her tell him about her past.

"Not that I need the reminder," she added bitterly. "Some things you can never forget."

A part of him wanted to tell her she didn't have to share those memories. He wanted to roll her underneath him and use his hands and mouth to distract her from opening up old wounds . . . and to keep her from opening up to him. If she shared her darkest years, would she expect him to do the same?

The other part of him needed her to continue. Dean wanted to know from her what had happened, not from some private investigator's report. But if she confided in him, did that mean she trusted him?

The decision wasn't his to make, however. He stayed quiet, tracing the memory on her hip as he waited for her to either explain or pull away as he had.

The seconds ticked by and turned into minutes, until finally she spoke again, her voice sounding tired and shaky.

"When I was eighteen I met the man I thought would make all my dreams come true. Dalton was older than I was, handsome, charming, and really sweet. I thought he was going to be the one to save me from the sadness I lived with after my parents' death. And he did for a while, but no good thing lasts forever.

"We had been together for a few months when one night I invited him to join Cali and me dancing. He sat at the table most of the night, brooding, so Cali and I danced while he watched. A guy started dancing with me. It was all innocent, but Dalton didn't see it that way.

"We dropped Cali off and went back to his place and . . . he was different. He started accusing me of leading the guy on and flirting with him, and when I tried to defend myself he got even angrier." She paused and drew in a deep breath. "I told him he was crazy and that's when he hit me. One slap; hard enough to bruise the side of my face and send me flying into his liquor shelf. I cut my hip when I fell on one of the broken whisky bottles."

"Son of a bitch," Dean said under his breath, hugging her closer to him.

"It just got worse from there."

"Novalee, why didn't you leave?" he asked, feeling angry. Why did smart women like his wife and mother let men abuse them? He didn't understand it one fucking little bit.

"I should have," she agreed. "But he knew all the right things to say and do to make me feel better. He knew how to make me believe it would never happen again."

"Even though you knew it would," he said.

"Yes."

"So why stay?"

"I don't know. I guess . . . I never thought it would get as bad as it did," she admitted. "I thought he loved me. I thought I loved him."

"The first time he put his hands on you should have been enough. You shouldn't have waited around to see how bad it would get," Dean scolded. Her only response was a quiet sniffle as she wiped tears from her eyes. "Why didn't Cali or her parents do something? Didn't they notice you were being beaten?"

"Of course they noticed," she snapped, defensive now that he had accused her family of turning the other cheek. "I denied it all the time, but they knew. It's not their fault I wouldn't seek help. In the end Cali did save me."

"You've said that before."

"One night Dalton and I got into an argument about the money I was going to inherit. He had all kinds of plans for it. I realize now he was probably only with me because of the money. When I finally stood up for myself and told him no, he almost killed me. It was Cali who found me and got me help before it was too late."

"How bad?" he asked, even though he knew the answer.

Novalee sighed. "Dean, it doesn't matter now."

"How bad?" he asked again though clenched teeth.

She hesitated before answering. "Broken bones including three ribs, a collarbone, and my right arm, plus a fractured hip and jaw. I also had some internal damage and a collapsed lung."

"What kind of internal damage?"

"I . . . there was . . ." She choked on the words, struggling to get the rest out, and Dean couldn't possibly imagine what could be worse than what she had already told him.

"It's okay." He soothed her, gently rubbing her back. "You don't have to tell me if it's too hard."

She shook her head.

"It's not that . . . well, maybe it is. I try not to think about it, much less talk about it."

"Like I said, it's okay if you don't want to tell me."

She was quiet for a moment and then said, "Because of the damage I might not be able to have children."

Dean rested his chin on top of her head. "I'm sorry."

The words sounded incredibly weak. What good was being sorry going to do? But he had no idea what else to say. He knew what he wanted to do. He wanted to find this Dalton bastard and rip the piece of shit limb from limb. Dean wanted him to know what it felt like to be afraid and in pain, left lying near death's door alone.

"I don't think about it. I mean, I never really thought about children before it all happened anyway, and now that there's a chance I can't have them, what's the point in thinking about it? Why want what you can't have?"

"You don't know that for sure."

She shrugged.

"It took a lot of healing and therapy, both mental and physical, to get me whole again. I'm okay with it. I'm alive at least." She traced the foreign characters of his tattoo again and said, "I've never talked about it with anyone before."

"Why tell me?" he asked.

"I have a feeling I'm not the only one with a dark past," she replied. "If you don't want to talk about it, that's fine. I don't expect you to understand what I went through, but . . . I trust you."

She trusted him. The knife in his gut twisted. He didn't fucking deserve her trust. He didn't deserve anything she had to offer him. How was she going to feel about sharing her past with him when she found out he had done nothing but lie to her?

"I understand better than you can imagine," he said.

She paused in her finger tracing and glanced at him.

"What do you mean?"

"My father was an abusive bastard, too."

The words hung in the air and he felt more vulnerable than ever before. Other than Abby, no one knew of the hell he lived in every day, but even his best friend couldn't understand what he had been through. Who would have thought the stranger he married in Vegas would understand him better than anyone in his life?

He should be the last person she should trust, and yet she did. And as much as it scared the shit out of him, he cared about her. She couldn't only know the lies about him if he wanted to be in her life after all this was over. The person she thought he was wasn't even close to the truth. If he didn't take this chance and let her in, let her know who he really was, how could he expect her to want him in the end?

And he wanted that. Dean wanted her to want him, wanted her to be with him after all this was said and done, when they could end their fraudulent marriage and move on. He wanted her more than he would ever be able to make her understand. More than even he could understand.

"Is that why you hate him?" she asked.

Dean covered her hand with his and held it on his chest. He could feel the pounding of his heart as he made the decision that could change everything.

"That tattoo means 'still I stand'. It defines the hell I witnessed growing up, my mom and sister's deaths, and everything else in my life

I've had to deal with and overcome to survive. It means in the end, no matter what kind of shit life throws at me, I'll take it and come out better because of it.

"And I hate my father because he killed my mom and sister."

Chapter 11

The tiny hairs on the back of her neck stood on end and a chill ran through her.

His father had killed his family?

She stared at Dean, too shocked to know what to say. The reasons she had imagined for why he hated his father so much didn't even come close to the truth. Here she had thought he wouldn't be able to relate to her past, yet she was the one left speechless.

Goosebumps rose on her skin and she felt very cold. She grabbed the covers and pulled them up to her chin, burying herself beneath the warmth of the blankets.

"I'm sorry if I've made you uncomfortable," he said, misreading her body language.

She shook her head.

"You haven't. I just . . . Dean, I don't know what to say." She looked at him. "Why is he still walking around free if he murdered your family?"

Dean sneered. "Because having blood on one's hands isn't enough to convict."

He glanced down at her and Novalee's brow furrowed in confusion and she shook her head again.

"He didn't actually pull the trigger," he explained, grimacing. "But he might as well have because it's his fault they're dead."

Novalee swallowed, trying to clear the bitter taste of bile.

"What does that mean? When did this happen? How? *Why?*" she asking, firing questions at him.

"It was sixteen years ago," he replied.

"So, you were . . ." She frowned, not realizing until that moment that she had no idea how old Dean was. "How old were you?"

"Seventeen."

Novalee sat up and faced him, tucking the sheet under her arms to keep it in place.

"Dean, I don't want to push you into talking about this, especially considering you didn't pressure me about my past, but I just don't understand. You said your father killed them, but then said he didn't actually do it. What does that mean?"

Dean briefly met her gaze before looking away and closing his eyes. His chest rose as he inhaled deeply and her eyes were drawn to the black scrawl above his heart.

"This is hard for me," he admitted quietly. "I appreciate how difficult it was for you to share your story with me, and as horrible as your experience was, mine is s a little different."

"That's fairly obvious."

He opened his eyes and looked at her sadly.

"My father wasn't always a monster. He seemed to change overnight. One day he and my mother were a happy, loving couple, and the next day I found her crying in the kitchen with a bruised face." His face suddenly changed and anger lit up his eyes. "And, just like you, she didn't try to stop it when it got worse; she didn't try to leave and save herself and us kids. She let him continue to hurt her until it was too late."

Novalee became rigid. She tilted her head and narrowed her eyes at him.

"What did you say?" she asked slowly, trying to keep the anger she felt building up at bay.

"Neither one of you tried to get out of a volatile situation. You took the shit and abuse as if you deserved it."

"You have no right—"

"I have every right!" he said, sitting up as well. "I admit I don't know everything you went through or how you felt except for what you told me, but I witnessed what it did to my mother, to my family, and I'll never understand why women don't get out after the first time."

Dean reached for her hand, but she jerked it out of his reach. Tears stung her eyes and she tried blinking them away, looking down at her lap.

"Novalee, I'm sorry," he said. "I don't want to upset you it's just . . . I lived through it, too, you know. He hit me, too, when I tried to save her . . . and she just let him get away with it."

She sniffed, wiping her tears. He reached for her hand again, this time grasping her fingers gently before she could pull away.

"Have you ever thought about how Cali felt, finding you like she did?" he asked.

Novalee looked up at him, surprised by the question.

Everyone had been so focused on her after it had happened, trying to help her recover and getting her through the process of charging Dalton, that she never considered how her best friend must have been feeling.

Novalee had seen the pictures that the police had taken as evidence of her broken body and she couldn't imagine finding Cali like that.

"I know how Cali must have felt," Dean said. "I . . . I'm the one that found my mom and sister."

"Dean." Fresh tears spilled down her cheeks when she thought of him discovering what she imagined to be a horrible scene. "I'm so sorry," she whispered.

He stared at their hands locked together and she stared at him. What had really happened? What had he seen that night?

"He didn't actually pull the trigger, but he might as well have because it's his fault they're dead."

Did that mean someone literally pulled the trigger?

There were so many questions Novalee wanted to ask, so many answers she needed to better understand what Dean had gone through, and was still going through. He hadn't pushed her into talking about Dalton, had only asked one or two questions about why she had stayed. She wanted to respect him the way he had her, and wait for him to confide in her in the same way she had felt confiding in him, but how long would that be? How long could she wait to know who this man was?

Before either of them could speak the sharp chirp of a cell phone broke through the silence of the room. Dean looked at her and then down at their hands again before pulling away and reaching over the side of the bed for his jeans. He fished the cell out of his pocket and glanced at the caller I.D. looking annoyed with the caller, and gave Novalee an apologetic look before answering the call.

"Yeah?" he answered sharply.

Novalee shifted her eyes around the room and ran her hands over her bare arms, feeling uncomfortable listening to him while he talked on the phone. She was going to get out of bed and give him some privacy, but he grabbed her hand when she went to leave. She peeked at him and he shook his head, holding up his finger indicating he'd only be a moment.

"How the hell did that happen, Abigail?" he asked, anger filling his voice.

Novalee kept her eyes on the bed, trying not to appear like she was listening, but really what choice did she have when he wouldn't let her leave and she was right there next to him?

Who was Abigail?

"That's less than a week." He paused, listening to the woman on the other end. "What the fuck am I supposed to do now?" he yelled, making Novalee jump s. He squeezed her hand again; a silent apology and she tried to relax. "I've . . . made some progress. It's not that simple anymore."

Okay, now she was more than curious about what was being said on the other end. Whatever this Abigail had done had definitely pissed Dean off.

And he obviously knew her well enough to call her by her first name.

Novalee scowled. It really was none of her business how well he knew this woman.

She tried to ignore the stab of jealousy she felt and focus on something else.

Was he working while he was here? Novalee couldn't remember him mentioning work, but he was doing something in order to make progress on it, and whatever it was had apparently become complicated.

She wondered if he would have to go back to Nevada to fix whatever mess had been made. Maybe it was hotel business. Perhaps Abigail was supposed to be managing things while he was away and had royally screwed up.

The jealousy she felt was nowhere near as close to unsettling as the twinge of sadness she felt when she thought of him leaving.

"Now is not a good time, let me get back to you."

He ended the conversation and hesitantly met her curious gaze.

"Problems?"

"Uh, yeah, you could say that," he said, and ran his hand down the side of his face, smiling weakly at her. "I've got to go."

"Right now? I thought we were talking—"

"We were," he said. Then seemed to regroup. "I mean, we are going to talk, but I've really got to handle this right now."

Novalee shifted her eyes away as he got out of bed and quickly dressed. She pulled the covers around her tighter, suddenly feeling very alone and exposed. She swallowed the lump in her throat and closed her eyes to fight back the tears that once again burned her eyes.

She didn't even acknowledge Dean when the bed dipped and he was sitting beside her again.

"Hey." Dean tucked his finger under her chin and gently lifted her head to face him. "Open your eyes, Novalee."

A childish part of her wanted to ignore him and keep them closed, pull her head away and sulk under the covers. He was leaving her with no explanation other than he had something to take care of this damn second and she was supposed to be okay with that.

But the reasonable, adult part, the part that told her throwing a tantrum complete with screaming and leg-kicking wouldn't look very attractive, made her open her eyes and look at him.

"I really am sorry," he said.

She nodded, afraid if she opened her mouth to say it was okay the childish part might win.

"It isn't the right time, anyway," he added. "You probably have to get to work soon."

Novalee glanced over her shoulder at the clock and sighed. "You're right."

"I want to explain things," he promised. "Can I come by after? Or is that too late?"

"Um . . ."

"Or you can stop by the hotel if you want."

"Can you meet me at the bar?" she asked. "I might be able to sneak out at a reasonable hour. I'll call and let you know."

"Sure." He leaned in, gently pecked her lips, and then stood. "I'll see you later."

Novalee nodded, keeping the small smile on her face until he left the room. She listened until she heard the front door open and close before flopping back on the bed, letting the tears she'd held back roll down the sides of her face.

She had just poured her heart out to him without any hesitation to make him feel like he could trust her the way she trusted him, and he walked out on her. She hadn't really been thinking when she'd started to tell him about Dalton, she just sensed he needed something else to think about, to focus on until he collected his thoughts. She hadn't had any intention at all of telling him about her past. But in that moment Novalee felt so much closer to him. For the first time in two years she had felt like she actually had a husband.

And now, when he should feel as if he could tell her anything and not have her sit in judgment, he ran.

Novalee still couldn't quite wrap her head around the little he had shared with her. If that wasn't reason enough for him to hate his father, she wasn't sure what was. Yet, she knew there was so much more to the hatred Dean felt, and if she was being honest with herself, it scared her to think of how much worse it could get.

Unfortunately, she was left hanging. He had dropped that bomb on her, practically dancing around the subject as best he could to avoid any real answers, and then bolted. Even though she knew there was a logical reason for him leaving, Novalee still couldn't help but feel as if it were just the excuse he'd been waiting for. He may have promised to explain everything, but she also felt a little bitter that this problem had suddenly come up was a convenient way to put some distance between them.

Novalee wiped the tears away, feeling silly to be lying there and crying for no real reason. It had been her decision to open up to Dean; he hadn't asked anything about her past. If he wasn't ready to talk about it, and clearly he wasn't or else he would have just told her and not spoken in circles, there wasn't anything she could do about it except wait.

But how long could she wait when their time together was limited? And if that phone call was any indication, their time together might be even shorter than she thought.

Frustrated now, she got up, wrapped her silk thigh-length robe around herself, and went to the kitchen to start a pot of much-needed coffee. She stared at the machine, watching as it made her own liquid heaven, until Jerry's soft whine reminded her she had other needs to take care of.

Novalee let him out, cleaned the kitty litter, and refilled both food and water dishes before letting him back in and finally grabbing her favorite mug from the cupboard. She clutched the ceramic with both hands, closed her eyes, and inhaled the aroma deeply.

A calm washed over her from the intoxicating scent, but she suddenly felt disappointed she wasn't sharing this first cup with Dean. She should be lying in bed basking in the afterglow of fabulous sex. It had been far too long and she deserved to bask, dammit! Instead she was alone, feeling confused, rejected, and frustrated.

She sighed and took a big gulp of coffee, wincing as it burned her tongue and throat, then opened her eyes and wandered back to her room, wanting nothing more than to crawl back into bed and sleep the day away. For the first time in years, Novalee didn't feel like dealing with work.

She grabbed her cell off the nightstand and shot a quick text to Cali, explaining that she was running late and asking if she would open up for her. Not waiting for a reply, Novalee dropped the phone on her bed and headed for the shower.

She closed her eyes as she lathered the shampoo into her hair, smiling as she thought of Dean. The warm water soothed the aching she felt in her joints, a pleasant reminder of last night and that morning's activities. Novalee's stomach gave a little flip as she thought of her boldness earlier. She had never been overly verbal in the bedroom, and especially wasn't confident enough ever before to say the things she had or do the things she'd done with Dean that morning.

Novalee had been young and naïve when it came to Dalton and sex. What she thought was great sex turned out to be nothing but mediocre compared to what she experienced later. Not that she'd had a whole lot of men to compare notes about. She had only been with two others after she'd started dating again, but it didn't take an experienced woman to know her sex life had been very much lacking with Dalton.

And as good as those other two men had been, and they really had been good, they were nothing compared to Dean. They hadn't made her body ache with everything they had done the way he had with just a single touch of his hand. They hadn't made her body come alive with a simple look like it did for him. The sound of their voices hadn't made her head spin and her stomach flutter like his did.

Novalee rinsed the shampoo out, realizing she was so screwed when it came to how she felt about Dean that she didn't know whether to laugh or cry.

She quickly finished washing, trying to push thoughts of Dean out of her mind for now, and grabbed one of her huge fluffy towels with which to dry herself off. She wrapped the towel around her and tucked the end into the top just under her arm to secure it in place.

Novalee grabbed her phone and shooed Ben off the bed. She ripped off the sheets, throwing them into the laundry basket to wash later when she had more time. Then she replaced them, loving the sweet scent of vanilla that wafted from the fresh sheets when she snapped them in place.

Glancing at the time, she quickly dressed, filled up a large travel mug with the remainder of the coffee, snatched her keys and purse off the coffee table, and rushed out the door. She needed to get there early so she could work around the lack-of-a-cook issue. If she had to she would take over the cooking duty herself. After all, if Dean could do it, so could she.

As she burst into the bar's kitchen, Novalee stopped in her tracks when she saw Tony working his magic at the chopping block.

"Um, hi?" She raised her eyebrows in question, waiting for him to explain why he was back in her kitchen.

"Oh. Hey." He smiled sheepishly at her. "Look, I'm sorry for yesterday. I know it's ballsy to show up today after I quit, but I was hoping you'd forgive me."

Novalee crossed her arms and studied the cook.

"*Forgive* may be pushing it, but I need a cook so I'll overlook it this one time."

"Cool." He smiled and went back to work as Novalee pulled open the door to the back stairs.

"Tony?" He lifted his head. "Don't bring your personal shit to work again. If you want to mess around with Cali, be prepared to deal with the consequences outside of here. Next time you won't have to worry about quitting because you'll be fired."

He nodded. "Got it."

Novalee hurried up the stairs and entered her office to find Cali sprawled out on the couch, waiting.

"Good afternoon?" Cali smirked, glancing at the clock.

Novalee ignored her as she set her purse down on her desk and took a seat. "Do you know why there's a Pony in my kitchen?"

Cali's smirk turned into a frown and she sat up with a sigh.

"Okay. I was feeling bad that you lost a pretty good employee and a little bit of that might have been my fault."

"A little bit?"

"Whatever." Cali rolled her eyes. "So, I went to see him and explained that his leaving left you in a sticky situation, and if he came back I'd . . . gooutonadatewithhim," she stammered in one breath as she glanced around the room.

"You said you'd what?" Novalee asked, leaning forward in her seat.

Cali glared at her. "That I'd go out with him."

"You bargained pity sex for work?"

"No! God no!" Cali said, eyes wide with horror. "I would never survive round two of monster dick. You might as well just order me a wheelchair now for my shattered pelvis."

Novalee laughed. "You're going out on a real date with Tony?"

"Yes. One date, no sex."

"Have you ever done that before? Dated without having sex?" Novalee

"This is where you thank me, Nov."

"Thank you for fixing your own mistake?"

"No, thank me because with Tony back our business is back."

"Hmm." Novalee pretended to ponder and then nodded. "Okay. Since you're taking one for the team, thanks."

"I would say 'no problem, any time', but I wouldn't really mean it." Cali grinned and Novalee knew the subject was about to change. "What happened last night after we left? Is that why you're late today?" She wiggled her eyebrows suggestively and Novalee blushed. "Oh my god, you had sex!"

"I'm not talking about this," Novalee stated, opening her books.

"The hell you aren't!" Cali stormed over to her desk and sat her ass down on the paperwork. "Did you get it on here? His hotel?"

"Cali."

"Novalee, you know I'll ride your ass until you spill, so just do it."

Novalee sighed and glared at her friend.

"My house. Twice," she added, unable to keep the grin from spreading across her face.

"Hot damn! Finally the woman gets some!" Cali hooted. "Is he a ten or closer to a one?"

"Huh?" Novalee looked at Cali blankly.

"Ten as in 'oh my god that won't fit' or one as in 'is it in yet?' "

Novalee rolled her eyes. "Why do I even ask?"

"He's got to be at least an eight," Cali mused.

"It's good. He's good." Novalee corrected quickly. "And that's all you're getting from me."

"But that's nothing!" Cali protested. "We're supposed to share these things."

"You over-share enough for the both of us," Novalee quipped, trying to tug the books out from under Cali's ass.

Cali crossed her arms, refusing to budge.

"Why are you here at work instead of wrapped in sweaty sheets at your place if he's so good, then?"

"He had something to take care of."

"Condom run?"

Novalee glared at her.

"No. Something work-related, I guess."

"He didn't explain?"

"I didn't ask."

"But it was a big enough problem for him to leave post-booty."

"Which is why it must be work related," Novalee said, annoyed. "Speaking of work, isn't there something you should be doing?"

"In a minute." Cali waved the comment away. "If it *is* because of work, and it *is* a major problem, that means he might have to leave."

Novalee's heart dropped to her stomach and that damn lump from before was back. Cali was watching her—too closely. She nodded and shrugged as if the thought hadn't crossed her mind and was no big deal.

"Guess so," she forced herself to say.

"Oh, no." Cali's grin turned into a frown.

"What?"

"This weepy look on your face?" Cali pointed her finger at her. "That's not good, Nov. You had great sex. Why can't you just leave it at that, sign the divorce papers, and move on?"

Novalee shook her head, slumped into her chair, and closed her eyes.

"It was more than great sex, wasn't it?" Cali asked after moment. Novalee nodded. "And now you think . . . what?"

"I don't know," she admitted. Novalee opened her eyes and looked at her best friend. "I told him about Dalton."

Cali was silent for a moment before asking, "Did it help?"

"Help what?" Novalee asked, confused.

"Did it help you to talk to someone that didn't have a biased opinion about what happened?"

Novalee bit her lip and shook her head.

"It wasn't about helping me," she replied. "I didn't intend to tell him anything. It . . . just happened."

"How does something like that just happen?" Cali asked. "It's not exactly normal everyday conversation. 'I like long walks on the beach, lying under the stars, chocolate, and, oh yeah, I spent a year in physical therapy because my ex beat me.' "

Novalee scowled, grabbed her purse, and threw it in the bottom desk drawer, then stood.

"It doesn't matter how it came up, it just did."

"It all matters if it's starting to make you think you're in love with him!" Cali said.

"What?" Novalee exclaimed, dumbfounded. "I never said that!"

"You didn't have to."

"Cali, get real," she scoffed. "He's been here, what, four days?"

"I don't think it just happened," Cali said.

"What the hell are you talking about?"

"You go away and come back totally different; you stop dating and having sex, and all this time you've been hiding that you got married. And now this image that you've been holding onto for the last two years suddenly shows up looking really fine and really hitched to you and gets under your skin so much that you open up to him about the most painful time of your life," Cali ranted.

"What's your point?"

"You wouldn't have told him about what happened if you didn't have feelings for this guy."

The two stood staring at one another until finally Novalee shook her head and looked away.

"I'm not in love with him," she said. "I like him . . . probably more than I should, but I'm not in love with Dean."

"Nov, I just don't want to see you hurt," Cali said gently as she took her hand and gave her a small smile. "It's okay to like him, and it's even okay to want something more with him. I just don't want to see you get attached and have him walk away without so much as a glance back."

"You were the one that told me to get out of my own way and give him a chance!" Novalee accused her, snatching her hand away. "And now that I've done it, you think I'm wrong?"

"No, not wrong. I—"

"You said that it wouldn't be real unless I got real, remember that?"

"Yes."

"So I told him something real because he needed to hear it. And why I did it is really none of your business," Novalee said when Cali opened her mouth. "Yes, I have feelings for Dean. Happy? But I'm *not* in love with him. I appreciate you looking out for me, and I love you like a sister, but there's nothing to worry about."

Cali nodded slowly and said, "Okay."

Novalee let out a long breath and also nodded. "Okay."

She thought that was the end of it, but at the door Cali turned around and said, "I don't believe you for one fucking second, but okay." And then she left.

Novalee fought the urge to hurl the stapler at the closed door and instead dropped back down and closed her eyes to stop the tears of frustration from spilling forth.

The problem was she didn't believe it for one fucking second either.

Novalee hid in her office the rest of the night. She didn't feel like plastering on a fake smile, handing out drinks, and making small talk with her regulars tonight. And she definitely didn't feel like having Cali observe her all night with her know-it-all smug little grin.

Novalee wanted to be alone, to lose herself in the mountain of bookwork that needed her attention in hopes that something would keep her mind off of Dean.

She sat there, pen in hand, staring at the print in front of her for hours until it all became one big blur. She yawned and rubbed her eyes, blinking a couple of times to bring them back into focus.

The noise from downstairs had lessened and she looked at the clock, surprised to see it was almost closing time. She chewed on her lip, debating if she should go down and help with the cleanup, but in the end deciding her employees could make do by themselves for one night. After all, that's what she paid them for, right?

Novalee yawned again as she raised her arms over her head and stretched. She closed her books, wanting nothing more than to curl up and go to sleep. She cast a glance at the couch that could easily be pulled out and made into a decent bed. The idea of just crashing and not having to drive home was very appealing, but she needed to get home to see to her boys.

Another yawn made the decision for her. She was staying put tonight.

She was just grabbing the afghan off the back of the couch when there was a knock on the door and Cali poked her head in. She looked from the knitted blanket to Novalee and raised an eyebrow.

"Just getting up or just going to bed?"

Novalee shrugged. "I don't really feel like driving home tonight."

"I can give you a lift," she offered.

"No. I'm going to stay."

"You okay?"

Novalee forced a tight smile. "I'm fine."

Cali stepped into the room and said, "Look, I'm sorry about earlier. I just don't want—"

"I know," Novalee said, not in the mood to hear about her good intentions again. "It's fine."

"I just want you to know that whatever happens, I'm here for you."

"I know," Novalee said again.

"Okay." Cali turned to leave and looked back once more. "You're sure you're okay?"

"I'm fine."

Cali nodded and was just about to leave when Novalee called to her.

"Could you do me a favor: swing by the house and let Jerry out?"

Cali gave her a small smile and mumbled a quiet, "Sure, no problem," and left without another word, closing the door softly behind her

Novalee kicked off her shoes and pulled her jeans off, but left her t-shirt on for something to sleep in, and slid under the afghan, too tired to even pull the bed out properly. The little throw pillow wasn't much, but it was better than using the couch arm. Her eyes were just drifting closed when there was another soft knock on the door. She glared at it, cursing Cali for not knowing when to just leave things be. She threw the cover off at the second knock and stomped to the door, yanking open.

"I said I was fine!" Dean's furrowed brow met her outburst. "Oh. Sorry, I thought you were Cali."

"She let me in." He held up his phone. "You didn't call, so I figured I'd just stop by."

"Oh." *Shit.* "I got caught up in some work and completely lost track of time," she explained. "I didn't intentionally blow you off."

He nodded.

"It's cool." His eyes roamed down her body, stopping at where the end of her t-shirt met her thigh and slowly traveled back up again. "I can see you're . . . busy?"

She laughed.

"I didn't feel like driving home, so slumber party for one in my office tonight," she joked.

"Just for one?" he asked his voice suddenly low and husky.

Novalee's stomach flipped.

How the hell did this man have that kind of effect on her? Just three little words in that gravelly voice and she was instantly turned on.

Novalee looked him up and down the same way he'd checked her out. She tried not to, but she paused on his crotch, remembering how he'd felt when he'd been inside her.

Dean reached out and rested his hand on her hip, pulling her closer to him. Novalee went willingly, pressing her body into his as she wrapped her arms around his neck and pulled him close, kissing him. He tasted like whiskey, and she wondered if he had nursed a couple of drinks downstairs while waiting for her.

He walked her backwards, slamming the door behind him, until she was pressed against the desk, the sharp edge cutting into the small of her back. Novalee wiggled against him, trying to tell him without having to break the kiss that it wasn't the most comfortable feeling.

Dean slid his hands under her shirt and hooked his fingers under the elastic of her panties, pulling them down and out of the way before lifting her onto the desk. He grasped her thighs and spread her legs apart as he dropped to his knees.

"Lean back on your hands, Novalee," he demanded.

She bit her lip and did as he asked, watching as he brought his face closer to the juncture of her thighs. Novalee cried out as his tongue dove into her and licked up to her clit, circling.

"Dean." She panted, closing her eyes and trying to arch her hips into his mouth.

He grabbed her hips and pulled her closer, lapping at her hungrily. He played with her, teasing her to the edge again and again until finally he sucked at her clit, flicking it quickly as she cried his name.

Dean stood and grabbed her waist and spun her around, grinding his jean-covered cock against her ass. He locked his mouth on her neck, nipping her ear. Novalee closed her eyes and sighed, tilting her head as she steadied herself on her shaky legs.

As his mouth played with her ear, he slipped one hand between her legs and gently teased her again. Novalee shifted her feet to widen her stance, silently asking him for what she wanted. Dean stroked her and Novalee bit her lip to keep from screaming as he slowly dragged his digit through her folds, teasing her entrance.

"Put your hands on the desk," Dean demanded.

Novalee fell forward and braced her hands, the action causing her bottom to press more firmly into his crotch. She rocked her hips, shuddering as he thrust a second finger inside her.

Dean pulled his hands away from her and Novalee heard the snap of his belt and jeans being unzipped and then the heavy material hit the floor as it pooled around his feet. He guided his cock between her legs, sliding it back and forth, coating it with her wetness.

"Dean, please, I need you."

His head rested against her and he held her hips.

"Tell me again," he said.

"I . . . I need you." She gasped, knowing she was voicing more than just sexual urgency.

Inch by agonizing inch, he pushed in until he was finally inside her. Novalee grasped the sides of the desk, her knuckles turning white from her grip as he slowly began to thrust.

Dean dragged his hands up her sides and under her shirt and tweaked her nipples, causing her to shudder and thrust her ass against him harder. He cupped her breasts as he pumped his hips faster.

"I need . . . you . . . too," he grunted with each thrust.

Novalee looked over her shoulder at him, meeting his eyes.

"Show me."

Without another word Dean moved his hands higher until he was gripping her shoulders from the front and increased the speed of his thrusts. He held her in place, her cries of pleasure encouraging him to go faster and harder.

"More! Just like that, Dean, but more." She gasped.

Dean gritted his teeth as he slammed his hips hard and she screamed. He froze, afraid he'd hurt her, and loosened his hold on her shoulders.

"No." She shook her head and looked at him again. "Don't stop. Please don't stop."

He moved his hands from her shoulders and rested them on her hips, holding her gently this time as he pulled out and thrust back into her. She gripped him in a way that made it almost impossible not to want to go harder and he groaned as she rocked her hips.

"Harder," she begged.

Dean pulled out, turned her to face him, and lifted her onto the desk again. Novalee spread her legs and he fit himself between them, rubbing the head of his cock against her until she was trembling from his touch as he sank back into her.

He stilled, just feeling her until she wrapped her legs around him, locking them behind his back. The action caused him to sink even deeper, and they both moaned.

Dean leaned his forehead against hers and Novalee closed her eyes, letting his breath wash over her as he slowly began to thrust again. He hooked his hands behind her knees and lifted them, which angled her better. Novalee rested her hands behind her on the cool surface of the desk to take some of the pressure off her tailbone as he thrust into her, harder now.

"Dean!" she cried out as shudder after shudder wracked her body.

He gave her a crushing kiss as he came with her, groaning his release against her lips.

As their breathing slowed back to normal, Dean gently lifted her off the desk and carried her to the couch. Novalee sighed contently as he threw the afghan on them and wrapped his arms around her, snuggling her close him.

She could barely keep her eyes open but asked, "Did you take care of your problem?"

He exhaled and kissed the top of her head.

"Later. Sleep now."

Even in her sleepy haze, Novalee heard the strain in his voice and wanted to protest and tell him he could talk to her and she'd listen to matter how tired she was.

But her eyes grew heavy and slowly closed on their own, and she fell asleep with her head on his chest, listening to the steady beat of his heart.

Chapter 12

Hours later, Dean was still awake, watching the slow rise and fall of Novalee's chest as he listened to her quiet breathing.

He wasn't surprised when she hadn't called him as she'd said she would. He knew when he'd left her house she was upset, but his only choice was to leave and try and do whatever he could to fix the fuck-ups that had become a normal part of his life recently.

Dean had been in his hotel room all day, making calls to every contact he had, pleading his case to give him a little more time and stick to the original court date. Somehow the bastard had convinced the judge to move up the hearing. From what Abigail had told him, Richard's lawyer claimed if Dean's marriage was genuine he didn't need an entire month to get his affairs in order and get his wife to Nevada.

Judge Benning, who was either tired of the entire ordeal or simply agreed with Charles, moved up the court date by a week, telling both Abigail and Andrew that their client had plenty of time to contact his wife and make arrangements.

"Charles made the motion as soon as our last court appearance was over," Abby had told him earlier that day. "They wanted to catch you off guard and give you as little time as possible to get everything together."

"So you've known about it this whole time?" Dean yelled.

"We've been working on it," she replied, sounding more bored than concerned with his anger level. "There was no point in telling you until we knew for sure what would happen."

"Fucking perfect," Dean spat, filling his glass half-full of Jack.

"You said you've made progress with her." Abby reminded him.

He swallowed the whisky, enjoying the burn, and stared at the almost empty glass.

"I also said it wasn't so simple anymore."

"Maybe if you learned to keep your dick in your pants it would be," she commented.

"Maybe you should do your damn job instead of worrying about my fucking life," he snapped.

"My damn job *is* your fucking life."

Dean took another shot of whisky and dropped the glass on the mini bar. The desire to lock himself away and drink straight from the bottle was strong. He'd been counting on having that extra week to be with Novalee, and now he had five days until he had to appear in court with her by his side or lose everything.

"Is there no way to get out of this?" he asked. "Can't we say she's out of the country or something?"

Abigail snorted. "I'm sure they'd buy that. Why don't we just have her write a note from her mother saying she's ill while we're at it?"

Dean ground his molars together, trying to hold back the harsh words that ate at his tongue.

"You knew going into this what had to be done, Dean."

"I just wish there was a way that she didn't have to be anywhere near this. That we could settle it without involving her," he replied.

"Why? So she wouldn't know about your part in using her?"

"So she wouldn't end up hurt. I can deal with the fallout when she finds out about my part," Dean answered, eyeing the bottle of whisky again.

"You'd better hope you can," Abigail said curtly. "Because if you fall apart, this falls apart, and then you can kiss everything goodbye, including your wife."

He would never admit it to Abby, but as he lay there holding a peacefully sleeping Novalee, he knew he would give up everything in that moment if it meant she wouldn't walk away from him. If Abby knew he would be willing to lose everything, she would be on the next plane to Montana to drag him back home by his balls before he had a chance to fuck everything up. Not to mention the heartbreak it would cause him to see all his grandfather's hard work squandered by his thoughtless father.

Novalee stirred in his arms and groggily looked up at him.

"Hey." Her voice was raspy from the little sleep she'd had.

"Hey." He brushed stray hairs off her face and smiled back at her.

"You can't be comfortable like this."

"Neither can you."

"You'd be surprised how comfortable I am," she answered with a sleepy little grin.

"It works both ways, sweetheart."

She stifled a yawn, looking sheepish as she asked, "Did you sleep at all?"

"A little," he lied. "I'm not all that tired."

Novalee gave him a look as if she didn't believe him and sat up.

"This pulls out, you know. The mattress isn't all that great, but it's got to be better than trying to sleep like this."

"Why don't you let me take you home?" he offered instead. "A few more hours of sleep in your bed has to sound better than pulling out this couch."

"Hmm." She smirked. "Is that your subtle way of getting yourself invited back to my bed?"

Dean grinned. "Darlin', if tonight has shown you anything it should be that I don't need a bed." He chuckled when she gave him an eye roll. "I can always just drop you off and come back later to talk."

She shook her head.

"No, I want you to stay."

Dean gently cupped her face and lightly kissed her lips.

"Get dressed," he said.

Novalee grabbed her neatly folded jeans and slipped them on *sans* panties. He watched her tug the denim slowly up her slim legs, his eyes traveling with her hands until they reached her thighs. His cock stirred when he saw her bare sex and he unconsciously licked his lips as he remembered the taste of her on his tongue.

His private show was over just as quickly as it had started as Novalee snapped her jeans closed and zipped them up. Dean cleared his throat and looked away before she caught him leering.

"I'll just be a second," she said and disappeared into the bathroom.

He stood and grabbed his discarded boxers and pants off the floor, tugging them on while he glared at the door hiding the woman that put him in a constant state of arousal. He was fucking hard over watching her get dressed. Everything about Novalee made his body feel like a teenager again; when everything and anything could be turned into something sexual and arousing. He was past the age where it was acceptable to be walking around with an unruly dick, dammit.

The bathroom door creaked open and Novalee walked out, meeting his tired gaze with one of her own.

"Ready?" he asked, holding out his hand to her.

She removed her purse from the desk and plucked her forgotten underwear off the floor, her cheeks turning a pale pink as she stuffed them into her bag, and nodded.

"Ready." She tucked her into his, locking their fingers together and let him lead her out of the office.

"We can take your car if you don't mind driving me back here later for the rental," he said as she locked up.

"I can drive myself, you know." She turned to face him and gave him a smile. "It's not that far and I'm not so tired that I'll fall asleep on the short drive home."

"I don't mind as long as you don't mind having to put up with me until you come back to work." He grinned and she rolled her eyes.

"The things I have to sacrifice to be chauffeured home," she teased, dropping the keys in his palm.

Novalee laughed at him when he pushed the seat back as far as it would go, but still ended up being cramped in the tiny car.

"Not meant for men with long legs." She giggled.

"I don't think it's meant for men at all," he grumbled, turning the volume down on the country station. Having to suffer through that shit once was enough.

"You don't like my taste in music," she observed as he pulled out of the lot.

"Maybe I just don't want anything to distract me from you." She gave him a don't-bullshit-me look and he chuckled. "No, I'm not a country music fan."

"What do you like then?"

"Something with a little more rock-and-roll. Who wants to constantly listen to songs about their wives leaving them and their dogs getting run over?"

Novalee threw her head back and laughed, "That's not what country music is about."

He smiled at her as he reached for her hand, driving in silence the rest of the way to her house.

Dean was about to cut the engine and leave the car parked in the driveway, but she reached over and hit the button above his head on the sun visor to open the garage door.

"I never leave the car in the drive," she told him, shifting her eyes away when he looked at her questioningly.

"Okay." He pulled into the garage and handed her the keys. "Never?"

She shook her head; digging in her purse for what he assumed was a distraction so she wouldn't have to look at him.

"Hey." He grabbed her hand again and gave her a gentle squeeze. "It's okay to tell me."

She looked at him and bit her lip before glancing out the passenger window.

"I still live in constant fear that he's out there waiting for me," she confessed, the quiver in her voice evident.

Dean clenched his jaw together, hating that he was right on his assumption that she felt just like his mother had all those years ago.

"I know it probably seems silly after all these years—"

"No, don't do that," he said a little too sharply if her startled look was any indication. "Sorry. I just mean don't dismiss how you feel. It's not silly or stupid; you have every reason to feel the way you do."

She turned and looked at him.

"Is it silly or stupid that I feel a lot better with you around?" she asked.

He wanted to tell her yes, it was. That even though he would never physically hurt her, the amount of trust she put in him was wrong, and he hadn't earned it yet. But he wanted to. He desperately wanted her to have every reason to trust him and feel safe with him and have no lies between them.

If he had known two years ago what he knew now, if he had thought for one second that he could actually come to care for the woman he married, there was no way in hell he would have gone through with it. He'd never even considered what would happen if he developed real feelings for her; the possibility had never crossed his mind. Who would have thought he would want a real shot with her? But here he sat wanting exactly that and more.

Fucking idiot.

Dean felt like he was about to lose what could possibly be the best thing to ever happen to him before he even had a chance to have it.

He gently cupped the back of her neck and leaned forward, kissing her.

"There are so many things I want to tell you," he said.

"So tell me," she whispered, resting her forehead against his.

"I'm afraid if I do . . ." His throat felt like it was closing up and he swallowed, trying to free his airway. What he wanted to say was one of the most honest things he could tell her since meeting her, and the words stuck in his throat.

Novalee grasped his wrists, holding onto him as he held her face close to his. He inhaled deeply through his nose, catching the light scent of the perfume she wore.

"I'm afraid if I do," he tried to explain again, his voice hoarse, "it will change the way you feel about me."

Novalee looked at him and sighed, "And I'm afraid if you don't, I won't know if what I feel is real."

Dean let his hands drop away from her face, hating the look of confusion that flashed in her eyes. He wanted to ask her how she felt, but what was the point? It would all change after the truth came out in a few days anyway, so maybe it was better not to fucking know than to be tortured with the knowledge of the truth later. But that didn't change the fact that he had to tell her what he could. He at least owed her that much honesty.

"Let's go inside," he suggested.

He felt her eyes on his back as he got out of the car, and it was only when he was waiting beside the passenger door for her that she did finally get out. She looked up at him but just as quickly looked away again. She unlocked the door, kicking off her shoes inside, and disappeared into the kitchen before he even had a chance to shut the door.

He frowned as he listened to her puttering around in the other room, wondering what he had done to obviously piss her off. He debated going in there, but decided against it and instead waited for her in the living room, giving her space.

Novalee finally came out a few minutes later, carrying a tray of coffee complete with toast, jam, and some fruit. She placed it on the coffee table in front of him and took a step back, looking uneasy.

"I can make you something more if you like, I just thought you might be hungry," she said.

"No, this is great." He smiled at her, hoping she would relax. He picked up his coffee from the tray and took a generous swallow.

She fiddled with the sugar and milk, stirring her coffee more than necessary until she finally looked at him.

"I didn't mean it like an ultimatum," she blurted. "In the car," she added when he gave her a blank look. "I didn't mean either you tell me about yourself or get out."

"I never thought that's what you meant," he said.

"Oh." She bit her lip and looked down at her mug.

Dean set his cup down and patted the space next to him. "Come here."

Novalee glanced up at him and, after placing her coffee next to his on the small table, scooted next to him. He wrapped his arm around her shoulders so her head rested against his chest.

He could feel his heartbeat quicken as he took a deep breath and prepared to tell her his dark secrets.

"My father has a gambling problem," he began and felt her tense against him. "And an alcohol problem, and an anger problem. Basically he's just an all-around fuck-up. But I guess I can't fault him for liking the drink considering I've developed a close friendship with it over the last couple of years."

"Do you have a problem?" Novalee asked.

He hesitated before answering. "I guess that would depend who you asked."

"I'm asking you."

"Then no, I don't think I do." He waited for her to comment further but she remained silent, so he continued. "His gambling is what started the fights between him and my mom. He got so far in debt that my grandfather pretty much cut him off except for an allowance of sorts that he gave him every month. That's when things started getting really bad at home. After a few years he started going to loan sharks and eventually got mixed up with the mob somehow.

"One night I came home late. I played high school football and we had a huge win that night so I was out celebrating with friends. I knew as soon as I pulled into the driveway something was wrong," Dean recalled as images of that night sixteen years ago flashed in his mind. "My mom always left lights on when I was out late and the house was completely dark. And when I went to the door it was . . ." He cleared his throat when his voice broke and Novalee reached for his hand. "The door had been kicked in."

"Dean." Novalee's voice quivered much like his own and she shivered.

"They were looking for Richard," he continued, even though he knew she was telling him he didn't have to. "But he was on another one of his benders and my mom and sister were there alone. I got there too late and I found them . . . I found them . . ." His throat closed and he choked on the words as images flashed through his mind. "There was so much fucking blood," he said, remembering the scene. "The walls . . ." His voice grew louder as he described what would forever be branded into his memory, and he balled is hands into fists. "They had been shot execution-style, and the walls, the fucking walls were covered in blood and brains and they were lying in pools of it! Lying together as if . . . as if they had died holding each other."

Dean felt something wet hit his arm and looked down to see Novalee quietly crying. The sight of her tears, of her looking so vulnerable and sad, made him loosen his fists and take a deep breath as he tried to calm himself.

"The smell," he continued in a softer tone, "of all that blood is something that you never forget. That *I'll* never forgot. I remember sliding to the floor and just staring at them, into their dead eyes. I sat there doing nothing for them until a neighbor found me and called the cops." He sneered. "The goddamn cops wrote it off as a robbery gone wrong, but they were killed as a message to my piece-of-shit father. He's just as responsible for their deaths as the bastards who killed them," he said gruffly.

"I'm so sorry," she whispered after a moment. "I can't even imagine . . . I wish there was something I could do or say to make it better."

He lifted her chin to meet her eyes and brushed the tears from her cheeks.

"You do," he said and then decided to go for broke. "When you told me that you feel a lot better with me around, the feeling is mutual. Novalee, I haven't been able to close my eyes without seeing blood-splattered walls for so many years now. I hate my father for making that the last memory I have of my mother and sister. But on Sunday, for the first time in far too long, I slept without the help of liquor or pills because of you. Because all I could think about was you."

"I think you give me too much credit," she replied.

Dean gave a half-smile and shook his head. "If anyone is getting too much credit, it's what you give me."

"Is that why your grandfather gave everything to you?" she inquired.

Dean roughly dragged his hand down his face and sighed. He knew she would be curious about that, but talking about why his grandfather did what he had was treading dangerous waters, especially since he couldn't tell her everything just yet. But he wanted to explain, and he definitely didn't want to fucking lie to her anymore.

"My grandfather, William, never trusted my father with very much responsibility, especially after he started gambling and drinking. I told you I went to live with him after . . . afterward and he took me under his wing and started showing me the ropes."

"Did you like being his second hand?" she asked.

Dean smiled. "Yeah, I did. I got to travel and people listened to what I had to say as if it was important. Like I was important," he added.

"It sounds like you are."

"I guess." He shrugged off the compliment, not comfortable with the praise when he felt like he didn't deserve it from her. "My father still inherited a large sum of money, but my grandfather knew his worth couldn't be trusted in Richard's hands, so he passed it along to me."

He saw the corners of her mouth turn down and knew there was another question coming before she asked it. "So, how come you're in court over the will, then? Isn't it legal?"

Fucking hell.

"There are some loose ends that Richard feels need to be tied up," Dean explained, thinking quickly. "He's contesting the will, claiming everything isn't authentic."

"Is it?" she asked, looking up at him.

Dean stared down into her blue eyes and slowly nodded. He knew she wouldn't understand just how significant his answer was, but his heart pounded just the same as said, "It feels like it is."

Novalee's eyes dropped to his lips and she asked, "What happens if you lose?"

"Then I've failed my grandfather."

And have lost you for nothing.

Novalee suddenly moved, straddling his lap as she wrapped her arms around his neck.

"Thank you for telling me," she said. "Kind of funny how we're not so different. We both have scars, whether emotional or physical, and they're there and not quite healed for either of us."

Dean slipped his arms around her waist and rested his head on the back of the couch.

"I wish we had different common ground," he said.

Novalee frowned. "It's not the greatest, is it?"

He ran his hands down her thighs and back up again, drawing them up and down her back and across her stomach as she closed her eyes and leaned into his touch. Touching her like this wasn't about sex, but his dick hardened from her squirming in his lap, and he knew it didn't go unnoticed as she ground her hips harder against him.

Dean slid his hands into her hair and pulled her mouth down so he could kiss her. Novalee placed her hands on the side of his face and slowly pulled away.

"You look like you need sleep," she said.

"Is that your subtle way of inviting me back to your bed?"

She rolled her eyes and slipped off his lap, grabbed his hand, and tugged. Dean stood and followed her to the bedroom and took her lead when she dropped to the bed. He didn't realize how dead on his feet he really felt until his head hit the pillow and he closed his eyes.

The aroma of something cooking woke him and he cracked his eyes open, glancing to the opposite side of the bed to see it was empty. The red numbers of the late hour glared at him from the bedside clock and he sat up, shocked he had been asleep so long. He rubbed his eyes, and wandered into the kitchen looking for Novalee.

He found her hunched over the stove, removing something from a large roaster that made his stomach growl. She turned and smiled at him as he rubbed his belly and grinned sheepishly.

"Whatever you're cooking, it's obvious my stomach is already a fan," he joked.

"It's just pot roast."

Dean walked over and leaned against the counter next to her.

"I didn't mean to crash so long," he apologized.

She shrugged. "You were tired; it's not a big deal."

"You're missing work."

She grinned. "I'm the boss; I can miss work if I feel like it. I'm not going in tonight."

"Didn't you sleep?" he asked, brushing her hair away from her face so he could see her better.

"I got a couple of hours. That's not the reason I'm playing hooky." She looked at him. "I'd rather spend time here alone with you right now."

Dean moved behind her, wrapped his arms around her waist, and rested his chin on her shoulder, watching as she worked. The embrace hit him as being extremely intimate. There was something secure about the act, something comfortable and routine about it.

Novalee moved her left hand and Dean's eyes were drawn to her ring finger. Without thinking he reached for her hand and caressed the bare skin, trying to picture what kind of wedding set would suit a woman like Novalee. He may have only known her a handful of days, but he knew she wasn't high-maintenance or flashy. He would be willing to bet anything that drew attention would make her feel uncomfortable and self-conscious.

He circled her finger with his thumb and he heard her breathing hitch as she watched him.

"What . . . what are you doing?" she asked sounding breathless.

Yeah, what the fuck are you doing, Philips? You have a better chance of a unicorn shooting out your ass than picking out an engagement ring.

Dean stopped stroking her finger and dropped her hand. He took a step back and shoved his hands in his pockets.

"Nothing," he said. "Do you, uh, need help with anything?"

Novalee opened her mouth to answer just as his cell rang.

"Perfect fucking timing as always," he said, knowing who it would be without pulling it from his pocket.

"Aren't you going to get that?" Novalee asked.

"No. It's probably just Abigail, anyway," he replied, grabbing the plates she had set out on the counter a little too roughly.

"Oh." Novalee turned back to the stove and Dean chuckled at the slight snit he heard in her tone.

"Abby's my attorney," he told her. And then added, "I feel like I should tell you we did have a . . . thing a few years ago."

He watched as she froze.

"A thing?" she asked softly.

"Before she became my attorney and was working as—elsewhere," he said, not needing to go into Abby's personal life as a dancer. "It didn't last very long, and honestly, it was purely sexual." He regretted the words as soon as he said them. "I mean, it was never anything serious."

She was silent for a moment before asking, "Why do you think I need to know this?"

"I just want you to know that there's nothing to worry about when it comes to me and Abby. It's been over for a long time and now she's just my attorney. We're still friends, but—"

"Dean, it's fine," Novalee said, turning to face him and giving him a small smile.

"Just as long as you know there's nothing to worry about," Dean said.

"Oh," she said. "Well, then you should definitely talk to her. It could be important."

"It's always important when Abby calls," he grumbled, taking the plates to the dining room and setting the table.

He yanked his cell from his pocket before going back into the kitchen and listening to the voicemail she left, rolling his eyes. Of course it was urgent, when wasn't it?

Novalee came in carrying a large serving plate and looked at him curiously.

"Everything okay?" she asked.

He stuffed the phone back in his pocket and sighed, "According to her, no."

"Then maybe you should—"

"No." He gently took the dish from her and set it down. "If I call her back now I'll be sucked into the drama that is my life and won't be able to enjoy this."

"But if it's important—"

"You're important."

Novalee bit her lip and shifted her eyes to the floor.

"Maybe it's about the divorce papers," she said.

Dean felt the invisible knife twist in his gut. He had actually forgotten that was supposed to be his purpose for being here with her. Here he was fucking thinking of *wedding rings*, divorce the farthest thing from his mind, yet it was obvious it was still high on her priority list.

What a fucking idiot he was.

Novalee looked up at him when he didn't say anything and narrowed her eyes at him.

"Have you heard anything about that?"

"I honestly haven't asked," he confessed, sitting down.

Novalee gripped the back of the chair and stared down at him.

"Why?"

He shrugged. "I guess it slipped my mind. We've been a little preoccupied." He winked and expected her to laugh or blush, but instead she suddenly looked offended and pissed off.

"You've stalled the divorce because we're having sex?"

"What?" he said. He would be amused by her accusation if he wasn't so surprised by it.

"Why? So the longer it drags out the more you get some?" She never raised her voice, but her anger was clear.

"Novalee, that's ridiculous," he scoffed. "And even more so I'm insulted you would even think that!"

"What else am I supposed to think?"

"How about that I forgot because I've enjoyed spending time with you? Do you think I would have told you what I did if all I wanted was sex from you?"

Novalee's grip on the chair loosened and she looked away, avoiding his eyes.

"What do you want from me?" she asked.

Dean reached out and grabbed her hand, pulling her forward until she stood in front of him with her knees pressed to his.

"I definitely don't just want sex from you," he answered. "And if that's what you really think then there's no damn way it's going to happen again."

"I don't really think that . . ."

"But?" he pressed.

She glanced at him, and then away again, and shrugged.

"I don't know what to think when it comes to us." She sighed. "It's confusing and complicated and totally fucking crazy."

"So you accuse me of using you for sex?"

"I never said that . . . exactly." She grimaced. "I'm sorry."

"Look—" Dean was cut off by his cell again and groaned. He fought the urge to smash it into a million pieces as he pulled it from his pocket, staring at the little screen as it lit up. "What the fuck could be so damn important?"

"You should get it," Novalee said, backing up.

"What?" he answered harshly.

"It's about fucking time you answer," Abigail barked. "Where the hell have you been?"

"Obviously avoiding your calls. What's so urgent, Abby?"

"You need to get your ass back home now," she demanded. "And when I say now, I mean this fucking second."

Dean's spine stiffened and a chill ran through his body. Abby didn't panic very often, but there was definitely a hint of hysteria in her voice that she was trying awfully hard to conceal.

"What's wrong?" he asked.

"Richard has moved into the penthouse at the hotel."

Dean rolled his eyes, the tension slowly leaving his body. That's what she was so fucking worked up about?

"I don't care," he said. "Let the bastard live there. I'll charge him rent."

"I'm not joking, Dean. He's causing disturbances with the guests, harassing the staff; he's even gotten into a few altercations with the security."

"Drunk?"

"Drunk isn't even the word for what he is right now. I wouldn't be surprised if he's on something else."

"Why isn't he living at his place?" Abigail remained silent and Dean felt the knot tighten in his stomach again. "Abby?"

"I think he's hiding out." She sighed. "When he showed up at the hotel he was in pretty bad shape physically."

"And he's bringing that shit around my hotel and innocent people again," Dean spat, his hands balling into a fist on their own.

"That's why you have to get back here. Now."

He glanced up at Novalee and saw she had moved into the living room. She was on the couch watching him, but far enough away to give him the space he needed.

"I'll call you back."

"No. You'll come home now."

"Have security watch him. If he causes any more problems have him thrown out. I still own the damn place, at least until Monday morning."

"Dean—"

"I'll be there as soon as I can." He promised and ended the call before she could reply.

Dean looked at Novalee from across the room and shook his head, frustration eating at him when he thought of having to leave her.

"So I take it you're leaving," she said, breaking the silence.

"My asshole father is causing a lot of problems. I would have had to go soon anyway, the hearing is on Monday."

She stopped pulling at the invisible strings on the couch cushion and stared at him.

"You mean the court case is this Monday?" He nodded. "Why didn't you tell me?"

He sighed heavily and stood, moving to sit down with her.

"I was going to tonight." He reached for her hand and gave it a gentle squeeze. "It's one of the reasons I didn't want any distractions tonight since it could very well be our last night together."

"And now it is," she concluded.

"Unless you came with me."

Dean's stomach rolled as the words left his mouth. He wanted her to say no just as much as he wanted her to say yes. If she said no then his chances of winning on Monday were shot to hell, but at least she wouldn't be dragged into the whole mess and could be kept in dark about how it all affected her.

If she said yes, his chances of the courts siding with him was in his favor. If she said yes, the chances of him losing her was even greater.

"You want me to come with you?" she asked, surprised.

"Yes."

No.

"Why?"

He swallowed down his guilt as he smiled and poured on the charm.

"Don't you deserve a few days away? What better place than with me in Vegas?"

Novalee laughed. "The last time I was in Vegas I met you, and that's how all this mess started."

"Look at it this way: you already did the drunken wedding, so how much worse can it get?"

"Well, when you think of it that way." Novalee rolled her eyes.

"I understand if you can't just drop everything and leave, but I'd really like it if you could come with him," he lied, the smile still plastered to his face as if he meant it.

She bit her lip and nodded thoughtfully.

"Let me talk to Cali," she said and Dean's heart sank as he nodded. "But first let me warm up that food 'cause it's bound to be cold by now."

He grabbed her hand again as she got up, stopping her from leaving.

"Novalee, I . . ."

All the things he wanted to say stuck in his throat. He wanted to explain things, tell her that he was sorry, and that if he had a choice he would go back and not let any of this happen. But all of that were just words, and words meant nothing if they weren't followed by actions, and really, what could he do?

"Thank you," he said.

"For what?" she asked, confused.

"For everything."

She gave him a small smile before pulling her hand free and he watched as she took the dish back into the kitchen to reheat.

Dean knew he needed her to come with him. As much as he hated it, even though his earlier thoughts had been about being willing to lose everything for her, his loyalty to his grandfather had to come first.

He also knew he was about to lose so much more by her accompanying him to Vegas than he would if she just stayed behind.

Chapter 13

Novalee dropped Dean off at his rental a few hours later, saying she would call him after she had talked to Cali and let him know if she could make it to Vegas. The look he'd given her as he'd driven away was so uncertain that she wondered if he really did want her to come.

She marched into the bar waving at a few regulars, stopping for idle chit-chat with others, as she roamed the crowed in search of Cali, finally spotting her serving a tray full of drinks to a corner booth full of businessmen. Excusing herself from the conversation, Novalee caught Cali on her way by and pulled her aside.

"I need to talk to you," she yelled over the crowed.

"Right now?" Cali pointed around the room. "It's a little busy if you haven't noticed."

"Meet me in my office when you can. It's important."

Two hours later Cali stumbled in, flopping down on the couch with a groan.

"I'm beat," she declared.

"Really? I never would have guessed."

"So what's so important?" Cali yawned.

"I need you to cover for me for a few days."

Cali rolled her head to the side and looked at her through partially open eyes.

"Why? What's wrong?"

"Nothing's wrong. I'm going Nevada with Dean." Novalee bit her lip, waiting for the lecture that was bound to happen.

Cali stared at her for a few moments, eyes wide open now "Friday's my date with Tony," she finally said.

"Tony?"

"Yeah. Your cook. Remember the deal I made?"

Novalee shook her head.

"Yeah, I remember. That's not what I meant. I tell you I'm going away with Dean and the only thing you say is you have a date with Tony?"

"What do you want me to say?" Cali sat up and shrugged. "It's your life, do what you want. If you need me to cover I will, but I won't be here all the time." She grinned. "You don't pay me enough for that."

Novalee frowned. "That's another thing I want to talk to you about."

"Oh God. If you tell me I'm about to take a pay cut after I've agreed to this date I'm going to send Pony Boy after you!"

"No." Novalee chuckled. "I want to talk to you about increasing your pay."

"Increasing my pay?" Cali raised an eyebrow.

"To that of what a partner would make."

"Are you asking me to be co-owner?" Disbelief was in her voice.

"Well, I'm not going to pay you that amount to bartend," Novalee replied with a laugh.

"Why?"

"Why not? You've covered for me enough to know what has to be done."

"But this is your baby! You love this place!"

"It can be *our* baby," Novalee pointed out. "I'm tired of being here all the time. I want some time to just chill and know it's being taken care of properly and not have to worry. You do three days I do three days. It'll give us both a lot more free time, especially if things work out with Tony." Novalee gave her a playful wink and Cali rolled her eyes.

"Please. That's a reason *not* to do it." She pursed her lips. "Does this have anything to do with Dean?"

"Why would it have anything to do with him?" Novalee hedged.

"Maybe so you have time to take more of these little trips?"

"I don't even know what's really going on between me and Dean. I'm not about to plan my life around something that may or may not happen. I'm doing this for me."

"Uh-huh."

Novalee sighed. "Just think about it, okay?"

Cali nodded. "Sure. Okay."

"And you're okay with covering?"

"No problem." Cali grinned wickedly. "Maybe it'll get so busy I'll have to cancel the date."

"Your dreams are pretty small, huh?" Novalee teased.

"You have no idea." Cali titled her head to the side thoughtfully and asked, "Just out of curiosity, how's the divorce coming?"

Novalee shifted her eyes away and shrugged one shoulder.

"I don't know. I guess that will be something we look into when we're away."

"Mm-hmm," Cali said, crossing her arms.

Novalee looked at her. "Mm-hmm what?"

"Has the divorce actually come up in conversation since he arrived or have you been too busy knocking boots to talk about it?"

"We've talked about it." Novalee dug around in her drawer to avoid to eye contact.

A very brief misunderstanding at dinner. But that was talking about it, right?

"Any possibility you'll be coming back home as the ex-Mrs. Philips?" Cali questioned.

"I guess anything is possible." Novalee huffed, slamming the drawer closed.

"Anything is possible but not probable."

"What? That doesn't make any sense."

"It's possible you could come back single, however, it's probably not likely because you really don't want to."

"I'm not even going to ask why you think that because I don't have the energy for your lunatic ideas," Novalee said.

"I don't think it's a lunatic idea at all. And you know I'm right." Cali grinned.

"I know it's possible I can kick your ass and I probably will if you don't get out so I can leave."

"Can you kick it hard enough so I can get out of this date Friday night?"

Novalee laughed as she sent off a quick text to Dean telling him everything was set and she was good to go on Friday. Seconds later her phone buzzed.

Come to the hotel?

Novalee bit her lip as she tapped out her response, hoping he wouldn't find the invite odd.

Check out and come to my place.

His reply was immediate and made Novalee grin.

Be there in fifteen.

"Are you even listening to me?" Cali whined.

"No." Novalee threw her phone in her purse and stood. "I need to get home."

"What's the sudden rush?"

"Dean is checking out and meeting me there."

Cali smirked. "Now you're living together?"

Novalee rolled her eyes and swept her arm toward the door. "Out."

Cali walked with her to her car, stopping for a quick hug before proceeding to hers.

"Be careful," she warned.

"I think all the damage that could possibly be done is done," Novalee commented, brushing off her concern.

Cali looked at her seriously and shook her head. "I wouldn't be so sure."

"What do you mean?"

"I think Dean's great . . . on the surface. And despite what he might have told you about himself just remember there's always more to a person. Sometimes it's not always so great." Cali gave her hand a tight squeeze and walked off.

A chill ran down Novalee's spine as she watched Cali get into her car and drive away. She sat there staring off into the night through her windshield, suddenly unable to shake off the bad feeling she had from her best friend's cautioning.

"Are you a nervous flyer?" Dean asked as they settled into their seats Friday morning.

Novalee shook her head, pulling the seatbelt strap as tight as she could, and took a deep breath, closing her eyes.

Dean chuckled. "Could have fooled me."

Novalee slowly released the trapped air from her lungs and gave him a tight smile.

"I don't like take-off or landing," she said.

"But once you're in the air you're fine?"

"Once we're in the air they sell booze," she stated.

Dean laughed and ran his hand up and down her thigh in a comforting manner.

"It's nine in the morning," he pointed out.

"And your point is?"

He leaned in and lightly kissed her ear and whispered, "My point is, I bet I can distract you better than any overpriced mini bottle of liquor."

Novalee shivered and sighed. "You think you can distract me for five hours?"

"I think I can distract you to the point that you feel exhausted and sleep the rest of the way." He winked. "I know you didn't get very much sleep last night."

"Maybe if someone wasn't such a bed hog, as well as a cover hog, I would have slept better," she teased back.

"I know. We really need to have a talk with Ben." He grinned.

Novalee laughed as her stomach did a silly little flip over the term *we*. She knew it was ridiculous since he was talking about her cat for God's sake, but he'd made it sound like he planned to stick around for a while. As if this trip wouldn't be the last time they were together.

"I'm surprised you don't have a private plane," Novalee commented. "Isn't that one of the perks to being richer than God?"

Dean glared at her. "I do have a private plane. I only use it for business, though. Sometimes it's just easier to fly this way."

"Yeah. Who would want to miss out on airport food and three-hour layovers?" she asked with a roll of her eyes.

Dean chuckled and softly patted her leg. "If you come with me one day, you'll see."

Novalee sat there surprised by what Dean just said, vaguely hearing the flight attendant greet them and begin her flight instructions.

Joking about talking to the cat was one thing, but inviting her to go with him on one of his business trips? That definitely sounded like long-term possibilities.

Or was it an invitation at all? He'd said "if" not "when" and he hadn't actually asked her if she wanted to, only that she would see the difference *if* she did. And even if it was an invitation, he could just mean as friends. They were still going to be friends after the divorce was over and done with, right? He wouldn't just disappear from her life, would he?

Novalee scowled, hating that she didn't know what was going on inside his head, and loathing even more that she didn't have the guts to ask him what was going to happen. She didn't want him to think of herself as needy and clinging if she asked what was going to happen after she went home. She highly doubted he was going to accompany her back to Montana, since he'd only come there to find her and start divorce proceedings, and they could now settle all that while she was in Nevada.

Once her mini-vacation was over, there would be no reason for them to be together. No legal papers hanging over their heads to sign and pronounce them ex-husband and wife. If they continued to see each other it would be because they wanted to, and not because they had to.

But did he want to? Were all those "we" and "ifs" hints that he wanted there to be more between them, or was he just making polite conversation to settle her nerves?

And she'd never know unless she sucked it up and just asked him what the hell he wanted from her. What he wanted for them.

"What's the frown for?" Dean asked, breaking into her thoughts.

"I was just thinking . . ."

"Don't worry. The chance of the plane crashing is very low." His smile brought out his dimples.

"Not about that!" Her frown deepened. "Well, it wasn't about that. Thanks a lot!"

"What then?"

"Nothing. Now all I can think about is having to use the floatation device beneath my seat," she grumbled.

"I don't think we'd crash in water so that's a problem you don't have to worry about."

Novalee swatted his arm as he laughed. "Oh, just shut up!"

The aircraft started its slow ascent and she sucked in a deep breath. Dean reached for her hand and gave it a comforting squeeze, shooting her a smile. After the plane was airborne Novalee relaxed immediately. She settled in her seat more comfortably and gave Dean a genuine smile.

"Better?" he asked.

"Yes. Although I could still go for that drink," she added.

"Ah." Dean rested his hand on her knee and started rubbed with his thumb. "I did promise distractions, didn't I?"

Novalee raised her eyebrows. "I think your distractions would be a little obvious. And there's no way you're going to convince me into that tiny little space they call a bathroom."

"You mean you don't want to join the Mile High Club?"

"Oh, I'm definitely interested in joining," Novalee said, her voice dropping seductively as she ran her hand up his thigh, stopping just before hitting his crotch. She leaned over and whispered into his ear, "But I'm afraid there are just too many prying eyes and not enough room for me to kneel between your legs and suck your cock the way I want to."

Dean's grip on her knee tightened and Novalee sat back with a wink.

"I guess there are pros to that private plane after all," she added, grinning.

"There are also pros to the limo that will be picking us up at the airport," he said in that deep voice that affected her right down to her toes and all the places in between.

He moved his hand higher, until his fingers brushed the seam of her jeans between her legs. He stroked her, lightly at first, and then moved his hand more firmly between her thighs.

She closed her eyes as he cupped her, rubbing his hand slowly up and down as he pressed her jeans against her sensitive skin until she was practically dry humping his hand.

She snapped her eyes open when his hand disappeared and he flashed a mischievous grin as the flight attendant stopped and asked if they needed anything.

Novalee flushed as she shook her head, embarrassed that their little grope could have been witnessed. And yet she as so frustrated and horny that if he asked her to straddle his lap right there in front of all these other people she would have a hard time saying no.

"Limo?" she asked, inquiring about his earlier comment.

"Yes. A limo that has a very spacious back seat and no prying eyes." His eyes twinkled as he asked, "You use peach-scented body wash, don't you?"

Novalee furrowed her brow at the off topic question. "Yes. Why?"

"Did you know when you're aroused, when *I* turn you on, Novalee, that peach scent is even stronger? When my face is buried between your legs and my tongue is teasing your clit that scent is so strong I swear I can almost taste that sweet fruit," he said. "And peaches are my favorite." He nuzzled his lips against her forehead, whispering, "I could eat them all . . ."—along her temple—"day . . ."—and down to her ear—"long."

Novalee's stomach fluttered. His voice alone turned her on in a way that no one else ever had but add the sexy talk and she was a goner. She knew without a doubt she'd be all for a long-distance relationship for the phone sex alone.

"Dean?" she asked, her voice raspy.

"Hmm?" he said as he continued to nip at her skin.

"How much longer until we land?"

His chuckle vibrated against her neck.

"Anxious, are we?"

"You have no idea," she muttered, turning her face so her lips met his.

Five hours and one layover in Seattle later, Novalee held tightly to Dean's hand as he led her through McCarran International to baggage claim. They were met by Dean's driver who, after collecting the bags, quickly whisked them out to the waiting limo.

"We'll be going to the house," Dean instructed the driver as he opened the door for Novalee and quickly urged her inside by patting her ass.

She tried to keep grin from spreading across her face due to his eagerness. Apparently she wasn't the only one who was anxious. She climbed into the luxurious car, spotting the bottle of champagne chilling on ice and couldn't help but roll her eyes at how cliché it all was.

Dean got in beside her, slamming the door at the same time he reached for her.

"The house?" Novalee asked through his frantic kisses.

"My grandfather's house. My house. Whatever. I don't live there anymore, I rarely even go there now," he added as he kissed down her neck.

"Why are we going now, then?"

He groaned and pulled away from her.

"Do you really want to talk about this now?" he practically whined.

Novalee laughed and swung her left leg over, settling into his lap. Dean slid his hands around her and spanned them over her ass, pulling her against him harder.

"I guess it can wait."

She leaned in and traced her tongue along his bottom lip, tasting the coffee he'd had earlier on the plane.

Dean cupped her face, holding her as he took what he wanted, tenderly nipping at the flesh as she tucked her hands between them and unbuckled his belt, snapped open his jeans, and tugged the zipper down. She spread the front open and slipped off his lap so she was kneeling in front of him.

Dean lifted his hips and Novalee pulled his jeans and boxers down.

She wrapped her hand around the base of him, loving how full and hard he felt in her palm. The salty taste of him washed over her tongue as she circled it around the head of his cock, slowly working her tongue, sliding it along the underside of him as she wrapped her lips around him tighter.

Dean groaned as she cupped his sack and gently massaged his balls. His hands fisted in her hair, pulling on the long strands as she sucked more of him into her mouth.

Novalee enjoyed the mild sting she felt at her roots. The sound vibrated through her mouth and over Dean's dick causing him to thrust his hips forward as he hissed.

"Jesus, Novalee," he groaned, placing his hands on either side of her head and carefully pulling her face away. "You have no idea how fucking good that feels, but I want more than just your mouth."

She looked up at him and quietly said, "You can have whatever you want."

Dean's eyes blazed as he reached for the fly on her jeans and roughly tugged it down. He snapped the button and slid his hand inside. Novalee sighed and arched her hips forward as he slipped his fingers beneath the lace of her panties.

"What do you want?" he asked as he dragged his finger through her.

"You." She gasped, rocking her hips as Dean drew his finger up to her clit and teasingly circled it before sliding back down and dipping into her.

He used his thumb to play with her clit, rubbing until she was crying for release.

"Dean, please," she begged.

Dean withdrew his hand and pushed her jeans and panties down her legs, hurriedly ridding her of the clothing. He pulled her up off the limo's floor and positioned her over his lap.

Dean locked eyes with her and in one smooth thrust he was deep inside her. Novalee held onto his shoulders, digging her nails into his skin through his shirt as she bucked her hips and rode him. He cupped the back of her head and pulled her lips down to his, sweeping his tongue along the inside of her mouth.

Dean dropped his hands to her hips, rocking her back and forth faster, needing to take everything she had to give.

Novalee's grip on his shoulders tightened and she kissed him harder. Dean's fingers dug into her ass as he squeezed and released her cheeks over and over again as their movements became almost frantic.

With one last rock of her hips, Novalee found the sweet release that only Dean could bring her to. She cried her pleasure against his lips just as he stiffened beneath her, arching into her body as deep as he could go.

Novalee collapsed on his chest and nestled her face into the crook of his shoulder as Dean wrapped his arms around her waist.

"That's quite the welcome to the state, Mr. Philips," she giggled against his neck.

Dean chuckled, kissing her temple. "Only for you, Mrs. Philips," he said. "Only for you."

Chapter 14

Dean nervously watched Novalee's reaction as they pulled into the circular drive of his house.

He had never brought anyone here before. Abby hadn't even set foot in this place for as long he'd known her. This house was special to Dean and inviting just anyone to explore the treasures that were to be found within its walls didn't feel right.

But having Novalee there with him did.

This was the house his grandfather had raised him in. This was the home that he had given Dean. Behind the gates that bordered the property was Dean's safe place. It was a place that wasn't tainted by his father or bad memories of abused years. It was a home filled with love and security; it was innocent and good.

It was everything he wanted to give his wife.

The limousine came to a stop and the driver quickly got out and opened the door for them. Dean climbed out first, holding his hand out to assist Novalee as she followed him.

"Wow," she said in awe, eyes wide as she took in her surroundings. "Dean, this is . . . amazing."

He shrugged, playing it off as not a big deal when really it was the world to him.

"It's just a house."

Novalee looked at him as if he was crazy.

"My place is just a house. This . . ." She shook her head. "This is incredible."

He took her hand and smiled, pulling her forward. "Wait until you see the rest of it, then."

Dean unlocked the front door and Novalee followed him in to the entry foyer. He couldn't help but feel his pride swell as he watched her looking around, obviously impressed. He glanced around his surroundings, not finding it hard to see it from her point of view.

"I think I'm out of my element," he heard her whisper.

"I think you belong in this element," he replied.

She glanced at him before walking toward the stairs to their immediate left, running her hands over the fine surface of the baby grand piano that was tucked away in the corner beneath the staircase.

"Do you play?" she asked.

"No. That one was strictly for show anyway. The one in here," he said, pointing to the family room to his right, "my grandmother used to play."

Novalee walked over to where he stood and glanced around the room he pointed out. A crystal chandelier hung from the middle of the ceiling, shooting rainbows of light all over the white furniture as the sun shone through the one wall made of patio glass doors.

"You never mentioned your grandmother before," she said, slipping her hand into his.

Dean looked down at their joined hands, comforted by the simple, intimate gesture.

"She passed away when I was ten," he said.

"You told me you don't live here anymore. Why not?"

Dean sighed and turned around, touring her through the other rooms in the house as he explained.

"I came to live here with my grandfather after I left New York. He'd actually only bought the house a year earlier. Until then he was still residing in the house he had lived in with my grandmother. It always felt like a home with him here, now it just feels empty. I have many great memories, but being here by yourself with only the ghosts of the past to keep you company can get pretty lonely."

"So you just stopped coming here altogether?"

Dean shrugged as he led her upstairs. "I haven't really been around much the last few months anyway. It was easier to throw myself into my work than really deal with the loss."

"So you never lived here with anyone? I mean, this isn't where you and your ex-fiancée lived?" she asked, shifting her eyes to one of the paintings on the wall.

Dean stopped walking and grabbed her other hand, forcing her to turn and face him and not avoid him by feigning interest in artwork.

"You are the only woman I've ever brought here, Novalee," he confessed. "You are the only woman I would want to bring here."

Novalee bit her lip and shook her head. "You don't have to say things you think I want to hear, Dean. I get that you had a life before you came looking for me and part of that life might have been in this house with someone else. It's okay if it was, I was just curious."

"The only life I had here was with my grandfather. I'm telling you the truth."

The guilty twist in his gut shot through his abdomen. His truths now would never make up for the lies that he had told. Even if those lies had good intentions behind them and brought both of them to where they stood now, there was never anything he could do or say that could make it right.

Dean dropped one of her hands and guided her farther down the hall. He stopped at a set of closed oak doors.

"I haven't moved into the master bedroom," he said, "so we'll be staying in what was my room."

"Ohhhhh." She drew out the word. "Is it full of playboy centerfolds and model cars?"

Dean laughed. "Not quite. I packed those away years ago." He winked and opened the doors, stepping back to allow her to enter first.

It was pretty plain compared to the rest of the house. He had never seen the need to make it fancy and go all out with decorating. It housed a king-size four-poster bed, dresser, and a loveseat in the sitting area that faced the fireplace. The attached bathroom had all the bells and whistles to make any girl swoon, but it was the view that Dean figured would get Novalee.

He threw open the balcony doors and stepped out, inhaling the air deeply. Novalee came up behind him and he pulled her to his side. The strip was laid out before them, just buildings of all shapes and sizes during the day, but at night it would light up and come alive.

"That's Red Rock Canyon in the distance," said. "It's really quite amazing."

"It is," she agreed.

"Have you been there?" She shook her head. "We'll have to try and get out there if you want. It's only about thirty minutes away."

"I'd like that."

"I hear it's very popular for weddings." He winked and she laughed.

"Damn, guess we missed out. Maybe next time."

"Next time, huh?" He spun her around and pressed her back against the balcony, bracing his arms on either side of her body.

Novalee shrugged one shoulder coyly.

"Not even divorced yet and already talking about next time," he said.

Dean's cell jingled in his pocket and he glanced at the watch on his left wrist.

"Business begins?" Novalee gave him a small smile.

He yanked the phone out and glanced at the text message. Leave it to Abby to bust his balls for not making the hotel his first fucking stop.

"Business begins." He sighed and shoved the phone back in his pocket. "I'll try and make it back fast."

"You're leaving me here?" she asked, surprised.

"Well, I just thought . . . I have all this shit to take care of and—"

"And you don't want me tagging along," Novalee finished, crossing her arms.

"No, it's not that I don't want you with me it's just . . ." *You can't be with me.* "It's business."

"Right. Look, I get that you came back here because of some crisis you have to take care of, but you asked me to come with you, remember? And really I have no idea why you did, because, like you said, it's business and that doesn't concern me."

If only she knew how much it all concerned her.

"I asked you to come because I want you here, but this is just something I have to take care of now." He dragged his hand through his hair, pulling at the roots in frustration. "If you don't want to wait around here that's fine. I'll have the car drop me off and you can take it and do whatever you want to pass the time until I'm done. I didn't mean you had to stay *here*."

"And I didn't mean to make it sound like I wanted you to take me with you, it's just that . . . you're going to be busy and I understand that. I just don't really get why you wanted me to come with you."

"Are you already regretting being here?"

"No!" She wrapped her arms around his waist and shook her head. "I'm glad I'm here with you."

"Okay, how about this? I'll leave the car here and that way if you decide you want to venture out you can. I'll call you when I'm done and we can make plans."

The corner of her mouth turned up into a half-smile and she nodded. Dean placed a soft kiss on her lips, lingered, and slowly pulled away.

"Make yourself at home," he said before hurrying off.

He had just reached the hotel when his cell went off again. He quickly parked before answering with a clipped, "Yes?"

"You'd better tell me you're either on your way or already fucking here," Abby said.

"Here as in Nevada, or here as in the hotel?" he asked, smiling despite the situation he was about to face.

"Don't be a smartass, Dean. Where are you?"

"I'm here."

There was a long pause and then Abby grumbled, "Here as in Nevada, or here as in the hotel?"

Dean laughed. "I'm exactly where you want me to be."

"Meet me in the bar," she instructed and hung up.

Dean found her a few minutes later, impatiently drumming her fingers on the bar as she waited for him.

"Where is he?" he asked, taking a seat next to her.

"Holed up in the penthouse. You see those men over there in the corner?" She flicked her eyes in their direction and Dean took a quick peek. "They've been here since he got here, waiting for him. Different ones come and go, but they never seem to leave."

"Why hasn't security hauled them out?" he asked, checking out the men again.

"They haven't done anything. The bastard knows he's safe up there. The only way in is if you know the security codes. You should be *very* grateful that you have employees who won't turn on you for a quick buck."

"Have they tried that?"

Abby shrugged. "I wouldn't put it past them."

"Maybe I should be grateful that none of the employees know the security codes."

"That too," she agreed.

Dean accepted the drink the bartender put down in front of him, but didn't drink.

"Do you think I should go up there and talk to him?" he asked, staring at the liquor.

"Do you want to?"

Dean rolled his eyes toward her.

"What the fuck do you think?" he snapped.

"I think it's astonishing you haven't polished off that drink yet."

Dean ignored the comment even though he silently agreed with her. A week ago talking about his father would have made him want to reach for an entire fucking bottle, not just a glass. But now the appeal to drown his sorrows in the hard stuff just wasn't there anymore.

"I think I want to meet this woman," Abigail declared. "Thank her for working whatever magic she has to have straightened you out."

"Fuck off, Abby." You make it sound like I was a danger to myself."

"You were." Dean glared at her and she shrugged. "I'm just telling it like it is."

"Well, how about you tell it like it is with some legal advice. Do you think I should go up there and talk to him?"

"There's no reason why you can't talk to him, legally speaking. However, I would advise against it since all it does is bring out the worst in both of you."

"He doesn't have another side. Not anymore."

"If you do go up there, Dean, you have to promise me you won't let your temper get the best of you. The last thing you need right now is an assault charge. In fact, if you do decide to talk to him, I'm coming with you just to be sure."

"I don't need a fucking babysitter!"

"No, you need your lawyer." She glanced at her watched and snapped her eyes back up to his. "Make it quick because we have to meet Andrew in an hour."

"Why?" Dean asked, mindlessly tracing the glass's rim.

"Your *wife* is here, is she not?"

He stopped and looked up to meet her black eyes.

"I can't bring her in. Not yet."

"You're going to have to, Dean," she said with annoyance. "There are things she has to know, questions we have to ask her, so she's prepared for Monday."

"I haven't told her anything yet!"

"What the hell are you waiting for? Your time is running out," she reminded him. "The whole purpose to get her here was to tell her so she'd help you."

"Not the whole purpose," Dean disagreed.

"Oh for Christ sake! You need to take your heart out of this for one fucking second and think with your head. Once this is over then you can proclaim your undying love and devotion and all that other bullshit, but right now I need you thinking straight."

"I am thinking straight!" His raised voice drew curious eyes their way and Dean lowered his voice as he leaned closer to Abby. "For the first time in two years I feel like I'm thinking straight. That's the fucking problem! I can't do a damn thing about it until all this mess goes away."

"And all this mess won't go away until you tell her, Dean." Abigail picked up her briefcase and purse and stood. "I'm tired of playing on this merry-go-round with you. You know what you have to do, so do it. Now, are we going up to speak to your father, or are we going to Andrew?"

Dean sucked in a deep breath, pushed away from the bar before he could change his mind about the alcohol, and stood.

"Upstairs."

Abby looked pissed but made no comment. Instead she turned and walked towards the private elevator that would take them to the top floor.

Dean glanced at the men in the corner and saw they were watching him closely. He should feel like shit that a part of him wanted to go over there and tell them what they wanted to know and hand his father over to them. Whatever they planned to do, the son-of-a-bitch deserved it.

But the other part, the sensible part, knew no matter how much he hated Richard he'd never be able to do it. If his father died from his own stupidity that was one thing, and he wouldn't shed a tear for the bastard. But he wasn't about to intentionally bring harm to the prick either. That would make Dean no better than the man he despised.

He followed Abby to the elevator and they rode up in silence. It wasn't until they were outside the penthouse door that she reminded him again to keep his cool.

"I'm not going to start throwing punches," he assured her.

"Sometimes your verbal attacks are just as bad as the physical ones."

He ignored her, slid his keycard into the door, and opened it.

"Richard?" he called.

"Who's there?"

Dean couldn't help but snicker when he heard the panic he heard in his father's voice. His old man was scared and the same part that wanted to drag him downstairs to the waiting men took sick pleasure in knowing he was.

"It's Dean." He glanced down at the woman to his right and added, "And Abigail."

Richard stumbled out of the bedroom, swaying as he tried to focus on the pair.

"Dean?"

Dean scowled at the sight before him, watching as his father tripped his way over to them. His usually cleaned-shaven father was scruffy as hell, his eyes red from too much booze and not enough sleep. His rumpled and stained clothes looked like they hadn't been changed in weeks, and the smell that was pouring off of him convinced Dean he hadn't seen a shower in just as long.

"Dean," he repeated, slurring, and then sneered up at his son. "What the fuck are you doing in my hotel?"

"Let's be glad it's not your hotel because if it was and you ran it like you run your life, it would be in shambles in a matter of minutes," Dean replied. "I would ask what *you're* doing in *my* hotel, but it's fairly obvious if those goons downstairs are any indication."

"I don't know what you're talking about," Richard said.

"Sure you do. You're hiding out, old man." Dean gave him the same sneer. "Only this time there's no one around to take the bullet for you, is there?"

"Dean," Abby hissed beside him.

"You no good for nothing—" Richard shot to his feet, and then fell over. He caught himself on the couch arm and glared up at Dean.

"You're so fucking pathetic, Richard," Dean said as his father tried to stand to his full height, holding onto the couch as support.

"We'll see who's pathetic come Monday, won't we, son?" Richard nodded, confirming whatever it was that he heard in his own head. "We'll see who's pathetic when I walk away with all of this and you're left with nothing."

"Oh, haven't you heard?" Dean asked, giving him a genuine smile. "When I came back to kick your ass out of here I didn't come back alone."

"Dean," Abby hissed again, warning him.

Richard eyed her before looking back at Dean.

"What the hell does that mean?"

"You know exactly what that means," Dean said, smugness in his tone. "My wife, the one you were so sure didn't exist is, in fact, here."

"I don't believe you!" Richard spat.

Dean shrugged. "I couldn't care less what you believe. You'll see for yourself on Monday."

"What the fuck have you done now?" Richard screamed, taking a step forward. "Who the fuck have you paid off to play this game?"

"That's enough, Dean. Let's go," Abby urged, grabbing his arm and trying to pull him towards the door.

"I'll let you stay here until Monday," Dean said, letting Abby lead him away. "But after that you're out. I don't care what happens to you then."

"It should have been you!" Richard screamed as Dean reached the door. "It should have been you that night! You. Not my girls."

Dean snapped. Turning around, he crossed the room in five strides and grabbed his father by the collar of his shirt as Abby cried for him to stop.

"Don't you dare pretend like you cared about my mother and sister!" Dean said through clenched teeth. "Don't you fucking stand here and call them 'my girls' with fake affection. Don't ever forget who saw the bruises; who witnessed and heard the sickening crack of bones as you broke her!" Dean tightened his grip on Richard's shirt, practically lifting him off the ground. "If anything, I should have found you that night and killed you myself," he seethed.

"That's enough, Dean," Abby said as she carefully touched his arm. "Let him go."

Dean stared into his father's eyes a few seconds longer before relaxing his body and dropping Richard onto the couch.

Abby grabbed his hand and walked backwards, gently tugging him along with her.

Richard laughed bitterly from the couch.

"You're no better than I am, boy. You might like to think you are, but you're not." Richard staggered to his feet. "I don't care what little bitch you got to play your game, it's not going to stop me from getting what's mine."

Abigail pushed Dean out into the hallway and slammed the door in Richard's face before another fight could start. She glared up at him and crossed her arms.

"You promised you weren't going to throw punches."

"I didn't. If I had he wouldn't still be standing," Dean responded.

Abby let her arms fall back to her sides and her face softened.

"I'm sorry he said that."

"It's not a secret he feels that way, Abby."

"You're not like him."

"Then why do I feel like him?" Dean asked. He looked at Abby and he hated the pity he saw in her face. "Can you get Andrew to fax whatever it is that he needs to the house? I just want to go home."

"You mean you just want to go back to Novalee," Abby corrected, following him to the elevator.

"That's what I said. I just want to go home," Dean said.

Abby remained silent until they reached the ground floor and then said, "I wish you hadn't told Richard she was here with you. I can't help but feel you're being a little too cocky and confident when it comes to all this. Don't underestimate him."

"Consider me warned. I'll see you later," he said, anxious to get back to the woman who waited for him.

"Dean," Abby called, and he turned around. "Good luck."

Dean nodded and hurried out of the building to his car, sending a quick text to Novalee telling her he was on his way back.

He found her asleep in his room when he arrived home. As quietly as he could Dean lay down beside her, but she opened her eyes as the bed shifted and she gave him a tired smile.

"Hey."

"Hey." He smiled, liking that they had fallen into somewhat of a routine even if it was just how they greeted each other.

"What time is it?"

"Early still."

Novalee rested her head on his chest and snuggled into his side.

"You weren't gone very long, then."

"No." He ran his fingers through her hair, playing with the strands. "I had a run-in with my father."

"Oh."

"If Abby hadn't been there I probably would have beaten the shit out of him," Dean confessed.

"Are you okay?" Novalee asked, raising her head off his chest and looking at him with concern.

He shrugged as he ran his hand from her hair and down her back. She had changed into shorts and a tank while he was gone and he trailed his fingers along the hem of the shorts, brushing her skin.

"I don't think you would have hurt him," Novalee suddenly said. "That's not the type of person you are."

"You don't know that," he said.

"I know you wouldn't intentionally hurt someone," she argued. "I know that you could never do the things you've told me your father has done."

When he didn't respond she sat up, kneeling beside him on the bed.

"You're a good man, Dean. You're nothing like him," she said as she leaned down and kissed him.

Dean knew he should stop her; tell her all the reasons she was wrong and let her walk away with her dignity. But he also knew his time limit to keep her safe in the world of lies he'd created was growing shorter. He didn't want their last time together to be raw, rushed sex in the back of some car.

Hell, he didn't want any time to be their last time together. But if this was it, if this was the last time he would get to hold her like this, he damn well was going to do it right.

Dean sat up slowly, not wanting to break the kiss, and ran his hands under her shirt, rubbing her stomach, stroking up her spine and back down again, enjoying how soft her skin felt. He softly brushed his fingertips over her chest, tracing the lace of her bra as her nipples hardened from his touch.

Novalee reached for the hem of her shirt and broke away from him just long enough to lift it over her head. Dean trailed his finger over her collarbone between her cleavage and down her stomach. Goosebumps rose on her skin and she shivered.

"I think you're wearing entirely too many clothes," she said, ridding him of his own shirt.

Dean let her pull it off him, crushing her to his body as soon as it was gone. He kissed along her jaw, dipping his tongue between the valley of her breasts, and she inhaled sharply as he ran his hands up her back to her bra clasp, unhooking it.

The cups fell away from her breasts as the straps slipped down her arms. Dean nudged the material out of the way with his nose as he continued to explore her flesh. He flicked her nipple with his tongue. Slowly he circled, drawing it into his mouth and gently scraping his teeth against the tip.

"Dean." Novalee sighed, sliding her hands through his hair and holding his mouth in place.

He lowered her to the bed, kissing his way down her stomach. He snaked his tongue inside her bellybutton and she trembled. As his tongue teased that little cavity he unbuttoned her shorts and slid them down her thighs.

Novalee squirmed beneath him, and as she kicked them off, Dean moved his mouth to her hip. She stilled beneath him and he shook his head.

"I don't want you to be self-conscious of this mark, Novalee," he whispered against her skin. "This isn't something to be ashamed of. It's a war wound, a battle you fought to survive and did. It should remind you of who you *are* and not what happened to you."

"Who do you think I am?" she asked.

Dean crawled back up to lie beside her. Stroking her cheek as he said, "You're a survivor. A fighter. You're a woman who has the knowledge to help others escape the same hell you lived. That's power. Never forget that you're strong, Novalee. And it's because you're strong that you survived."

Novalee blinked away the tears before they had a chance to roll down her cheeks.

"That's who you think I am?" she asked.

"That's who I *know* you are," he corrected.

"And how do you know that?"

"Because I figure we're a lot alike and I ain't no pussy," he declared, breaking the heavy mood and making her laugh.

Upon hearing her laugh, his heart actually hurt. The sound made him smile and he couldn't imagine never hearing it again.

He skimmed his fingers down her sides and over her hip, resting his palm on her thigh. Her sigh told him without words that she liked the way he teased her. That sigh, the little moans she made and the way she cried out his name told him he had learned how to make her body come alive in just the few short days they had been together.

Just as she had learned to map his body and give him a pleasure that no one else had been able to do, the kind of comfort they felt with each other went beyond the bedroom. They fucking knew each other. It wasn't the knowledge of what movies made her cry or what pet peeves pissed him off; it was knowing the deeper part of a person's soul.

Dean knew the darkness of her past just as Novalee knew his. That meant more than anything they would ever learn about each other.

It was because of that knowledge that Dean was positive the way he felt for her wasn't just some infatuation or lust at first sight bullshit. It was real and he wanted it. The only thing that was stopping him from telling her how he felt about her was the truth about everything that he had done.

If he wanted her to believe him about the way he felt, he needed to be honest about his lies first.

"I need to tell you something." His voice came out sounding hoarse and shaky to his own ears, but Novalee must have missed it.

"Can you show me rather than tell me?" she asked, moving his hand from her thigh to between her legs.

"Not this I can't," he groaned.

"Tell me later then," she whispered. "And take those off now."

A stronger man might have said no, but he was weak and Dean did as she asked.

He stripped the little scrap of lace from her body as she worked at getting him out of his jeans. Dean hovered over her as her legs fall open, offering him to take what he wanted. His tongue swept her mouth at the same time he slowly slipped inside her. With every thrust Dean made, Novalee raised her hips to meet him, moaning as he seemed to go even deeper, each time more than the last.

There were no frenzied movements, no begging for more of this or harder of that. Silently they gave each other what they needed. She clung to him as they both climaxed.

Afterward, Dean pulled her close, laying her across his chest as he listened to her breathing slowly go back to normal.

"What did you want to tell me?" she asked, breaking the comfortable silence they had fallen into.

Dean's stomach rolled and he felt sick. It felt wrong to tell her now even though he knew he had to, but it couldn't be here after what they had just shared. He knew it was just an excuse for more time, but he had to get her out of the house, away from this moment so nothing could tarnish it.

"I want to take you out tonight."

Novalee laughed and rolled her head to the side to look at him.

"That's what you had to tell me?"

He forced a tight smile and shrugged.

"Hey, will you take me somewhere?" she asked, suddenly sounding excited.

"That would be the general idea of taking you out," he replied.

Novalee rolled her eyes.

"No, I mean somewhere specific. Will you take me to the casino where we met?"

The request caught him off guard. Of all the places she could ask to go, that wasn't one that had crossed his mind for her to ask.

"Do you remember which one it was?" he asked, dodging the question.

A little frown appeared as she thought.

"Not really. Do you?"

Like it was yesterday.

"No, that night is a little foggy for me too," he lied. "But I can take you to another casino if you want."

She shrugged. "It doesn't matter. I just thought it might be fun to go back there." Her eyes suddenly lit up with another idea. "Will you show me your hotel?"

Fuck!

The last place he wanted to take her was to the one place Richard was. It was a little too dangerous to have her so close to him, even if the chance of him risking his safety by coming out of hiding was low.

"Um, that's where my father is right now," he admitted.

"Oh." Her face fell, but she nodded. "Okay, I get why you don't want to go there."

He watched her fiddle with the sheet, hating to disappoint her. Maybe it wouldn't be such a bad idea to show her what he was fighting for. Maybe if she saw what his grandfather had built she would understand why he had to do whatever he could to hang onto it.

They could be in and out without Richard even knowing they had been there at all. Anyway, Dean doubted he'd be wandering the building while there were men waiting to jump him the second they got the chance.

"Get dressed," he said.

She looked up at him, surprised. "Where are we going?"

"WIP Hotel, Mrs. Philips. You should see what you're giving up. It might change your mind," he teased.

Novalee rolled her eyes. "Change my mind about divorcing you, or not taking half of what you're worth?"

"You tell me."

"I'm not going to change my mind about taking anything of yours, Dean," she said firmly.

"Then I guess I can always hold out hope for the first one."

An hour later they were wandering around the hotel as Dean gave her the grand tour.

"It's amazing," she said, stopping to look into a ballroom. "I can tell your grandfather put a lot of thought and detail into it."

"That he did," Dean agreed.

"What does WIP stand for?" she asked as they made their way back around to the bar.

"William Isaac Philips."

"Clever." She smiled and looped her arm through his as he led her out onto one of the patios.

"Do you want a drink before we go?" he asked, needing a little bit of liquid courage for what he was about to do.

"Sure."

"I'll be right back." He kissed her cheek and left her watching over the pool grounds as he went back to the bar.

He ordered a glass of champagne and a scotch straight up, downing the scotch in two large swallows as soon as it was placed in front of him. He signaled for another to take outside with him and turned to head back to Novalee, but as he reached the patio he stopped dead in his tracks.

Dean's hold on his scotch glass tightened and he fought to keep the panic that was rising inside him at bay. He suddenly felt lightheaded and was sure he had broken out into a sweat. The drink from earlier threatened to come back up as he watched the nightmare in front of him unfold, powerless to stop it.

There, standing with his wife with a sly grin on his face, was his father.

Chapter 15

"What's a beautiful woman like you doing out here all alone?"
Novalee turned to look at the owner of the voice and was struck with
such familiarity that it made her uneasy. She knew she had never met the
man was who standing beside her, but there was something about him that
she recognized.

"I'm waiting for my husband," she answered, taking a small step to the
side so he wasn't so close.

There was something about this man that didn't sit well with her. After
ignoring her instincts for so long when she was younger, she had learned to
trust her gut and go with it, and right now red flags were definitely going
up.

His eyes flickered to her left hand and he pointed to her finger.

"You don't wear a ring. You're not just trying to get rid of me by
claiming to be taken, are you?" He grinned, no doubt thinking he was being
charming when really all he did was make her skin crawl.

Novalee smiled politely, not wanting to make a scene if there was no
need to, and shook her head. "I guess rings just aren't our thing."

He leaned against the patio's brick wall and leered at her.

"How long have you been married?"

Novalee narrowed her eyes at the man and answered with, "Not long."

"I'm sorry," he apologized. "I didn't mean to make you uncomfortable,
Mrs. . . . ?"

She hesitated a minute before answering, "Novalee."

A wicked glint flashed in his eyes and his sleazy grin widened. She
couldn't explain it, but she was suddenly frightened.

"How unusual. You know, that's my daughter-in-law's name."

A cold shiver suddenly ran down Novalee's spine and it felt like a fist was tightening around her heart. Her legs felt weak and she feared they would give out at any second.

"Is that right?" she said, her tongue feeling like it had swollen to twice the normal size.

"Forgive me, Novalee. I'm Richard. Richard Philips."

Novalee stared at him, the familiar feeling she had now making sense. Dean and his father didn't look a lot alike, but there were certain resemblances in their features if you looked closely. Their jaw lines were similar and their eye colors were very close to the same shade, but other than that they were nothing alike.

"I can tell by your speechlessness that my son has told you about me. Don't worry, it can't all be true."

"I highly doubt that," Novalee responded, glancing around looking for Dean.

"I think I'm at the disadvantage here, Novalee," Richard said. "You have all this knowledge about me, as distorted as it might be, and yet you have been a well-kept mystery to all of us for all these years."

Novalee snapped her eyes back to Richard. The cold that had first enveloped her heart now dropped to her stomach.

"All these . . . years?" she asked, the question coming out a whisper.

"Correct me if I'm wrong, but you and Dean just celebrated your two-year anniversary, did you not?" He shrugged, as if the details weren't important anyway. "It would have been nice to know the woman my son married instead of having him keep her away all this time."

Novalee opened her mouth, wanting to say something, but nothing would come out. She shook her head, not understanding what she was being told.

Richard knew about her marriage to Dean. He even knew how long they had been married. If he knew then that meant . . .

Novalee closed her eyes against the wave of nausea that overtook her. She leaned against the patio wall, ready to heave into the rose bushes at any second. Tears of anger and betrayal burned her lids as she tried to keep her composure.

"What the fuck are you doing?" Dean said as he appeared beside her, draping an arm around her shoulders.

She wanted to pull away from his touch, but her legs were barely keeping her standing as it was and she was afraid any sudden movement would land her on her ass.

"I'm just getting acquainted with your wife," Richard answered gleefully. "It seems I've said something to upset her."

"Get out," Dean snarled, taking a step away toward him. "Get the fuck out of my sight!"

"I do hope she'll be all right. It would be a shame if she couldn't appear in court for you on Monday."

Novalee heard him walk away and Dean was by her side again,

leaning over to see her face.

"Novalee?" He touched the small of her back, only this time she jerked away.

"Don't touch me," she rasped, the emotion she felt closing her throat.

"Novalee, please." His voice was quiet when he said, "You have to listen to me. I need to explain."

She pushed away from the wall and glared at him.

"So it's true? You've been lying to me this entire time. When you walked into my office and claimed to have just found out you knew the whole time!"

Dean swallowed, slowly nodding.

"I'm sorry."

"Everything you've told me, everything that I believed from you was a lie. Every fucking thing, Dean! You knew; you knew, and you made me think you were the innocent victim in all of this!"

He reached for her, but she stepped away, brushing his attempt away.

"I wanted to tell you," he said. "I wanted to, but—"

"No. If you wanted to then you would have," she accused.

"I couldn't, not right away. I brought you here tonight to tell you everything," he said.

"You didn't want to bring me here tonight," she reminded him. "I was the one that asked, so don't give me that bullshit."

"It's not!"

"So what's the truth?" She crossed her arms and cocked her hip to the side. "What the hell is really going on because apparently I'm the only one who doesn't know?"

"Let me take you home and we'll talk about it," he suggested.

"No. I'm not going anywhere with you. You had your chance to tell me back there. You'll tell me here and now."

Dean ran his hand down the side of his face and sighed, "Please, Novalee, come back to the house and we'll talk there. If you want to leave after that . . . I won't stop you."

"Afraid to make a scene?" she seethed. "You planned to tell me here anyway, right? What the fuck's stopping you now?"

"I just . . . I'm sorry. Please," he rambled. "We'll have more privacy at the house."

Novalee finally nodded and Dean exhaled a relieved breath. He reached for her hand, but she pulled away, stepping out of his reach. The ache in her chest grew when she saw the rejected look on his face and she had to turn away to keep him from seeing the tears that threatened to spill down her cheeks.

She refused to cry in front of him. She refused to give him that power over her, to let him see how much he had truly hurt her. She wasn't going to give him the satisfaction of knowing she cared so much for him that he had just broken her heart into more pieces than she ever thought possible

"I didn't want you to find out his way," Dean said.

"I don't know anything yet." She hated that her voice trembled, that the sobs were so close to breaking through the surface.

"Will you at least look at me?" he pleaded.

"I can't. Please, just take me back to the house." She walked past him, keeping her head down as she left the patio.

Dean walked besides her, making sure to keep some space between them. He opened the car door for her, brushing her back as she got in and the slight touch made her want to break down and cry right there. She knew she would never feel that touch from him again after tonight, and she hadn't realized until that moment just how much she had come to need it.

Dean got in and quickly exited the parking lot as Novalee sat staring out the passenger window, losing the battle with her emotions as silent tears rolled down her cheeks and dripped off her chin.

"I never meant to hurt you," Dean said.

"I wish I could believe you."

"You think I wanted all this to happen?"

"I don't know," she whispered. "I guess I won't know until you tell me what's really going on."

Dean pulled into the driveway and parked in front of the house. Novalee bolted from the car as soon as it stopped, needing more space than the tiny confinement the vehicle allowed. Dean was right behind her, unlocking the door and ushering her inside.

As soon as the door closed behind him, Novalee turned and demanded answers.

"You got me here, now tell me."

"Will you sit?" he asked, nodding toward the family room.

"I'd rather stand." She swallowed over the lump in her throat, forcing herself to stay calm and not have the emotional breakdown she wanted to. "Tell me the truth, Dean."

He walked past her and into the room, stopping at the bar to pour himself a drink. With his back to her he confessed, "I've known about our marriage since it happened. I remember everything about that night."

Novalee forced herself to move and stand in the room with him.

"I don't understand," she said weakly. "If you knew, why did you come to my office that day and pretend like you had no idea? Why would you lie about it?"

"I had my reasons."

"Which were?" Her heart hammered in her chest as she asked the question, dreading the answer but needing to hear it.

"I told you why my grandfather didn't want my father to inherit anything. Remember?" Novalee nodded even though his back was still to her. "Needless to say my father wasn't happy about that, so he requested that my grandfather put a stipulation in the will."

"What kind of stipulation?"

Dean turned to face her as he said, "I had to be married."

Novalee furrowed her brow and shook her head. "Okay, but you were going to be married, right? I mean, you were engaged—"

"I was never engaged. There was no fiancée, no other woman," Dean admitted. "I just needed an excuse to see you, a reason why I was suddenly showing up after all this time."

Novalee stood there speechless for a second as what he said sunk in.

"You were never engaged," Novalee recited. The knowledge of that shouldn't have mattered to her, but it did. Somewhere, buried deep beneath the hurt and anger, it mattered to her that he hadn't planned to tie himself to another woman.

And she hated that it did.

"No. I haven't been with any other women since we were married. I didn't want anyone else."

And she most definitely hated how much that delighted her.

"What does all this have to do with me?" she asked, trying to ignore the way she felt.

"The night we met, my grandfather had a heart attack. They didn't know if he was going to make it and . . ." He paused, looking at her with what was clearly regret. "I wasn't married."

"Oh my god," Novalee said, dropping her hand to her stomach as if that would stop it from rolling as she pieced some of it together. "You . . . you married me . . . you used me to get . . . ," she stammered.

"I didn't use you," he disagreed quickly.

"What would you call it?"

"I didn't take anything from you, Novalee. I didn't want anything from you. I just needed someone to help me."

"To help you?" She laughed mockingly. "If you need help you ask for it, you don't trick someone into marrying you!"

"I was desperate! Don't you see? Can't you understand why I did what I did?" he begged.

"So you just decide to get the random woman you're having a conversation with drunk and drag her to the altar?"

"It wasn't like that. You knew what you were doing."

"How the hell could I know what I was doing when I don't even fucking remember doing it!"

"You knew. I swear to you that you knew . . . sort of."

Novalee snorted. "Sort of? That makes me feel so much better."

"When we were talking you were drinking. You weren't drunk, but you were definitely feeling it." He smiled, but it quickly left his face when she glared at him. "After a couple of hours of flirtatious conversation and some casino games, you told me that it was the first time in a long time that you'd let loose, and you wanted to do something crazy and out of character."

"I never would have married you despite how crazy I wanted to be," she contradicted.

"Not a legal marriage, no, but you agreed to a phony one," he informed her.

She stared at him as if he was speaking a foreign language. "What?"

"There's a chapel on the strip that does both real and fake weddings," he revealed.

"Fake weddings?"

"Yeah, like gag weddings. Just something fun you can do to freak out your family or friends. You know, look-what-I-did-in-Vegas type shit."

"Oh my god." Novalee slumped to the couch and dropped her head in her hands.

"I convinced you it would be something fun to do. No harm could come from it, and you agreed. So we did it. Only I got the real package and you were a little too inebriated to notice."

"Oh my god," Novalee repeated, taking a deep breath as the panic started to rise again.

"We had a few more drinks afterwards in celebration and went up to the room," Dean finished.

Novalee's head snapped up and she felt sick.

"I remember waking up in that room. We . . . how could you . . ." Novalee shook her head, swallowing the bile that rose in her throat. "It takes a special kind of twisted bastard to trick someone into what they think is a phony marriage, but then to have sex—"

"No!" Dean said, taking a step towards her. "Fuck, Novalee, never! I promise you, if you ever believe anything I say to you, believe that we never had sex that night."

"But . . . but I woke up naked!"

"You wanted to. You tore off your clothes before I could stop you, but you passed out right after that."

"Why the hell should I believe you?"

"What I did was wrong and you have no idea how sorry I am for that, but I swear I never would take advantage of you, or anyone else, if they were that drunk."

She shook her head as tears burned her eyes again and she looked away. She did believe him. She hated him for what he was telling her, but she believed him nonetheless.

"Why didn't you have the marriage annulled when your grandfather recovered?" she asked.

Dean sat beside her but didn't reach for her, and she was grateful.

"He wasn't the same. He needed someone to take over and I could only be power of attorney with that simple, complicated paper I handed over. I couldn't have our marriage dissolved and then it went on too fucking long, and six months ago when he passed away Richard contested the will and we've been in court ever since. I needed for us to stay married until all this shit was over with."

"And then what was the plan?" Novalee asked bitterly. "You'd mail me divorce papers and set yourself free?"

"Yes," he admitted.

Novalee looked at him, too surprised to say anything.

"But then the judge wanted physical proof that we were married since no one had ever met you," he added.

"So you had to come find me," she concluded. Dean nodded. "That's what your father meant by me being in court for you on Monday."

Dean drew in a deep breath and nodded again. "If you don't show up, Richard wins."

"So it all comes down to me." Dean remained silent. "Either I help you or you lose it all." Novalee looked at him coldly. "Why the hell should I help you?"

"You shouldn't," he said. "I don't expect you to."

"No, you don't fucking get to do that!" she yelled, jumping up from the couch. "You don't get to sit there and act all noble and tell me I can just walk away from all this and you'll be fine with it. You don't get to make me feel sorry for you and make me think I was right to believe you're a decent guy!"

"What the hell do you want me to say?" he said. "I fucked up. I married some woman I didn't give a damn about until I got to know her and now she's the best thing I could ask for to be in my life and I've fucked it up with all of this bullshit!"

Novalee dug her teeth into her bottom lip as she fought the urge to cover her ears and scream at him to shut up. The last thing she wanted was to hear this now. It just made the hurt she felt that much more painful.

"What do you expect me to do? Beg you to help me? Ask you to forgive and forget and move on from this mess? I'm not going to do that, Novalee. I would do anything to take it back, but I can't. The only thing I *can* do is act all noble, as you put it, and give you a way out."

"That's not a way out," she snapped. "That's a guilt trip."

"It's not meant to be."

"You sit there and spew this shit about me being the best thing in your life and yet all I am is a pawn in this game with your father! I'm nothing more than the winning piece."

"You're so much more than that."

"You can't expect me to believe anything you say," she said. "Your words don't mean anything anymore."

"Do you want me to prove it?" Dean stood. "I'll call Abby right now and have her bring the damn divorce papers over and sign them right here and now and you can walk away. If that will prove to you that I'm sorry about how this all turned out, I'll do it in a heartbeat. If losing everything to the one person I hate the most in this world will prove to you that you're not just a means to an end, I'll do it with no regrets."

"You'd be doing it for no reason," Novalee said hoarsely. "It wouldn't mean a thing to me because I don't want anything from you. I don't want any grand gestures or declarations of affection. It means nothing now."

"Novalee—"

"I've been honest with you from the start and I thought you were doing the same. Turns out you had a whole hidden agenda for getting to know me, for being with me. Hell, for even sleeping with me."

"No." Dean gently grabbed her arm before she had a chance to pull away. "I didn't sleep with you because of this. What we shared was real. That was us. Why do you think I was so fucking hesitant to have anything happen between us? I never wanted you to think I was with you intimately so you'd help me."

Novalee looked down, biting her lip as she let the tears fall freely down her face, not caring if he saw them now.

"There is no 'us'," she whispered. "There never was. There can't be when everything was built on lies and deception."

"Not everything I told you was a lie. My life, my family, and the way I feel about you is all true." He gently pulled her into his arms and held her as she sobbed against his chest, soaking the front of his shirt with her tears.

She grabbed his shirt, balling her hands into fists and holding on tightly as the sobs rocked her body.

"I knew this was going to happen when I told you," he whispered against her temple. "I knew you'd be angry and hurt and you have every right to be."

Novalee stayed in his arms, letting him hold her. He murmured apologies and promises as he stroked her hair and placed soft kisses on the top of her head, the strong steady beat of his heart drowning out his voice and making it no more than a hum.

His heart was still whole. It heart still beat every beat. It hadn't just been broken, causing him more agony than any physical pain could.

And while her heart still beat, she felt like it had been ripped from her chest.

"I never meant to hurt you like this, Novalee."

"But you did." She sniffed. "And I swore that I would never let another man hurt me again." She finally pulled out of his arms and wiped the tears from her cheeks.

"What I did and what *he* did . . . it's not the same," Dean pleaded.

"No. It's worse." Novalee sucked in a deep breath and looked Dean in the eye. "This hurts so much more than anything Dalton ever did to me. I hope all this is worth it when you're left with nothing but the knowledge that you're capable of causing more pain than someone who beat me and left me to die."

Dean's face paled as he took a step back, his mouth open, yet silent. She meant every word she said, but the devastated look on his face still tore at her heart and she had to look away, fleeing the room and hurrying upstairs to grab her belongings.

As she was carelessly throwing her things into her suitcase, her eyes fell on the bed where only hours before she had been ready to confess her feelings for him. Dean had made her feel like she had so much worth when he'd spoken of what he saw in the scar on her hip. For the first time ever she didn't see it as a disfigurement. She saw what he told her it was—a testament to her inner strength.

Novalee might have put up with the abuse for far longer than another woman might have, and she still fought to deal with the fear from that day, but she hadn't let it defeat her. She got up every day and faced the day, fear and all, and moved forward. She didn't wallow in self-pity or let it define who she was. She'd picked up the pieces of her shattered life and moved on. That was strength.

And Dean had made her understand that with just a few simple words. He had helped her see how far she had come and what she was capable of when it came to dealing with her past.

It was ironic that the man who made her feel whole again was the same man who just shattered her into a million pieces.

Novalee angrily wiped her tears away and grabbed her luggage. She expected to find Dean waiting for her downstairs, but only his driver stood at the front door.

"Mrs. Philips—"

"Jensen," Novalee snapped at the man. "It's Ms. Jensen, or Novalee or anything but *Mrs. Philips*."

"Forgive me, Ms. Jensen." He quickly snatched up her bag. "I have the car out front whenever you're ready," he informed her.

Novalee narrowed her eyes at him.

"I never called you."

"No, Mr. Philips did. He told me to take you wherever you needed to go."

Novalee ground her teeth together. It occurred to her to tell him to shove the car up his ass and she'd rather walk then accept any help from his son-of-a-bitch employer. She should call a taxi, but the idea of waiting around any longer than she had to and risk seeing Dean again held less appeal than taking his damn car.

"I need to go home," she said. "Can you do that?"

"To the airport, then, ma'am?" he asked.

Novalee nodded and followed him out to the waiting car. She was just about to get in when a thought crossed her mind and made her pause.

"Do you know Dean's attorney? Abigail . . . whatever?" she asked with a flip of her hand.

"Ms. Knight?" He nodded.

"Do you know how I can get in touch with her?"

He hesitated, before nodding again.

"I have her numbers in case of an emergency."

"Well this is an emergency. I need those numbers," she demanded and got into the back of the car.

There was one thing she had to take care of before heading back to Montana. She wasn't about to leave the state again still being Mrs. Dean Philips, and she sure as hell didn't trust Dean to take care of it. And as much as she didn't trust anyone that worked for him either, especially when it came to legal matters since it was obvious they were all in on his little plot, she knew this Abigail would have what she needed.

"Do you still want to go to the airport, ma'am?" the driver asked.

"No, to a hotel, please. I don't care which; the first one you see will be fine," she said.

"Mr. Philips's hotel, perhaps?"

"No!" Novalee glared at him. How could he possibly think she would want to go there? "Anywhere but there."

He closed the door and Novalee leaned her head back against the leather seat, fighting hard to control the sobs that wanted to take over her again. Crying wasn't going to do a damn thing to help the situation. The only thing she could do now that would make a difference was get her hands on those divorce papers and have them filed as soon as possible.

Sadly, she knew it wouldn't do one bit of good to help lessen the hurt and betrayal she felt, but the sooner she was no longer married to the pompous ass was one step closer to putting this whole mess behind her.

Novalee snorted. Even she wasn't so naïve to believe that this was something she could just forget and move on from.

She jumped when the car door opened a few minutes later. She had been so caught up in her own thoughts that she hadn't realized the driver had stopped in front of the hotel that would be her home for the night. She looked up at the building, not caring which one it was as long as it wasn't *his*, before getting out of the sleek car.

The chauffer handed her a business card, explaining it was Abby's and her cell was written on the back since the office would be closed at this hour.

Novalee took the card, brushing off his assistance when he went to grab her bag, and thanked him.

After checking in she grabbed her cell and immediately called the number of the person she needed more than anything right that second.

After three rings she was greeted with, "All is fine. The building still stands and I haven't run off with any of your secret stash yet."

Novalee smiled as the ball in the pit of her stomach stopped rolling for a minute when she heard of her best friend's voice.

"How do you know I have a secret stash?" Novalee asked, trying to keep the mood light, but her trembling voice gave her away and Cali suddenly went serious.

"What's wrong? And don't give me no bullshit nothing answer," she warned. "Something's up."

Novalee opened her mouth to deny it, but the only sound that came out was a sob.

"Oh, honey." Cali tried to soothe her. "What did he do?"

Through the tears and cries, Novalee broke and told Cali everything. She wept her way from beginning to end as Cali stayed quiet until she finished.

"I'm going to cut off his balls and use them as pom-poms as I dance and cheer around his mangled body," Cali seethed.

Novalee half-laughed as she wiped her cheeks with her hoodie sleeve and slumped back against the pillows on the bed.

"I don't know what to do, Cali." She sighed.

"Yes, you do. You divorce the fucker and take him for all he's worth."

Novalee frowned. "I can't do that. I don't *want* to do that."

"You should," was Cali's response. "He'd deserve it."

"I just want to come home and forget about it all."

"That's not likely."

"I know." Novalee closed her eyes, wincing at how tender her puffy eyes felt from all the crying she'd done.

"Nov, I hate to even ask because I'm going to be pissed if your answer is yes, but are you planning to help him on Monday?"

Novalee stayed quiet, biting her lip as she pondered the question. Her heart and her head were pulling her in two different directions. She knew she should get on the first plane out of there, papers in hand, and never look back. But her heart, her damn heart that ached from what he did to her, still felt for Dean and broke for everything that he'd told her and didn't want to walk away and let him lose to his father.

"Novalee." Cali sighed. "How can you even consider helping him now?"

"You don't know what he's lived through."

"I don't care what he's lived through. I care about what he's putting *you* through. How the hell can you defend him now?"

"I'm not defending him, Cali. I just . . . despite what he's done, I know what he's told me and I can't forget that."

"How do you know it's the truth?" Cali questioned. "How do you know this sad sob story he's told you is really true? He's lied to you since the second he met you, why would you give him the benefit of the doubt now?"

"I believe him when it comes to this."

"Just like you believed him when he told you he just found out you two were married?"

"I didn't call you for a lecture, Cali, or for you to question my intelligence," Novalee snapped. "And if I recall, *you* were the one that told me he was a good guy."

"Well, what the hell do I know?"

Novalee sighed and shook her head.

"I don't know what to do," she repeated.

Jennifer Schmidt

"I'm not trying to lecture you, and I'm definitely not questioning your intelligence, I'm just trying to look out for you."

"Because obviously I can't look out for myself."

"I didn't say that."

"You didn't have to. It's pretty clear from the crappy choices I make." She took a deep breath. "How did the date go?" she asked, needing to focus on something else.

"Oh. Um . . . it was good." Cali hedged. "But this is more important than some date."

"Oh, no. You don't get away that easy. It was *good*? Not awful and complete torment but good?"

"Yeah. You know, it was fine."

"Cali?" Novalee couldn't help the little grin that spread across her face.

"What?" And that tone meant Cali knew it.

"Did you actually have *fun* with Tony?"

"He's not that bad when he's not trying to split me in half," Cali said defensively. "I think the problem is no one can get past the rabbit speed long enough to really get to know him."

Novalee laughed so hard tears were burning her already cried-out eyes again.

"Fine, laugh at my misfortune," Cali grumbled. "But I'm telling you, he's not a bad guy."

"Where have I heard that before?" Novalee said, her voice in mock wonder, not having to see Cali to know the question had just earned her an eye roll.

"Maybe I can groom him," Cali thought out loud.

"Please tell me that doesn't mean what I think it does."

"Think about it. He has what it takes to interest a woman intellectually, and he definitely has what it takes to please them sexually, *if* he wasn't in such a rush to prove it."

"I don't want to hear this." Novalee groaned. "He works for me."

"Works for us," Cali corrected.

Novalee smiled. "So you're agreeing to be partners?"

"I think it's something we should talk about when you get home."

"Hmm . . . I can't believe Tony is interesting enough to hold your attention."

Cali laughed. "I know, right? Who would have thought?"

"You and Pony Boy, a couple? That's not something I ever expected, no."

"One date a couple does not make," Cali said quickly.

"Well, just don't get drunk and wake up married to the guy," Novalee said dryly.

"Damn. That's number one on my bucket list." Cali paused. "You know what you have to do, right?"

"I know."

"Call me with your flight info and I'll pick you up at the airport."

"You don't have to."

"Yes, I do. You might decide to marry the cabbie on the way home to keep him from being deported," she teased.

Novalee rolled her eyes. "Go to hell."

Cali laughed. "I'll see you soon. Love you."

Novalee sighed. "Me, too," she said, and ended the call.

She sat on the bed, staring at the rectangular piece of paper she had been given, the numbers glaring back at her.

With shaky hands and a heavy heart she punched in the numbers of Abigail Knight's cell phone.

"Abigail Knight," a clipped voice answered.

"Ms. Knight?" Novalee swallowed, coating her dry throat. Her heart pounded in her chest as she thought about what she was about to do, and she feared she wouldn't be able to hold a conversation with this woman without bursting into tears again.

"Can I help you?" She sounded both curious and annoyed about being disturbed so late at night, and Novalee suddenly wished she had waited until morning.

"My name is Novalee Jensen. I'm your . . . I'm Dean's . . . wife." The last word came out almost in a whisper as she struggled to get it out.

There was a thirty second moment of silence and then Abigail said, "I've been expecting your call. I assume Dean has filled you in on everything."

Novalee was surprised by how direct the woman was. For all she knew Novalee had come across her number and decided to call her regarding the divorce proceedings, not having a clue about Dean's lies.

Unless Dean had called her and told her what happened.

"I'm sorry for calling so late. I probably should have waited until morning—"

"We don't exactly have a lot of time on our hands," Abigail said, interrupting her. "It's good you called tonight. The more time we have to prep you, the better."

"Prep me?"

"Yes. For Monday." The attorney spoke slowly as if she was worried Novalee couldn't keep up. "We need to make sure that your and Dean's stories are the same. There's information you need and matters we need to go over."

A wave of anger washed over Novalee over Abigail's nerve to just assume that she would be taking the stand for Dean. The woman hadn't even *asked* her how she felt about the situation or what *she* planned to do. It was as if her decision had been made for her and she had no say whatsoever.

"I'm afraid there's been a misunderstanding," Novalee said coldly. "I only called you for the divorce papers."

Another pause on Abigail's end, and then she said, "I don't understand. Are you saying you have no intention of helping your husband?"

Novalee's laugh was just as cold as her words. "My husband? If by that you mean the son-of-a-bitch who lied and tricked me into a fake marriage, then no, I don't think I have any intention of helping him."

"You do understand what he stands to lose if you don't, right?" she asked, the hardness gone from her voice.

"I don't care." Her stomach rolled at lie. "Would you care, Ms. Knight, if you were in my situation? Or would you be so pissed and upset that you would just want out as fast as you could?"

"I understand what he did was wrong," Abigail responded instead of answering the question. "*He* knows it was wrong. Novalee, I'm not just his attorney but his best friend as well. And no one can tell you as well as I can just how sick this whole thing has made him."

"Now I'm supposed to have sympathy for him?"

"I believe you do, yes."

"Why do you think that?" Novalee asked, wanting the question to sound like she was asking out of boredom rather than out of the interest she had for the other woman's thoughts.

"Because he told you what happened to him. He told you what he's lived through, what he dealt with, and what he still deals with. Despite the lies about how you were married, you know everything else he's said is the truth."

Novalee blinked away the tears that threatened to betray her. "I am sorry for everything he's lost."

"And yet you're going to walk away and let him lose all he has left."

"How can I help him now, after what he's done?"

"I wasn't talking about his material possessions, Novalee. I mean you."

"I don't mean anything to him other than a way he can benefit himself," Novalee replied.

"That's a bunch of bullshit and you know it," Abigail snapped. "I've never seen Dean fight harder for anything than what he's done to make sure William's will stays intact. And yet, you come along and he's willing to let it all slip away as long as you don't. Don't tell me you don't mean anything to him."

"I just want the divorce papers," Novalee said, trying to ignore the effect Abigail's words had on her.

Abby sighed, "Fine. Tell me where you are and I'll bring them to you tonight."

Novalee gave her the name of the hotel, reading the pad on the desk. Abigail told her she wasn't too far and she'd be there soon.

Novalee forced herself to get up a few minutes later and wash her tear-streaked face so she would look at least half-presentable. The reflection that stared back at her in the bathroom mirror was a complete mess. Her hair looked tangled in places from running her fingers through it too much. Her eyes were red and puffy with dark circles forming under them, and she looked even paler than usual against the black cotton of her hoodie.

Novalee looked away, splashing cold water on her face and gently patting it off with the soft hand towel. Her stomach growled in protest from being ignored for so long, but she doubted she would be able to keep any food down even if she wanted to.

Twenty minutes later there was a sharp knock on her door. Novalee sucked in a deep breath before opening it, immediately feeling self-conscious about the way she looked when she saw the well-put-together woman standing in front of her. She crossed her arms, already feeling defensive when it came to Abigail Knight, but gave her a small, tight smile in greeting to be polite.

"You're not what I expected at all," Abigail said as she looked her up and down.

Novalee frowned. So much for being polite.

"Excuse me?"

"Don't get me wrong. I've seen pictures of you so I knew what you looked like, but to find you here moping and depressed is not what I expected."

Novalee bristled. "You've seen pictures of me?"

Abigail rolled her eyes. "Of course. We sent a private detective after you. I know more about you than you probably like, Novalee."

The anger returned as Novalee learned of the invasion of privacy. She felt sick knowing there had been someone out there watching her every move, logging what she did and when she did it, snapping pictures of her. It was as if one of her worst fears had come true and she had been stalked.

"You had someone follow me? Do you know how sick that is?"

Abigail shrugged as if her feelings about it didn't matter one way or another.

"We had to see who Dean married. He had no part in it, just so you know. He refused to even look at the report until a week ago."

"Wow. That makes me feel so much better."

Abigail raised a perfectly-shaped eyebrow. "Can I come in, or are you going to keep me out in the hallway?"

Novalee stepped back and waved her in, watching the other woman look around the room as she placed her briefcase on the small table by the window.

"What do you know about me?" Novalee couldn't help but ask.

"Everything," she said with another shrug. "If you really want to know the dirt we dug up I can give you a copy."

Novalee bit her lip, afraid to ask the only thing she really wanted to know. Abigail turned and nodded as if she had asked a question.

"Yes, I know about the abuse you survived, too."

A cold chill ran through her body and she wrapped her arms around her middle again. Did that mean Dean knew about what happened to her before she'd told him? Had he known all her secrets before he'd earned the right to know them? Did it mean anything to him that she had lived through a hell of her own, or was sympathizing with her just part of his plan to get closer to her so she'd trust him?

Novalee felt not only hurt over his betrayal, but irritated at herself for believing everything he'd told her and having no clue what the truth really was. As much as she wanted to get the hell away from him, it pissed her off that by leaving she'd never really know all the answers.

Not that she would really believe anything he told her now, anyway.

"Did you bring the divorce papers?" Novalee asked, breaking the silence.

Abigail turned back to the table. She rifled through her briefcase until she pulled out a large yellow envelope and faced Novalee again.

"I'm sure you'll want your lawyer to look it over," Abigail advised as she held it out to her.

Novalee took it, shaking her head as she said, "I'll look it over myself."

Surprise filled Abby's face.

"Do you think that's wise?" She crossed her arms and tilted her head to the side. "Don't you want your lawyer to read it and make sure I'm not screwing you?"

"I'm sure it's all straightforward, isn't it? What's his is his, right?" Novalee scowled. "Don't worry, Ms. Knight, I don't want anything from him."

Abigail didn't comment. Instead she pulled another file out from her briefcase and held it out.

"What's that?" Novalee asked.

"All the information you'll need on Dean. I'm sure you know the intimate details, but it will give you other little things that a spouse should know."

Novalee stared at the folder and shook her head.

"I don't need that," she all but whispered.

Abigail lowered her arm and sighed. "You're really going to just walk away?"

"Walk away from a bunch of lies? Yes."

"And feed him to the wolves in the process?"

"That's not my problem."

"But can you live with yourself knowing that's what you did?"

"What I did? All I'm guilty of is not annulling a drunken marriage. I didn't set out to hurt anyone. I didn't lie and trick someone into a commitment to benefit myself! And I wasn't the one that turned up and fabricated even more lies, and faked attraction and feelings to gain trust!"

"You think he faked his attraction for you? Trust me, honey, I was the

one person in this whole thing he was honest with and there is nothing fake about his feelings for you. In fact, I was pissed at him for getting emotionally attached to you. I hated that he was compromising the case by developing real feelings for you."

"Are you sure you weren't pissed because he was developing feelings for someone other than you?" Novalee snapped, letting Abigail know she knew about her and Dean's affair.

The other woman raised her eyebrows at the snarky comment, but a smile crept across her lips.

"You've got more backbone than I thought."

Novalee crossed her arms and glared.

"Just because you've read a file about me doesn't mean you know shit about me. That's all just paper work. You have no idea what I'm capable of."

Abigail pursed her lips and slowly nodded.

"Very true." She watched Novalee for a moment before sighing and giving a weak shrug. "Yes, Dean and I had our fifteen minutes of sexual bliss." Novalee tried not to show how much it bothered her to hear another woman talk about being with her husband. "It was years ago and it was over before it really began. I care about him, as he does me, but that's it. We make better friends than lovers and there will never be anything between us again.

"Trust me. His feelings for you are real and not just a sexual itch he wanted to scratch like it was with me."

Novalee snorted. "You'd say anything to sway my opinions. You work for him; you want him to win and you need me in order to make that happen. That doesn't exactly scream 'trust' to me."

"You're right, I could be telling you anything. And honestly, I would if I thought it would help. But you're a smart woman, Novalee, and I think deep down you know I'm not bullshitting you."

Novalee rolled her eyes. "If I was so smart I wouldn't be in this mess right now."

"It's only a mess if you want it to be," Abigail said.

Novalee looked as she set the folder about Dean on the bed and grabbed her briefcase.

"In case you change your mind," she said and walked to the door. "If you have any questions call me."

"Abigail," Novalee called just as she was about to leave. "Would you do it?" she asked, meeting her eyes.

Abby's smile was small but soft, as was her voice when she said, "If a man loved me as much as he does you, I think I would."

As much as she hated it, Novalee's body reacted to what she said. Her heart beat quickened, her throat closed, and she found it hard to breathe. The knot that had been in her stomach since earlier that evening suddenly uncoiled and the butterflies were going crazy.

"He doesn't love me," Novalee said, wishing her voice didn't sound so damn breathless.

"I've known Dean for a good ten years," Abigail said. "I've seen him at his worst just as I've seen him at his best. But I've never seen him as happy or sound as hopeful as he has these past few days."

"That doesn't mean he loves me," Novalee argued.

"Do you love him?" Abby pressed.

Novalee hesitated. "I don't know him."

"You know the parts that count. He has his faults, Novalee, but so do you. We all do. And when he met you he really was just trying to save someone he loved. I know he hurt you, but if one of his faults is doing whatever it takes to make the people he loves happy, how horrible is that?"

"And what about the people like me who are hurt in the process?"

"What about the people like Richard who will profit from all the pain he's caused?" Abby asked. "Wouldn't that be like letting your own abuser win?"

Novalee was about to tell her she could stuff her opinions when it came to that part of her life, but Abigail held up her hand. "All I'm saying is he needs you, just like you needed the support system you had. He can't beat his assailant alone, either. You're all the hope he has."

Abby opened the door, turning to face her one last time as she said, "He does love you, or else he would be here trying to convince you to stay and help him. Instead, he's willing to let you go to prove that you aren't just some way for him to beat his father. And if you feel even half of what he feels for you, you won't let that happen."

Novalee watched her leave, gripping the yellow envelope as if her life depended on it. Then it occurred to her that a life did depend it, but that life wasn't hers. It was Dean's; everything he had, everything she knew that mattered to him, was in her hands.

And she had no idea how to feel about that.

Chapter 16

Dean sat in what had been his grandfather's home office, his only company the single glass of whisky he held in his hand.

The shades were drawn and the lights off, blanketing the room in darkness. The appearance of the room fit his mood: dark, dreary, lifeless.

He brought the glass to his nose, inhaling the hard liquor deeply as he swished it around in the glass. His throat burned for that first taste, his mouth almost watering at the thought of shooting back the drink. The desire to get wasted out of his fucking mind was a tempting one. He didn't care that Abigail was probably on her way over right now. He didn't care that in a few short hours he would have to face his father and a judge that would take everything away from him. Christ, he didn't even care that everything *would* be taken away from him.

He only cared that she was gone. The only thing that fucking mattered in his life had walked away from him. And he only had himself to blame.

If he thought for one second that drowning his sorrows in alcohol would help anything, he would have started drinking the night she left. It might have dulled the pain for a while, but it could never take away the image of how hurt she had been. There was no amount of booze that could erase that look from his memory. It would be forever burned there, haunting him every day, reminding him of the pain he caused the one woman he loved.

Dean scoffed. Love. What the fuck good was it to know you loved someone when there was no way you could ever tell her? It would just stay with him, eating at him every day, knowing the woman he wanted to spend the rest of his life with, the woman he was already fucking married to, would never know how he truly felt.

It killed him that Novalee left thinking she was nothing more than the winning game piece in the fight with his father. It killed him even more that she could actually believe she was nothing to him after everything they had shared in the week they had been together.

A week? All it had been was a fucking week?

Dean stared into the glass, the aroma hitting his nose every time he moved his hand. It sure as hell didn't feel like a week. Dean felt like he had been with her for years. People didn't feel what he did for her in only a week, did they? It didn't seem possible.

He had never been one to believe in that love-at-first-sight shit. All too often love was confused with lust and once the lust was gone, what did you have left? Nothing but two strangers waking up next to each other wondering how the hell they had let themselves get to that point.

Love was earned. It was built over a long period of time between two people who really knew each other, who trusted and believed in one another. It didn't just happen with someone that you had only been with for seven days.

That's what he would have told anyone if they had asked him a week ago. But now . . . Dean knew different. Love was still earned; it had to be worked on and built between two people who were committed to only each other, but there was no time limit as to when it could happen.

Sometimes it just happened.

Jesus, what the fuck was wrong with him? Sitting in the dark playing Russian roulette with a glass of whisky was bad enough, but now he was giving himself romantic advice? What kind of pansy-ass-self-loathing-fuck had he turned into?

Dean set the whisky on the desk and ran his hands down his stubble-covered cheeks with a groan. This wasn't helping anything. He had locked himself away from the world, hoping that if he ignored Abby and Andrew's calls, he could avoid what he had to do this morning.

The angry voice mail messages and texts let him know his attorneys were not happy with him blowing off last-minute meetings. Dean didn't see the point in dragging his ass out to them when their one shot of winning had flown out of state. And frankly, he didn't give a damn about it all anymore.

The guilt he felt over basically handing everything over to Richard was just as bad as the guilt he felt over lying to Novalee. He couldn't help but feel he was letting his grandfather down by giving up. If William had taught him anything it was to give it his all, win or lose, because at least he could walk away knowing he had done his best.

Dean may have done his best in the beginning, but by hiding out the last two days he had admitted defeat before it was even over. His grandfather must be rolling in his grave over his cowardly actions.

The door suddenly burst open and Dean slowly raised his eyes, not at all surprised by his uninvited guest.

"So this is what you've been doing?" Abigail said. "Drinking yourself stupid."

"Good morning to you too, Abby," he drawled.

"Fuck you, Dean. While you've been playing possum, Andrew and I have been working our asses off to try and save yours!"

"That's what I pay you the big bucks for, darlin'," he said, sliding his glass back and forth across the desk. "And I don't recall inviting you here."

"Well, that's just too damn bad, isn't it? I respected your need for some space and I know when you're here it's supposed to be off-limits, but screw that. I haven't done all this work for you to sit in here and throw it all away."

"You make it sound like there's still any hope that this could turn out in our favor."

"We'll never know if you don't put down the booze, now will we?"

Dean lifted his eyes and said, "I haven't touched a drop."

"And I just seduced the pope," she retorted.

Dean chuckled, amazed she could deliver the line with such a straight face.

"Did you rock his world as well as his little go-cart?"

Abby rolled her eyes and walked into the room. She picked up the glass and held it up in front of his face.

"Haven't touched a drop, huh?"

"Poured it, didn't touch it."

She set the glass back down and crossed her arms.

"I'm not going to just let you give up, Dean. You're going to get your ass out of that chair, go upstairs, and get ready to come with me to court. Or I'm prepared to take you like you are, it's your choice."

Dean leaned back in the chair, folded his hands, and placed them on his stomach as he closed his eyes.

"I appreciate your efforts, but we both know we're fucked."

"Even if that's true, is this really how you want to go out?" she questioned. "Hiding in the dark instead of facing the prick? I never took you for a coward, Dean."

His eyes snapped open and he glared at her.

"I may be a lot of things, but a coward isn't one of them."

"Get up and prove it," she challenged.

Dean stared at her. What she said irked him, mainly because there was some truth to it. He wasn't a fucking coward. He didn't run away from the difficulties in his life, he stood and faced them as his grandfather had taught him. But even he had to admit he had stuck his head in the sand and blocked out the rest of the world after watching Novalee walk out.

His gut twisted thinking about her and he looked away from Abby's stare.

"Have you talked to her?" he asked quietly. She didn't respond and Dean took her silence to mean what he already knew.

"Whatever choice she made is on her," Abby finally said. "Just like whatever choice you make right now is on you. But I swear to all that is holy, Dean, if you make me walk out of this house by myself I will find you after it's all over and kick you so hard in the nuts they'll never be able to retrieve them. And then I'll quit."

Dean snorted and shook his head. "Well, I would hate for you to quit."

He sat there for a few more minutes, contemplating his options. Abby waited as patiently as she could, but finally the silence got to her and she started to get angry. Dean peered at her from the corner of his eye, made her wait a while longer, and then stood. He was sure he heard her breathe a sigh of relief as he rounded the desk.

"You need to keep your skirt on while I get ready," he said with a grin.

"Oh, I'm used to not having time to get out of my clothes with you, Dean. It was usually over pretty quick," she quipped.

Dean laughed and surprised them both by pulling her into a quick hug.

"Thank you for threatening my balls so often," he said and she laughed this time.

"I take great pleasure in it."

Dean left her waiting in the office and hurried to shower and dress. As he was staring into the mirror looping his tie, he thought about how different he would be feeling if Novalee had been next to him fixing the noose around his neck, as they got ready to face the day together. One smile from her would have been enough to ease the shakes that felt like were taking over his body.

Dean braced his hands on the sink's edge and leaned over the counter, inhaling deeply as he stared into the porcelain basin. A sudden wave of nausea hit him and his forehead dampened from a cold sweat. He exhaled the trapped air slowly and swallowed, hoping to stop the dry heaves before they started. He closed his eyes and counted to five, inhaling and exhaling every few seconds. Then he grabbed the glass he kept by the sink and filled it with cold water, taking a small enough sip to wet his parched mouth and test his stomach.

When the water didn't come back up, Dean straightened and looked at his pale reflection. He hated that he looked so weak going into this thing, even if that's how he felt. He made a mental note to stop for coffee, hoping it would bring some color back to his cheeks so he wouldn't look so fucking pathetic.

Dean grabbed his suit jacket off the bed and shrugged it on as he went downstairs. Abby waited for him at the bottom, pacing back and forth impatiently. She looked up at him when she heard him approach and grimaced.

"You look like shit," she stated.

"Always great to hear compliments from you, Abs," he said as he fixed his cuff. "It's a damn expensive suit, what more do you want?"

"The suit is fine," she said. "I mean you."

He sighed. "Can we just go and get this over with?"

Abigail made no further comments as she turned on her heel and marched out the door. She grumbled when he requested a pit stop for coffee, but did it anyway. The first shot of caffeine rushed through his system, the warmth of the drink calming his nerves.

Abigail rambled on beside him, filling him in as fast as she could about what he had missed while he'd been avoiding his responsibilities. He rolled his eyes when she gave him instructions on how to behave in court as if he was a child that might throw a temper tantrum at any second.

"None of that bullshit like what happened at the penthouse," she warned him.

"Don't beat him down in front of the judge," Dean answered. "Got it."

She narrowed her eyes and he winked.

"When the judge makes his decision," she continued, "if it's not in your favor—"

"*If* it's not in my favor?" He laughed. "You hold out high hopes, don't you?"

Abby turned her attention back in front of her as the light turned green and she sped away.

"When it comes to this I refuse to lose hope until the decision is final," she confessed.

"Novalee getting on the plane was like putting the nail in the coffin," he replied. "It's over. I played a stranger, ended up fucking up everything William worked for, and got to know my wife and fell in love as she walked away. It's so fucking over, Abigail."

"Dean . . ."

"Once this is settled I think I'm going to take off for a while," he said. "I can't stick around and watch as Richard runs everything into the ground, or lose it to the mob or whatever the fuck he's mixed up in now."

"Where will you go?"

"I don't know, but wherever it is it has to be better than here." Dean looked out the window, watching as Vegas passed by him.

Andrew was waiting for them outside the courtroom, nodding a greeting as Dean and Abby approached him. Dean scanned the hallway, his eyes falling on every person but never finding the one he was looking for, and the little hope he'd secretly held in his heart, died.

"Richard and Charles are already in there," Andrew said.

Abigail shook her head, silently telling the other attorney it wasn't Richard or Charles he was searching for.

"Oh." Andrew sighed and tried to muster up the confidence all lawyers seemed to have. "We'll do this, with or without the help, Dean."

Dean rolled his shoulders, biting back the remark that they both knew they were royally screwed.

"Well, then, let's do it," he said.

He followed Andrew into the room, pausing when he noticed Abigail had been pulled aside by the guard at the door. He raised his eyebrows in question and she shook her head, indicating he should go in.

He took his seat, leaving the middle chair for Abigail to sit next to Andrew. He chanced a quick look at his father who was sitting back, smiling smugly, noticing Dean was alone. Dean's hands fisted as he wished he could wipe that grin off the bastard's face.

"Keep your cool, Dean," Andrew advised him, noticing the strain in his posture.

Dean nodded, dropping his eyes to the table as his body vibrated with rage.

Abigail sat next to him, leaning in to whisper something in Andrew's ear that brought a genuine smile to the man's face.

"What's that about?" Dean asked.

"What's what about?" she asked coyly, giving him a small smile.

"What are you up to, Abby?" he asked, some of the tension leaving his body because of her change of mood.

"The only thing I'm up to is winning, Dean. Only winning." She winked at him and he furrowed his brow.

"What the fuck is going on?"

Before she could respond they were asked to stand and Judge Benning appeared. Dean took his seat again and watched him as he looked around the courtroom and frowned.

"Mr. Percy, Ms. Knight, your client was instructed to have his wife appear in court with him today, was he not?" the judge asked, looking at them over the rim of his glasses.

Abigail stood.

"Request permission to approach the bench, Your Honor," she said.

Dean looked up at her, over at Andrew, back up at her, and then at Judge Benning who waved his hand, letting council know they could approach the bench.

Dean strained to hear what the whispering was about, and a look over at Richard told him he had no idea what was going on, either. As soon as they all sat back down Richard was all over Charles, who didn't look at all happy.

"What's going on, Abby?" he hissed again in her ear.

"Shut up."

"Bailiff, would you call in the witness?"

Dean's head whipped to the judge and his heart stopped.

The witness?

He followed the bailiff with his eyes as he walked out of the courtroom. Dean's palms grew damp and his heart finally started beating again, getting faster with each second that passed as he waited for the door to open again. Unconsciously, he started bouncing his leg, only noticing what he was doing when Abby placed her hand on his knee.

"I need you to stay calm. Act normal," she whispered just as the door opened.

Dean turned in his seat, shifting his eyes from Abby to the woman who followed the bailiff into the courtroom.

If he hadn't been warned to stay calm, and if Abby hadn't been digging her nails into his leg to restrain him, he would have jumped up, taken Novalee in his arms and shown her just how fucking happy he was to see her. And not because her being there saved his ass. He was just happy to see *her*, something he feared he'd never get to do again.

Novalee passed him, keeping her eyes ahead of her as she followed the bailiff to the stand. She was sworn in and told to have a seat, all of which she did without a glance at him.

Dean swallowed over the lump in his throat, his heart still beating a mile a minute as he looked at her, willing her to meet his eyes.

The fact that she was there had to mean something, right? She wouldn't have come if she didn't care, would she? Did she forgive him? Want to speak to him? Why didn't she call him and let him know she had stayed and had decided to appear for him?

Dean quickly glanced at Abby, narrowing his eyes at his attorney. Something told him she knew more about Novalee's decision to stay than she would admit.

A commotion to his left made him look over at his father who was waving at Novalee and Dean as his hushed whispers grew louder and Charles tried to settle him down.

"I'd advise you get your client under control, Mr. Tanner," the judge warned before turning to Novalee. "We'll get to the questioning in a moment, but first I would like you to acknowledge to the court that you are, and have been since August fifteenth, married to Dean Philips. Remember, you are under oath, Ms. Jensen," Judge Benning reminded. "Do you acknowledge your marriage to be authentic in the eyes of the law?"

Novalee slowly lifted her eyes and finally looked at Dean, but what he saw didn't warm his heart like he'd hoped it would. They looked vacant; the life that had been in them since the day he'd met her was gone. They were glassy as if she was about to burst into tears at any second and the dark circles told him she hadn't been sleeping. A sharp twist in his gut reminded him he had done that to her, and he feared that he was looking into the same eyes she had had after the suffering she endured with Dalton.

"Ms. Jensen? Do you acknowledge your marriage to be authentic in the eyes of the law?" the judge repeated.

Dean listened to her sharp intake of breath and she nodded as she looked away from him.

"I do."

Dean sat listening as Novalee was questioned by the judge, by Charles, and finally by both Andrew and Abigail. He heard every answer she gave, surprised by how much she knew, and even more surprised by how well she pulled off the lie. But what he didn't hear was the emotion behind her answers; it was as if she was just answering automatically, reciting information that she studied.

Apparently he was the only one that heard the robotic tone of her answers, though. The judge nodded every once in a while, seemingly satisfied with what she was telling him. Charles frantically searched through papers as Richard sat stewing next to him, the anger rolling off of him. And Abigail winked at him discreetly as Novalee spun her tale.

Finally, after what seemed like hours, Judge Benning dismissed Novalee from the stand. Dean wanted to jump up and protest as she quickly exited the courtroom, afraid that if she wasn't made to stay inside she would disappear before he got a chance to speak with her.

He was so focused on getting out and getting to her that he didn't hear the judge declare his decision until Richard's angry cry snapped him back to his surroundings.

"Congratulations, Dean," Andrew said, grasping his hand and patting him on the back. "You owe it all to that little wife of yours."

"I told you we'd pull it off." Abby beamed.

Dean forced a smile at both of them as he pushed passed them.

"Sorry. I'll stop by the office and discuss this later, but right now I really need to go," he said, backing away. "Thanks for everything."

He turned to hurry out of the room and slammed into Richard.

"I don't know how you did it, or what you paid the bitch, but you'll regret it," he said.

Dean snorted. "You're finished, old man. Your threats mean nothing to me anymore. Get the fuck out of my way, and stay out of my life. And if you ever call my wife a bitch again, *you'll* regret it," Dean threatened, knocking him out of the way with his shoulder as he walked away.

Dean hurried out into the hallway, prepared to have to search to find her, but she was waiting on the bench just outside the courtroom. She stood when he approached, crossing her arms and looking uncomfortable as she stopped in front of her.

"Hey," he greeted, falling into their normal habit.

Novalee shifted her eyes away, glancing at the people around him before looking at him again.

Dean never knew he could feel so rejected by not hearing one simple word.

"Did you . . . is it over?" she asked.

Dean nodded. "He lost. Because of you," he added with a smile. "Thank you."

Novalee shrugged, looking down at her arms.

It killed him. He wanted to reach out and take her in his arms and hold her. But her body language was speaking loud and clear and it was telling

Dean to back the fuck off.

"Why did you come back?" he asked.

"I never left," she revealed. "I've been staying at–at a hotel."

"What changed your mind?"

"I don't know. I was set to go, I even went to the airport, but I couldn't board the plane." She glanced at him, only to look away again. "I couldn't leave knowing it was going to be because of me that you lost something that means so much to you."

Her hair fell over one eye and he automatically reached out to brush it out of the way. Novalee flinched as his fingers brushed her skin and he dropped his hand, shoving them into his pockets.

"Thank you," he said again.

"That's what my role was this entire time, right?" she asked, anger and hurt flashing in her eyes.

"Novalee—"

"Here." She pulled the purse strap off her shoulder and dug around in the oversized bag, pulling out an envelope. She held it out to him. "Give this to Abigail for me?"

He took the envelope slowly, asking, "What is it?"

"Divorce papers," she answered. "I've signed them; they just need your signature."

The envelope suddenly felt like a hundred pounds as he realized what this meant. He looked from the yellow packet up to the woman he needed more than air and shook his head.

"Novalee—"

"I did this for you, Dean, now will you do something for me?"

"Anything," he promised quickly.

Novalee looked up at him, her eyes glassy from tears he knew she was holding back and said, "Leave me alone."

"I . . . What?" he asked, hoping he heard her wrong.

"I want you to leave me alone," she repeated. "I want you to file those papers so I'm free of you and can move on with my life. I want it to be like we never met."

"Novalee," he whispered, his closing throat making it impossible to speak any louder. "Please, if you would just let me try and make it right . . ."

She shook her head, biting her lip as she flicked tears off her cheek.

"I can't," she said. "I can't get past being lied to like that. I can't be with you, constantly wondering if what you're telling me is the truth."

"I have no more to hide," he tried to assure her. "You know everything. It's just us from now on. Just you and me with nothing left to come between us."

"I think this would always be between us," she confessed. "I can't do it."

"Novalee, I lo—"

"Please, Dean," she said, drawing eyes their way. She glanced at the people around them and shook her head, lowering her voice, "Please don't. Don't say another word. I did this for you. Do this for me."

He stared at her, all the things he wanted to say to her dying on his tongue as she looked up at him and begged with tears in her eyes for him to leave her alone. There was a pain in his chest, a pain so fucking sharp it felt like someone had placed a thousand pound weight on him and was cracking every single bone in his body. He felt like he couldn't breathe; the air was slowly being sucked out of his body and he was powerless to stop it.

Novalee stared at him, waiting for him to answer, but Dean knew he wouldn't be able to find his voice even if he wanted to. And the last thing he wanted to do was actually fucking tell her he would leave her alone.

So he simply nodded and watched as she closed her eyes in what he assumed could only be relief.

Novalee turned to walk away, but stopped and faced him once more time. She hesitated for a moment before standing on her toes to reach up and kiss his cheek.

"I'm glad you won, Dean," she said against his skin and then was gone.

Dean stood watching where she disappeared around the corner until Abigail came up beside him and wrapped an arm around his waist as she laid her head on his shoulder. The action was so out of character that it shocked Dean.

"I'm sorry," she said.

Dean nodded, not trusting his voice just yet as he passed the envelope to her. She took it, opening the flap, and pulling out the papers. She flipped through them and looked up at Dean.

"She signed them."

"That's what she said," he croaked, clearing his throat.

"What do you want me to do with them?" Abby asked.

His brow wrinkled as he looked at her, confused by her question. "What do you mean?"

"Well, I mean do you actually want me to file them?"

"Why wouldn't you?"

"For one, you haven't signed them, and two you're in love with her."

Dean grabbed the papers from her and walked over to the nearest person with a pen. He scrawled his name on each line where it needed to be, handed the pen back to the surprised owner, and stalked back to Abby.

"There." He thrust the papers back into her hand. "It's done."

Abigail raised her brows in disbelief.

"Just like that?" she finally managed to ask.

"Just like that," he mimicked.

"But, Dean—"

"She asked me to leave her alone, Abby. She doesn't want me, she doesn't want this, and I don't blame her."

"So, you're just going to let her walk away?"

"Yes. I'm giving her her life back. The life she had before I fucked it up for her. It's what she wants and how can I deny her that one simple thing when she just saved me?"

"I understand that, but—"

"Abby." He sighed. "For once can you just shut up?" He smiled to take the sting out of his words. "You did good, kid. I'll be happy to write you that big fat check and you can take that beach vacation you want. You deserve it."

"You deserve it, too, Dean. And I don't mean a beach vacation," she said, giving him a tight smile as she squeezed his arm and walked away.

Dean went back to the house that night, wandering the empty rooms as he breathed easy for the first time in two years. This really was his place and that wasn't going to change. He ended up in the master suite that night for the first time ever, lying on the bed and staring at the ceiling as he thought of Novalee and how he wished she was here to celebrate the win with him. It was all because of her, and he couldn't even show her how grateful he was.

His eyes were just beginning to grow heavy when his cell rang and for a split second he couldn't stop the hope that swelled inside him that it might be her. The unknown number flashed on his screen as he answered.

"Hello?"

"Dean Philips?" a soft voice asked.

"Yes."

"I'm calling from the hospital regarding your father, Richard."

Dean sat up and turned on the bedside lamp.

"Is he dead?" The words were out before Dean realized what he said and the silence on the other end told him just how bad it sounded. "I mean, is he in critical condition or anything?"

"He was brought in by ambulance and is fairly beaten up, but he should be fine."

"Not to be rude or anything, but I couldn't care less about my father. Why are you calling me?"

"I, well, he asked me to," was the flustered response.

"Why?"

"I'm not sure, sir." She gave him the information on where to find him if he was interested in coming and hung up.

Dean stared at the phone as if it would magically come to life and tell him what his father wanted from him.

"Fuck," he swore under his breath as he threw off the covers and got dressed.

He was at the hospital within fifteen minutes, following the nurse's directions as to which floor to find the old man. When he entered the room he stopped in his tracks, startled by what he saw.

Richard was propped up, both an arm and a leg in casts, his face badly bruised and swollen and three fingers on his unbroken hand wrapped in bandages. He raised his puffy eyes to Dean as he stood there and a sneer twisted his busted lips.

"Guess you think I got what I deserved, huh?" he rasped.

"Not really. You're still alive," Dean replied, not moving any farther into the room.

"I'm surprised you came."

Dean shrugged. "Maybe I was hoping they would need someone to pull the plug."

Richard made a half-snort, half-cough sound and closed his eyes until his breathing returned to normal. He opened them again and stared at Dean.

"Don't you want to know what happened?" he asked.

"I think I can figure it out. You promised the wrong people you were going to score big today and came up empty-handed. I'm assuming this is just a warning and next time I'll be here to claim your body."

"I need money, Dean," he said, not even looking a bit sorry for asking for a handout.

Dean laughed bitterly. "Of course you need money. Why the hell else would you have called me here?"

"If you don't give it to me they'll kill me next time."

"I guess you should make sure your affairs are in order then."

Father and son stared at each until one broke.

"I know you hate me for what happened," Richard said. "Trust me, son, you can't hate me anymore than I hate myself."

"You're a fucking liar and a bad one at that." Dean glared at him. "You have no remorse. If you did, you would have straightened up your life in honor of them. Instead, you just keep digging your own grave, and this time you're going to fill it."

"They only left me alive because I told them I could get the money from you," Richard confessed.

"Jesus fucking Christ, Richard," Dean shouted. "Don't you fucking dare bring me into this mess of yours! This is all on you."

"I just need a little help. Just to get them off my back," his father pleaded.

"How much do you owe?"

Richard licked his lips, wincing.

"Over a hundred grand."

Dean shook his head, clenching his jaws as he muttered a string of curse words.

"That's nothing for you. It's pennies compared to what you have."

"And you think that's a reason to just give it to you?" Dean yelled.

Richard remained silent.

Dean dragged his hand down his face and glared at him. "You deserve every fucking broken bone and bruise you have. I have absolutely no sympathy for you. I hate you. I've hated you since the day I found out you were beating mom. But I'll tell you what I'll do. I'll give you half a million if you pay off your debts and get the fuck out of here. Leave. I don't care where you go as long as I never have to see you again."

"You're going to give me half a million dollars?"

"It's not out of the goodness of my heart, trust me," Dean said coldly. "If you die by your own stupidity that's your fault and I won't give a damn, but as much as I want to, I can't walk out of this fucking room knowing if I do you'll die and it will be on my hands. So take the money and get lost. What happens to you after that is on you."

"How fast can you get me it?" Richard questioned.

"I'll have it ready for you by tomorrow. Andrew will bring it by. I don't want to hear from you after tonight. Do you understand?"

"I can see you're good at paying people off, Dean. Did the efforts turn out well for the little woman you got to play your wife?"

"I would be grateful if I were you."

"Why should I be grateful? It's the least you can do considering you got everything that's mine."

"Fuck you, Richard," Dean said. "I hope you enjoy burning in hell."

He turned to leave but not before he heard the reply, "I'm sure I'll see you there, son. You'll get what you deserve, too."

Dean had to smile as he left the room. For once he agreed with the bastard.

He did deserve what was coming to him.

And he didn't care how long it took; he was going to get it.

Chapter 17

Novalee stared at the lettering on the large white envelope, feeling as if the words were taunting her.

She had received the piece of mail six weeks ago, a month after she'd left Las Vegas and everything that had happened there, behind her. She had let it sit, too afraid to rip open the seal and actually see what she already knew was inside.

On a whim she had grabbed it that afternoon before heading to work, promptly stuffing it into the bottom drawer of her office desk, hoping that she would forget about it. But as the hours wore on she knew it was no use. She knew she had to open it.

She had gotten as far as taking it out of the drawer, but it felt hot in her hands and she quickly dropped it onto the desk where it still sat waiting for her to get some courage.

Novalee bit her lip, glaring at the large reminder of what had happened ten weeks ago. She knew it was coming, she knew she would eventually get a copy of it, and she hated the part of herself that wanted to cry that it had actually happened. She hated the part of herself that had hoped he wouldn't go through with it.

It was the same part that made her breathing quicken every time the phone rang, or her heart stop every time the door opened at the bar and the man that entered was hidden in the shadows.

It was the part that Novalee feared would always yearn for Dean Philips.

She sighed and leaned her head back in the chair, closing her eyes. It would be easy to blame that part for her decision to help Dean, but as much as she wished she could convince herself it was nothing more than a weak moment, she knew it wasn't.

Despite what Dean had done, Novalee hadn't been able to see him lose his life to the likes of Richard. She had been one step away from boarding the plane, one step away from leaving Dean and all his lies behind, when she turned and bolted from the airport. She had checked back into the hotel she had checked out of only hours before, and spent the next two days learning all she could about her husband. She had been prepared to help him. What she hadn't been prepared for was seeing him.

The cowardly part of Novalee won out when she asked the court guard to tell Abigail when she arrived that she was waiting for her. She couldn't face Dean. She couldn't walk into the courtroom with him and pretend to be his loving wife when all she was to him was his match point.

She should have left right after the judge dismissed her. She should have given the divorce papers to Abigail and fled as her head told her to. But her heart made her stay. Her damned heart made her sit outside the courtroom biting her lip to nothing but a chapped mess as she waited to find out if her good deed had paid off.

And for a minute, as she watched Dean emerge from behind the closed doors, she worried he had lost. He looked so sad and alone . . . until he saw her.

It was that look that made her heart break all over again. He seemed so hopeful, so delighted to see her there waiting for him that it made her rethink giving him the divorce papers at all.

But she knew it was just another thing she had to do. Just like showing up for him that day. She didn't do it out of loyalty or because she had forgiven him for the lies he had told her. She did it because she felt obligated. She couldn't walk away knowing if she did she was handing over everything Dean's grandfather had worked so hard for, something that meant everything to do Dean, to a man who would piss it away.

Helping Dean was just something she had to do.

Just like asking him to leave her alone was something she had to do. Novalee couldn't move on with her life if she thought for one second he could show up again. She couldn't spend her days waiting to see if he'd come back to her, holding her breath every day hoping today would be the day he would show up. She had spent too long feeling as if her life had been on pause, waiting for the day that her husband would show up and reveal her secret marriage. And she couldn't spend any longer waiting for her husband to show up and decide to have a marriage with her now.

It had killed her to ask Dean to leave her alone. Even as she was saying the words she hoped that he would try his hardest to stop her. But he let her go, just as she asked.

And she hated that he did.

"You okay?"

Novalee opened her eyes and turned her head to face the door. She gave Cali a small smile and nodded. "Fine."

"Liar." Cali walked into the office and perched herself on the edge of the desk. She glanced down at the envelope and frowned. "Still haven't opened it?"

Novalee shrugged.

"What's the point? I know what it is. I know what I'll see."

"So if you know, why does it bother you so much?"

Novalee stayed silent, staring at her desk.

"You made a choice, Novalee," Cali said. "This is just part of it."

"I know."

"On second thought, you don't *have* to open it. It's not like you have to sign anything and send it back."

"Nope."

"But I still think it would give you some kind of closure."

Novalee rolled her eyes and Cali chuckled.

"Wanna come out with Tony and me tonight?"

"And play the third wheel? No thanks."

Honestly, Novalee couldn't believe that there was a third wheel to play when it came to Cali and Tony. What was supposed to be a one-time date had turned into an actual relationship between them. Although no one seemed more surprised by it than Cali herself.

"How are things going with you two?" Novalee asked.

Cali shrugged. "They're going. I mean, I'm not planning a trip to Vegas any time soon or anything." She winked at Novalee who rolled her eyes again. "I like him."

"Like?" Novalee raised a questioning eyebrow.

Cali shifted her eyes away and said, "Yes, like. I'm in no hurry to venture into deep feelings and shit."

"Maybe you'll have to teach me how to groom a man," Novalee teased.

Cali laughed. "Oh, Nov, if you knew how much effort went into that you'd know why I'm not about to let him get away so easily."

Novalee shook her head, not desperate enough for a distraction to listen to Cali's new and improved sex life.

Cali shimmied off the desk.

"Are you sure you don't want to come?" she asked again.

"The things you're probably planning to do at this hour with Tony aren't something I want to be a part of," Novalee said.

Cali grinned. "Trust me, you're missing out now."

"I have two males waiting at home who adore me."

Cali snorted. "That's kind of pathetic."

"I know." Novalee sighed.

"You could call him, you know."

Novalee glared at her friend. "No, I can't."

"Oh, come on, Novalee, you're miserable," Cali said. "You know you miss him, you know you regret asking him to leave you alone, so why not just end it all and call him?"

"Since when are you on his side? What happened to dancing around his mangled body?"

"Hey, I would gladly dance around his mangled body," Cali said, "if you didn't want to be with him. But you do."

"I can't be."

"That's bullshit and you know it."

"He lied to me, Cali! How can you expect me to just forgive him for that?"

"I don't." Cali shrugged and pulled out the cell phone that had just buzzed in her pocket "But the Novalee I know wouldn't just give up on what she wanted, even if it meant working for it."

Novalee looked up at her best friend, suddenly needing an answer to the question Dean had asked her all those nights ago. "Cali?"

"Hmm?" she hummed, playing with her cell phone.

"What was it like when you found me that night?" Novalee asked softly.

Cali's fingers stilled on the phone and she slowly raised her eyes to meet Novalee's.

"You've never asked that before," she all but whispered.

"I know, and I think that was selfish of me," Novalee admitted. "After everything was over and Dalton was charged I just wanted to forget about it. But you went through something, too, and I never gave it a second thought."

Cali pressed her lips together and inhaled deeply, slowly releasing the trapped breath.

"Are you sure you want to talk about it now?" she asked.

Novalee nodded.

Cali sat back down on the edge of the desk and looked down at the cell, avoiding Novalee's gaze.

"I thought you were dead," Cali told her softly. "After you guys dropped me off that night something didn't feel right. I had this . . . ache, like a knot in the pit of my stomach telling me something bad was going to happen." She looked up and Novalee saw the tears glistening in her eyes.

"Cali . . ." She reached for her, putting a hand on her knee.

"I shouldn't have waited so long to go check on you," Cali said, wiping away the tears as they slid down her cheeks. "If I had left a little earlier, if I had listened to my gut, I might have been able to stop him. I could have called the cops, or done something, anything, to stop him."

"Cali, you can't blame yourself for what happened," Novalee told her gently.

"I know, but my instincts told me something wasn't right and I ignored them for too long." She grabbed Novalee's hand and squeezed. "When I got there he was gone already, and you . . ." A sob escaped her as she recalled that night. "There was so much blood, Novalee. You were so bruised and battered . . . I couldn't recognize you. I thought you were dead," she repeated as she cried.

Novalee waited until Cali had calmed a little and then asked the question she knew she had to, even though she really didn't want to.

"How did you know I wasn't?"

Cali blinked away her tears and locked eyes with her.

"When I knelt down beside you I . . . I brushed the bloody hair away from your face and you moaned." Cali swallowed and shook her head. "I called 911 right away, and just sat beside you, holding you until they arrived."

Novalee stood and wrapped her arms around her friend.

"You know you saved my life," Novalee said. "You are the one who saved me that night because you did listen to your instincts."

"I'll always wish I had gotten there sooner," she mumbled into Novalee's shoulder.

"We all have regrets, but that can't be one of yours."

Cali pulled away from her and wiped her tear-streaked face with the sleeve of her shirt.

"And letting Dean get away can't be one of yours," she said.

Novalee sighed and sat back down.

"It's not the same thing," she muttered. "And we're not talking about Dean."

"Well, I'm not talking about that other shit anymore," Cali said stubbornly. "It's in the past, and we can't change the past, but we do have a say in our future. Novalee," Cali reached for her hand again, "you deserve to be happy, and despite the fucked-up way you and Dean got together, he makes you happy."

"Cali—"

"Go home. I think you'll find your answer there." Cali gave her a tight smile, bent to kiss her cheek and walked to the door.

Novalee waited until Cali left, closing the door behind her, before taking a deep breath and reaching for the offensive envelope. She grabbed a letter opener, stabbing it into the paper and ripping away her frustration.

She pulled out the contents, skimming through them, not bothering to really read them again since she had already done so weeks ago. She paused when she saw Dean's signature, an unreadable scrawl on the dotted lines, and tears suddenly formed in her eyes. Seeing both of their names made it that much more real.

Novalee was finally a divorced woman.

She threw the papers on the desk and blinked away the tears. She didn't need Dean Philips. She didn't need to have the title *Mrs.* before her name. It's not as if she'd actually had it before, so why cry over it now? She didn't need to be any man's wife. Especially not a man who lied and tricked her into loving him. Who wanted to be married to that man?

Novalee grabbed her purse, shoving the divorce papers into it angrily and locked up the office. She quickly made her way to her car, slamming the door harder than necessary in frustration and drove home a little faster than she should have.

Stupid ex-husband. Stupid best friend. Stupid woman to fall in love with said ex-husband.

Novalee scowled as she let herself into the house, ignoring Jerry's whining as she kicked off her shoes.

"Just give me a minute, boy," she grumbled as he poked her with his nose when she dropped to the couch.

She had just closed her eyes, not planning to walk the few steps to her bedroom tonight, when a crash from the kitchen made her snap her eyes open.

"Ben!" she yelled, jumping from the couch and stomping into the kitchen. "I'm not in the mood for your mischievous shit tonight, cat. I swear I'll string you up by your tail—"

Novalee stopped short as she entered the kitchen, shocked by what she saw. Ben twirled around her feet as she stood there, mouth open, heart hammering at the sight before her.

Dean smiled sheepishly as he picked up the pot from the floor and set it on the counter.

"It's not Ben's tail you should threaten this time," he joked.

Ben meowed as if agreeing with him.

"What the hell are you doing here?" Novalee said. "How the hell did you get in my house?"

"I had some help from Cali."

"Cali?" Novalee shook her head, pushing her hair back from her face as she tried to comprehend what was going on. "Cali let you in?"

"It took some convincing, and she mentioned something about hairy pom-poms, but I finally managed to get her to help me."

"Cali let you into my house?" Novalee asked again. Dean nodded. "Why the hell would she do that? And why are you here?"

Dean looked around the kitchen and Novalee followed his gaze, seeing for the first time the bags of groceries on the counter and the meal he was preparing.

"You're cooking?" Novalee had to bite back her smile as she asked, "I helped you out, Dean, why would you want to torture me as payback?"

Dean laughed as he turned down a burner on the stove.

"I'll have you know I've taken some classes."

"Cooking classes?" Novalee inched her way closer to him, still not fully grasping what the hell was going on.

"Yes, cooking classes. I thought I'd put some of those big bucks I have to use." He winked at her and her stomach flipped.

"And you thought it was okay to just come into my house?" Novalee asked, crossing her arms.

Dean glanced up at her as he carefully sliced a pepper and frowned.

"No. That's why I asked Cali."

"Um, I'm sorry, but I don't think Cali's name is on the mortgage. Shouldn't it be up to me who's invited into my house?"

"I wanted to surprise you," Dean said quietly, not looking up from the counter. "I wanted to make some grand gesture and sweep you off your feet in hopes you'd forgive me."

"And you thought your cooking would do that?" Novalee asked, feeling more amused than she wanted to be.

"Not entirely," Dean admitted. "But I thought it might be a start."

Novalee sighed. "What are you really doing here, Dean? I asked you to leave me alone."

Dean set down the knife and finally looked up at her. "I know and I tried. I tried to move on and focus on work and forget everything that happened. I tried to forget I had a wife who I let go, just like that, with no fight for her at all. I tried to forget that the only person other than my family I've ever loved was gone. I couldn't."

Novalee's heart jumped in her chest at his words and she suddenly felt weak in the knees. She inhaled, sucking in as much air as she could as she scolded herself for feeling like a teenager whose crush just passed her a note in class.

"Dean—"

"I know what I did was horrible," he continued, "but you have no idea how much I hope it's not unforgivable."

"Dean," Novalee tried again, "I asked you to stay away because I can't do this. I can't want to be with you. It hurts too much. And you showing up here like this," Novalee waved her arms around at the mess in her kitchen, "it's not fair."

"I know I messed up. I know what I did was wrong and that I hurt you —"

"No, I don't think you do," Novalee disagreed. "Because if you did you wouldn't be here right now."

Dean walked toward her and Novalee fought every instinct she had to throw herself into his arms. Instead she wrapped hers around herself to keep from reaching for him and dropped her eyes to the floor to keep him from seeing how much she wanted him.

"You deserve a man who you can trust," Dean said. "You deserve a man who will make you fall but catch you once you do. You deserve a man who will love you like there's no tomorrow every day. I want to be that man, Novalee."

Novalee shook her head.

"I don't think you can be," she whispered as the tears she tried to hold back slowly slid down her cheeks.

"But you won't know for sure unless you give me a chance."

"And then what?" Novalee wiped the tears from her face and looked up at him. "I'm blindsided by more of your secrets?"

"There are no more secrets," Dean promised.

"How do I know that? How fair is it to ask me to give you a chance when I could spend the entire time wondering what else is out there to surprise me?"

Dean exhaled noisily as he stared at her. "The only thing I can do is prove it to you, but I can't do that unless you let me." He reached out and wiped a tear from her cheek, giving her a small smile.

Novalee closed her eyes, tilting her head, and he cupped her cheek, stroking her skin.

She sighed as a shiver ran down her spine. She'd missed his touch, missed the sound of his voice, missed those damn dimples that flashed her every time he smiled and made her stomach do funny things. It would be so easy to give in to what they both wanted, but she had to wonder at what price.

"When we met you were just a pretty face that I could slap my name behind and call to save my ass," Dean admitted. "You were just an easy piece of paper I could present to keep my father out."

Novalee stiffened and pulled her face away from his hand, but Dean grabbed her arms and kept her from moving away.

"You have no idea how many times during those two years I thought about you, wondering who the woman was I married."

Novalee scowled. "I find that hard to believe, considering you had an entire file on me from your P.I."

Dean's eyes widened in surprise, but he quickly shook his head.

"No, my attorneys had an entire file on you. I never looked at it," he said.

"Never?" Novalee raised a skeptical eyebrow.

Dean shifted his eyes away and then sighed. "Okay, I did. But only after I came here, and I didn't really read it. I mostly just skimmed it."

"So you knew about my past before I ever told you?" she accused, narrowing her eyes.

Dean swallowed hard as he nodded.

"Yes. I knew the details."

Novalee pulled out of his grasp and moved to the opposite side of the kitchen. She spun around to face him, angry again by how violated she felt.

"Do you know how hard it was for me to tell you about that time in my life? Do you know how much trust I had in you to be able to share that? And you knew the entire time! You knew and played that against me to gain my sympathy with your own past."

"No! I would never use what happened against you in any way. Remember, I lived it too."

"The difference is you chose to tell me about it; my choice to share with you was taken away. That hurts more than the lies."

"I never asked for that report. I never hired the P.I. I thought about you often, wondering if what I'd done was stopping you from having a real life, a real relationship. Dreading the day that you might show up and demand a divorce so you could move on with someone else, yet hoping for it at the same time."

"Why would you hope for it? Wouldn't that ruin your little plan?" Novalee asked, bitterly.

"Yes, but you would have been free. And it would have freed me as well." Dean dragged his hand down the side of his face and sighed. "I was a mess after our marriage. I drank too much and slept too little. I tried to stay away from home as much as possible because it all just reminded me of my mistakes, but I couldn't run away from it. You haunted me the entire time."

"You weren't the only one that was haunted, Dean. That first year I expected to see you, positive the stranger that I shared not only a bed with, but promised a lifetime to, would show up angry and looking for answers or revenge. You didn't, but the second I started breathing a little easier, you did. And now this." Novalee glanced around the kitchen and shook her head. "You can't do this to me."

"I'm not trying to do anything *to* you, I want to do it *with* you," Dean said, walked toward her again. "I want to be *with* you, Novalee. I want to see if we can make this work for real and not just because it was down on paper."

"You signed the divorce papers."

"You signed them first," Dean answered.

"I'm not the one saying I want to make a relationship work," Novalee countered.

"I signed them so we could have a relationship. A fresh start. Something not based on manipulation and lies. I want to make something with you. I want to make it real and make it last."

"Why?" Novalee asked. She knew why, just as she knew hearing the words would make it that much harder to walk away. Just as she knew that she felt the same exact way and it scared the hell out of her.

Dean held her gaze and made it impossible for her to look away as he said, "Because I love you. Maybe I've always loved you. Maybe I just needed to be with you, to spend that little bit of time with you to realize it."

Novalee bit her lip to stop it from quivering as she tried to blink back tears again, then tore her eyes away and shook her head. "Maybe you're just caught up in everything that happened and you feel like you owe me."

"You believe I think I owe you love?" he asked, surprise raising his voice.

"Not love. Maybe you feel as if you owe it to me, or to us or whatever, to try and have a relationship after all this."

"Novalee Jensen, I love you. Not because of some failed fraudulent marriage, not because I feel guilty for making you wait on a husband that was never around, and not because I feel obligated to make it work with you. What I feel is all about you and not what happened in our fucked-up past."

"Dean . . ."

"I get that you're scared. I get that you're not sure if taking the risk will be worth it since I've already let you down without a real relationship on the line. But I took a chance coming here tonight because I *know* it's worth it. We're worth it."

"I don't know if I can take that risk," Novalee confessed.

Dean moved closer to her. "That disastrous night that I worked for you was the best time of my life." Novalee half-laughed as she wiped at the tears. "I mean it. I might have screwed up royally, but I had a blast doing it because it was for you. I want to spend the rest of my life doing things like that for you. I want to spend it helping you out of tight jams, making you smile, and coming home with you at the end of the night to a crowded bed with Ben."

Novalee laughed again, smiling through the damn tears that just wouldn't stop.

"But I need you to be willing to take that risk with me, Novalee. I can't do it alone."

"What if it doesn't work?" she asked.

Dean smiled. "Then at least we'll know and won't have to spend the rest of our lives wondering."

Novalee inhaled a shaky breath and stared at her ex-husband.

"It's last call, Novalee. Come get what you want or walk away."

Novalee licked her lips. Her heart pounded in her chest because of what she was about to do and her stomach was flipping like crazy.

"I want you, Dean," she whispered. "I love you."

Dean crossed the space between them in one stride and swept her into his arms as she wrapped her arms around his neck and her legs around his waist, kissing him passionately.

Dean spun them around, heading for her bedroom as she pulled her mouth away just long enough to laugh. "What about your grand gesture dinner?"

He grinned. "I never intended for you to actually eat it. Despite the lessons, my culinary skills didn't improve very much."

"What a disappointment. Here I planned to put you to work tomorrow," Novalee teased.

"I think you should call in sick the next couple of nights," Dean suggested with a wiggle of his eyebrows.

"Good thing I have Cali to cover for me. Remind me to take my spare key away from her, though."

"Remind me to buy her the biggest, most expensive gift I can find as a thank you."

"She'll love you forever for that."

"There's only one woman I'm interested in loving me forever," Dean replied.

"Forever is a long time."

"It's not nearly long enough when it comes to loving you."

CPSIA information can be obtained at www.ICGtesting.com
Printed in the USA
244896LV00007B/4/P